Riverside College Classics

THE AMERICAN

BY

HENRY JAMES

TOVT
BIEN OV
RIEN

HOUGHTON MIFFLIN COMPANY

BOSTON · NEW YORK · CHICAGO · DALLAS

SAN FRANCISCO

The Riverside Press Cambridge

The Riverside Press
CAMBRIDGE · MASSACHUSETTS
PRINTED IN THE U. S. A.

THE AMERICAN

I

ON a brilliant day in May, of the year 1868, a gentleman was reclining at his ease on the great circular
divan which at that period occupied the centre of the
Salon Carré, in the Museum of the Louvre. This
commodious ottoman has since been removed, to the
extreme regret of all weak-kneed lovers of the fine
arts; but our visitor had taken serene possession of its
softest spot, and, with his head thrown back and his
legs outstretched, was staring at Murillo's beautiful
moon-borne Madonna in deep enjoyment of his posture. He had removed his hat and flung down beside
him a little red guide-book and an opera-glass. The
day was warm; he was heated with walking, and he
repeatedly, with vague weariness, passed his hand-
kerchief over his forehead. And yet he was evidently
not a man to whom fatigue was familiar; long, lean,
and muscular, he suggested an intensity of unconscious resistance. His exertions on this particular day,
however, had been of an unwonted sort, and he had
often performed great physical feats that left him
less jaded than his quiet stroll through the Louvre.
He had looked out all the pictures to which an asterisk
was affixed in those formidable pages of fine print in
his Bädeker; his attention had been strained and his
eyes dazzled; he had sat down with an æsthetic

headache. He had looked, moreover, not only at all the pictures, but at all the copies that were going forward around them in the hands of those innumerable young women in long aprons, on high stools, who devote themselves, in France, to the reproduction of masterpieces; and, if the truth must be told, he had often admired the copy much more than the original. His physiognomy would have sufficiently indicated that he was a shrewd and capable person, and in truth he had often sat up all night over a bristling bundle of accounts and heard the cock crow without a yawn. But Raphael and Titian and Rubens were a new kind of arithmetic, and they made him for the first time in his life wonder at his vaguenesses.

An observer with anything of an eye for local types would have had no difficulty in referring this candid connoisseur to the scene of his origin, and indeed such an observer might have made an ironic point of the almost ideal completeness with which he filled out the mould of race. The gentleman on the divan was the superlative American; to which affirmation of character he was partly helped by the general easy magnificence of his manhood. He appeared to possess that kind of health and strength which, when found in perfection, are the most impressive — the physical tone which the owner does nothing to "keep up." If he was a muscular Christian it was quite without doctrine. If it was necessary to walk to a remote spot he walked, but he had never known himself to "exercise." He had no theory with regard to cold bathing or the use of Indian clubs; he was neither an oarsman, a rifleman nor a fencer — he had never had time for these amusements — and he was quite unaware that the saddle is recommended for certain forms of indigestion. He was by inclination a temperate man; but he had supped the night before his visit to the Louvre at the Café Anglais — some one had told him it was an experience not to be omitted — and he had slept none the less the sleep of the just. His usual attitude and carriage had a liberal looseness, but when, under a special inspiration, he straightened himself he looked a grenadier on parade. He had never tasted tobacco. He had been assured — such things are said — that cigars are excellent for the health, and he was quite capable of believing it; but he would no more have thought of "taking" one than of taking a dose of medicine. His complexion was brown and the arch of his nose bold and well-marked. His eye was of a clear, cold grey, and save for the abundant droop of his moustache he spoke, as to cheek and chin, of the joy of the matutinal steel. He had the flat jaw and the firm, dry neck which are frequent in the American type; but the betrayal of native conditions is a matter of expression even more than of feature, and it was in this respect that our traveller's countenance was supremely eloquent. The observer we have been supposing might, however, perfectly have measured its expressiveness and yet have been at a loss for names and terms to fit it. It had that paucity of detail which is yet not emptiness, that blankness which is not simplicity, that look of being committed to nothing in particular, of standing in a posture of general hospitality to the chances of life, of being very much at one's own disposal, characteristic of American faces of the clear strain. It was the eye, in this case, that chiefly told the story; an eye in which the unacquainted and the expert were singularly blended. It was full of contradictory suggestions; and though it was by no means the glowing orb of a hero of romance you could find in it almost anything you looked for. Frigid and yet friendly, frank yet cautious, shrewd yet credulous, positive yet sceptical, confident yet shy, extremely intelligent and extremely good-humoured, there was something vaguely defiant in its concessions and something profoundly reassuring in its reserve. The wide yet partly folded wings of this gentleman's moustache, with the two premature wrinkles in the cheek above it, and the fashion of his garments, in which an exposed shirt-front and a blue satin necktie of too light a shade played perhaps an obtrusive part, completed the elements of his identity. We have approached him perhaps at a not especially favourable moment; he is by no means sitting for his portrait. But listless as he lounges there, rather baffled on the æsthetic question and guilty of the damning fault (as we have lately discovered it to be) of confounding the aspect of the artist with that of his work (for he admires the squinting Madonna of the young lady with the hair that somehow also advertises "art," because he thinks the young lady herself uncommonly taking), he is a sufficiently promising acquaintance. Decision, salubrity, jocosity, prosperity, seem to hover within his call; he is evidently a man of business, but the term appears to confess, for his particular benefit, to undefined and mysterious boundaries which invite the imagination to bestir itself.

As the little copyist proceeded with her task, her attention addressed to her admirer, from time to time, for reciprocity, one of its blankest, though not of its briefest, missives. The working-out of her scheme appeared to call, in her view, for a great deal of vivid by-play, a great standing off with folded arms and head dropping from side to side, stroking of a dimpled chin with a dimpled hand, sighing and frowning and patting of the foot, fumbling in disordered tresses for wandering hair-pins. These motions were accompanied by a far-straying glance, which tripped up, occasionally, as it were, on the tall arrested gentleman. At last he rose abruptly and, putting on his hat as if for emphasis of an austere intention, approached the young lady. He placed himself before her picture and looked at it for a time during which she pretended to be quite unconscious of his presence. Then, invoking her intelligence with the single word that constituted the strength of his French vocabulary, and holding up one finger in a manner that appeared to him to illuminate his meaning, "*Combien?*" he abruptly demanded.

The artist stared a moment, gave a small pout, shrugged her shoulders, put down her palette and brushes and stood rubbing her hands.

"How much?" said our friend in English. "*Combien?*"

"Monsieur wishes to buy it?" she asked in French.

"Very pretty. *Splendide. Combien?*" repeated the American.

"It pleases monsieur, my little picture? It's a very beautiful subject," said the young lady.

"The Madonna, yes; I'm not a real Catholic, but I want to buy it. *Combien?* Figure it right there." And he took a pencil from his pocket and showed her the fly-leaf of his guide-book. She stood looking at him and scratching her chin with the pencil. "Isn't it for sale?" he asked. And as she still stood reflecting, probing him with eyes which, in spite of her desire to treat this avidity of patronage as a very old story, added to her flush of incredulity, he was afraid he had offended her. She was simply trying to look indifferent, wondering how far she might go. "I haven't made a mistake — *pas insulté*, no?" her interlocutor continued. "Don't you understand a little English?"

The young lady's aptitude for playing a part at short notice was remarkable. She fixed him with all her conscious perception and asked him if he spoke no French. Then *"Donnez!"* she said briefly, and took the open guide-book. In the upper corner of the fly-leaf she traced a number in a minute and extremely neat hand. On which she handed back the book and resumed her palette.

Our friend read the number: "2000 francs." He said nothing for a time, but stood looking at the picture while the copyist began actively to dabble with her paint. "For a copy, isn't that a good deal?" he inquired at last. *"Pas beaucoup?"*

She raised her eyes from her palette, scanned him from head to foot, and alighted with admirable sagacity upon exactly the right answer. "Yes, it's a good deal. But my copy is extremely *soigné*. That's its value."

The gentleman in whom we are interested understood no French, but I have said he was intelligent, and here is a good chance to prove it. He apprehended, by a natural instinct, the meaning of the young woman's phrase, and it gratified him to find her so honest. Beauty, therefore talent, rectitude; she combined everything! "But you must finish it," he said. "*Finish*, you know;" and he pointed to the unpainted hand of the figure.

"Oh, it shall be finished in perfection — in the perfection of perfections!" cried mademoiselle; and to confirm her promise she deposited a rosy blotch in the middle of the Madonna's cheek.

But the American frowned. "Ah, too red, too red!" he objected. "*Her* complexion," pointing to the Murillo, "is more delicate."

"Delicate? Oh it shall be delicate, monsieur; delicate as Sèvres *biscuit*. I'm going to tone that down; I promise you it shall have a surface! And where will you allow us to send it to you? Your address."

"My address? Oh yes!" And the gentleman drew a card from his pocket-book and wrote something on it. Then hesitating a moment: "If I don't like it when it is finished, you know, I shall not be obliged to pay for it."

The young lady seemed as good a guesser as himself. "Oh, I'm very sure monsieur's not capricious!'

"Capricious?" And at this monsieur began to laugh. "Oh no, I'm not capricious. I'm very faithful. I'm very constant. *Comprenez?*"

"Monsieur's constant; I understand perfectly. It's not the case of all the world. To recompense you, you shall have your picture on the first possible day; next week — as soon as it's dry. I'll take the card of monsieur." And she took it and read his name: "Christopher Newman." Then she tried to repeat it aloud and laughed at her bad accent. "Your English names are not *commodes* to say!"

"Well, mine's partly celebrated," said Mr. Newman, laughing too. "Did you never hear of Christopher Columbus?"

"*Bien sûr!* He first showed Americans the way to Europe; a very great man. And is he your patron?"

"My patron?"

"Your patron saint, such as we all have."

"Oh, exactly; my parents named me after him."

"Monsieur is American then too?"

"Does n't it stick right out?" monsieur enquired.

"And you mean to carry my dear little picture away over there?" She explained her phrase with a gesture.

"Oh, I mean to buy a great many pictures — *beaucoup, beaucoup*," said Christopher Newman.

"The honour's not less for me," the young lady answered, "for I'm sure monsieur has a great deal of 'aste."

"But you must give me your card," Newman went on; "your card, you know."

The young lady looked severe an instant. "My father will wait on you."

But this time Mr. Newman's powers of divination were at fault. "Your card, your address," he simply repeated.

"My address?" said mademoiselle. Then, with a little shrug: "Happily for you, you're a stranger — of a distinction *qui se voit.* It's the first time I ever gave my card to a gentleman." And, taking from her pocket a well-worn flat little wallet, she extracted from it a small glazed visiting-card and presented the latter to her client. It was neatly inscribed in pencil, with a great many flourishes, "Mlle. Noémie Nioche." But Mr. Newman, unlike his companion, read the name with perfect gravity; all French names to him were equally *incommodes.*

"And precisely — how it happens! — here's my father; he has come to escort me home," said Mademoiselle Noémie. "He speaks English beautifully. He'll arrange with you." And she turned to welcome a little old gentleman who came shuffling up and peering over his glasses at Newman.

M. Nioche wore a glossy wig, of an unnatural colour, which overhung his little meek, white, vacant face, leaving it hardly more expressive than the unfeatured block upon which these articles are displayed in the barber's window. He was an exquisite image of shabby gentility. His scant, ill-made coat, desperately brushed, his darned gloves, his highly polished boots, his rusty, shapely hat, told the story of a person who had "had losses" and who clung to the spirit of nice habits even though the letter had been hopelessly effaced. Among other things M. Nioche had lost courage. Adversity had not only deprived him of means, it had deprived him of confidence — so frightened him that he was going through his remnant of life on tiptoe, lest he should wake up afresh the hostile fates. If this strange gentleman should be saying anything improper to his daughter M. Nioche would entreat him huskily, as a particular favour, to forbear; but he would admit at the same time that he was very presumptuous to ask for particular favours.

"Monsieur has bought my picture," said Mademoiselle Noémie. "When it's finished you'll carry it to him in a cab."

"In a cab!" cried M. Nioche; and he stared, in a bewildered way, as if he had seen the sun rising at midnight.

"Are you the young lady's father?" said Newman "I think she said you speak English."

"Spick English — yes." The old man slowly rubbed his hands. "I'll bring it in a cab."

"Say something then," cried his daughter. "Thank him a little — not too much."

"A little, my daughter, a little?" he murmured in distress. "How much?"

"Two thousand!" said Mademoiselle Noémie. "Don't make a fuss or he'll take back his word."

"Two thousand!" gasped the old man; and he began to fumble for his snuff-box. He looked at Newman from head to foot; he looked at his daughter and then at the picture. "Take care you don't spoil it!" he cried almost sublimely.

"We must go home," said Mademoiselle Noémie. 'This is a good day's work. Take care how you carry it!" And she began to put up her utensils.

"How can I thank you?" asked M. Nioche. "My English is far from sufficing."

"I wish I spoke French half so well," said Newman good-naturedly. "Your daughter too, you see, makes herself understood."

"Oh sir!" and M. Nioche looked over his spectacles with tearful eyes, nodding out of his depths of sadness. "She has had an education — *très-supérieure!* Nothing was spared. Lessons in pastel at ten francs the lesson, lessons in oil at twelve francs. I didn't look at the francs then. She's a serious worker."

"Do I understand you to say that you've had a bad time?" asked Newman.

"A bad time? Oh sir, misfortunes — terrible!"

"Unsuccessful in business?"

"Very unsuccessful, sir."

"Oh, never fear; you'll get on your legs again," said Newman cheerily.

The old man cast his head to one side; he wore an expression of pain, as if this were an unfeeling jest: whereupon "What is it he says?" Mademoiselle Noémie demanded.

M. Nioche took a pinch of snuff. "He says I shall make my fortune again."

"Perhaps he'll help you. And what else?"

"He says thou hast a great deal of head."

"It's very possible. You believe it yourself, my father."

"Believe it, my daughter? With this evidence!" And the old man turned afresh, in staring, wondering homage, to the audacious daub on the easel.

"Ask him then if he'd not like to learn French."

"To learn French?"

"To take lessons."

"To take lessons, my daughter? From thee?"

"From thee."

"From me, my child? How should I give lessons?"

"*Pas de raisons!* Ask him immediately!" said Mademoiselle Noémie with soft shortness.

M. Nioche stood aghast, but under his daughter's eye he collected his wits and, doing his best to assume an agreeable smile, executed her commands. "Would it please you to receive instruction in our beautiful language?" he brought out with an appealing quaver.

"To study French?" Newman was rather struck.

M. Nioche pressed his finger-tips together and slowly raised his shoulders. "A little practice in conversation!"

"Practice, conversation — that's it!" murmured Mademoiselle Noémie, who had caught the words. "The conversation of the best society."

"Our French conversation is rather famous, you know," M. Nioche ventured to continue. "It's the genius of our nation."

"But — except for your nation — isn't it almost impossible?" asked Newman very simply.

"Not to a man of *esprit* like monsieur, an admirer of beauty in every form!" And M. Nioche cast a significant glance at his daughter's Madonna.

"I can't fancy myself reeling off fluent French!" Newman protested. "And yet I suppose the more things, the more names of things, a man knows, the better he can get round."

"Monsieur expresses that very happily. The better he can get round. *Hélas, oui!*"

"I suppose it would help me a great deal, knocking about Paris, to be able to try at least to talk."

"Ah, there are so many things monsieur must want to say: remarkable things, and proportionately difficult."

"Everything I want to say is proportionately difficult. But you're in the habit of giving lessons?"

Poor M. Nioche was embarrassed; he smiled more appealingly. "I'm not a regular professor," he admitted. "I can't *pourtant* tell him I've a diploma," he said to his daughter.

"Tell him it's a very exceptional chance," answered mademoiselle; "an *homme du monde* — one perfect gentleman conversing with another. Remember what you are. Remember what you *have* been."

"A teacher of languages in neither case! Much more *dans le temps* and much less to-day! And if he asks the price of the lessons?"

"He won't ask it," said the girl.

"What he pleases, I may say?"

"Never! That's bad style."

"But if he wants to know?"

Mademoiselle Noémie had put on her bonnet and was tying the ribbons. She smoothed them out, her shell-like little chin thrust forward. "Ten francs," she said quickly.

"Oh my daughter! I shall never dare."

"Don't dare then! He won't ask till the end of the lessons, and you'll let me make out the bill."

M. Nioche turned to the confiding foreigner again and stood rubbing his hands with his air of standing convicted of almost any counsel of despair. It never occurred to Newman to plead for a guarantee of his skill in imparting instruction; he supposed of course M. Nioche knew the language he so beautifully pronounced, and his brokenness of spring was quite the perfection of what the American, for vague reasons, had always associated with all elderly foreigners of the lesson-giving class Newman had never reflected upon philological processes. His chief impression with regard to any mastery of those mysterious correlatives of his familiar English vocables which were current in this extraordinary city of Paris was that it would be simply a matter of calling sharply into play latent but dormant muscles and sinews. "How did you learn so much English?" he asked of the old man.

"Oh, I could do things when I was young — before my miseries. I was wide awake then. My father was a great *commerçant;* he placed me for a year in a counting-house in England. Some of it stuck to me, but much I 've forgotten!"

"How much French can I learn in about a month?"

"What does he say?" asked mademoiselle; and then when her father had explained: "He 'll speak like an angel!"

But the native integrity which had been vainly exerted to secure M. Nioche's commercial prosperity flickered up again. "*Dame*, monsieur!" he answered. "All I can teach you!" And then, recovering himself at a sign from his daughter: "I 'll wait upon you at your hotel."

"Oh yes, I should like to converse with elegance," Newman went on, giving his friends the benefit of any vagueness. "Hang me if I should ever have thought of it! I seemed to feel it too far off. But you've brought it quite near, and if you could catch on at all to our grand language — that of Shakespeare and Milton and Holy Writ — why should n't I catch on to yours?" His frank, friendly laugh drew the sting from the jest. "Only, if we're going to converse, you know, you must think of something cheerful to converse about."

"You're very good, sir; I'm overcome!" And M. Nioche threw up his hands. "But you've cheerfulness and happiness for two!"

"Oh no," said Newman more seriously. "You must be bright and lively; that's part of the bargain."

M. Nioche bowed with his hand on his heart. "Very well, sir; you've struck up a tune I could almost dance to!"

"Come and bring me my picture then; I'll pay you for it, and we'll talk about that. That will be a cheerful subject!"

Mademoiselle Noémie had collected her accessories and she gave the precious Madonna in charge to her father, who retreated backwards, out of sight, holding it at arm's length and reiterating his obeisances. The young lady gathered her mantle about her like a perfect Parisienne, and it was with the "Au revoir, monsieur!" of a perfect Parisienne that she took leave of her patron.

II

THIS personage wandered back to the divan and seated himself, on the other side, in view of the great canvas on which Paul Veronese has spread, to swarm and glow there for ever, the marriage-feast of Cana of Galilee. Weary as he was his spirit went out to the picture; it had an illusion for him; it satisfied his conception, which was strenuous, of what a splendid banquet should be. In the left-hand corner is a young woman with yellow tresses confined in a golden head-dress; she bends forward and listens, with the smile of a charming person at a dinner-party, to her festal neighbour. Newman detected her in the crowd, admired her and perceived that she too had her votive copyist — a young man whose genius, like that of Samson, might have been in his bristling hair. Suddenly he was aware of the prime throb of the mania of the "collector." He had taken the first step — why should he not go on? It was only twenty minutes before that he had bought the first picture of his life, and now he was already thinking of art-patronage as a pursuit that might float even so heavy a weight as himself. His reflexions quickened his good-humour and he was on the point of approaching the young man with another "*Combien?*" Two or three facts in this relation are noticeable, although the logical chain that connects them may seem imperfect. He knew

Mademoiselle Nioche had asked too much; he bore
her no grudge for doing so, and he was determined to
pay the young man exactly the proper sum. At this
moment, however, his attention was attracted by a
gentleman who had come from another part of the
room and whose manner was that of a stranger to the
gallery, though he was equipped neither with guide-
book nor with opera-glass. He carried a white sun-
umbrella lined with blue silk, and he strolled in front
of the great picture, vaguely looking at it but much
too near to see anything but the grain of the canvas.
Opposite Christopher Newman he paused and turned,
and then our friend, who had been observing him, had
a chance to verify a suspicion roused by an imperfect
view of his face. The result of the larger scrutiny
was that he presently sprang to his feet, strode across
the room and, with an outstretched hand, arrested
this blank spectator. The gaping gentleman gaped
afresh, but put out his hand at a venture. He was
large, smooth and pink, with the air of a successfully
potted plant, and though his countenance, orna-
mented with a beautiful flaxen beard carefully divided in the middle and brushed outward at the sides,
was not remarkable for intensity of expression, it was
exclusive only in the degree of the open door of an
hotel — it would have been closed to the undesirable.
It was for Newman in fact as if at first he had been
but invited to "register."

"Oh come, come," he said, laughing; "don't say
now you don't know me — if I've *not* got a white
parasol!"

His tone penetrated; the other's face expanded to

its fullest capacity and then broke into gladness.
"Why, Christopher Newman — I'll be blowed!
Where in the world — ? Who would have thought?
You've carried out such extensive alterations."

"Well, I guess you've not," said Newman.

"Oh no, I hold together very much as I was. But
when did you get here?"

"Three days ago."

"Then why did n't you let me know?"

"How was I to be aware — ?"

"Why, I've been located here quite a while."

"Yes, it's quite a while since we last met."

"Well, it *feels* long — since the War."

"It was in Saint Louis, at the outbreak. You
were going for a soldier," Newman said.

"Oh no, not I. It was you. Have you forgotten?"

"You bring it unpleasantly back."

"Then you did take your turn?"

"Oh yes, I took my turn. But that was nothing,
I seem to feel, to *this* turn."

"How long then have you been in Europe?"

"Just seventeen days."

"First time you've been?"

"Yes, quite immensely the first."

Newman's friend had been looking him all over.
"Made your everlasting fortune?"

Our gentleman was silent a little, and then with
a tranquil smile, "Well, I've grubbed," he answered.

"And come to buy Paris up? Paris *is* for sale, you
know."

"Well, I shall see what I can do about it. So they
carry those parasols here — the men-folk?"

"Of course they do. They're great things, these parasols. They understand detail out here."

"Where do you buy them?"

"Anywhere, everywhere."

"Well, Tristram, I'm glad to get hold of you. I guess you can tell me a good deal. I suppose you know Paris pretty correctly," Newman pursued.

Mr. Tristram's face took a rosy light. "Well, I guess there are not many men that can show me much. I'll take care of you."

"It's a pity you were not here a few minutes ago. I've just bought a picture. You might have put the thing through for me."

"Bought a picture?" said Mr. Tristram, looking vaguely round the walls. "Why, do they sell them?"

"I mean a copy."

"Oh, I see. These"—and Mr. Tristram nodded at the Titians and Vandykes—"these, I suppose, are originals?"

"I hope so," said Newman. "I don't want a copy of a copy."

"Ah," his friend sagaciously returned, "you can never tell. They imitate, you know, so deucedly well. It's like the jewellers with their false stones. Go into the Palais Royal there; you see 'Imitation' on half the windows. The law obliges them to stick it on, you know; but you can't tell the things apart. To tell the truth," Mr. Tristram continued — and his grimace seemed a turn of the screw of discrimination — "I don't do so very much in pictures. They're one of the things I leave to my wife."

"Ah, you've acquired a wife?"

"Did n't I mention it? She's a very smart woman. You must come right round. She's up there in the Avenue d'Iéna."

"So you're regularly fixed — house and children and all?"

"Yes; a tip-top house, and a couple of charming cubs."

"Well," sighed Christopher Newman, stretching his arms a little, "you affect me with a queer feeling that I suppose to be envy."

"Oh no, I don't," answered Mr. Tristram, giving him a little poke with his parasol.

"I beg your pardon; you do."

"Well, I shan't then, when — when — !"

"You don't certainly mean when I've seen your pleasant home?"

"When you've made *yours*, my boy. When you've seen Paris. You want to be in light marching order here."

"Oh, I've skipped about in my shirt all my life, and I've had about enough of it."

"Well, try it on the basis of Paris. That makes a new thing of it. How old may you be?"

"Forty-two and a half, I guess."

"*C'est le bel âge*, as they say here."

Newman reflected. "Does that mean the age of the belly?"

"It means that a man should n't send away his plate till he has eaten his fill."

"It comes to the same thing. I've just made arrangements, anyhow, to take lessons in the language."

"Oh, you don't want any lessons. You'll pick it

right up. I never required nor received any instruction."

"You speak it then as easily as English?"

"Easier!" said Mr. Tristram roundly. "It's a splendid language. You can say all sorts of gay things in it."

"But I suppose," said Christopher Newman with an earnest desire for information, "that you must be pretty gay to begin with."

"Not a bit: that's just the beauty of it!"

The two friends, as they exchanged these remarks, which dropped from them without a pause, had remained standing where they met and leaning against the rail which protected the pictures. Mr. Tristram at last declared that he was overcome with lassitude and should be happy to sit down. Newman recommended in the highest terms the great divan on which he had been lounging, and they prepared to seat themselves. "This is a great place, is n't it?" he broke out with enthusiasm.

"Great place, great place. Finest thing in the world." And then suddenly Mr. Tristram hesitated and looked about. "I suppose they won't let you smoke?"

Newman stared. "Smoke? I'm sure I don't know. You know the regulations better than I."

"I? I never was here before."

"Never! all your six years?"

"I believe my wife dragged me here once when we first came to Paris, but I never found my way back."

"But you say you know Paris so well!"

"I don't call this Paris!" cried Mr. Tristram with

assurance. "Come; let's go over to the Palais Royal and have a smoke."

"I don't smoke," said Newman.

"What's that for?" Mr. Tristram growled as he led his companion away. They passed through the glorious halls of the Louvre, down the staircases, along the cool, dim galleries of sculpture and out into the enormous court. Newman looked about him as he went, but made no comments; and it was only when they at last emerged into the open air that he said to his friend: "It seems to me that in your place I'd have come here once a week."

"Oh no, you wouldn't!" said Mr. Tristram. "You think so, but you wouldn't. You wouldn't have had time. You'd always mean to go, but you never *would* go. There's better fun than that here in Paris. Italy's the place to see pictures; wait till you get there. There you *have* to go; you can't do anything else. It's an awful country; you can't get a decent cigar. I don't know why I went into that place to-day. I was strolling along, rather hard up for amusement. I sort of took in the Louvre as I passed, and I thought I might go up and see what was going on. But if I hadn't found you there I should have felt rather sold. Hang it, I don't care for inanimate canvas or for cold marble beauty; I prefer the real thing!" And Mr. Tristram tossed off this happy formula with an assurance which the numerous class of persons suffering from an overdose of prescribed taste might have envied him.

The two gentlemen proceeded along the Rue de Rivoli and into the Palais Royal, where they seated themselves at one of the little tables stationed at the door of the café which projects, or then projected, into the great open quadrangle. The place was filled with people, the fountains were spouting, a band was playing, clusters of chairs were gathered beneath all the lime-trees and buxom, white-capped nurses, seated along the benches, were offering to their infant charges the amplest facilities for nutrition. There was an easy, homely gaiety in the whole scene, and Christopher Newman felt it to be characteristically, richly Parisian.

"And now," began Mr. Tristram when they had tasted the decoction he had caused to be served to them,—"now just give an account of yourself. What are your ideas, what are your plans, where have you come from and where are you going? In the first place, where are you hanging out?"

"At the Grand Hotel."

He put out all his lights. "That won't do! You must change."

"Change?" demanded Newman. "Why, it's the finest hotel I ever was in."

"You don't want a 'fine' hotel; you want something small and quiet and superior, where your bell's answered and your personality recognised."

"They keep running to see if I've rung before I've touched the bell," said Newman, "and as for my personality they're always bowing and scraping to it."

"I suppose you're always tipping them. That's very bad style."

"Always? By no means A man brought me something yesterday and then stood loafing about in a beggarly manner. I offered him a chair and asked him if he'd sit down. Was that bad style?"

"I'll tell my wife!" Tristram simply answered.

"Tell the police if you like! He bolted right away, at any rate. The place quite fascinates me. Hang your 'superior' if it bores me. I sat in the court of the Grand Hotel last night until two o'clock in the morning, watching the coming and going and the people knocking about."

"You're easily pleased. But you can do as you choose — a man in your shoes. You've made a pile of money, hey?"

"I've made about enough."

"Happy the man who can say that! But enough for what?"

"Enough to let up a while, to forget the whole question, to look about me, to see the world, to have a good time, to improve my mind and, if my hour strikes, to marry a wife." Newman spoke slowly, with a quaint effect of dry detachment and with frequent pauses. This was his habitual mode of utterance, but it was especially marked in the words just recorded.

"Jupiter, there's an order!" cried Mr. Tristram. 'Certainly all that takes money, especially the wife; unless indeed she gives it, as mine did. And what's the story? How have you done it?"

Newman had pushed his hat back from his forehead, folded his arms and stretched his legs. He listened to the music, he looked about him at the bustling crowd, at the plashing fountains, at the nurses and the babies. "Well, I have n't done it by sitting round this way."

Tristram considered him again, allowing a finer curiosity to measure his generous longitude and retrace the blurred lines of his resting face. "What have you been in?"

"Oh, in more things than I care to remember."

"I suppose you're a real live man, hey?"

Newman continued to look at the nurses and babies; they imparted to the scene a kind of primordial, pastoral simplicity. "Yes," he said at last, "I guess I am." And then in answer to his companion's enquiries he briefly exposed his record since their last meeting. It was, with intensity, a tale of the Western world, and it showed, in that bright alien air, very much as fine dessicated, articulated "specimens," bleached, monstrous, probably unique, show in the high light of museums of natural history. It dealt with elements, incidents, enterprises, which it will be needless to introduce to the reader in detail; the deeps and the shallows, the ebb and the flow, of great financial tides. Newman had come out of the war with a brevet of brigadier-general, an honour which in this case — without invidious comparisons — had lighted upon shoulders amply competent to carry it. But though he had proved he could handle his men, and still more the enemy's, with effect, when need was, he heartily disliked the business; his four years in the army had left him with a bitter sense of the waste of precious things — life and time and money and ingenuity and opportunity; and he had addressed himself to the pursuits of peace with passionate zest and energy. His "interests," already mature, had meanwhile, however, waited for him, so that the capital at

his disposal had ceased to be solely his whetted, knife-
edged resolution and his lively perception of ends and
means. Yet these were his real arms, and exertion and
action as natural to him as respiration: a more completely healthy mortal had never trod the elastic soil
of great States of his option. His experience moreover
had been as wide as his capacity; necessity had in his
fourteenth year taken him by his slim young shoulders
and pushed him into the street to earn that night's
supper. He had not earned it, but he had earned the
next night's, and afterwards, whenever he had had
none, it was because he had gone without to use the
money for something else, a keener pleasure or a finer
profit. He had turned his hand, with his brain in it,
to many things; he had defied example and precedent
and probability, had adventured almost to madness
and escaped almost by miracles, drinking alike of the
flat water, when not the rank poison, of failure, and of
the strong wine of success.

A born experimentalist, he had always found something to enjoy in the direct pressure of fate even when
it was as irritating as the haircloth shirt of the medi-
æval monk. At one time defeat had seemed inexorably
his portion; ill-luck had become his selfish bed-fel-
low, and whatever he touched had turned to ashes
out of which no gleaming particle could be raked. His
most vivid conception of a supernatural element in the
world's affairs had come to him once when he felt
his head all too bullyingly pummelled; there seemed
to him something stronger in life than his personal,
intimate will. But the mysterious something could
only be a demon as personal as himself, and he accord-

ingly found himself in fine working opposition to this rival concern. He had known what it was to have utterly exhausted his credit, to be unable to raise a dollar and to find himself at nightfall in a strange city, without a penny to mitigate its strangeness. It was under these circumstances that he had made his entrance into San Francisco, the scene subsequently of his most victorious engagements. If he did not, like Dr. Franklin in Philadelphia, march along the street munching a penny loaf it was only because he had not the penny loaf necessary to the performance. In his darkest days he had had but one simple, practical impulse — the desire, as he would have phrased it, to conclude the affair. He had ended by concluding many, had at last buffeted his way into smooth waters, had begun and continued to add dollars to dollars. It must be rather nakedly owned that Newman's only proposal had been to effect that addition; what he had been placed in the world for was, to his own conception, simply to gouge a fortune, the bigger the better, out of its hard material. This idea completely filled his horizon and contented his imagination. Upon the uses of money, upon what one might do with a life into which one had succeeded in injecting the golden stream, he had up to the eve of his fortieth year very scantly reflected. Life had been for him an open game, and he had played for high stakes. He had finally won and had carried off his winnings; and now what was he to do with them? He was a man to whom, sooner or later, the question was sure to present itself, and the answer to it belongs to our story. A vague sense that more answers were possible than his philosophy had hitherto dreamt of had already taken possession of him, and it seemed softly and agreeably to deepen as he lounged in this rich corner of Paris with his friend.

"I must confess," he presently went on, "that I don't here at all feel my value. My remarkable talents seem of no use. It's as if I were as simple as a little child, and as if a little child might take me by the hand and lead me about."

"Oh, I'll be your little child," said Tristram jovially; "I'll take you by the hand. Trust yourself to me."

"I'm a grand good worker," Newman continued, "but I've come abroad to amuse myself; though I doubt if I very well know how."

"Oh, that's easily learned."

"Well, I may perhaps learn it, but I'm afraid I shall never do it by rote. I've the best will in the world about it, but my genius does n't lie in that direction. Besides," Newman pursued, "I don't want to work at pleasure, any more than ever I played at work. I want to let myself, let everything go. I feel coarse and loose and I should like to spend six months as I am now, sitting under a tree and listening to a band. There's only one thing: I want to hear some first-class music."

"First-class music and first-class pictures? Lord, what refined tastes! You've what my wife calls a rare mind. I have n't a bit. But we can find something better for you to do than to sit under a tree. To begin with, you must come to the club."

"What club?"

on the way. Perhaps I had, but in that case my sacrifice of them has become, in another way, my biggest stroke of business. I spent the morning looking at the first green leaves on Long Island. I had been so hot that it seemed as if I should never be cool enough again. As for the damned old money, I 've enough, already, not to miss it — you see how that spoils my beauty. I seemed to feel a new man under my old skin; at all events I longed for a new world. When you want a thing so very badly you probably had better have it and see. I did n't understand my case in the least, but gave the poor beast the bridle and let him find his way. As soon as I could get out of harness I sailed for Europe. That's how I come to be sitting here."

"You ought to have bought up that hack," said Tristram; "it is n't a safe vehicle to have about. And you 've really wound up and sold out then? you 've formally retired from business?"

"Well, I 'm not at present transacting any — on any terms. There 'll be plenty to be done again if I don't hold out, but I shall hold out as long as possible. I dare say, however, that a twelvemonth hence the uncanny operation will be repeated in the opposite sense and the pendulum swing back again. I shall be sitting in a gondola or on a dromedary, or on a cushion at the feet of Beauty, and all of a sudden I shall want to clear out. But for the present I 'm perfectly free. I 've even arranged that I 'm to receive no business letters."

"Oh, it's a real *caprice de prince*," said Tristram. "I back out; a poor devil like me can't help you to

"The Occidental. You 'll see all the Americans there; all the best of them at least. Of course you play poker?"

"Oh, I say," cried Newman, with energy, "you 're not going to lock me up in a club and stick me down at a card-table! I have n't come all this way for that."

"What the deuce then *have* you come for? You were glad enough to play poker in Saint Louis, I recollect, when you cleaned me out."

"I 've come to see Europe, to get the best out of it I can. I want to see all the great things and do what the best people do."

"The 'best' people? Much obliged. You set me down then as one of the worst?"

Newman was sitting sidewise in his chair, his elbow on the back and his head leaning on his hand. Without moving he played a while at his companion his dry, guarded, half-inscrutable and yet altogether good-natured smile. "Introduce me to your wife!"

Tristram bounced about on his seat. "Upon my word I 'll do nothing of the sort. She does n't want any help to turn up her nose at me, nor do you either."

"I don't turn up my nose at you, my dear fellow; nor at any one nor anything. I 'm not proud, I assure you I 'm not proud. That's why I 'm willing to take example by the best."

"Well, if I 'm not the rose, as they say here, I 've lived near it. I can show you some rare minds too. Do you know General Packard? Do you know C. P. Hatch? Do you know Miss Kitty Upjohn?"

"I shall be happy to make their acquaintance. I want to cultivate society."

Tristram seemed restless and suspicious; he eyed his friend askance, and then, "What are you up to, anyway?" he demanded. "Are you going to write a heavy book?"

Christopher Newman twisted one end of his moustache in silence and finally made answer. "One day, a couple of months ago, something very curious happened to me. I had come on to New York on some important business; it's too long and too low a story to tell you now — a question of getting in ahead of another party on a big transaction and on information that was all my own. This other party had once played off on me one of the clever meannesses the feeling of which works in a man like strong poison. I owed him a good one, the best one he was ever to have got in his life, and as his chance here — for he was after it, but on the wrong tip — would have been a remarkably sweet thing, a matter of half a million, I saw my way to show him the weight of my hand. The good it was going to do me, you see, to feel it come down on him! I jumped into a hack and went about my business, and it was in this hack — this immortal historical hack — that the curious thing I speak of occurred. It was a hack like any other, only a trifle dirtier, with a greasy line along the top of the drab cushions, as if it had been used for a great many Irish funerals. It's possible I took a nap; I had been travelling all night and, though I was excited with my errand, I felt the want of sleep. At all events I woke up suddenly, from a sleep or from a kind of reverie,

with the most extraordinary change of heart — a me[n]tal disgust for the whole proposition. It came up[on] me like *that!*" — and he snapped his fingers — "[as] abruptly as an old wound that begins to ache. [I] could n't tell the meaning of it; I only realised I ha[d] turned against myself worse than against the ma[n] I wanted to smash. The idea of *not* coming by tha[t] half-million in that particular way, of letting it utterly slide and scuttle and never hearing of it again, became the one thing to save my life from a sudden danger. And all this took place quite independently of my will, and I sat watching it as if it were a play at the theatre. I could feel it going on inside me. You may depend upon it that there are things going on inside us that we understand mighty little about."

"Jupiter, you make my flesh creep!" cried Tristram. "And while you sat in your hack watching the play, as you call it, the other man looked in and collared your half-million?"

"I have n't the least idea. I hope so, poor brute, but I never found out. We pulled up in front of the place I was going to in Wall Street, but I sat still in the carriage, and at last the driver scrambled down off his seat to see whether his hack had n't turned into a hearse. I could n't have got out any more than if I *had* been a corpse. What was the matter with me? Momentary brain-collapse, you'll say. What I wanted to get out of was Wall Street. I told the man to drive to the Brooklyn ferry and cross over. When we were over I told him to drive me out into the country. As I had told him originally to drive for dear life down town, I suppose he thought I had lost my wits spend such very magnificent leisure as that. You should get introduced to the crowned heads."

Newman considered a moment and then with all his candour, "How does one do it?" he asked.

"Come, I like that!" cried Tristram. "It shows you're in earnest."

"Of course I'm in earnest. Did n't I say I wanted the best? I know the best can't be had for mere money, but I'm willing to take a good deal of trouble."

"You're not too shrinking, hey?"

"I have n't the least idea — I must see. I want the biggest kind of entertainment a man can get. People, places, art, nature, everything! I want to see the tallest mountains, and the bluest lakes, and the finest pictures, and the handsomest churches, and the most celebrated men, and the most elegant women."

"Settle down in Paris then. There are no mountains that I know of, higher than Montmartre, and the only lake's in the Bois de Boulogne and not particularly blue. But there's everything else: plenty of pictures and churches, no end of celebrated men, and several elegant women."

"But I can't settle down in Paris at this season, just as summer's coming on."

"Oh, for the summer go right up to Trouville."

"And what may Trouville be?"

"Well, a sort of French Newport — as near as they can come. All the Americans go."

"Is it anywhere near the Alps?"

"About as near as Newport to the Rocky Mountains."

"Oh, I want to see Mont Blanc," said Newman,

"and Amsterdam, and the Rhine, and a lot of places Venice in particular. I've grand ideas for Venice."

"Ah," said Mr. Tristram, rising, "I see I shall have to introduce you to my wife. She'll have grand ideas for you!"

III

He performed that ceremony the following day, when, by appointment, Christopher Newman went to dine with him. Mr. and Mrs. Tristram lived behind one of those chalk-coloured façades which decorate with their pompous sameness the broad avenues distributed by Baron Haussmann over the neighbourhood of the Arc de Triomphe. Their apartment was rich in the modern conveniences, and Tristram lost no time in calling his visitor's attention to their principal household treasures, the thick-scattered gas-lamps and the frequent furnace-holes. "Whenever you feel homesick," he said, "you must come right up here. We'll stick you down before a register, under a good big burner, and —"

"And you'll soon get over your homesickness," said Mrs. Tristram.

Her husband stared; this lady often had a tone that defied any convenient test; he could n't tell for his life to whom her irony might be directed. The truth is that circumstances had done much to cultivate in Mrs. Tristram the need for any little intellectual luxury she could pick up by the way. Her taste on many points differed from that of her husband; and though she made frequent concessions to the dull small fact that he had married her it must be confessed that her reserves were not always muffled in pink gauze. They were founded upon the

35

vague project of her some day affirming herself in her totality; to which end she was in advance getting herself together, building herself high, enquiring, in short, into her dimensions.

It should be added, without delay, to anticipate misconception, that if she was thus saving herself up it was yet not to cover the expense of any fore-seen outlay of that finest part of her substance that was known to her tacitly as her power of passion. She had a very plain face and was entirely without illusions as to her appearance. She had taken its measure to a hair's breadth, she knew the worst and the best, she had accepted herself. It had not been indeed without a struggle. As a mere mortified maiden she had spent hours with her back to her mirror, crying her eyes out; and later she had, from desperation and bravado, adopted the habit of pro-claiming herself the most ill-favoured of women, in order that she might — as in common politeness was inevitable — be contradicted and reassured. It was since she had come to live in Europe that she had begun to take the matter philosophically. Her observation, acutely exercised here, had suggested to her that a woman's social service resides not in what she is but in what she appears, and that in the labyrinth of appearances she may always make others lose their clue if she only keeps her own. She had encountered so many women who pleased with-out beauty that she began to believe she had discov-ered her refuge. She had once heard an enthusiastic musician, out of patience with a gifted bungler, de-clare that a fine voice is really an obstacle to singing properly; and it occurred to her that it might perhaps be equally true that a beautiful face is an obstacle to the acquisition of charming manners. Mrs. Tristram then undertook to persuade by grace, and she brought to the task no small ingenuity.

How well she would have succeeded I am unable to say; unfortunately she broke off in the middle. Her own excuse was the want of encouragement in her immediate circle. But she had presumably not a real genius for the charming art, or she would have pursued it for itself. The poor lady was after all incomplete. She fell back upon the harmonies of dress, which she thoroughly understood, and contented herself with playing in its lock that key to the making of impressions. She lived in Paris, which she pretended to detest, because it was only in Paris that one could find things to exactly suit one's complexion. Besides, out of Paris it was always more or less of a trouble to get ten-button gloves. When she railed at this serviceable city and you asked her where she would prefer to reside she returned some very unexpected answer. She would say in Copenhagen or in Barcelona; having, while making the tour of Europe, spent a couple of days at each of these places. On the whole, with her poetic furbelows and her misshapen, intelligent little face, she was, when known, a figure to place, in the great gallery of the wistful, somewhere apart. She was naturally timid, and if she had been born a beauty she would (content with it) probably have taken no risks. At present she was both reckless and diffident; extremely reserved sometimes with her friends and strangely expansive with strangers. She overlooked her husband; overlooked him too much, for she had been perfectly at liberty not to marry him. She had been in love with a clever man who had eventually slighted her, and she had married a fool in the hope that the keener personage, reflecting on it, would conclude that she had had no appreciation of his keenness and that he had flattered her in thinking her touched. Restless, discontented, visionary, without personal ambitions but with a certain avidity of imagination, she was interesting from this sense she gave of her looking for her ideals by a lamp of strange and fitful flame. She was full — both for good and for ill — of beginnings that came to nothing; but she had nevertheless, morally, a spark of the sacred fire.

Newman was fond, in all circumstances, of the society of women; and now that he was out of his native element and deprived of his habitual interests he turned to it for compensation. He took a great fancy to Mrs. Tristram; she frankly repaid it, and after their first meeting he passed a great many hours in her drawing-room. Two or three long talks had made them fast friends. Newman's manner with women was peculiar, and it required some diligence on a lady's part to discover that he admired her. He had no gallantry in the usual sense of the term; no compliments, no graces, no speeches. Fond enough of a large pleasantry in his dealings with men, he never found himself on a sofa beside a member of the softer sex without feeling that such situations appealed, like beautiful views, or celebrated operas, or fine portraits, or handsome "sets" of the classics, or even elegant "show" cemeteries, to his earnest side. He was not shy and, so far as awkwardness proceeds from a struggle with shyness, was not awkward: grave, attentive, submissive, often silent, he was simply swimming in a sort of rapture of respect. This emotion was not at all theoretic, it was not even in a high degree romantic; he had thought very little about the "position" of women, and he was not familiar, either sympathetically or otherwise, with the image of a President in petticoats. His attitude was simply the flower of his general good-nature and a part of his instinctive and genuinely democratic assumption of every one's right to lead an easy life. If a shaggy pauper had a right to bed and board and wages and a vote, women, of course, who were weaker than paupers, and whose physical tissue was in itself an appeal, should be maintained, sentimentally, at the public expense. Newman was willing to be taxed for this purpose, largely, in proportion to his means. Moreover many of the common traditions with regard to women were with him fresh personal impressions. He had never read a page of printed romance.

He spent a great deal of time in listening to advice from Mrs. Tristram; advice, it must be added, for which he had never asked. He would have been incapable of asking for it, inasmuch as he had no perception of difficulties and consequently no curiosity about remedies. The complex Parisian world about him seemed a very simple affair; it was an

immense, surprising spectacle, but it neither inflamed his imagination nor irritated his curiosity.
He kept his hands in his pockets, looked on good-
humouredly, desired to miss nothing important,
observed a great many things in detail, and never
reverted to himself. Mrs. Tristram's "advice"
was a part of the show and a more entertaining
element of her free criticism than any other. He
enjoyed her talking about *him* — it seemed a part
of her beautiful culture ; but he never made an
application of anything she said or remembered
it when he was away from her. For herself, she
appropriated him : he was the most interesting
thing she had had to think about for many a month.
She wished to do something with him — she hardly
knew what. There was so much of him; he was so
rich and robust, so easy, friendly, well-disposed,
that he kept her imagination constantly on the alert.
For the present the only thing she could do was to
like him. She told him he was beyond everything
a child of nature, but she repeated it so often that it
could have been but a term of endearment. She led
him about with her, introduced him to fifty people,
took extreme satisfaction in her conquest. Newman
accepted every proposal, shook hands universally
and promiscuously, and seemed equally unversed
in trepidation and in " cheek." Tom Tristram complained of his wife's rapacity, declaring he could
never have a clear five minutes with his friend. If
he had known how things were going to turn out he
never would have brought him to the Avenue d'Iéna.
The two men had formerly not been intimate, but

Newman recalled his earlier impression of his host
and did Mrs. Tristram, who had by no means taken
him into her confidence, but whose secret he presently discovered, the justice to admit that her
husband had somehow found means to be degenerate
without the iridescence of decay. People said he was
very sociable, but this was as much a matter of
course as for a dipped sponge to expand; and it was
a sociability affirmed, on its anecdotic side, too
much at the expense of those possible partakers
who were not there to guard their interest in it. He
was patient at poker; he was infallible upon the
names and the other attributes of all the *cocottes;*
his criticism of cookery, his comparative view of the
great "years" of champagne, enjoyed the authority
of the last word. And then he was idle, spiritless,
sensual, snobbish. He irritated our friend by the
tone of his allusions to their native country, and
Newman was at a loss to understand wherein such
a country, as a whole, could fall short of Mr. Tristram's stomach. He had never been a very systematic
patriot, but it vexed him to see the United States
treated as little better than a vulgar smell in his
friend's nostril, and he finally spoke up for them
quite as if it had been Fourth of July, proclaiming
that any American who ran them down ought to be
carried home in irons and compelled to live in Boston
— which for Newman was putting it very vindic-
tively. Tristram was a comfortable man to snub;
he bore no malice and he continued to insist on
Newman's finishing his evenings at the Occidental
Club. The latter dined several times in the Avenue

d'Iéna, and his host always proposed an early adjournment to this institution. Mrs. Tristram protested, declaring as promptly that her husband exhausted a low cunning in trying to displease her.

"Oh no, I never try, my love," he answered; "I know you loathe me quite enough when I take my chance." But their visitor hated to see a married couple on these terms, and he was sure one or other of them must be very unhappy. Yet he knew it was not Tristram. The lady had a balcony before her windows, upon which, during the June evenings, she was fond of sitting, and Newman used frankly to say that he preferred the balcony to the club. It had a fringe of perfumed plants in tubs and enabled you to look up the broad street and see the Arch of Triumph vaguely massing its heroic sculptures in the summer starlight. Sometimes he kept his promise of following Mr. Tristram in half an hour to the Occidental and sometimes forgot it. His companion asked him a great many questions about himself, but on this subject he was an indifferent talker. He was not "subjective," though when he felt her interest sincere he made a real effort to meet it. He told her many things he had done, and regaled her with pictures of that "nature" as the child of which he figured for her; she herself was from Philadelphia and, with her eight years in Paris, talked of herself as a languid Oriental. But some other person was always the hero of the tale, though by no means always to his advantage; and the states of Newman's own spirit were but scantily chronicled. She had an especial wish to know whether he had ever been in love — seriously, passionately — and, failing to gather any satisfaction from his allusions, at last closely pressed him. He hesitated a while, but finally said "Hang it then, no!" She declared that she was delighted to hear it, as it confirmed her private conviction that he was a man of no real feeling.

"Is that so?" he asked very gravely. "But how do you recognise a man of real feeling?"

"I can't make out," said Mrs. Tristram, "whether you're very simple or very deep."

"I'm very deep. That's a fact."

"I believe that if I were to tell you with a certain air that you're as cold as a fish you would implicitly believe me."

"A certain air?" Newman echoed. "Well, try your air and see."

"You'd believe me, but you wouldn't care," said Mrs. Tristram.

"You've got it all wrong. I should care immensely, but I shouldn't believe you. The fact is I have never had time to 'feel' things so very beautifully. I've had to *do* them, had to make myself felt."

"Oh, I can imagine indeed that you may have sometimes done that tremendously."

"Yes, there's no mistake about that."

"When you're in one of your furies it can't be pleasant."

"Ah, I don't have to get into a fury to do it."

"I don't, nevertheless, see you always as you are now. You've *something* or other behind, beneath. You get harder or you get softer. You're more displeased — or you're more pleased."

"Well, a man of any sense does n't lay his plans to be angry," said Newman, "and it's in fact so long since I've been displeased that I've quite forgotten it."

"I don't believe," she returned "that you're never angry. A man *ought* to be angry sometimes, and you're neither good enough nor bad enough always to keep your temper."

"I lose it perhaps every five years."

"The time's coming round then," said his hostess. "Before I've known you six months I shall see you in a magnificent rage."

"Do you mean to put me into one?"

"I should n't be sorry. You take things too coolly. It quite exasperates me. And then you're too happy. You've what must be the most agreeable thing in the world — the consciousness of having bought your pleasure beforehand, having paid for it in advance. You've not a day of reckoning staring you in the face. Your reckonings are over."

"Well, I suppose I'm happy," said Newman almost pensively.

"You've been odiously successful."

"Successful in copper," he recalled, "but very mixed in other mining ventures. And I've had to take quite a back seat on oil."

"It's very disagreeable to know how Americans have come by their money," his companion sighed. "Now, at all events, you've the world before you. You've only to enjoy."

"Oh, I suppose I'm all right," said Newman. "Only I'm tired of having it thrown up at me.

Besides, there are several drawbacks. I don't come up to my own standard of culture."

"One does n't expect it of you," Mrs. Tristram answered. Then in a moment: "Besides, you do come up. You *are* up!"

"Well, I mean to have a good time, wherever I am," said Newman. "I find I take notice as I go, and I guess I shan't have missed much by the time I 've done. I feel something under my ribs here," he added in a moment, "that I can't explain — a sort of strong yearning, a desire to stretch out and haul in."

"Bravo!" Mrs. Tristram cried; "that's what I want to hear you say. You 're the great Western Barbarian, stepping forth in his innocence and might, gazing a while at this poor corrupt old world and then swooping down on it."

"Oh come," Newman protested; "I'm not an honest barbarian either, by a good deal. I'm a great fall-off from *him*. I 've seen honest barbarians, I know what they are."

"I don't mean you 're a Comanche chief or that you wear a blanket and feathers. There are different shades."

"I have the instincts — have them deeply — if I have n't the forms of a high old civilisation," Newman went on. "I stick to that. If you don't believe it I should like to prove it to you."

Mrs. Tristram was silent a while. "I should like to make you prove it," she said at last. "I should like to put you in a difficult place."

"Well, put me!" said Newman.

"Vous ne doutez de rien!" his companion rejoined.

"Oh," he insisted, "I've a very good opinion of myself."

"I wish I could put it to the test. Give me time and I will." And Mrs. Tristram remained silent a minute, as if trying to keep her pledge. It didn't appear that evening that she succeeded; but as he was rising to take his leave she passed suddenly, as she was very apt to do, from the tone of ingenious banter to that of almost tremulous sympathy. "Speaking seriously," she said, "I believe in you, Mr. Newman. You flatter my latent patriotism."

"Your latent —?"

"Deep within me the eagle shrieks, and I've known my heart at times to bristle with more feathers than my head. It would take too long to explain, and you probably wouldn't understand. Besides, you might take it — really you might take it — for a declaration. Yet it has nothing to do with you personally; the question is of what you almost unconsciously represent. Fortunately you don't know all that, or your conceit would increase insufferably." And then as Newman stood wondering what this great quantity might be: "Forgive all my meddlesome chatter and forget my advice. It's very silly in me to undertake to tell you what to do. When you're embarrassed do as you think best, and you'll do very well. When you're in a difficulty judge for yourself. Only let it then be all you."

"I shall remember everything you've told me." he made answer. "There are so many twists and turns over here, so many forms and ceremonies —"

"Forms and ceremonies are what I mean of course."

"Ah, but I don't want not to take account of them," he declared. "Have n't I as good a right as another? They don't scare me, and you need n't give me leave to ignore them. I want to know all about 'em."

"That's not what I mean. I mean that you're to deal with them in your own way. Settle delicate questions by your own light. Cut the knot or untie it, as you choose."

"Oh, if there's ever a big knot," he returned — "and they all seem knots of ribbon over here — I shall simply pull it off and wear it!"

The next time he dined in the Avenue d'Iéna was a Sunday, a day on which Mr. Tristram left the cards unshuffled, so that there was a trio in the evening on the balcony. The talk was of many things, and at last Mrs. Tristram suddenly observed to their visitor that it was high time that he should take a wife.

"Listen to her: she has the *toupet!*" said Tristram, who on Sunday evenings was always a little peevish.

"I don't suppose you've made up your mind not to marry?" Mrs. Tristram continued.

"Heaven forbid!" cried Newman. "I'm quite viciously bent on it."

"It's a very easy mistake," said Tristram; "and when it's made it's made."

"Well then," his wife went on, "I suppose you don't mean to wait till you're fifty."

"On the contrary, I'm in an almost indecent hurry."

"One would never guess it. Do you expect a lady to come and propose to you?"

"No; I'm willing to put the case before her myself. I think a great deal about it."

"Tell me some of your thoughts."

"Well," said Newman slowly, "I want to marry about as well as you *can*."

"'Well' in what sense?"

"In every sense. I shall be hard to suit."

"You must remember that, as the French proverb puts it, the finest girl in the world can give but what she has."

"Since you ask me," said Newman, "let me be frank about it — I want quite awfully to marry. It's time, to begin with; before I know it I shall be forty-five. And then I'm lonely, and I really kind of pine for a mate. There are things for which I want help. But if I marry now, so long as I did n't do it in hot haste when I was twenty, I must do it, you see, with my eyes open. I want to set about it rather grandly. I not only want to make no mistakes, but I want to make a great hit. I want to take my pick. My wife must be a pure pearl. I've thought an immense deal about it."

"Perhaps you think too much. The best thing's simply to fall in love."

"When I find the woman who satisfies me I shall rise to the occasion. My wife shall be as satisfied as I shall."

"You begin grandly enough," said Mrs. Tristram. "There's a chance for the pure pearls!"

"You're not fair," Newman presently broke out. "You draw a fellow on and put him off his guard and then you gibe at him."

"I assure you," she answered, "that I'm very serious. To prove it I make you a proposal. Should you like me, as they say here, to marry you?"

"To hunt up a wife for me?"

"She's already found. I'll bring you together."

"Oh come," said Tristram, "we don't keep a *bureau de placement*. He'll think you want your commission."

"Present me to a woman who comes up to my notion," Newman declared, "and I'll marry her to-morrow."

"You've a strange tone about it, and I don't quite understand you. I did n't suppose you could be so cold-blooded."

Newman was silent a while. "Well, I want a great woman. I stick to that. That's one thing I *can* treat myself to, and if it's to be had I mean to have it. What else have I toiled and struggled for all these years? I've succeeded, and now what am I to do with my success? To make it perfect, as I see it, there must be a lovely being perched on the pile like some shining statue crowning some high monument. She must be as good as she's beautiful and as clever as she's good. I can give my wife many things, so I'm not afraid to ask certain others myself. She shall have everything a woman can desire; I shall not even object to her being too good for me. She may be cleverer and wiser than I can understand, and I shall only be the better pleased. I want, in a word, the best article in the market."

"Why did n't you tell a fellow all this at the outset?" Tristram demanded. "I've been trying so to make you fond of *me!*"

"It's remarkably interesting," said Mrs. Tristram "I like to see a man know his own mind."

"I've known mine for a long time," Newman went on. "I made up my mind tolerably early in life that some rare creature all one's own is the best kind of property to hold. It's the greatest victory over circumstances. When I say rare I mean rare all through — grown as a rarity and recognised as one. It's a thing every man has an equal right to; he may get it if he *can* get it. He does n't have to be born with certain faculties on purpose; he needs only to be — well, whatever he really *is*. Then he need only use his will, and such wits as he can muster, and go in."

"It strikes me," said Mrs. Tristram, "that your marriage is to be rather a matter of heartless pomp."

"Well, it's certain," Newman granted, "that if people notice my wife and admire her I shall count it as part of my success."

"After this," cried Mrs. Tristram, "speak of any man's modesty!"

"But none of them will admire her so much as I."

"You really have the imagination of greatness."

He hesitated as if in fear of her mockery, but he kept it up, repeating his dry formula: "I want the best thing going."

"And I suppose you've already looked about you a good deal."

"More or less, according to opportunity."

"And you've seen nothing that has tempted you?"

"No," said Newman half reluctantly, "I'm bound to say in honesty that I've seen nothing that has come up to my idea."

"You remind me of the heroes of the French romantic poets, Rolla and Fortunio and all those other insatiable gentlemen for whom nothing in this world was handsome enough. But I see you're in earnest, and I *should* like to help you," Mrs. Tristram wound up.

"Who the deuce is it, darling, that you're going to palm off upon him?" her husband asked. "We know a good many pretty girls, thank goodness, but nobody to be mentioned in *that* blazing light."

"Have you any objections to a foreigner?" Mrs. Tristram continued, addressing their friend, who had tilted back his chair and, with his feet on a bar of the balcony railing and his hands in his pockets, sat looking at the stars.

"No Irish need apply," said Tristram.

Newman remained pensive. "Just as a foreigner, no. I've no prejudices."

"My dear fellow, you've no suspicions!" Tristram cried. "You don't know what terrible customers these foreign women are; especially those grown, as you call it, for the use of millionaires. How should you like an expensive Circassian with a dagger in her baggy trousers?"

Newman administered a vigorous slap to his knee. "I'd marry a Patagonian if she pleased me."

"We had better confine ourselves to Europe," said Mrs. Tristram. "The only thing is then that the young person herself should square with your tremendous standard?"

"She's going to offer you an unappreciated governess!" Tristram groaned.

"Of course I won't deny that, other things being equal, I should like one of my own countrywomen best," Newman pursued. "We should speak the same language, and that would be a comfort. But I'm not afraid of any foreigner who's the best thing in her own country. Besides, I rather like the idea of taking in Europe too. It enlarges the field of selection. When you choose from a greater number you can bring your choice to a finer point."

"Sardanapalus!" Tristram sighed.

"Well, you've come to the right market," Newman's hostess brought out after a pause. "I happen to number among my friends the finest creature in the world. Neither more nor less. I don't say a very charming person or a very estimable woman or a very great beauty: I say simply the finest creature in the world."

"I'm bound to say then," cried Tristram, "that you've kept very quiet about her. Were you afraid of *me*?"

"You've seen her," said his wife, "but you've no perception of such quality as Claire's."

"Ah, her name's Claire? I give it up."

"Does your friend wish to marry?" Newman asked.

"Not in the least. It's for you to make her change her mind. It won't be easy; she has had one husband and he gave her a low opinion of the species."

"Oh, she's a widow then ?"

"Are you already afraid ? She was married at eighteen, by her parents, in the French fashion, to a man with advantages of fortune, but objectionable, detestable, on other grounds, and many years too old. He had, however, the discretion to die a couple of years afterwards, and she's now twenty-eight."

"So she's French ?"

"French by her father, English by her mother. She's really more English than French, and she speaks English as well as you or I — or rather much better. She belongs, as they say here, to the very top of the basket. Her family, on each side, is of fabulous antiquity; her mother's the daughter of an English Catholic peer. Her father's dead, and since her widowhood she has lived with her mother and a married brother. There's another brother, younger, who I believe is rather amusing but quite impossible. They have an old hôtel in the Rue de l'Université, but their fortune's small and they make, for economy's sake, a common household. When I was a girl of less than fifteen I was put into a convent here for my education while my father made the tour of Europe. It was a fatuous thing to do with me, but it had the advantage that it made me acquainted with Claire de Bellegarde. She was younger than I, yet we became fast friends. I took a tremendous fancy to her, and she returned my adoration so far as she could. They kept such a tight rein on her that she could do very little, and when I left the convent she had to give me up. I was not of her *monde;* I'm not now either, but we sometimes meet. They're terrible

people — her *monde;* all mounted upon stilts a mile
high and with pedigrees long in proportion. It's the
skim of the milk of the old noblesse. Did you ever
hear of such a prehistoric monster as a Legitimist or
an Ultramontane? Go into Madame de Cintré's
drawing-room some afternoon at five o'clock and
you'll see the best-preserved specimens. I say go,
but no one is admitted — to intimacy — who can't
show good cause in the form of a family tree."

"And this is the lady you propose to me to marry?"
asked Newman. "A lady I can't even approach?"

"But you said just now that you recognised no
reasons against you."

Newman looked at Mrs. Tristram a while, stroking
his moustache. "Is she a very great beauty?" he
demanded

She hung fire a little "No."

"Oh then it's no use —!"

"She's not a very great beauty, but she's very,
very beautiful; two quite different things. A beauty
has no faults in her face; the face of a beautiful
woman may have faults that only deepen its charm."

"I remember Madame de Cintré now," said Tristram. "She's as plain as a copy in a copy-book —
all round o's and uprights a little slanting. She just
slants toward *us.* A man of your large appetite
would swallow her down without tasting her."

"In telling how little use *he* has for her my husband
sufficiently describes her," Mrs. Tristram pursued.

"Is she good, is she clever?" Newman asked.

"She's perfect! I won't say more than that. When
you're praising a person to another who's to know

her, it's bad policy to go into details. I won't exaggerate, I simply recommend her. Among all the
women I've known she stands alone; she's of a
different clay."

"I should like to see her," said Newman simply.

"I'll try to manage it. The only way will be to
invite her to dinner. I've never invited her before,
and I'm not sure she'll be able to come. Her old
feudal countess of a mother rules the family with an
iron hand and allows her to have no friends but of her
own choosing and to visit only in a certain sacred
circle. But I can at least invite her."

At this moment Mrs. Tristram was interrupted; a
servant stepped out upon the balcony and announced
that there were visitors in the drawing-room. When
she had gone in to receive her friends Tom Tristram
approached his guest.

"Don't put your foot into *this*, my boy," he said,
puffing the last whiffs of his cigar. "There's nothing
in it!"

Newman eyed him with oblique penetration. "You
tell another story, eh?"

"I say simply that Madame de Cintré's a great
white doll of a woman and that she cultivates quiet
haughtiness."

"Ah, she's *really* haughty, eh?"

"She looks at you as if you were so much thin air,
and blows you away as easily."

"She's *really* proud, eh?" Newman pursued with
interest.

"Proud? As proud as they make 'em over here."

"And not good-looking?"

Tristram shrugged his shoulders. "She leaves me cold. She's as cold herself as a porcelain stove, and has about as much expression. But I must go in and amuse the company."

Some time elapsed before Newman followed his friends into the drawing-room. When he at last joined them there he remained but a short time, and during this period sat perfectly silent, listening to a lady to whom Mrs. Tristram had straightway introduced him and who treated him, without drawing breath, to the full force of an extraordinarily high-pitched voice. He could but gaze and attend. Presently he came to bid his hostess good-night. "Who is that lady?"

"Miss Dora Finch. How do you like her?"

"Well, as I like the gong that sounds for dinner. She's good for a warning."

"She's thought so sweet! Certainly you have ideas," said Mrs. Tristram.

He hung about, but at last, "Don't forget about your friend," he said, "the lady of the proud people. Do make her come, and give me good notice." And with this he departed.

Some days later he came back; it was in the afternoon. He found Mrs. Tristram in her drawing-room and entertaining a visitor, a woman young and pretty and dressed in white. The two had risen and the visitor was apparently taking leave. After Newman had approached he received from Mrs. Tristram, who had turned to her companion, a glance of the most vivid significance, which he was yet not immediately able to interpret. "This is a good friend of

ours, Mr. Christopher Newman. I've spoken of you
to him, and he has an extreme desire to make your
acquaintance. If you had consented to come and dine
I should have offered him an opportunity."

The stranger presented her face with a still brightness of kindness. He was not embarrassed, for his
unconscious equanimity was boundless; but as he
became aware that this was the proud and beautiful
Madame de Cintré, the finest creature in the world,
the promised perfection, the proposed ideal, he made
an instinctive movement to gather his wits together.
Through the slight preoccupation it produced he had
a sense of a longish fair face and of the look of a pair
of eyes that were both intense and mild.

"I should have been most happy," said Madame
de Cintré. "Unfortunately, as I have been telling
Mrs. Tristram, I go next week to the country."

Newman had made a solemn bow. "I'm very very
sorry."

"Paris is really getting too hot," Madame de
Cintré added, taking her friend's hand again in farewell.

Mrs. Tristram seemed to have formed a sudden
and somewhat venturesome resolution, and she
smiled more gaily, as women do when they become
more earnest. "I want Mr. Newman to know you,"
she said, dropping her head on one side and looking
at Madame de Cintré's bonnet-ribbons.

Christopher Newman stood gravely silent, and
his native penetration admonished him. Mrs. Tristram was determined to force her friend to address
him a word of encouragement which should be more

than one of the common formulas of politeness; and if she was prompted by charity it was by the charity that begins at home. Madame de Cintré was her dearest Claire and her especial admiration; but Madame de Cintré had found it impossible to dine with her and Madame de Cintré should for once be forced gently to render tribute to Mrs. Tristram. "It would give me great pleasure," she said, looking at Mrs. Tristram.

"That's a great deal," cried the latter, "for Madame de Cintré to say!"

"I'm very much obliged to you," said Newman. "Mrs. Tristram can speak better for me than I can speak for myself."

Madame de Cintré turned on him again her soft lustre. "Are you for long in Paris?"

"We shall keep him," said Mrs. Tristram.

"But you're keeping *me!*" And Madame de Cintré disengaged her hand.

"A moment longer," said Mrs. Tristram.

Madame de Cintré looked at Newman again; this time without her smile. Her eyes lingered a little. "Will you come and see me?"

Mrs. Tristram kissed her at this; Newman acknowledged it more formally, and she took her departure. Her hostess went with her to the door, leaving Newman briefly alone. Presently she returned, clasping her hands together and shaking them at him. "It was a fortunate chance. She had come to decline my invitation. You triumphed on the spot, making her ask you, at the end of three minutes, to her house."

"It was you who triumphed," said Newman "You must n't see too much in her."

Mrs. Tristram stared. "What do you mean?"

"She did n't strike me as so very proud. I should call her quite timid."

"I should call *you* quite deep! And what do you think of her face?"

"Well, I guess I like her face," said Newman.

"I should think you might! May I guess, on my side, that you'll go and see her?"

"To-morrow!" cried Newman.

"No, not to-morrow; next day. That will be Sunday; she leaves Paris on Monday. If you don't see her it will at least be a beginning." And she gave him Madame de Cintré's address.

He walked across the Seine late in the summer afternoon and made his way through those grey and silent streets of the Faubourg Saint Germain whose houses present to the outer world a face as impassive and as suggestive of the concentration of privacy within as the blank walls of Eastern seraglios. Newman thought it a perverse, verily a "mean" way for rich people to live; his ideal of grandeur was a splendid façade, diffusing its brilliancy outward too, irradiating hospitality. The house to which he had been directed had a dark, dusty, painted portal, which swung open in answer to his ring. It admitted him into a wide, gravelled court, surrounded on three sides with closed windows; here was a doorway facing the street, approached by three steps and surmounted by a tent-like canopy. The place was all in the shade; it answered to Newman's conception of a convent. The portress couldn't say if Madame de Cintré were visible; he would please to apply at the further door. He crossed the court; a gentleman was sitting, bareheaded, on the steps of the portico, in play with a beautiful pointer. He rose as Newman approached, and, as he laid his hand on the bell, said, almost sociably, in English, that he was ashamed a visitor should be kept waiting: the servants were scattered; he himself had been ringing; he didn't know what the deuce was in them. This gentleman was young; his English was excellent, his expression easy. Newman pronounced the name of Madame de Cintré.

"I dare say," said the young man, "that my sister will be visible. Come in, and if you'll give me your card I'll carry it to her myself."

Newman had been accompanied on his present errand by a sentiment I will not say of defiance — a readiness for aggression or for defence, as either might prove needful — but rather of meditative, though quite undaunted and good-humoured suspicion. He took from his pocket, while he stood on the portico, a card upon which, under his name, he had written the words "San Francisco," and while he presented it he looked warily at his interlocutor. His glance found quick reassurance: he liked the young man's face; it strongly resembled that of Madame de Cintré, whose brother he would clearly be. The young man, on his side, had made a rapid inspection of Newman's person. He had taken the card and was about to enter the house with it when another figure appeared on the threshold — an older man, of a fine presence, habited in evening-dress. He looked hard at Newman and Newman met his examination. "Madame de Cintré," the younger man repeated as an introduction of the visitor. The other took the card from his hand, read it in a sustained stare, looked again at Newman from head to foot, hesitated a moment and then said, gravely but urbanely: "Madame de Cintré is not at home."

The younger man made a gesture and turned to Newman. "I'm very sorry, sir."

Newman gave a friendly nod, to show that he bore him no malice, and retraced his steps. At the porter's lodge he stopped; the two men were still standing on the portico. "Who may the gentleman with the dog be?" he asked of the old woman who reappeared. He had begun to learn French.

"That's Monsieur le Comte."

"And the other?"

"That's Monsieur le Marquis."

"A marquis?" said Christopher in English, which the old woman fortunately did not understand. "Oh then he's not the major-domo!"

IV

EARLY one morning, before he was dressed, a little old man was ushered into his apartment, followed by a youth in a blouse who carried a picture in a shining frame. Newman, among the distractions of Paris, had forgotten M. Nioche and his accomplished daughter; but this was an effective reminder.

"I was afraid you had given me up, sir," M. Nioche confessed after many apologies and salutations. "We have made you wait so many days. You accused us perhaps of a want of respectability, of bad faith, what do I know? But behold me at last! And behold also the pretty 'Madonna.' Place it on a chair, my friend, in a good light, so that monsieur may admire it." And M. Nioche, addressing his companion, helped him to dispose the work of art.

It had been endued with a layer of varnish an inch thick, and its frame, of an elaborate pattern, was at least a foot wide. It glittered and twinkled in the morning light and looked to Newman's eyes wonderfully splendid and precious. He thought of it as a very happy purchase and felt rich in his acquisition. He stood taking it in complacently while he proceeded with his dressing, and M. Nioche, who had dismissed his own attendant, hovered near, smiling and rubbing his hands.

"It has wonderful *finesse,*" he critically pronounced. "And here and there are marvellous touches; you probably perceive them, sir. It attracted great attention on the Boulevard as we came along. And then a gradation of tones! That's what it is really to know how to paint. I don't say it because I'm her father, sir; but as one man of taste addressing another I can't help observing that you've acquired an object of price. It's hard to produce such things and to have to part with them. If our means only allowed us the luxury of keeping it! I in fact may say, sir" — and M. Nioche showed a feebly insinuating gaiety — "I really may say that I envy you your privilege. You see," he added in a moment, "we've taken the liberty of offering you a frame. It increases by a trifle the value of the work and it will save you the annoyance — so great for a person of your delicacy — of going about to bargain at the shops."

The language spoken by M. Nioche was a singular compound, which may not here be reproduced in its integrity. He had apparently once possessed a certain knowledge of English, and his accent was oddly tinged with old cockneyisms and vulgarisms, things quaint and familiar. But his learning had grown rusty with disuse and his vocabulary was defective and capricious. He had repaired it with large patches of French, with words anglicised by a process of his own, with native idioms literally translated. The result, in the form in which he in all humility presented it, would be scarcely comprehensible to the reader, so that I have ventured to attempt for it some approximate notation. Newman only half followed, but he was always amused, and the old man's decent

forlornness appealed to his democratic instincts.
The assumption of any inevitability in the depressed
state always irritated his strong good-nature — it was
almost the only thing that did so; and he felt the
impulse to pass over it the dipped sponge of his own
prosperity. Mademoiselle Noémie's parent, however,
had apparently on this occasion been vigorously in-
doctrinated and showed a certain tremulous eagerness
to cultivate unexpected opportunities.

"How much do I owe you then with the frame?"
Newman asked.

"It will make in all three thousand francs," said
the old man, smiling agreeably but folding his hands
in instinctive suppliance.

"Can you give me a receipt?"

"I've brought one," said M. Nioche. "I took the
liberty of drawing it up in case monsieur should happen to desire to discharge his debt." And he drew
a paper from his pocket-book and presented it to his
patron. The document, Newman judged, had the
graces alike of penmanship and of style. He laid
down the money, and M. Nioche dropped the napoleons one by one, solemnly and lovingly, into
an old leathern purse.

"And how's your young lady?" he proceeded.
"She made a great impression on me."

"An impression? monsieur is very good. Monsieur finds her —?" the old man quavered.

"I find her remarkably pretty."

"Alas, yes, she's very very pretty!"

"And what's the harm in her being so?"

M. Nioche fixed his eyes upon a spot in the carpet and shook his head. Then raising them to a more intimate intelligence: "Monsieur knows what Paris is. Dangerous to beauty when beauty has n't the sou."

"Ah, but that's not the case with your daughter. Is n't she rich now?"

"We're rich — yes, for six months. But if my daughter were less attractive I should sleep none the worse."

"You're afraid of the young men?"

"The young and the old!"

"She ought to get a husband."

. "Ah, monsieur, one does n't get a husband for nothing. Her husband must take her as she is; I can't give her a *liard*. But the young men don't see with that eye."

"Oh," said Newman, "her talent's in itself a good outfit."

"*Heuh*, for that it needs first to be converted into specie!" — and M. Nioche slapped his purse tenderly before he stowed it away. "The miracle does n't take place every day."

"Well, your young men have very little grit; that's all I can say. They ought to pay for your daughter," Newman said, "and not ask money themselves."

"Those are very noble ideas, monsieur; but what will you have? They're not the ideas of this country. We want to know where we are when we marry."

"Well, how much will it take to show where your daughter is?" M. Nioche stared as if he wondered what might be coming next; but he promptly recovered himself, at a venture, and replied that he knew a very nice young man, employed by an insurance company, who would content himself with fifteen thousand francs. "Let your daughter paint half a dozen pictures for me," his benefactor then resumed, "and you can offer him his figure."

"Half a dozen pictures — his figure? Monsieur is n't speaking inconsiderately?"

"If she 'll make me six or eight copies in the Louvre as pretty as that 'Madonna,' I 'll pay her the same price," said Newman.

Poor M. Nioche was speechless a moment, with amazement and gratitude; after which he seized Newman's hand and pressed it between his own ten fingers, gazing at him with watery eyes. "As pretty as that? They shall be a thousand times prettier — they shall be perfect little loves. Ah, if I only knew how to paint myself, sir, so that I might lend a hand! What can I do to thank you? *Voyons!*" — and he pressed his forehead while he tried to think of something.

"Oh, you 've thanked me enough," said Newman.

"Ah, here it is, sir!" cried M. Nioche. "To express my gratitude I 'll charge you nothing for our lessons!"

"Our lessons? I had quite forgotten them. Listening to your English," Newman laughed, "is really quite a lesson in French."

"Ah, I don't profess to teach English, certainly," said M. Nioche. "But for my own admirable tongue I 'm still at your service."

"Since you 're here then we 'll begin. This is a very good hour, I 'm going to have my coffee. Come every morning at half-past nine and have yours with me."

"Monsieur offers me my coffee also?" cried M. Nioche. "Truly my *beaux jours* are coming back."

"*Allons, enfants de la patrie*," said Newman; "let's begin! The coffee's ripping hot. How do you say that in French?"

Every day then, for the following three weeks, the minutely respectable figure of M. Nioche made its appearance, with a series of little enquiring and apologetic obeisances, among the aromatic fumes of Newman's morning beverage. I know not what progress he made; but, as he himself said, if he did n't learn a great deal, at least he did n't learn much harm. And it amused him; it gratified that irregularly sociable side of his nature which had always expressed itself in a relish for ungrammatical conversation and which often, even in his busy and preoccupied days, had made him sit on rail fences in the twilight of young Western towns and gossip scarce less than fraternally with humorous loafers and obscure fortune-seekers. He had notions, wherever he went, about talking with the natives; he had been assured, and his judgement approved the advice, that in travelling abroad it was an excellent thing to look into the life of the country. M. Nioche was very much of a native, and though his life might not be particularly worth looking into he was a palpable and smoothly-rounded unit in that "stiff" sum of civilisation and sophistication which offered our hero so much easy entertainment and proposed so many curious problems to his idle but active mind

Newman had a theory that his intelligence was lying down, but at least it could n't sleep. He was fond of statistics; he liked to know how things were done; it gratified him to learn what taxes were paid, what profits were gathered, what commercial habits prevailed, how the battle of life was fought. M. Nioche, as a reduced capitalist, was familiar with these considerations, and he formulated his information, which he was proud to be able to impart, in the neatest possible terms and with a pinch of snuff between finger and thumb. As a Frenchman — quite apart from Newman's napoleons — M. Nioche loved conversation, and even in his decay his urbanity had not declined. As a Frenchman too he could give a clear account of things, and — still as a Frenchman — when his knowledge was at fault he could supply its lapses with the most convenient and ingenious hypotheses. The small shrunken bourgeois rejoiced, ever, to have questions asked him, and he scraped together information by frugal processes, he took in his little greasy pocket-book notes of matters that might interest his munificent friend. He read old almanacks at the book-stalls on the quays and began to frequent another café, where more newspapers were taken and his post-prandial *demi-tasse* cost him a penny extra, and where he used to con the tattered sheets for curious anecdotes, freaks of nature and strange coincidences. He would relate with solemnity the next morning that a child of five years of age had lately died at Bordeaux, whose brain had been found to weigh sixty ounces — the brain of a Napoleon or a Washington! or that Madame X,

charcutière in the Rue de Clichy, had found in the
wadding of an old petticoat the sum of three hundred
and sixty francs, which she had lost five years before.
He pronounced his words with great pomp and circumstance, and Newman assured him that his way
of dealing with the French tongue was very superior
to the bewildering chatter that he heard in other
mouths. Upon this M. Nioche's accent became
more flutelike than ever; he offered to read extracts
from Lamartine and protested that, although he did
endeavour according to his feeble lights to cultivate
authority of diction, monsieur, if he wanted the real
thing, should go to the Comédie.

Newman took an interest in the wondrous French
thrift and conceived a lively admiration for Parisian
economies. His own economic genius was so entirely
for operations on a larger scale, and, to move at his
ease, he needed so imperatively the sense of great
risks and great prizes, that he found diversion akin
to the watching of ants in the spectacle of fortunes
made by the aggregation of copper coins and in the
minute subdivision of labour and profit. He questioned M. Nioche about his own manner of life and
felt a friendly mixture of compassion and respect
for the mystery of these humilities. The worthy
man told him how he and his daughter had at one
period supported existence comfortably on the sum
of fifteen sous *per diem;* recently, having succeeded
in dragging ashore the last floating fragments of the
wreck of his fortune, his budget had been a trifle
more ample. But they still had to butter their bread
very thin, and M. Nioche intimated with a sigh that

his young companion didn't bring to this task the zealous co-operation that might have been desired. "But what will you have? One is in the flower of youth, one is pretty, one needs new dresses and fresh gloves; one can't wear shabby gowns among the splendours of the Louvre."

"Yet she must earn what will pay for her clothes," Newman felt enlisted enough to suggest.

M. Nioche looked at him with weak, uncertain eyes. He would have liked to be able to say that his daughter's talents were appreciated and that her crooked little daubs commanded a market; but it seemed a scandal to abuse the credulity of this free-handed stranger, who, without a suspicion or a question, had admitted him to equal social rights. He compromised, he declared that while it was obvious that Mademoiselle Noémie's reproductions of the old masters had only to be seen to be coveted, the prices which, in consideration of their altogether peculiar degree of finish, she felt obliged to ask for them, had kept purchasers at a respectful distance. "Poor little cherished one!" said M. Nioche with a sigh; "it's almost a pity that her work's so perfect! It would be in her interest to be a bit of an impostor."

"But if she has this spark of the flame," Newman benevolently reasoned, "why should you have those fears for her that you spoke of the other day?"

M. Nioche meditated; there was an inconsistency in his position; it made him particularly uncomfortable. Though he had no desire to destroy the goose with the golden eggs — Newman's benevolent confidence — he felt a weary need to speak out all his trouble. "Ah, she has a spark of that flame, my dear sir, most assuredly. But, to tell you the truth, she has also more than a mere spark of another. She's a *franche coquette* if there ever was one. I'm sorry to say," he added in a moment, shaking his head with a world of accepted melancholy, "it was to come to her as straight as a letter in the post. Her poor mother had that sad vice."

"Why, you weren't happy with your wife?" Newman almost incredulously asked.

M. Nioche gave half a dozen little backward jerks of his head. "She was my heavy cross, monsieur!"

"She wasn't very good?"

"She was good for some things and some people, but not for a poor man like me. She deceived me, under my nose, year after year. I was too stupid, and the temptation was too great. But I found her out at last. I've only been once in my life a man to be afraid of; I know it very well: it was in that hour! Nevertheless I don't like to think of it. I loved her — I can't tell you why nor how much. Oh, she was — if I must say so — bad."

"She's not living?"

"She's gone to her account."

"Her influence on your daughter then," said Newman encouragingly, "is not to be feared."

"She cared no more for her daughter than for the wind in the chimney. But Noémie has no more use for bad examples than for good. She's sufficient to herself. She's stronger than I."

"She doesn't mind what you say?"

"There isn't much to mind, sir — I say so little

What's the use of my saying anything? It would only irritate her and drive her to some *coup de tête*. She's very clever, like her poor mother; she would waste no time about it. As a child — when I was happy, or supposed I was — she studied drawing and painting with first-class professors, and they assured me she had the gift. I was delighted to believe it, and when I went into society I used to carry her little water-colours with me in a portfolio and hand them round to the company. I remember how a lady once thought I was offering them for sale and that I took it very ill. We don't know what we may come to! Then came my dark days and my final rupture with Madame Nioche. Noémie had no more twenty-franc lessons; but in the course of time, when she grew older and it became highly expedient that she should do something that would help to keep us alive, she bethought herself of her palette and brushes. Some of our friends in the *quartier* pronounced the idea fantastic: they recommended her to try bonnet-making, to get a situation in a shop, or — if she was more ambitious — to advertise for a place of *dame de compagnie*. She did advertise, and an old lady wrote her a letter and bade her come and see her. The old lady liked her and made her an offer of her living and six hundred francs a year; but Noémie discovered that she passed her life in her arm-chair and had only two visitors, her confessor and her nephew: the confessor very strict, and the nephew a man of fifty, with a broken nose and a government clerkship of two thousand francs. She threw her old lady over, bought a paint-box, a canvas and a new dress, and went and set up her easel in the Louvre. There, in one place and another, she has passed the last two years; I can't say it has made us millionaires. But she tells me Rome was n't built in a day, that she's making great progress, that I must leave her to her own devices. The fact is, without prejudice to her 'gift,' that she has no idea of burying herself alive. She likes to see the world and to be seen of the world. She says herself that she can't work in the dark. Her appearance itself holds up the lamp for others! Only I can't help worrying and trembling — I can't help wondering what may happen to her there all alone, day after day, amid that prowling of people from the ends of the earth. I can't be always at her side. I go with her in the morning, and I come to fetch her away, but she won't have me near her in the interval; she says I give on her nerves. As if it did n't give on mine to keep walking up and down outside! Ah, if anything were to happen to her!" cried M. Nioche, clenching his two fists and jerking back his head again portentously.

"Oh, I guess she'll come out all right," his friend soothingly returned.

"I believe I should shoot her otherwise!" said the old man solemnly.

"Well, we'll marry her quick enough," insisted Newman — "since that's how you manage it; and I'll go and see her to-morrow at the Louvre and pick out the pictures she's to copy for me."

M. Nioche had brought a message from his daughter in acceptance of their patron's magnificent commission, the young lady declaring herself his most devoted servant, promising her most zealous endeavour and regretting that the proprieties forbade her coming to thank him in person. The morning after the conversation just narrated Newman reverted to his intention of meeting his young friend at the Louvre. M. Nioche appeared preoccupied and left his budget of anecdotes unopened; he took a great deal of snuff and sent certain oblique, appealing glances toward his stalwart pupil. At last, when taking his leave, he stood a moment, after he had polished his hat with his calico pocket-handkerchief, and fixed his small pale eyes strangely on that personage.

"Well, what's the matter?"

"Pardon the solicitude of a father's heart! You inspire me with boundless confidence, but I can't help making you an appeal. After all you're a man, and so fine a one; you're young and at liberty. Let me beseech you then to respect an innocence—!"

Newman had wondered what was coming, yet had already burst into mirth. He was on the point of pronouncing his own innocence the more exposed, but he contented himself with promising to treat the young lady with nothing less than veneration. He found her, awaiting him, seated on the great divan of the Salon Carré. She was not in the garb of labour, but wore her bonnet and gloves and carried her parasol in honour of the occasion. These articles had been selected with unerring taste, and a fresher, prettier image of youthful alertness and blooming discretion was not to be conceived. She made Newman a most respectful curtsey, she expressed her gratitude for his liberality in the neatest of little speeches. It annoyed him to have so charming a girl stand there thanking him, and it made him feel uncomfortable to think that this perfect young lady, with her excellent manners and her finished intonation, was literally in his pay. He assured her, in such French as he could muster, that the thing was not worth mentioning and that he regarded her services as a particular favour.

"Whenever you please then," she said, "we'll pass the review."

They walked slowly round the room and then into the others; they strolled about with high dignity for half an hour. His companion evidently relished her situation and had no desire to bring to a close her public interview with a patron of such striking type. Newman perceived that prosperity agreed with her and that the little firm-lipped, peremptory air with which she had addressed her father on the occasion of their former meeting had given place to the prettiest, easiest prattle.

"What sort of pictures have you in mind?" she asked. "Sacred or profane?"

"Oh, a few of each. But I want something bright and gay."

"Something gay? There's nothing very gay in this solemn old Louvre. But we'll see what we can find. You speak French to-day like a charm. My father has done wonders."

' Oh, I'm a thankless subject," said Newman. "I'm too old to learn a language."

"Too old? *Quelle folie!*" she cried with a clear

shrill laugh. "You're a very *beau jeune homme!*
And how do you like my father?"

"He's a very nice old gentleman. He never laughs
at my blunders."

"He's very *comme il faut*, dear papa," said Mademoiselle Noémie, "and as honest as the day. Oh,
a probity that would take a prize! You could trust
him with millions."

"Do you always mind what he says?" asked
Newman.

"'Mind' it?"

"Do you do what he bids you."

The girl stopped and looked at him; she had a
spot of colour in either cheek, and in her prompt
French eye, too protrusive for perfect beauty, was a
sharp spark of freedom. "Why do you ask me
that?"

"Because I want to know."

"You think me a bad little girl?" And she gave
a strange smile.

Newman looked at her a moment; he saw she was
pretty, but he was not in the least dazzled. He remembered poor M. Nioche's solicitude for her innocence, and he laughed out again as his eyes met this
odd quantity. Her face was a rare mixture of youth
and maturity, and beneath her clear, charming forehead her searching little smile seemed to contain a
world of ambiguous intentions. She was pretty
enough, certainly, to make her father uneasy; but
as regards her innocence Newman felt ready on the
spot to affirm that she had never yet sacrificed it.
She had simply never had any to lose; she had been

looking at the wonderful world about her since she was ten years old, and he would have been a wise man who could tell her any secret of the town. In her long mornings at the Louvre she had not only studied Madonnas and Saint Johns; she had kept an eye upon the variously-embodied human nature in which the scene no less abounded, and she had formed her conclusions. In a degree, it seemed to Newman, M. Nioche might be at rest; if his daughter should assert her liberty in some unmistakeable way she would yet never publish her imprudence. Newman, with his long-drawn, leisurely smile and his articulation that suggested confidence in nothing but its motive, was always mentally taking his time; so he asked himself now what she was looking at him in that way for. He had an impression she would like him to confess that he did think her a wretch. "Oh no," he said at last; " it would be very impolite in me to judge you in any such way. I don't know you."

"But my father has complained to you."

"He says you're a free spirit."

"He should n't go about saying such things to gentlemen! But you don't believe it?"

"Well," said Newman conscientiously, "I don't believe he meant any harm by it."

She looked at him again, gave a shrug and a smile, and then pointed to a small Italian picture, a Marriage of Saint Catherine. "How should you like that?"

"It does n't please me," he presently answered. "The young lady in the yellow dress is n't pretty enough."

77

"Ah, you're a great connoisseur!" his companion sighed.

"In pictures? Oh no; I'm only picking up the rudiments of knowledge."

"In pretty women then?"

"In that I may be coming on, but I've ground to make up."

"What do you say to this?" the girl asked, indicating a superb Italian portrait of a lady. "I'll do it for you on a smaller scale."

"On a smaller scale? Why not as large as the original?"

She glanced at the glowing splendour of the Venetian masterpiece and gave a toss of her head. "I don't like that woman. She looks stupid."

"Well, she makes an impression on me," said Newman. "Decidedly I must have her, and as large as life. And just as shiningly stupid as she stands there."

The girl fixed her eyes on him again, and with her mocking smile: "It certainly ought to be easy for me to make her look stupid!" And then as he but opposed his vagueness she gave another shrug. "Seriously, you *want* that portrait — the golden hair, the purple satin, the pearl necklace, the two magnificent arms?"

"Everything — just as it is."

"Would nothing else do instead?"

"Oh, I want some other things, but I want that too."

She turned away a moment, walked to the other side of the hall and stood there looking vaguely about her. At last she came back. "It must be charming to be able to order pictures at such a rate. Venetian portraits as large as life! You go at it *en prince*. And you're going to travel about Europe that way?"

"Yes, I intend to travel," said Newman.

"Ordering, buying, spending money?"

"Of course I shall spend a certain amount of money."

"You're very happy to have it. And you're perfectly free?"

"How do you mean, free?"

"You have nothing to *embêter* you — no father, no family, no wife, no *fiancée*?"

"Yes, I'm tolerably free."

"You're very very happy," said Mademoiselle Noémie gravely.

"*Je le veux bien!*" said Newman, proving that he had learned more French than he admitted.

"And how long shall you stay in Paris?" the girl went on.

"Only a few days more."

"Why do you go away?"

"It's getting hot, and I must go to Switzerland."

"To Switzerland? That's a fine country. I would give the clothes on my back to see it! Lakes and mountains, deep green valleys, *ranz-des-vaches!* Oh I congratulate you! Meanwhile I shall sit here through all the hot summer daubing at your pictures."

"Ah, take your time about it," Newman urged "Do them at your convenience."

They walked further and looked at a dozen other things. He pointed out what pleased him, and Mademoiselle Noémie generally criticised it and proposed something else. Then suddenly she diverged into the intimate. "What made you speak to me the other day in the Salon Carré?"

"I admired your picture."

"But you hesitated a long time."

"Oh, I do nothing foolish," he said.

"Yes, I saw you watching me. But I never supposed you were going to speak to me. I never dreamed I should be walking about here with you to-day. It's very remarkable."

"It's sufficiently natural," he calmly pleaded.

"Ah, I beg your pardon: not to me. 'Free spirit' — in other words horrid creature — as you think me, I have never walked about in public with a gentleman before. What was my father thinking of when he consented to our interview?"

"He was repenting of his unjust accusations," Newman returned.

Mademoiselle Noémie remained silent; at last she dropped into a seat. "Well then, for those five it's fixed," she presently said. "Five copies as brilliant and beautiful as I can make them. We've one more to choose. Should n't you like one of those great Rubenses — the Marriage of Marie de Médicis? Just look at it and see how handsome it is."

"Oh yes; I should like that," he allowed. "Finish off with that."

"Finish off with that — good!" she laughed. She sat a moment looking at him, then suddenly rose and stood before him with her arms expressively folded. "*Ah ça*, I don't understand you," she bravely broke out. "I don't understand how a man can be so ignorant."

"Oh, I'm ignorant certainly." And he put his hands in his pockets.

"It's too ridiculous! I don't know how to paint *pour deux sous*."

"You don't know how?"

"I paint like a cat; I can't draw a straight line. I never sold a picture until you bought that thing the other day." And as she offered this surprising information she continued to smile.

Newman met it with a grimace of his own. "Why do you make that statement?"

"Because it irritates me to see a clever man so *bête*. My copies are grotesque."

"And the one I possess —?"

"That one's the flower of the dreadful family."

"Well," said Newman, "I never outgrew a mistake but in my own time and in my own way."

She looked at him askance. "Your patience is very *gentille;* it's my duty to warn you before you go further. This *commande* of yours is impossible, you know. What do you take me for? It's work for ten strong men. You pick out the six most difficult pictures in the place, and you expect me to go to work as if I were sitting down to hem a dozen pocket handkerchiefs. I wanted to see how far you'd go."

Newman considered her in some perplexity. In spite of the blunder of which he stood convicted he was very far from being a simpleton, and he had a lively suspicion that her burst of confidence was not essentially more honest than her original pretence. She was playing a great game; she was not simply taking pity on the bloom of his barbarism. What was it she expected to gain? The stakes were high and the risk not small; the prize therefore must have been commensurate. But even granting that the prize might be great Newman could scarce resist a movement of admiration for his young friend's intrepidity. She was throwing away with one hand, whatever she might intend to do with the other, a substantial sum of money. "Are you joking or serious?"

"Oh, *d'un sérieux!*" she cried, but with her extraordinary smile.

"I know very little about pictures or how they're really painted. If you can't do all, why then do what you conveniently can."

"It will all be bad *à faire pleurer*," said Mademoiselle Noémie.

"Oh," Newman laughed, "if you want to swindle me of course you can. But why do you go on painting badly?"

"I can do nothing else; I've neither eye nor hand nor training. Above all I have n't patience."

"You're deceiving your father then."

The girl just hesitated. "He perfectly knows."

"No," Newman declared; "I'm sure he believes in you"

"He's afraid of me, poor dear. I go on painting badly, as you say, because it passes the time. I like being here; it's a place to come to every day; it's better than sitting in a little dark damp room on a court or than selling buttons and whalebones over a counter."

"Of course it's much more amusing," said Newman. "But for a poor girl is n't it rather an expensive amusement?"

"Oh, I'm very wrong; there's no doubt about that," she answered. "But rather than earn my living as some girls do — toiling with a needle in little black holes out of the world — I'd throw myself into the Seine."

"There's no need of that," he presently observed. "Your father must have mentioned to you the reason of my offer?"

"The reason — ?"

"He wants you to marry, and I told him I'd give you a chance to earn your *dot*."

"He told me all about it, and you see the account I make of it! Why should you take such an interest in my marriage?"

"My interest was in your father. I hold to my engagement. Do what you can, and I'll buy what you do."

She stood some time in thought, her eyes on the ground. At last looking up, "What sort of a husband can you get for twelve thousand francs?" she asked.

"Your father tells me he knows some very good young men."

"Grocers and butchers and little *maîtres de cafés?* I won't marry at all if I can't marry more *proprement* than that."

"I'd advise you not to be too fastidious," said Newman. "That's all the advice I can give you."

"I'm vexed at what I've said!" cried his companion. "It has done me no good. But I could n't help it."

"What good did you expect it to do you?"

"I could n't help it, simply."

He looked at her a moment. "Well, your painting may be a fraud, but you're too honest for me all the same. I don't understand you. Good-bye!" And he put out his hand.

She made no response, she granted him no farewell. She turned away and seated herself sidewise on a bench, leaning her head on the back of her hand, which clasped the rail in front of the pictures. Newman stood near her another moment, then he turned on his heel and retreated. He had understood her better than he confessed; this singular scene was a practical commentary upon her father's description of her as a free spirit.

V

WHEN he had told Mrs. Tristram the story of his fruitless visit to Madame de Cintré she urged him not to be discouraged, but to carry out his plan of "seeing Europe" during the summer — after which he might return to Paris for the autumn and then settle down comfortably for the winter. "Claire de Cintré will be kept in a cool place for you," she reasoned; "she's not a woman who'll change her condition from one day to another." Newman made no distinct affirmation that he would come back to Paris; he even talked about Rome and the Nile, and abstained from professing any especial interest in Madame de Cintré's continued widowhood. This was a little of a false note in his usual distinctness, and may perhaps be regarded as characteristic of the incipient stage of that passion which is more particularly known as the romantic one. The truth is that the expression of a pair of eyes, that were both intense and mild, had become very familiar to his memory, and he would not easily have resigned himself to the prospect of never looking into them again. He communicated to Mrs. Tristram a number of other facts, of greater or less importance, as you choose; but on this particular point he kept his own counsel. He took a kindly leave of M. Nioche, having assured him that so far as he was concerned the blue-cloaked Madonna herself might have been present at his interview with Mademoiselle Noémie; and left the old man nursing his breast-pocket in an ecstasy which the sharpest paternal discomposure might have been defied to dissipate.

He started on his travels with all his usual appearance of slow-strolling leisure and all his essential directness and intensity of aim. No man seemed less in a hurry and yet no man enabled brief periods to serve him more liberally. He had practical instincts which signally befriended him in his trade of tourist. He found his way in foreign cities by divination, his memory was excellent when once his attention had been at all cordially given, and he emerged from dialogues in foreign tongues, of which he had formally not understood a word, in full possession of the particular item he had desired to elicit. His appetite for items was large, and although many of those he noted might have seemed woefully dry and colourless to the ordinary sentimental traveller, a careful inspection of the list would have shown that his toughness had sensitive spots. In the charming city of Brussels — his first stopping-place after leaving Paris — he asked a great many questions about the street-cars and took extreme satisfaction in the reappearance of this familiar symbol of American civilisation; but he was also greatly struck with the beautiful Gothic tower of the Hôtel de Ville and wondered if they might n't "get up" something like it in San Francisco. He stood long in the crowded square before this edifice, in imminent danger from carriage-wheels, listening to a toothless old cicerone mumble in broken English the touching history of

Counts Egmont and Horn; and he wrote the names
of these gentlemen — for reasons best known to himself — on the back of an old letter.

At the outset, on his leaving Paris, his curiosity
had not been intense; passive entertainment, in the
Champs Elysées and at the theatres, seemed about
as much as he need expect of himself, and although,
as he had said to Tristram, he wanted to see the
mysterious and satisfying *best*, he had not the grand
tour in the least on his conscience and was not given
to worrying the thing that amused him. He believed
serenely that Europe was made for him and not he
for Europe. He had said he wanted to improve his
mind, but he would have felt a certain embarrassment, a certain shame even — a false shame possibly — if he had caught himself looking intellect-
ually into the mirror. Neither in this nor in any other
respect had he a high sense of responsibility; it was
his prime conviction that a man's life should be a
man's ease and that no privilege was really great
enough to take his breath away. The world, to his
vision, was a great bazaar where one might stroll
about and purchase handsome things; but he was
no more conscious, individually, of social pressure
than he admitted the claim of the obligatory purchase. He had not only a dislike but a sort of moral
mistrust of thoughts too admonitory; one should n't
hunt about for a standard as a lost dog hunts for
a master. One's standard was the idea of one's own
good-humoured prosperity, the prosperity which
enabled one to give as well as take. To expand
without too much ado — without "mean" timidity

on one side or the bravado of the big appetite on the other — to the full compass of any such experience as was held to stir men's blood represented his nearest approach to a high principle. He had always hated to hurry to catch railroad-trains, and yet had always caught them; and just so an undue solicitude for the right side seemed a sort of silly dawdling at the station, a proceeding properly confined to women, foreigners and invalids. All this admitted, he enjoyed his journey, when once he had fairly entered the current, as intimately as if he had kept a diary of raptures. He lounged through Belgium and Holland and the Rhineland, through Switzerland and Northern Italy, planning about nothing and seeing all things. The guides and *valets de place* found him an excellent subject. He was always approachable, for he was much addicted to large lapses and long intervals, to standing about in the vestibules and porticoes of inns, and he availed himself little of the opportunities for impressive seclusion so liberally offered in Europe to gentlemen travelling with long purses. When an excursion, a church, a gallery, a ruin was proposed to him the first thing he usually did, after surveying his postulant in silence and from head to foot, was to sit down at a little table and order some light refreshment, of which he more often than not then forgot to partake. The cicerone during this process, commonly retreated to a respectful distance; otherwise I am not sure that Newman would not have bidden him sit down and share, sit down and tell him as a decent creature if his church or his gallery were really worth one's trouble. At last he rose and stretched his long legs, beckoned to the man of monuments, looked at his watch and fixed his eye on his adversary "What is it and how far?" And whatever the case, though he might seem to hesitate he never declined He stepped into an open cab, made his conductor sit beside him to answer questions, bade the driver go fast (he had a particular aversion to slow driving), and rolled, in all probability through a dusty suburb, to the goal of his pilgrimage. When the goal was a disappointment, when the church was meagre or the ruin a heap of rubbish, he never protested nor berated his adviser; he looked with an impartial eye upon great monuments and small, made the guide recite his lesson, listened to it religiously, asked if there were nothing else to be seen in the neighbourhood, and drove back again at a rattling pace. It is to be feared that his perception of the difference between the florid and the refined had not reached the stage of confidence, and that he might often have been seen — as we have already seen him — gazing with culpable serenity at inferior productions. The wrong occasion was a part of his pastime in Europe as well as the right, and his tour was altogether a pastime. But there is sometimes nothing like the imagination of those people who have none, and Newman now and then, in an unguided stroll through a foreign city, before some lonely, sad-towered church or some angular image of one who had rendered civic service in an unknown past, had felt a singular deep commotion. It was not an excitement, not a perplexity; it involved an extraordinary sense of recreation.

He encountered by chance in Holland a young American with whom he fell for a time into a tacit travellers' partnership. They were men of different enough temper, but each in his way so true to his type that each might seem to have something of value to contribute to the association. Newman's comrade, whose name was Babcock, was a young Unitarian minister; a small, spare, neatly-attired man, with a strikingly candid countenance. He was a native of Dorchester, Massachusetts, and had spiritual charge of a small congregation in another suburb of the New England capital. His digestion was weak and he lived chiefly on Graham bread and hominy — a regimen to which he was so much attached that his tour seemed to him destined to be blighted when, on landing on the Continent, he found these delicacies fail to flourish under the *table d'hôte* system. In Paris he had purchased a bag of hominy at an establishment which called itself an American Agency and at which the New York illustrated papers were also to be procured, and he had carried it about with him and shown extreme serenity and fortitude in the somewhat delicate position of having his hominy prepared for him and served on odd occasions at the hotels he successively visited. Newman had once spent a morning, in the course of business, at Mr. Babcock's birthplace, and, for reasons too recondite to unfold, the memory of his visit always pressed the spring of mirth. To carry out his joke, which certainly seems poor so long as it is not explained, he used often to address his companion as "Dorchester." Fellow-aliens cling together, on a strange soil, in spite of themselves; but it was probable that at home these unnatural intimates must have met only to part. They had indeed by habit and form as little in common as possible. Newman, who never reflected on such matters, accepted the situation with great equanimity, but Babcock used to meditate over it privately; used often indeed to retire to his room early in the evening for the express purpose of considering it conscientiously and, as he would have said, with detachment. He was not sure it was a good thing for him to have given himself up so unreservedly to our hero, whose way of taking life was so little his own.

Newman was a spirit of easy power; Mr. Babcock even at times saw it clear that he was one of nature's noblemen, and certainly it was impossible not to feel strongly drawn to him But would it not be desirable to try to produce an effect on him, to try to quicken his moral life and raise his sense of responsibility to a higher plane? He liked everything, he accepted everything, he found amusement in everything; he was not discriminating, his values were as vague and loose as if he had carried them in his trousers pocket. The young man from Dorchester accused Newman of a fault that he considered very grave and did his best himself to avoid — of what he would have called a want of moral reaction. Poor Mr. Babcock was extremely fond of pictures and churches, and kept Mrs. Jameson's volumes in his trunk; he regarded works of art as questions and his relations with them as experiences, and received peculiar impressions from everything he saw. But

nevertheless in his secret soul he detested Europe
and felt an irritated need to protest against Newman's
easy homage to so compromised a charmer, mistress
of a cynicism that appeared at times to have made him
cynical. Mr. Babcock's moral *malaise*, I am afraid,
lay deeper than where any definition of mine can
reach it. He mistrusted the "European" tempera-
ment, he suffered from the "European" climate, he
hated the "European" dinner hour; "European"
life seemed to him unscrupulous and impure. And
yet he had what he called an intimate sense of the
true beautiful in life, and as this element was often
inextricably associated with the above displeasing
conditions, as he wished above all to be just and
dispassionate and as he was furthermore extremely
bent on putting his finger on the boundary-line, in
the life of a School, between the sincere time and the
insincere, he could not bring himself to decide that
the kingdoms of the earth were utterly rotten. But
he thought them in a bad way, and his quarrel with
Newman was over some of the elements, insidious
forms of evil, that this promiscuous feeder at the
feast could swallow with no wry face. Babcock himself really knew as little about the forms of evil, in
any quarter of the world, as about the forms of bank-
ing; his most vivid realisation of the most frequent
form had been the discovery that one of his college
classmates, a student of architecture in Paris, was
carrying on a love-affair with a young woman who
did n't in the least count on his marrying her. Babcock had described this situation to Newman, and
our hero had applied an epithet marked by a rough

but not unfriendly justice to the girl. The next day his companion asked him if he were certain he had used exactly the right word to characterise the young architect's mistress. Newman wondered and seemed amused. "There are a great many words to express that idea," he said; "you can take your choice!"

"Oh, I mean," said Babcock, "was she possibly not to be considered in a different light? Don't you think she really *had* believed in his higher nature?"

"I'm afraid I don't know," Newman replied. "Very likely she had; I've no doubt she judged it by her own." He was willing to meet his friend on any view of her.

"I didn't mean that either," said Babcock; "I'm not sure that she *has* a higher nature I'm not sure — not *very* sure — every one has. I was only afraid I might have seemed yesterday not to remember — not to consider. Well, I think I'll write to Percival about it."

And he had written to Percival (who had answered him in a manner that *was* indubitably cynical) and had reflected that Newman ought n't to be encouraged, after all, to read a cheap idealism into flagrant cases of immorality. The levity and brevity of his comrade's judgements very often shocked and depressed him. He had a way of damning people without further appeal, or else of appearing almost in sympathy with their sinister side, which seemed unworthy of a man whose conscience could still pretend to a squirm. And yet poor Babcock yearned toward him and remembered that even if, decidedly, his sensibility

would never work straight, this was not a reason for
giving him up. Goethe recommended seeing human
nature in the most various forms, and Mr. Babcock
thought Goethe perfectly splendid. He often tried in
odd half-hours of conversation to explain what he
meant by some of his principal doubts, but it was
like offering to read from a technical treatise. The
volume might deal lucidly with Mr. Babcock's subject, but what was Mr. Babcock's subject without
Mr. Babcock's interest in it? Newman could entertain a respect for any man's subject and thought his
friend fortunate to have so special a one He accepted
all the proofs of its importance that were thus anxiously offered him, and put them away in what he
supposed a very safe place; but poor Babcock never
afterwards recognised his gifts among the articles that
Newman had in daily use.

They travelled together through Germany and
into Switzerland, where for three or four weeks they
trudged over rough passes and smooth and lounged
by the edge and on the bosom of blue lakes. At last
they crossed the Simplon and made their way to
Venice. Mr. Babcock had become gloomy and even
a trifle irritable; he seemed moody, absent, preoccupied; he got his plans into a tangle and talked
one moment of doing one thing and the next of doing
another. Newman led his own usual life, recklessly
made acquaintances, took his ease in the galleries
and churches, spent an unconscionable amount of
time in strolling in Piazza San Marco, bought several
spurious pictures and for a fortnight enjoyed Venice
grossly. One evening, coming back to his inn, ne

found Babcock waiting for him in the little garden beside it. The young man walked up to him, looking very dismal, thrust out his hand and said with solemnity that he was afraid they must part. Newman expressed his surprise and regret; he wondered why a parting had become necessary. "Don't be afraid I'm tired of you," he said.

"You're not tired of me?" his companion asked, fixing him with clear but almost tragic eyes.

"Why the deuce should I be? You're a very nice man. Besides, I don't break down so easily."

"We don't understand each other," said poor Dorchester.

"Don't I understand you?" cried Newman. "Why, I hoped I did. But what if I don't; where's the harm?"

"I don't understand *you*," said Babcock. And he sat down and rested his head on his hand and looked up mournfully at his immeasurable friend.

"But why should you mind that if I don't?"

"It's very distressing to me. It keeps me in a state of unrest. It irritates me; I can't settle anything. I don't think it's good for me."

"You worry too much; that's what's the matter with you," said Newman.

"Of course it must seem so to you. You think I take all questions too hard, and I think you take them too superficially. We can never agree."

"But we've agreed very well all along."

"No, *I* have n't agreed," said Babcock, shaking his head. "I'm very uncomfortable. I ought to have separated from you a month ago."

"Oh, shucks! I'll agree to anything!" cried Newman.

Mr. Babcock buried his head in both hands. At last, looking up, "I don't think you appreciate my position," he observed. "I try to arrive at the truth about everything. And then you go too fast. There are things of which you take too little account. I feel as if I ought to go over all this ground we've traversed again by myself. I'm afraid I have made a great many mistakes."

"Oh, you need n't give so many reasons," said Newman. "You've simply had enough of me. You've all your right to that."

"No, no, I've *not* had enough of you!" his friend insisted. "It would be very wrong of me to have had enough."

"I give it up!" laughed Newman. "But of course it will never do to go on making mistakes. Go your way, by all means. I shall miss you; but you've seen I make friends very easily. You'll be lonely yourself; but drop me a line when you feel like it, and I'll wait for you anywhere."

"I think I'll go back to Milan. I'm afraid I did n't do justice to Luini."

"Poor old Luini!" said Newman.

"I mean I'm afraid I went too far about him. I don't think he's as *true* as he at first seems."

"Luini?" Newman exclaimed. "There's something in the look of his genius that's like the face of a beautiful woman. It's as if she were coming straight *at* you, or standing very close."

His companion frowned and winced. And it must

be added that this was, for Newman, an unusually metaphysical flight, though in passing through Milan ne had found a great attraction in the painter. "There you are again!" said Mr. Babcock. "Yes, we had better separate." And on the morrow he retraced his steps and proceeded to his revisions of judgement. But presently Newman heard from him.

My dear Mr. Newman, — I am afraid that my conduct at Venice a week ago seemed to you strange and ungrateful, and I wish to explain my position, which, as I said at the time, I do not think you appreciate. I had long had it on my mind to propose that we should part company, and this step was not really so abrupt as it appeared. In the first place, you know, I am travelling in Europe on funds supplied by my congregation, who kindly offered me a vacation and an opportunity to enrich my mind with the treasures of nature and art in these countries. I feel therefore that I ought to use my time to the very best advantage. I've a high sense of responsibility. You appear to care only for the pleasure of the hour, and you give yourself up to it with a violence which I confess I'm not able to emulate. I consider that I must arrive at some conclusion and fix my convictions on certain points. Art and Life seem to me intensely serious things, and in our travels in Europe we should especially remember the rightful, indeed the solemn, message of Art. You seem to hold that if a thing amuses you for the moment this is all you need ask of it; and your relish for mere amusement is also much higher than

mine. You put moreover a kind of reckless finality
into your pleasures which at times, I confess, has
seemed to me — shall I say it? — almost appalling
Your way, at any rate, is not my way, and it's un-
wise that we should attempt any longer to pull together. And yet let me add that I know there is
a great deal to be said for your way; I have felt its
attraction, in your society, very strongly. Save for this
I should have left you long ago. But I was so deeply
perplexed. I hope I have not done wrong. I feel as
if I had a great deal of lost time to make up. I beg
you take all this as I mean it, which heaven knows
is not harshly. I have a great personal esteem for
you and hope that some day when I have recovered
my balance we shall meet again. But I *must* recover
my balance first. I hope you will continue to enjoy
your travels; only *do* remember that Life and Art
are extremely solemn.

Believe me your sincere friend and well-wisher,

BENJAMIN BABCOCK.

P. S. I am very unhappy about Luini.

This letter produced in Newman's mind a singular
mixture of exhilaration and awe. Mr. Babcock's
tender conscience at first seemed to him as funny as
a farce, and his travelling back to Milan only to get
into a deeper muddle to be, for reward of his ped-
antry, exquisitely and ludicrously just. Then he
reflected that these are mighty mysteries; that possibly he himself *was* indeed almost unmentionably
"appalling," and that his manner of considering the
treasures of art and the privileges of life lacked the

last, or perhaps even the very first, refinement. Newman had a great esteem, after all, for refinement, and that evening, during the half-hour that he watched the star-sheen on the warm Adriatic, he felt rebuked and humiliated. He was unable to decide how to answer this communication. His good-nature checked his snubbing his late companion's earnestness, and his tough, inelastic sense of humour forbade his taking it seriously. He wrote no answer at all, but a day or two after he found in a curiosity-shop a grotesque little statuette in ivory, of the sixteenth century, which he sent off to Babcock without a commentary. It represented a gaunt, ascetic-looking monk, in a tattered gown and cowl, kneeling with clasped hands and pulling a portentously long face. It was a wonderfully delicate piece of carving, and in a moment, through one of the rents of his gown, you espied a fat capon hung round the monk's waist. In Newman's intention what did the figure symbolise? Did it mean that he was going to try to be as impressed with the solemnity of things as the monk looked at first, but that he feared he should succeed no better than this personage proved on a closer inspection to have done? It is not supposable he intended a satire on Babcock's own asceticism, for this would have been a truly cynical stroke. He at any rate made his late companion a valuable little present.

He went, on leaving Venice, through the Tyrol to Vienna and then returned, westward, through South Germany. The autumn found him at Baden-Baden, where he spent several weeks. The charming

place kept him from day to day; he was looking
about him and deciding what to do for the winter.
His summer had been very full, and as he sat under
the great trees beside the miniature river that trickles
past the Baden flower-beds he slowly rummaged it
over. He had seen and done a great deal, enjoyed
and observed a great deal; he felt older, yet felt it
somehow, even at the age he had reached, as an
advantage. He remembered Mr. Babcock and his
desire to learn the great lesson, and he remembered
also that he had profited little by his friend's exhorta-
tion to cultivate the same respectable habit. Could n't
he scrape together a few great lessons? Baden-
Baden was the prettiest place he had seen yet, and
orchestral music in the evening, under the stars, was
decidedly a great institution. This was the lesson
that was clearest. But he went on to reflect that he
had done very wisely to pull up stakes and come
abroad; the world was apparently such an interesting thing to see. He had drawn a few morals of his
own; he could n't say just which, but he had them
there under his hat-band. He had done what he
wanted; he had tackled the great sights and closed
with the great occasions, he had given his mind a
chance to "improve" if it would. He fondly believed
it had improved a good deal. Yes, these waters of the
free curiosity were very soothing, and he would
splash in them till they ran dry. Forty-two years as
he was on the point of numbering, he had a long
course in his eye, and if the haze of the future was
thick it was that of a golden afternoon. Where should
he take the world next? I have said he remembered

the eyes of the lady whom he had found standing in
Mrs. Tristram's drawing-room; four months had
elapsed and he had not forgotten them yet. He had
looked — he had made a point of looking — into a
great many other eyes in the interval, but the only
ones he thought of now were Madame de Cintré's.
If he wanted to make out where the golden afternoon
hung heaviest would n't the place perhaps be in
Madame de Cintré's eyes? He would certainly find
something of interest there, call it all bravely bright
or call it engagingly obscure.

But there came to him sometimes too, through this
vague rich forecast, the thought of his past life and
the long array of years (they had begun so early)
during which he had had nothing in his head but his
possible "haul." They seemed far away now, for
his present attitude was more than a holiday, it was
almost a repudiation. He had told Tom Tristram
the pendulum was swinging back, and the backward swing, visibly, had not yet ended. Still, the
possibility of hauls, which had dropped in the other
quarter, wore to his mind a different aspect at different
hours. In its train a thousand forgotten episodes
came trooping before him. Some of them he looked
complacently enough in the face; from some he
averted his head. They were old triumphs of nerve,
even of bluff, mere cold memories of the heat of
battle, the high competitive rage. Some of them, as
they lived again, he felt decidedly proud of; he admired himself as if he had been looking at another
man. And in fact many of the qualities that make
a great deed were there; the decision, the resolution

the courage, the celerity, the clear eye and the firm hand. Of certain other performances it would be going too far to say he was ashamed of them, for he had doubtless never had a stomach for dirty work. He had been blessed from the first with a natural impulse to disfigure with a direct unreasoning blow the painted face of temptation In no man, verily, could a want of the stricter scruple have been less excusable. Newman knew the crooked from the straight at a glance, and the former had received at his hands, early and late, much putting in its place. None the less, however, some of his memories wore at present a graceless and sordid mien, and it struck him that if he had never incurred any quite ineffaceable stain he had never on the other hand followed the line of beauty, as a sought direction, for a single mile of its course. He had spent his years in the unremitting effort to add thousands to thousands, and now that he stood so well outside of it the business of mere money-getting showed only, in its ugliness, as vast and vague and dark, a pirate-ship with lights turned inward It is very well, of a truth, to think meanly of money-getting after you have filled your pockets, and our friend, it may be said, should have begun somewhat earlier to moralise with this superiority. To that it may be answered that he might have made another fortune if he chose ; and we ought to add that he was not exactly moralising. It had come back to him simply that what he had been looking at all summer was a very brave and bristling world, and that it had not all been made by men "live" in his old mean sense.

During his stay at Baden-Baden he received a
letter from Mrs. Tristram, scolding him for the
scant tidings he had sent his friends and begging to
be definitely assured that he had not even thought of
not wintering within call of the Avenue d'Iéna.
Newman replied as to the blast of a silver bugle.

"I supposed you knew I was a miserable letter-
writer and did n't expect anything of me. I guess
I've not struck off twenty letters of pure friendship
in my whole life; in America I conducted my cor-
respondence altogether by telegrams and by dictation to a shorthand reporter. This is a letter of
friendship undefiled; you've got hold of a curiosity —
you could really get something for it. If you want to
know everything that has happened to me these three
months the best way to tell you, I think, would be to
send you my half-dozen guide-books with my pencil
marks in the margin. Wherever you find a scratch or
a cross or a 'Beautiful!' or a 'So true!' or a 'Too
thin!' you may know that I've had some one or other
of the sensations I was after. That has been about
my history ever since I left you. Belgium, Holland,
Switzerland, Germany, Italy — I've taken the whole
list as the bare-backed rider takes the paper hoops
at the circus, and I'm not even yet out of breath.
I carry about six volumes of Ruskin in my trunk;
I've seen some grand old things and shall perhaps
talk them over this winter by your fireside. You see
my face is n't altogether set against Paris. I have had
all kinds of plans and visions, but your letter has
blown most of them away. '*L'appétit vient en mange-
ant*,' says your proverb, and I find that the more

sweet things I taste the more greedily I look over the
table. Now that I'm in the shafts why should n't
I trot to the end of the course? Sometimes I think
of the far East and keep rolling the names of Eastern
cities under my tongue; Damascus and Bagdad,
Trebizond, Samarcand, Bokhara. I spent a week
last month in the company of a returned missionary
who told me I ought to be ashamed to be loafing
about Europe when there is such a treat to be had
out there. I do want more treats, but I think frankly
I should like best to look for them in the Rue de
l'Université. Do you ever hear from that handsome
tall lady? If you can get her to promise she'll be at
home the next time I call I'll go back to Paris straight.
So there you have a bargain. I'm more than ever
in the state of mind I told you about that evening;
I want a companion for life and still want her to be
a star of the first magnitude. I've kept an eye on all
the possible candidates for the position who have
come up this summer, but none of them has filled
the bill or anything like it. I should have enjoyed the
whole thing a thousand times more if I had had
the lady just mentioned under my arm. The nearest
approach to her was a cultivated young man from
Dorchester Mass., who, however, very soon demanded of me a separation for incompatibility of
temper. He told me I had n't it in me ever to raise
a "tone," and he really made me half-believe him.
But shortly afterwards I met an Englishman with
whom I struck up an acquaintance which at first
seemed to promise well — a very bright man who
writes in the London papers and knows Paris nearly

as well as Tristram. We knocked about for a week together, but he very soon gave me up in disgust. He pronounced me a poor creature, incapable of the joy of life — he talked to me as if *I* had come from Dorchester. This was rather bewildering. Which of my two critics was I to believe? I did n't worry about it and very soon made up my mind they don't know everything. You come nearer that than any one I've met, and I defy any one to pretend I'm wrong when I'm more than ever your faithful friend   **C N.**"

VI

HE gave up Bagdad and Bokhara and, returning
to Paris before the autumn was over, established
himself in rooms selected by Tom Tristram in accordance with the latter's estimate of his "social
standing." When Newman learned that this occult
attribute was to be taken into account he professed
himself utterly incompetent and begged Tristram to
relieve him of the care of it. "I did n't know I 'stood,'
socially, at all — I thought I only sat round inform-
ally, rather sprawling than anything else. Is n't
a social standing to know some two or three thousand people and invite them to dinner? I know you
and your wife and little old Mr. Nioche, who gave
me French lessons last spring. Can I invite you to
dinner to meet each other? If I can you must come
to-morrow."

"That's not very grateful to me," said Mrs. Tristram, "who introduced you last year to every creature of my acquaintance."

"So you did; I had quite forgotten. But I thought
you wanted me to forget," said Newman in that
tone of surpassing candour which frequently marked
his utterance and which an observer would not have
known whether to pronounce a whimsical affectation
of ignorance or a modest aspiration to knowledge.
"You told me you yourself disliked them all."

"Ah, the way you remember what I say is at least

very flattering. But in future," added Mrs. Tristram, "pray forget all the 'mean' things and remember only the good. It will be easily done and won't fatigue your memory. Only I forewarn you that if you trust my husband to pick out your rooms you're in for something hideous."

"Hideous, darling?" her husband cried.

"To-day I utter nothing base; otherwise I should use stronger language."

"What do you think she would say, Newman?" Tristram asked. "If she really tried now? She can polish one off for a wretch volubly — in two or three languages; that's what it is to have high culture. It gives her the start of me completely, since I can't swear, for the life of me, except in pure Anglo-Saxon. When I get mad I have to fall back on our dear old mother tongue. There's nothing like it after all."

Newman declared that he knew nothing about tables and chairs and would accept, in the way of a lodging, with his eyes shut, anything that Tristram should offer him. This was partly pure veracity on our hero's part, but it was also partly charity. He knew that to pry about and count *casseroles* and make people open windows, to poke into beds and sofas with his cane, to gossip with landladies and ask who lived above and who below — he knew that this was of all pastimes the dearest to his friend's heart, and he felt the more disposed to put it in his way as he was conscious he had suffered the warmth of their ancient fellowship somewhat to abate. He had besides no taste for upholstery; he had even no very exquisite sense of comfort or convenience. He had a relish for luxury and splendour, but it was satisfied by rather gross contrivances. He scarcely knew a hard chair from a soft, and used an art in stretching his legs which quite dispensed with adventitious aids. His idea of material ease was to inhabit very large rooms, have a great many of them, and be conscious in them of a number of patented mechanical devices, half of which he should never have occasion to use. The apartments should be clear and high and what he called open, and he had once said that he liked rooms best in which you should want to keep on your hat. For the rest he was satisfied with the assurance of any respectable person that everything was of the latest model. Tristram accordingly secured for him an habitation over the price of which the Prince of Morocco had been haggling. It was situated on the Boulevard Haussmann, was a first floor, and consisted of a series of rooms gilded from floor to ceiling a foot thick, draped in various light shades of satin and chiefly furnished with mirrors and clocks. Newman thought them magnificent, did n't haggle, thanked Tristram heartily, immediately took possession, and had one of his trunks standing for three months in the drawing-room.

One day Mrs. Tristram told him that their tall handsome lady had returned from the country and that she had met her three days before coming out of the church of Saint Sulpice; she herself having journeyed to that distant quarter in quest of an obscure lace-mender of whose skill she had heard high praise.

"And how were those intense mild eyes?" Newman asked.

"They were red with weeping — neither more nor less. She had been to confession."

"It does n't tally with your account of her," he said, "that she should have sins to cry about."

"They were not sins — they were sufferings."

"How do you know that?"

"She asked me to come and see her. I went this morning."

"And what does she suffer from?"

"I did n't press her to tell me. With her, somehow, one is very discreet. But I guessed easily enough. She suffers from her grim old mother and from the manner in which her elder brother, the technical head of the family, abets and hounds on the Marquise. They keep at her hard, they keep at her all the while. But I can almost forgive them, because, as I told you, she's simply a saint, and a persecution is all that she needs to bring out what I call her quality."

"That's a comfortable theory for *her*. I hope you'll never mention it to the old folks. But why does she *let* them persecute her? Is n't she, as a married woman, her own mistress?"

"Legally yes, I suppose; but morally no. In France you may never say Nay to your mother, whatever she requires of you. She may be the most abominable old woman in the world and make your life a purgatory; but after all she's *ma mère,* and you've no right to judge her. You've simply to obey. The thing has a fine side to it. Madame de Cintré bows her head and folds her wings."

"Can't she at least make her brother quit?"

"Her brother's the *chef de la famille*, the head of the clan. With those people the family's everything; you must act not for your own pleasure but for the advantage of your race and name."

"But what do they want to get out of our lovely friend?" Newman asked.

"Her submission to another marriage. They're not rich, and they want to bring more money into the house."

"There's where *you* come in, my boy!" Tristram interposed

"And Madame de Cintré does n't see it?" Newman continued.

"She has been sold for a price once; she naturally objects to being sold a second time. It appears that the first time they greatly bungled their bargain. M. de Cintré, before he died, managed to get through almost everything."

"And to whom do they want then to marry her now?"

"I thought it best not to ask; but you may be sure it is to some horrid old nabob or to some dissipated little duke."

"There's Mrs. Tristram as large as life!" her husband cried. "Observe the wealth of her imagination. She has not asked a single question — it's vulgar to ask questions — and yet she knows it all inside out. She has the history of Madame de Cintré's marriage at her fingers' ends. She has seen the lovely Claire on her knees with loosened tresses and streaming eyes and the rest of them standing over her with spikes and goads and red-hot irons, ready to come down if she refuses Bluebeard. The simple truth is that they've made a fuss about her milliner's bill or refused her an opera-box."

Newman looked from Tristram to his wife with a certain reserve in each direction. "Do you really mean," he asked of the latter, "that your friend is being really hustled into a marriage she really shrinks from?"

"I think it extremely probable. Those people are very capable of that sort of thing."

"It's like something in a regular old play," said Newman. "That dark old house over there looks as if wicked things had been done in it and might be done again."

"They have a still darker old house in the coun-try, she tells me, and there, during the summer, this scheme must have been hatched."

"*Must* have been; mind that!" Tristram echoed.

"After all," their visitor suggested after a pause, "she may be in trouble about something else."

"If it's something else then it's something worse." Mrs. Tristram spoke as with high competence.

Newman, silent a while, seemed lost in meditation. "Is it possible," he asked at last, "that they can do that sort of thing over here? that helpless women are thumb-screwed — sentimentally, socially, I mean — into marrying men they object to."

"Helpless women, all over the world, have a hard time of it," said Mrs. Tristram. "There's plenty of the thumb-screw for them everywhere."

"A great deal of that kind of thing goes on in

New York," said Tristram. "Girls are bullied or coaxed or bribed, or all three together, into marrying, for money, horrible cads. There's no end of that always going on in Fifth Avenue, and other bad things besides. The Morals of Murray Hill! Some one ought to show them up."

"I don't believe it!"—Newman took it very gravely. "I don't see how, in America, such cases can ever have occurred; for the simple reason that the men themselves would be the first to make them impossible. The American man sometimes takes advantage—I've known him to. But he does n't take advantage of women."

"Listen to the voice of the spread eagle!" cried Tristram.

"The spread eagle should use his wings," said his wife. "He should fly to the rescue of the woman of whom advantage is being taken!"

"To her rescue—?" Newman seemed to wonder.

"Pounce down, seize her in your talons and carry her off. Marry her yourself."

Newman, for some moments, answered nothing; but presently, "I guess she has heard enough of marrying," he said. "The kindest way to treat her would be to care for her and yet never speak of it. But that sort of thing's infamous," he added. "It's none of my business, but it makes me feel kind of swindled to hear of it."

He heard of it, however, more than once afterwards. Mrs. Tristram again saw Madame de Cintré and again found her looking very very sad. But on these occasions there had been no tears; the intense mild eyes were clear and still. "She's cold, calm and hopeless," Mrs. Tristram declared, and she added that on her mentioning that her friend Mr. Newman was again in Paris and was faithful in his desire to make Madame de Cintré's acquaintance, this lovely woman had found a smile in her despair and expressed her regret at having missed his visit in the spring and her hope that he had not lost courage. "I told her something about you," Newman's hostess wound up.

"That's a comfort," he patiently answered. "I seem to *want* people to know about me."

A few days after this, one dusky autumn afternoon, he went again to the Rue de l'Université. The early evening had closed in as he applied for admittance at the stoutly-guarded Hôtel de Bellegarde. He was told that Madame la Comtesse was at home, on which he crossed the court, entered the further door and was conducted through a vestibule, vast, dim and cold, up a broad stone staircase with an ancient iron balustrade, to an apartment on the first floor. Announced and ushered in, he found himself in a large panelled boudoir, at one end of which a lady and a gentleman were seated by the fire. The gentleman was smoking a cigarette; there was no light in the room save that of a couple of candles and the glow from the hearth. Both persons rose to welcome Newman, who in the firelight recognised Madame la Comtesse. She gave him her hand with a smile which seemed in itself an illumination, and, pointing to her companion, murmured an allusion, "One of my brothers." The gentleman struck Newman as taking him, with great good-nature, for a friend already made, and our hero then perceived him to be the young man he had met in the court of the hotel on his former visit, the one who had appeared of an easy commerce. "Mrs. Tristram has often mentioned you to us." It had an effect of prodigious benignity as Madame de Cintré resumed her former place.

Newman, noticing in especial her "us," began, after he had seated himself, to consider what in truth might be his errand. He had an unusual, unexpected sense of having wandered into a strange corner of the world. He was not given, as a general thing, to "borrowing trouble" or to suspecting danger, and he had had no social tremors on this particular occasion. He was not without presence of mind, though he had no formed habit of prompt chatter. But his exercised acuteness sometimes precluded detachment; with every disposition to take things simply he could n't but feel that some of them were less simple than others. He felt as one feels in missing a step, in an ascent, where one has expected to find it. This strange pretty woman seated at fireside talk with her brother in the grey depths of her inhospitable-looking house — what had he to say to her? She seemed enveloped in triple defences of privacy; by what encouragement had he presumed on his having effected a breach? It was for a moment as if he had plunged into some medium as deep as the ocean and must exert himself to keep from sinking. Meanwhile he was looking at Madame la Comtesse and she was settling herself in her chair and drawing in her long dress and vaguely, rather indirectly, turning her face to him. Their eyes met; a moment later she looked away and motioned to her brother to put a log on the fire. But the moment, and the glance that lived in it, had been sufficient to relieve Newman of the first and the last fit of sharp personal embarrassment he was ever to know. He performed the movement frequent with him and which was always a symbol of his taking mental possession of a scene — he extended his long legs. The impression his hostess had made on him at their first meeting came back in an instant; it had been deeper than he knew. She took on a light and a grace, or, more definitely, an interest; he had opened a book and the first lines held his attention.

She asked him questions as if unable to do less: how lately he had seen Mrs. Tristram, how long he had been in Paris, how long he expected to remain there, how he liked it. She spoke English without an accent, or rather with that absence of any one of those long familiar to him which on his arrival in Europe had struck him as constituting by itself a complete foreignness — a foreignness that in women he had come to like extremely. Here and there her utterance slightly exceeded this measure, but at the end of ten minutes he found himself waiting for these delicate discords. He enjoyed them, marvelling to hear the possible slip become the charming glide. "You have a beautiful country of your own," she safely enough risked.

"Oh, very fine, very fine. You ought to come over and see it."

"I shall never go over and see it," she answered with a smile.

"Well, why should n't you?"

"We don't travel; especially so far."

"But you go away sometimes; you don't always stay right here?"

"I go away in summer — a little way, to the country."

He wanted to ask her something more, something personal and going rather far — he hardly knew what. "Don't you find it rather lifeless here," he said; "so far from the street?" Rather "lonesome" he was going to say, but he deflected nervously, for discretion, and then felt his term an aggravation

"Yes, it's very lifeless, if you mean very quiet; but that's exactly what we like."

"Ah, that's exactly what you like," he repeated. He was touched by her taking it so.

"Besides, I've lived here all my life."

"Lived here all your life," Newman found he could but echo.

"I was born here, and my father was born here before me, and my grandfather and my great-grandfathers. Were they not, Valentin?" — and she appealed to her brother.

"Yes, it seems a condition of our being born at all," the young man smiled as he rose and threw the remnant of his cigarette into the fire. He remained leaning against the chimney-piece, and an observer would have guessed that he wished to take a better look at their guest, whom he covertly examined while he stroked his moustache.

"Your house is tremendously old then?" Newman pursued.

"How old is it, brother?" asked Madame de Cintré.

The young man took the two candles from the mantel, lifted one high in each hand and looked up, above the objects on the shelf, toward the cornice of the room. The chimney-piece was in white marble of the Louis-Quinze period, but much aloft was a panelling of an earlier date, quaintly carved, painted white and here and there gilded. The white had turned to yellow and the gilding was tarnished. On the top the figures ranged themselves into a shield, on which an armorial device was cut. Above it, in relief, was a number — 1627. "There you have a year," said the young man. "That's old or new, according to your point of view."

"Well, over here," Newman replied, "one's point of view gets shifted round considerably." And he threw back his head and looked about. "Your house is of a very fine style of architecture."

"Are you interested in questions of architecture?" asked the gentleman at the chimney-piece.

"Well, I took the trouble this summer to examine — as well as I can calculate — some four hundred and seventy churches. Do you call that interested?"

"Perhaps you're interested in religion," said his amiable host.

Newman thought. "Not actively." He found himself speaking as if it were a railroad or a mine; so that the next moment, to correct this, "Are you a

Roman Catholic, madam?" he inquired of Madame de Cintré.

"I'm of the faith of my fathers," she gravely replied.

He was struck with a sort of richness in the effect of it — he threw back his head again for contemplation. "Had you never noticed that number up there?" he presently asked.

She hesitated a moment and then, "In former years," she returned.

Her brother had been watching Newman's movement. "Perhaps you would like to examine the house."

Our friend slowly brought down his eyes for recognition of this; he received the impression that the young man at the chimney-piece had his forms, and sought his own opportunities, of amusement. He was a handsome figure of a young man; his face wore a smile, his moustachios were curled up at the ends and there was something — more than the firelight — that played in his eyes. "Damn his French impudence!" Newman was on the point of inwardly growling. "What the deuce is he grinning at?" He glanced at Madame de Cintré, who was only looking at the floor. But she raised her eyes, which again met his, till she carried them to her brother. He turned again to this companion and observed that he strikingly resembled his sister. This was in his favour, and our hero's first impression of Count Valentin had moreover much engaged him. His suspicion expired and he said he should rejoice to see the house.

The young man surrendered to gaiety, laying his hand again on a light. "It will repay your curiosity. Come then."

But Madame de Cintré rose quickly and grasped his arm. "Ah Valentin, what do you mean to do?"

"To show Mr. Newman the house. It will be very amusing to show Mr. Newman the house."

She kept her hand on his arm and turned to their visitor with a smile. "Don't let him take you; you won't find it remarkable. It is a musty old house like any other."

"Ah, not like any other," the Count still gaily protested. "It's full of curious things. Besides a visit like Mr. Newman's is just what it wants and has never had. It's a rare chance all round."

"You're very wicked, brother," Madame de Cintré insisted.

"Nothing venture, nothing have!" cried the young man. "Will you come?"

She stepped toward Newman, clasping her hands and speaking, to his sense, with an exquisite grave appeal. "Would n't you prefer my society here by my fire to stumbling about dark passages after — well, after nothing at all?"

"A hundred times! We'll see the house some other day."

The young man put down his light with mock solemnity, and, shaking his head, "Ah, you've defeated a great scheme, sir!" he sighed.

"A scheme? I don't understand," said Newman.

"You'd have played your part in it all the better. Perhaps some day I shall have a chance to explain it."

"Be quiet and ring for tea," Madame de Cintré gently concluded.

Count Valentin obeyed, and presently a servant brought in a tray, which he placed on a small table. Madame de Cintré, when he had gone, busied herself, from her place, with making tea. She had but just begun when the door was thrown open and a lady rushed in with a loud rustling sound. She stared at Newman, gave a little nod and a "Monsieur!" and then quickly approached Madame de Cintré and presented her forehead to be kissed. Madame de Cintré saluted her, but continued to watch the kettle. The rustling lady was young and pretty, it seemed to Newman; she wore her bonnet and cloak and a train of royal proportions. She began to talk rapidly in French. "Oh, give me some tea, my beautiful one, for the love of God! I'm *anéantie*, annihilated." Newman found himself quite unable to follow her; she spoke much less distinctly than M. Nioche.

"That's my wonderful sister-in-law," the young man mentioned to him.

"She's very attractive," Newman promptly responded.

'Fascinating," the Count said; and this time again his guest suspected him of latent malice. His sister-in-law came round to the other side of the fire with her tea in her hand, holding it out at arm's length so that she might n't spill it on her dress and uttering little cries of alarm. She placed the cup on the chimney and began to unpin her veil and pull off her gloves, looking meanwhile at Newman. "Is there anything I can do for you, my dear lady?" the young man asked with quite extravagant solicitude.

"Present me to monsieur," said his sister-in-law. And then when he had pronounced their visitor's name: "I can't curtsey to you, monsieur, or I shall spill my tea. So Claire receives strangers like this?" she covertly added, in French to her brother-in-law.

"Apparently! Isn't it fun?" he returned with enthusiasm.

Newman stood a moment and then approached Madame de Cintré, who looked up at him as if she were thinking of something to say. She seemed to think of nothing, however — she simply smiled. He sat down near her and she handed him his cup. For a few moments they talked about that, and meanwhile he kept taking her in. He remembered what Mrs. Tristram had told him of her "perfection" and of her having, in combination, all the brilliant things that he dreamed of finding. This made him consider her not only without mistrust, but without uneasy conjectures; the presumption, from the first moment he looked at her, had been so in her favour. And yet if she was beautiful it was not from directly dazzling him. She was tall and moulded in long lines; she had thick fair hair and features uneven and harmonious. Her wide grey eyes were like a brace of deputed and garlanded maidens waiting with a compliment at the gate of a city, but they failed of that lamplike quality and those many-coloured fires that light up, as in a constant celebration of anniversaries, the fair front of the conquering type. Madame de Cintré was of attenuated substance and might pass for younger than she probably was. In her whole person was something still young and still passive, still uncertain and that seemed still to expect to depend, and which yet made, in its dignity, a presence withal, and almost represented, in its serenity, an assurance. What had Tristram meant, Newman wondered, by calling her proud? She was certainly not proud, now, to him; or if she was it was of no use and lost on him. she must pile it up higher if she expected him to mind it. She was a clear, noble person — it was very easy to get on with her. And was she then subject to that application of the idea of "rank" which made her a kind of historical formation? Newman had known rank but in the old days of the army — where it had not always amounted to very much either; and he had never seen it attributed to women, unless perhaps to two or three rather predominant wives of generals. But the designations representing it in France struck him as ever so pretty and becoming, with a property in the bearer, this particular one, that might match them and make a sense — something fair and softly bright, that had motions of extraordinary lightness and indeed a whole new and unfamiliar play of emphasis and pressure, a new way, that is, of not insisting and not even, as one might think, wanting or knowing, yet all to the effect of attracting and pleasing. She had at last thought of something to say. "Have you many friends in Paris — so that you go out a great deal?"

He considered — about going out. "Do you mean if I go to parties — ?"

"Do you go *dans le monde*, as we say?"

"I've seen a good many people. Mrs. Tristran at least tells me I have. She has taken me about. I do whatever she bids me."

"By yourself then you're not fond of amusements?"

"Oh yes, of some sorts. I'm not fond of *very* fast rushing about, or of sitting up half the night; I'm too old and too heavy. But I want to be amused; I came to Europe for that."

She appeared to think a moment, and then with a smile: "But I thought one can be so much amused in America."

"I couldn't; perhaps I was too much part of the show. That's never such fun, you know, for the animals themselves."

At this moment young Madame de Bellegarde came back for another cup of tea, accompanied by Count Valentin. Madame de Cintré, when she had served her, began to talk again with Newman and recalled what he had last said. "In your own country you were very much occupied?"

"I was in active business. I've been in active business since I was fifteen years old."

"And what was your active business?" asked Madame de Bellegarde, who was decidedly not so pretty as Madame de Cintré.

"I've been in everything," said Newman. "At one time I sold leather; at one time I manufactured wash-tubs."

Madame de Bellegarde made a little grimace. "Leather? I don't like that. Wash-tubs are better. I prefer the smell of soap. I hope at least they made your fortune." She rattled this off with the air of a woman who had the reputation of saying everything that came into her head, and with a strong French accent.

Newman had spoken with conscientious clearness, but Madame de Bellegarde's tone made him go on, after a meditative pause, with a certain light grimness of pleasantry. "No, I lost money on wash-tubs, but I came out pretty square on leather."

"I've made up my mind, after all," said the Marquise, "that the great point is — how do you call it? — to come out square. I'm on my knees to money and my worship is as public as you like. If you have it I ask no questions. For that I'm a real radical — like you, monsieur; at least as I suppose you. My *belle-sœur* is very proud; but I find that one gets much more pleasure in this sad life if one does n't make too many difficulties."

"Goodness gracious, chère madame, how you rush in!" Count Valentin gaily groaned.

"He's a man one can speak to, I suppose, since my sister receives him," the lady more covertly answered. "Besides, it's very true; those are my ideas."

"Ah, you call them ideas?" the young man returned in a tone that Newman thought lovely.

"But Mrs. Tristram told me you had been in the army — in your great war," his beautiful sister pursued.

"Yes, but that was not business — in the paying sense. I could n't afford it often."

"Very true!" said Count Valentin, who looked at our hero from head to foot with his peculiar facial play, in which irony and urbanity seemed perplexingly commingled. "Are you a brave man?"

"Well, try me."

"Ah then, there you are! In that case come again."

"Dear me, what an invitation!" Madame de Cintré murmured with a smile that betrayed embarrassment.

"Oh, I want Mr. Newman to come — particularly," her brother returned. "It will give me great pleasure. I shall feel the loss if I miss one of his visits. But I maintain he must be of high courage. A stout heart, sir, and a firm front." And he offered Newman his hand.

"I shall not come to see you; I shall come to see Madame de Cintré," said Newman, bent on distinctness.

"You 'll need, exactly for that, all your arms."

"Ah de grâce!" she appealed.

"Decidedly," cried Madame de Bellegarde, "I 'm the only person here capable of saying something polite! Come to see me; you 'll need no courage at all, monsieur."

Newman gave a laugh which was not altogether an assent; then, shaking hands all round, marched away. Madame de Cintré failed to take up her sister's challenge to be gracious, but she looked with a certain troubled air at the retreating guest.

VII

ONE evening very late, about five days after this episode, Newman's servant brought him a card which proved to be that of young M. de Bellegarde. When a few moments later he went to receive his visitor he found him standing in the middle of the greatest of his gilded saloons and eyeing it from cornice to carpet. Count Valentin's face, it seemed to him, expressed not less than usual a sense of the inherent comedy of things. "What the devil is he laughing at now?" our hero asked himself; but he put the question without acrimony, for he felt in Madame de Cintré's brother a free and adventurous nature, and he had a presentiment that on this basis of the natural and the bold they were destined to understand each other. Only if there was food for mirth he wished to have a glimpse of it too.

"To begin with," said the young man as he extended his hand, "have I come too late?"

"Too late for what?"

"To smoke a cigar with you."

"You would have to come early to do that," Newman said. "I don't know how to smoke."

"Ah, you're a strong man!"

"But I keep cigars," he added. "Sit down."

His visitor looked about. "Surely I may n't smoke here."

"What's the matter? Is the room too small?"

"It's too large. It's like smoking in a ball-room or a church."

"That's what you were laughing at just now?" Newman asked; "the size of my room?"

"It's not size only, but splendour and harmony, beauty of detail. It was the smile of sympathy and of admiration."

Newman looked at him harder and then, "So it is very ridiculous?" he enquired.

"Ridiculous, my dear sir? It's sublime."

"That of course is the same thing," said Newman. "Make yourself comfortable. Your coming to see me, I take it, is an act of sympathy and a sign of confidence. You were not obliged to. Therefore if anything round here amuses you it will be all in a pleasant way. Laugh as loud as you please; I like to have my little entertainment a success. Only I must make this request: that you explain the joke to me as soon as you can speak. I don't want to lose anything myself."

His friend gave him a long look of unresentful perplexity. He laid his hand on his sleeve and seemed on the point of saying something, but suddenly checked himself, leaned back in his chair and puffed at his cigar. At last, however, breaking silence, "Certainly," he began, "my coming to see you is the frank demonstration you recognise. I have been, nevertheless, in a measure encouraged — or urged — to the step. My sister, in a word, has asked it of me, and a request from my sister is, for me, a law. I was near you just now and I observed lights in what I supposed to be your rooms. It was not a ceremonious hour for making a call, but I was not sorry to do something that would show me as not performing a mere ceremony."

"Well, here I am for you as large as life," said Newman as he extended his legs.

"I don't know what you mean," the young man went on, "by giving me unlimited leave to laugh. Certainly I'm a great laugher; it's the only way, in general, is n't it? not to — well, not to *crever d'ennui*. But it's not in order that we may laugh together — or separately — that I have, I may say, sought your acquaintance. To speak with a confidence and a candour which I find rapidly getting the better of me, you have interested me without having done me the honour, I think, in the least to try for it — by having acted so consistently in your own interest: that, I mean, of your enlightened curiosity." All this was uttered, to Newman's sense, with a marked proficiency, as from a habit of intercourse that was yet not "office" intercourse, and, in spite of the speaker's excellent English, with the perfect form, as our friend supposed, of the superlative Frenchman; but there was at the same time something in it of a more personal and more pressing intention. What this might prove to have for him Newman suddenly found himself rather yearning to know. M. de Bellegarde was a foreigner to the last roll of his so frequent rotary *r;* and if he had met him out in bare Arizona he would have felt it proper to address him with a "How-d'ye-do, Mosseer?" Yet there was that in his physiognomy which seemed to suspend a bold bridge of gilt wire

over the impassable gulf produced by difference of
race. He was but middling high and of robust and
agile aspect. Valentin de Bellegarde, his host was
afterwards to learn, had a mortal dread of not keeping the robustness down sufficiently to keep the
agility up; he was afraid of growing stout; he was
too short a story as he said, to afford an important
digression. He rode and fenced and practised gym-
nastics with unremitting zeal, and you could n't
congratulate him on his appearance without making
him turn pale at your imputation of its increase. He
had a round head, high above the ears, a crop of
hair at once dense and silky, a broad, low forehead,
a short nose, of the ironical and enquiring rather
than of the dogmatic or sensitive cast, and a moustache as delicate as that of a page in a romance. He
resembled his sister not in feature, but in the expression of his fair open eyes, completely void, as
they were in his case, of introspection, and in the fine
freshness of his smile, which was like a gush of crys-
talline water. The charm of his face was above all
in its being intensely, being frankly, ardently, gallantly alive. You might have seen it in the form of
a bell with the long "pull" dangling in the young
man's conscious soul; at a touch of the silken cord
the silver sound would fill the air. There was something in this quick play which assured you he was
not economising his consciousness, not living in a
corner of it to spare the furniture of the rest. He was
squarely encamped in the centre and was keeping
open house. When he flared into gaiety it was the
movement of a hand that in emptying a cup turns

it upside down; he gave you all the strength of the liquor. He inspired Newman with something of the kindness our hero used to feel in his earlier years for those of his companions who could perform strange and clever tricks — make their joints crack in queer places or whistle at the back of their mouths. "My sister told me," he said, "that I ought to come and remove the impression I had taken such apparent pains to produce on you; the impression of my labouring under some temporary disorder. Did it strike you that what I said did n't make a sense?"

"Well, I thought I had never seen any one like you in real life," Newman returned. "Not in real quiet *home* life."

"Ah then Claire's right." And Count Valentin watched his host for a moment through his smoke-wreaths. "And yet even if it is the case I think we had better let it stand. I had no idea of putting you off by any violence of any kind; I wanted on the contrary to produce a favourable impression. Since I did nevertheless make a fool of myself I was perhaps luckily inspired, for I must n't seem to set up a claim for consistency which, in the sequel of our acquaintance, I may by no means justify. Set me down as a shocking trifler with intervals of high lucidity and even of extraordinary energy."

"Oh, I guess you know what you're about," said Newman.

"When I'm sane I'm very sane; that I admit," his guest returned. "But I did n't come here to talk about myself. I should like to ask you a few questions. You allow me?"

"Well, give me a specimen."

"You live here all alone?"

"Absolutely. With whom should I live?"

"For the moment," smiled M. de Bellegarde, "I'm asking questions, not answering them. You've come over to Paris for your pleasure?"

Newman had a pause. "Every one asks me that!" he said with his almost pathetic plainness. "It sounds quite foolish — as if I were to get my pleasure somehow under a writ of extradition."

"But at any rate you've a reason for being here."

"Oh, call it for my pleasure!" said Newman. "Though it represents me as trying to reclaim a hopeless absentee it describes well enough the logic of my conduct."

"And you're enjoying what you find?"

"Well, I'm keeping my head."

Count Valentin puffed his cigar again in silence. "For myself," he resumed at last, "I'm entirely at your service. Anything I can do for you will make me very happy. Call on me at your convenience. Is there any one you wish to know — anything you wish to see? It's a pity you should n't fully avail yourself of Paris."

"Well, I guess I avail myself," said Newman serenely. "I'm much obliged to you."

"Honestly speaking," his visitor went on, "there's something absurd to me in hearing myself make you these offers. They represent a great deal of good-will, but they represent little else. You're a successful man, and I am a *raté* — by which we mean a dead failure — and it's a turning of the tables to talk as if I could lend you a hand."

"How does it come that you have n't succeeded?" Newman ingenuously asked.

"Oh, I'm not a failure to wring your heart," the young man returned. "I've not fallen from a height, and my fiasco has made no noise and luckily no scandal. But you stand up, so very straight, for accomplished facts. You've made a fortune, you've raised an edifice, you're a financial, practical power, you can travel about the world till you've found a soft spot and lie down on it with the consciousness of having earned your rest. And all — so fabulously! — in the flower of your magnificent manhood. Is not that true? Well, imagine the exact reverse of all that and you have *votre serviteur*. I've done nothing, and there's not a poor pitiful thing for me to do."

"Why what's the matter with all the things?"

"It would take me time to say. Some day I'll tell you. Meanwhile I'm right, eh? You're a horrid success? You've made more money than was ever made before by one so young and so candid? It's none of my business, but in short you're beastly rich?"

"That's another thing it sounds foolish to say," said Newman. "Do you think that's *all* I am?"

"No, I think you're original — that's why I'm here. We're very different, you and I, as products, I'm sure; I don't believe there's a subject on which we judge or feel alike. But I rather guess we shall get on, for there's such a thing, you know, as being — like fish and fowl — too different to quarrel."

"Oh, I never quarrel," said Newman rather shortly.

"You mean you just shoot? Well, I notify you that *till* I'm shot," his visitor declared, "I shall have had a greater sense of safety with you than I have perhaps ever known in any relation of life. And as a sense of danger is clearly a thing impossible to *you*, we shall therefore be all right."

With the preamble embodied in these remarks he paid our hero a long visit; as the two men sat with their heels on Newman's glowing hearth they heard the small hours of the morning strike larger from a far-off belfry. Valentin de Bellegarde was by his own confession at all times a great chatterer, and on this occasion the habit of promptness of word and tone was on him almost as a fever. It was a tradition of his race that people of its blood always conferred a favour by their attentions, and, as his real confidence was as rare as his general surface was bright, he had a double reason for never fearing his friendship could be importunate. Late blossom though he might be, moreover, of an ancient stem, tradition (since I have used the word) had in his nature neither visible guards nor alarms, but was as muffled in sociability and urbanity as an old dowager in her laces and strings of pearls. Valentin was by the measure of the society about him a *gentilhomme* of purest strain, and his rule of life, so far as it was definite, had been to keep up the character. This, it seemed to him, might agreeably engage a young man of ordinary good parts. But he attained his best values by instinct rather than by theory, and the amiability of his character was so great that certain of the aristocratic virtues lost, at his touch, their rigour without losing, as it were, their temper. In his younger years he had been suspected of low tastes, and his mother had greatly feared from him some such slip in the common mire as might bespatter the family shield. He had been treated therefore to more than his share of schooling and drilling, but his instructors had not succeeded in mounting him upon stilts. They had never troubled his deepest depths of serenity, and he had remained somehow as fortunate as he was rash. He had long been tied with so short a rope, however, that he had now a mortal grudge against family discipline. He had been known to say within the limits of the family that, featherhead though he might be, the honour of the name was safer in his hands than in those of some of its other members, and that if a day ever came to try it they would see. He had missed no secret for making high spirits consort with good manners, and he seemed to Newman, as afterwards young members of the Latin races often seemed to him, now almost infantile and now appallingly mature. In America, Newman reflected, "growing" men had old heads and young hearts, or at least young morals; here they had young heads and very aged hearts, morals the most grizzled and wrinkled.

"What I envy you is your liberty," Count Valentin found occasion to observe; "your wide range, your freedom to come and go, your not having a lot of people, who take themselves all too seriously, expecting something of you. I live," he added with a sigh, "beneath the eyes of my admirable mother."

"Is n't it then your own fault? What's to hinder your ranging?" Newman asked.

"There's a delightful simplicity in that question. Everything in life is to hinder it. To begin with I have n't a penny."

"Well, I had n't a penny when *I* began to range."

"Ah, but your poverty was your capital! Being of your race and stamp, it was impossible you should remain what you were born, and being born poor — do I understand it? — it was therefore inevitable you should become as different from that as possible. You were in a position that makes one's mouth water; you looked round you and saw a world full of things you had only to step up to and take hold of. When I was twenty I looked round me and saw a world with everything ticketed 'Don't touch,' and the deuce of it was that the ticket seemed meant only for me. I could n't go into business, I could n't make money, because I was a Bellegarde. I could n't go into politics because I was a Bellegarde — the Bellegardes don't recognise the Bonapartes. I could n't go into literature because I was a dunce. I could n't marry a rich girl because no Bellegarde had for ages married a *roturière* and it was n't urgent I should deviate. We shall have to face it, however — you 'll see. Marriageable heiresses, *de notre bord*, are not to be had for nothing; it must be name for name and fortune for fortune. The only thing I could do was to go and fight for the Pope. That

I did, punctiliously, and received an apostolic flesh-wound at Castelfidardo. It did neither the Holy Father nor me any good that I could make out Rome was doubtless a very amusing place in the days of Heliogabalus, but it has sadly fallen off since. I was immured for three years, like some of the choicest scoundrels in history, in the castle of Saint Angelo, and then I came back to secular life."

Newman followed very much as he had followed *ciceroni* through museums. "So you've no active interest ? — you do absolutely nothing ?"

"As hard as ever I can. I'm supposed to amuse myself and to pass my time, and, to tell the truth, I've had some good moments. They come somehow, in spite of one, and the thing is then to recognise them. But you can't keep on the watch for them for ever. I'm good for three or four years more perhaps, but I foresee that after that I shall spring a leak and begin to sink. I shan't float any more, I shall go straight to the bottom. Then, at the bottom, what shall I do ? I think I shall turn monk. Seriously, I think I shall tie a rope round my waist and go into a monastery. It was an old custom and the old customs were very good. People understood life quite as well as we do. They kept the pot boiling till it cracked, and then put it on the shelf altogether."

"Do you attend church regularly ?" asked Newman in a tone which gave the enquiry a quaint effect.

His friend evidently appreciated this element, yet looked at him with due decorum. "I'm a very good Catholic. I cherish the Faith. I adore the blessed Virgin. I fear the Father of Lies."

"Well then," said Newman, "you're very well fixed. You've got pleasure in the present and paradise in the future: what do you complain of?"

"It's a part of one's pleasure to complain. There's something in your own situation that rubs me up. You're the first man about whom I've ever found myself saying 'Oh, if I were he —!' It's singular, but so it is. I've known many men who, besides any factitious advantages that I may possess, had money and brains into the bargain, yet they've never disturbed my inward peace. You've got something it worries me to have missed. It's not money, it's not even brains — though evidently yours have been excellent for your purpose. It's not your superfluous stature, though I should have rather liked to be a couple of inches taller. It's a sort of air you have of being imperturbably, being irremoveably and indestructibly (that's the thing!) at home in the world. When I was a boy my father assured me it was by just such an air that people recognised a Bellegarde. He called my attention to it. He didn't advise me to cultivate it; he said that as we grew up it always came of itself. I supposed it had come to me because I think I've always had the feeling it represents. My place in life had been made for me and it seemed easy to occupy. But you who, as I understand it, have made your own place, you who, as you told us the other day, have made and sold articles of vulgar household use — you strike me, in a fashion of your own, as a man who stands about at his ease and looks straight over ever so many high walls. I seem to see you move everywhere like a big stockholder on his favourite railroad. You make me feel awfully my want of shares. And yet the world used to be supposed to be ours. What is it I miss?"

"It's the proud consciousness of honest toil, of having produced something yourself that somebody has been willing to pay you for — since that's the definite measure. Since you speak of my wash-tubs — which were lovely — is n't it just they and their loveliness that make up my good conscience?"

"Oh no; I've seen men who had gone beyond wash-tubs, who had made mountains of soap — strong-smelling yellow soap, in great bars; and they've left me perfectly cold."

"Then it's just the regular treat of being an American citizen," said Newman "That sets a man right up."

"Possibly," his guest returned; "but I'm forced to say I've seen a great many American citizens who did n't seem at all set up or in the least like large stockholders. I never envied them. I rather think the thing's some diabolical secret of your own."

"Oh come," Newman laughed, "you'll persuade me against my humility."

"No, I shall persuade you of nothing. You've nothing to do with humility any more than with swagger: that's just the essence of your confounded coolness. People swagger only when they've something to lose, and show their delicacy only when they've something to gain."

"I don't know what I may have to lose," said Newman, "but I can quite see a situation in which I should have something to gain."

His visitor looked at him hard. "A situation —?"

Newman hesitated. "Well, I'll tell you more about it when I know you better."

"Ah, you'll soon know me by heart!" the young man sighed as he departed.

During the next three weeks they met again several times and, without formally swearing an eternal friendship, fell, for their course of life, instinctively into step together. Valentin de Bellegarde was to Newman the typical, ideal Frenchman, the Frenchman of tradition and romance, so far as our hero was acquainted with these mystic fields. Gallant, expansive, amusing, more pleased himself with the effect he produced than those (even when they were quite duly pleased) for whom he produced it; a master of all the distinctively social virtues and a votary of all the agreeable sensations; a devotee of something mysterious and sacred to which he occasionally alluded in terms more ecstatic even than those in which he spoke of the last pretty woman, and which was simply the beautiful though somewhat superannuated image of personal Honour; he was irresistibly entertaining and enlivening, and he formed a character to which Newman was as capable of doing justice when he had once been placed in contact with it as he was unlikely, in musing upon the possible combinations of the human mixture, mentally to have foreshadowed it. No two parties to an alliance could have come to it from a wider separation, but it was what each brought out of the queer dim distance that formed the odd attraction for the other.

Valentin lived in the basement of an old house in the Rue d'Anjou Saint Honoré, and his small apartments lay between the court of the house and a garden of equal antiquity, which spread itself behind – one of those large, sunless, humid gardens into which you look unexpectedly in Paris from back windows, wondering how among the grudging habitations they find their space. When Newman presently called on him it was to hint that such quarters were, though in a different way, at least as funny as his own. Their oddities had another sense than those of our hero's gilded saloons on the Boulevard Haussmann. the place was low, dusky, contracted, and was crowded with curious bric-à-brac. Their proprietor, penniless patrician though he might be, was an insatiable collector, and his walls were covered with rusty arms and ancient panels and platters, his doorways draped in faded tapestries, his floors muffled in the skins of beasts. Here and there was one of those uncomfortable tributes to elegance in which the French upholsterer's art is prolific; a curtained recess with a sheet of looking-glass as dark as a haunted pool; a divan on which, for its festoons and furbelows, you could no more sit down than on a dowager's lap; a fireplace draped, flounced, frilled, by the same analogy, to the complete exclusion of fire. The young man's possessions were in picturesque disorder, and his apartment pervaded by the odour of cigars, mingled, for inhalation, with other dim ghosts of past presences. Newman thought it, as a home, damp, gloomy and perverse, and was puzzled by the romantic incoherence of the furniture.

The charming Count, like most of his countrymen, hid none of his lights under a bushel and made little of a secret of the more interesting passages of his personal history. He had inevitably a vast deal to say about women, and could frequently indulge in sentimental and ironical apostrophes to these authors of his joys and woes. "Oh, the women, the women, and the things they've made me do!" he would exclaim with a wealth of reference. "*C'est égal*, of all the follies and stupidities I've committed for them there is n't one I would have missed!" On this subject Newman maintained an habitual reserve; to make it shine in the direct light of one's own experience had always seemed to him a proceeding vaguely analogous to the cooing of pigeons and the chattering of monkeys, and even inconsistent with a fully-developed human character. But his friend's confidences greatly amused and rarely displeased him, for the garden of the young man's past appeared to have begun from the earliest moment to bloom with rare flowers, amid which memory was as easy as a summer breeze. "I really think," he once said, "that I'm not more depraved than most of my contemporaries. They're *joliment* depraved, my contemporaries!" He threw off wonderfully pretty things about his female friends and, numerous and various as they had been, declared that his curiosity had survived the ordeal. "But you're not to take that as advice," he added, "for as an authority I must be misleading. I'm prejudiced in their favour; I'm a *sentimental* — in other words a donkey." Newman listened with an uncommitted smile and was glad, for his own sake, that he had fine feelings; but he mentally repudiated the idea of a Frenchman's having discovered any merit in the amiable sex he himself did n't suspect. Count Valentin, however, was not merely anecdotic and indiscreet; he welcomed every light on our hero's own life, and so far as his revelations might startle and waylay Newman could cap them as from the long habit of capping. He narrated his career, in fact, from the beginning, through all its variations, and whenever his companion's credulity or his "standards" appeared to protest it amused him to heighten the colour of the episode. He had sat with Western humourists in circles round cast-iron stoves and seen "tall" stories grow taller without toppling over, and his imagination had learnt the trick of building straight and high. The Count's regular attitude became at last that of lively self-defence; to mark the difference of his type from that of the occasionally witless he cultivated the wit of never being caught swallowing. The result of this was that Newman found it impossible to convince him of certain time-honoured verities.

"But the details don't matter," Valentin said, "since you've evidently had some such surprising adventures. You've seen some strange sides of life, you've revolved to and fro over a continent as I walk up and down the Boulevard. You're a man of the world to a livelier tune than ours. You've spent some awful, some deadly days, and you've done some extremely disagreeable things: you've shovelled sand, as a boy, for supper, and you've eaten boiled cat in a gold-digger's camp. You've stood casting up figures for ten hours at a time and you've sat through Methodist sermons for the sake of looking at a pretty girl in another pew. It can't all have been very *folichon*. But at any rate you've done something and you *are* something; you've used your faculties and you've developed your character. You've not *abruti* yourself with debauchery, and you've not mortgaged your fortune to social conveniencies. You take things as it suits you, and you've fewer prejudices even than I, who pretend to have none, but who in reality have three or four that stand in my way. Happy man, you're strong and you're free — nothing stands in yours. But what the deuce," he wound up, "do you propose to do with such advantages? Really to use them you need a better world than this. There's nothing worth your while here."

"Oh, I guess there's something," Newman said.

"What is it?"

"Well," he sighed, "I'll tell you some other time!"

In this way he delayed from day to day broaching a subject he had greatly at heart. Meanwhile, however, he was growing practically familiar with it; in other words he had called again, three times, on Madame de Cintré. On but two of these occasions had he found her at home and on each of them she had other visitors. Her visitors were numerous and, to our hero's sense, vociferous, and they exacted much of their hostess's attention. She found time none the less to bestow a little of it on the stranger, a quantity represented in an occasional vague smile — the very vagueness of which pleased him by allowing him to fill it out mentally, both at the time and afterwards, with such meanings as most fitted. He sat by without speaking, looking at the entrances and exits, the greetings and chatterings, of Madame de Cintré's guests. He felt as if he were at the play and as if his own speaking would be an interruption; sometimes he wished he had a book to follow the dialogue; he half expected to see a woman in a white cap and pink ribbons come and offer him one for two francs. Some of the ladies gave him a very hard or a very soft stare, as he chose; others seemed profoundly unconscious of his presence. The men looked only at the mistress of the scene. This was inevitable, for whether one called her beautiful or not she entirely occupied and filled one's vision, quite as an ample, agreeable sound filled one's ear. Newman carried away after no more than twenty distinct words with her an impression to which solemn promises could not have given a higher value. She was part of the play he was seeing acted, as much a part of it as her companions, but how she filled the stage and how she bore watching, not to say studying and throwing bouquets to! Whether she rose or seated herself; whether she went with her departing friends to the door and lifted up the heavy curtain as they passed out and stood an instant looking after them and giving them the last nod; or whether she leaned back in her chair with her arms crossed and her eyes quiet, her face listening and smiling, she made this particular guest desire to have her always before him

moving through every social office open to the genius
of woman, or in other words through the whole range
of exquisite hospitality. If it might be hospitality *to*
him it would be well; if it might be hospitality *for*
him it would be still better. She was so high yet so
slight, so active yet so still, so elegant yet so simple,
so present yet so withdrawn! It was this unknown
quantity that figured for him as a mystery; it was
what she was off the stage, as he might feel, that
interested him most of all. He could not have told
you what warrant he had for talking of mysteries;
if it had been his habit to express himself in poetic
figures he might have said that in observing her he
seemed to see the vague circle sometimes attending
the partly-filled disc of the moon. It was not that
she was effaced, and still less that she was "shy";
she was, on the contrary, as distinct as the big figure
on a banknote and of as straightforward a profession. But he was sure she had qualities as yet
unguessed even by herself and that it was kept for
Christopher Newman to bring out.

He had abstained for several reasons from saying
some of these things to her brother. One reason was
that before proceeding to any act he was always cir-
cumspect, conjectural, contemplative; he had little
eagerness, as became a man who felt that whenever
he really began to move he walked with long steps.
And then it just pleased, it occupied and excited him,
not to give his case, as he would have said, prematurely
away. But one day Valentine — as Newman conveniently sounded the name — had been dining with
him on the boulevard and their sociability was such

that they had sat long over their dinner. On rising from it the young man proposed that, to help them through the rest of the evening, they should go and see Madame Dandelard. Madame Dandelard was a little Italian lady married to a Frenchman who had proved a rake and a brute and the torment of her life. Her husband had spent all her money and then, lacking further means for alien joys, had taken, in his more intimate hours, to beating her. She had a blue spot somewhere which she showed to several persons, including the said Valentine. She had obtained a legal separation, collected the scraps of her fortune, which were meagre, and come to live in Paris, where she was staying at an *hôtel garni*. She was always looking for an apartment and visiting, with a hundred earnest questions and measurements, those of other people. She was very pretty and child-like and made very extraordinary remarks. Valentin enjoyed her acquaintance, and the source of his interest in her was, according to his declaration, an anxious curiosity as to what would become of her. "She's poor, she's pretty and she's silly," he said; "it seems to me she can go only one way. It's a pity, but it can't be helped. I'll give her six months. She has nothing to fear from me, but I'm watching the process. It's merely a question of the how and the when and the where. Yes, I know what you're going to say; this horrible Paris hardens one's heart. But it quickens one's wits, and it ends by teaching one a refinement of observation. To see this little woman's little drama play itself out is now for me a pleasure of the mind."

"If she's going to throw herself away," Newman had said, "you ought to stop her."

"Stop her? How stop her?"

"Talk to her; give her some good advice."

At which the young man laughed. "'Some'? How much? Heaven deliver us both! Imagine the situation. Try giving her yourself exactly the right amount."

After which it was that Newman had gone with him to see Madame Dandelard. When they came away Valentin reproached his companion. "Where was your famous advice? I didn't hear a word of it."

"Oh, I give it up," Newman simply answered.

"Then you're as bad as I!"

"No, because I don't find it a pleasure of the mind to watch her prospective adventures. I don't in the least want to see her going down hill. I had rather look the other way. But why," our friend asked in a moment, "don't you get your sister to go and see her?"

His companion stared. "Go and see Madame Dandelard— my sister?"

"She might talk to her to very good purpose."

Valentin shook his head with sudden gravity. "My sister doesn't have relations with that sort of person. Madame Dandelard's nothing at all; they'd never meet."

"I should think," Newman returned, "that Madame de Cintré might see whom she pleased." And he privately resolved that, after he should know her a little better, he would ask her to go and pick up, for such "pressing" as might be possible, the little spotted blown leaf in the dusty Parisian alley. When they had dined, at all events, on the occasion I have mentioned, he demurred to the latter's proposal that they should go again and "draw" the lady on the subject of her bruises. "I've something better in mind; come home with me and finish the evening before my fire."

Valentin always rose to any implied appeal to his expository gift, and before long the two men sat watching the blaze play over the pomp of Newman's high saloon.

VIII

'Look here — I want to know about your sister,"
the elder abruptly began.

His visitor arched fine eyebrows. "Now that I
think of it you've never yet made her the subject of
a question."

"Well, I guess I know why."

"If it's because you don't trust me, you're very
right," said Valentin. "I can't talk of her rationally.
I admire her too much."

"Talk of her as you can," Newman returned,
"and if I don't like it I'll stop you."

"Well we're very good friends; such a brother
and sister as haven't been known since Orestes and
Electra. You've seen her enough to have taken her
in: tall, slim, imposing, gentle, half a *grande dame*
and half an angel; a mixture of 'type' and simplicity, of the eagle and the dove. She looks like
a statue that has failed as cold stone, resigned itself
to its defects and come to life as flesh and blood, to
wear white capes and long soft trains. All I can say
is that she really possesses every merit that the face
she has, the eyes she has, the smile she has, the
tone of voice she has, the whole *way* she has, lead
you to expect; and isn't it saying quite enough? As
a general thing when a woman seems from the first
as *right* as that, she's altogether wrong — you've
only to look out. But in proportion as you take

Claire for right you may fold your arms and let
yourself float with the current; you're safe. You'll
only never imagine a person so true and so straight.
She's so honest and so *gentille*. I've never seen a
woman half so charming. She has every blessed
thing a man wants and more; that's all I can say
about her. There!" Valentin concluded: "I told you
how much I should bore you."

Newman uttered no assurance that he was not
bored; he only said after a little: "She's remarkably *good*, eh?"

"She'd have invented goodness if it did n't exist."

"It seems to me," Newman remarked, "that you'd
have invented *her*—! But it's all right," he added
— "I'd have invented *you!* Is she clever?" he then
asked.

"Try her with something you think so yourself.
Then you'll see."

"Oh, how can I try her?" sighed Newman with
a lapse. But he picked himself up. "Is she fond of
admiration?"

"*Pardieu!*" cried Valentin. "She'd be no sister
of mine if she were n't. What woman's not?"

"Well, when they're too fond of it," Newman
heard himself hypocritically temporise, "they commit all kinds of follies to get it."

"I did n't say she was 'too' fond!" Valentin ex
claimed. "Heaven forbid I should say anything so
idiotic. She's not *too* anything. If I were to say she's
ugly I should n't mean she's 'too' ugly. She's fond
of pleasing, and if you're pleased she leaves it so. If
you're not pleased she lets it pass, and thinks the

worse neither of you nor of herself. I imagine, though, she hopes the saints in heaven are, for I'm sure she's incapable of trying to please by any means of which they'd disapprove."

"Is she happy then?" Newman presently pursued.

"Oh, oh, oh! That's much to ask."

"Do you mean for me — ?"

"I mean for her. What should she be happy about?"

Newman wondered. "Then she has troubles?"

"My dear man, she has what we all have — even you, strange to say. She has a history."

"That's just what I want to hear," said Newman.

Valentin hesitated — an embarrassment rare with him. "Then we shall have to appoint a special séance, with music or refreshments or a turn outside between the acts. Suffice it for the present that my sister's situation has been far from *folichonne*. She made, at eighteen, a marriage that was expected to be brilliant, but that, like a lamp that goes out, turned all to smoke and bad smell. M. de Cintré was fifty-five years old and *pas du tout aimable*. He lived, however, but three or four years, and after his death his family pounced upon his money, brought a law-suit against his widow, pushed things very hard. Their case was good, for M. de Cintré, who had been trustee for some of his relatives, appeared to have been guilty of some very irregular practices. In the course of the suit some revelations were made as to his private history which my sister found so little to her taste that she ceased to defend herself and washed her hands of all her interests. This required some strength of conviction, for she was between two fires, her husband's family opposing her and her own family denouncing. My mother and my brother wished her to cleave to what they regarded as her rights. But she resisted firmly and at last bought her freedom — obtained my mother's assent to her compromising the suit at the price of a promise."

"What was the promise?"

"To do anything else whatever, for the next ten years, that might be asked of her — anything, that is, but marry."

"She had disliked her husband very much?"

"No one knows how much!"

"The marriage had been made in your vicious French way," Newman continued — "by the two families and without her having a voice?"

"It was a first act for a melodrama. She saw M. de Cintré for the first time a month before the wedding, after everything, to the minutest detail, had been arranged. She turned white when she looked at him and white she remained — I shall never forget her face — till her wedding-day. The evening before the ceremony her nerves completely gave way and she spent the whole night in sobs. My mother sat holding her two hands and my brother walked up and down the room. I declared it was revolting and told my sister publicly that if she would really hold out I would stand by her against all comers. I was sent about my business and she became Comtesse de Cintré."

"Your brother," said Newman reflectively, "must be a very nice young man."

"He's very nice, though he's not very young. He's now upwards of fifty; fifteen years my senior. He has been a father to my sister and me. He's a type apart; he has the best manners in France. He's extremely clever; indeed he's full of accomplishment. He's writing a history of The Unmarried Princesses of the Maison de France." This was said by Valentin with extreme gravity, in a tone that betokened no mental reservation — or that at least almost betokened none.

Our friend perhaps discovered there what little there was, for he presently said: "You could struggle along without your brother."

"I beg your pardon" — the young man still as gravely protested. "A house like ours is inevitably *one*."

"Then you want some one to come right in and break it up."

"*Hein?*" said Valentin.

On which Newman, after an instant, put the matter another way. "Well, I'm glad *I'm* free not to like him!"

"Wait till you know him!" Valentin returned — and this time he smiled.

"Is your mother also then a type apart?" his friend asked after a pause.

"For my mother," the young man said, now with intense gravity, "I have the highest admiration. She's a very extraordinary person. You can't approach her without feeling it."

"She's the daughter, I believe, of an English nobleman?"

"Of Lord Saint Dunstans."

"And was *he* very grand?"

"Not as grand as we. They date only from the sixteenth century. It is on my father's side that we go back — back, back, back. The family antiquaries themselves lose breath. At last they stop, panting and fanning themselves, somewhere in the ninth century, under Charlemagne. That's where we begin."

"There is no mistake about it?" Newman demanded.

"I'm sure I hope not. We've been mistaken at least for several centuries."

"And you've always married into — what do you call them? — 'ancient houses'?"

"As a rule; though in so long a stretch of time there have been some exceptions. Three or four Bellegardes, in the seventeenth and eighteenth centuries, took wives out of the *bourgeoisie* — accepted lawyers' daughters."

"A lawyer's daughter — that's a come-down?" Newman went on.

"A condescension. But one of us, in the Middle Ages, did better: he married a beggar-maid, like King Cophetua. That was really more convenient; it was like pairing with a bird or a monkey; one did n't have to think about her family at all. Our women have always done well; they've never even gone into the *petite noblesse*. There is, I believe, not a case on record of a misalliance among *ces dames*."

Newman turned this over a while and then at last: "You offered, the first time you came to see

me, to render me any service you could. I told you
I'd sometime mention something you might do. Do
you remember?"

"Remember? I've been counting the hours."

"Very well; here's your chance. Do what you
can to make your sister think well of me."

The young man had a strange bright stare. "Why,
I'm sure she thinks as well of you as possible already."

"An opinion founded on seeing me three or four
times? That's putting me off with very little. I want
something more. I've been thinking of it a good deal
and at last I've decided to tell you. I should like
very much to marry Madame de Cintré."

Valentin had been looking at him with quickened
expectancy and with the smile with which he had
greeted his allusion to the promised request. At this
last announcement he kept his eyes on him, but their
expression went through two or three curious phases.
It felt, apparently, an impulse to let itself go further;
but this it immediately checked. Then it remained
for some instants taking counsel with the danger of
hilarity — at the end of which it decreed a retreat.
It slowly effaced itself and left a sobriety modified
by the desire not to be rude. Extreme surprise had
in fine come into M. de Bellegarde's face; but he had
reflected that it would be uncivil to leave it there.
And yet what the deuce was he to do with it? He got
up in his agitation and stood before the chimney-
piece, still looking at his host. He was a longer time
thinking what to say than one would have expected.

"If you can't render me the service I ask," New-

man pursued, "don't be afraid to tell me, for I ll
be hanged if I won't get on without you."

"Let me hear it again distinctly, the service you
ask. It's very important, you know," Valentin went
on. "I'm to plead your cause with my sister because you want — you want to marry her? That's
it, eh?"

"Oh, I don't say plead my cause exactly; I shall
try and do that myself. But say a good word for me
now and then — let her know at least what *you* take
me for."

This *was*, visibly, for the young man, a droll
simplification. "I shall have first, my dear fellow, to
know myself!"

But Newman went on unheeding. "What I want
chiefly, after all, is just to make you aware of what
I have in mind. I suppose that's what you all expect,
making you formally aware, is n't it? I want always
to do, over here, what's customary, what you've
been used to. You seem more lost without what
you've been used to than we are. If there's anything
particular to be done let me know and I'll make it
right. I would n't for the world approach Madame
de Cintré save by schedule. I'd go in to her on all-
fours if that's what's required. If I ought to speak
to your mother first why I'll speak to her. If I ought
to speak even to your brother I'll speak to *him*.
I'll speak to any one you like, to the porter in his
lodge or the policeman on his beat. As I don't know
any one else I begin by speaking to you. But that, if
it 's a social obligation, is a pleasure as well."

"Yes, I see — I see," said Valentin, lightly strok·

ing his chin. "You've a very right feeling about it, but I'm glad you've begun with me." He paused, hesitated, and then turned away and walked slowly the length of the room. Newman got up and stood leaning against the chimney with his hands in his pockets and his eyes on his friend's evolution. This personage came back and stopped in front of him. "I give it up. I'll not pretend I'm not — well, impressed. I am — hugely! *Ouf!* It's a relief."

"That sort of news is always a surprise," said Newman. "No matter what you've done, people are never prepared. But if you're impressed I hope at least you're impressed favourably."

"Come!" the young man broke out; "I'm going to let you have it. I don't know whether it lays me flat or makes me soar."

"Well, if it corners you too much I'm afraid you've got to stay there, for I assure you I mean myself to fight out in the open."

"My dear man, Samson was in the open when he pulled down the temple, but there wasn't much left of any one else." To which Valentin added: "You're perfectly serious?"

"Am I a futile Frenchman that I shouldn't be?" Newman asked. "But why is it, by the by — come to talk — that you *are* prostrated?"

The Count raised his hand to the back of his head and rubbed his hair quickly up and down, thrusting out the tip of his tongue as he did so. "Well, for instance you're not, as we call it, if I'm not mistaken, 'born.'"

"The devil I'm not!" Newman exclaimed.

"Oh," said his friend a little more seriously, ' I did n't know you had — well, your quarterings."

"Ah, your quarterings are your little local matter!"

Valentin just hesitated. "But are n't we all — is n't my admirable sister in particular — our little local matter?"

Newman met his eyes with a long, hard look — exhaling at last, however, a sigh as long. "Do you mean that I must *claim* a social standing and hang out my sign? What sort of swagger's that? If it's a question of pretensions — pretensions, that is, to effectively existing — let me make, to meet you on your own ground, the very highest. Only it is n't, it seems to me, for me vulgarly to make them; it's for you, assuming them, to invalidate them. On you, in other words, the burden of disproof."

Valentin's fine smile suffered a further strain. "Have n't you manufactured and placed in the market certain admirable wash-tubs?"

"With great temporary success. But it is n't a question of my achievements — it's a question of my failures. You might catch me," said our friend, "on two or three of those. Only then, you know," he added, "I should have the right to ask you about yours."

"Oh, ours have partaken of our general brilliancy! They have n't at any rate prevented the great thing."

"And what do you call the great thing?"

"Well," Valentin smiled, "our being interesting."

Newman considered. "To yourselves?"

"To the world. That *has* been our value — that

we've had the world's attention. We've been felt to be worth it."

"Oh," said Newman, "if it's but a question of what you're worth — !" He hung fire an instant, and then, "Should you like to know what *I* am?" he demanded.

He had held his companion by his pause, and his words prolonged a little the situation. "No, thanks," Valentin then replied. "It's none of my business. It's enough for me that you're worth, delightfully, my acquaintance and my wonder."

In recognition of these last words Newman for a moment said nothing. He only coloured as with a flush of hope. Then he raised his eyes to the ceiling and stood looking at one of the rosy cherubs painted on it. "Of course I don't expect to marry any woman for the asking," he observed at last: "I expect first to make myself acceptable to her. She must like me to begin with. But what I feel is how she *must* — from the moment she knows me as I want."

"As the prince of husbands?"

"Well yes — call it the prince, as you speak of such people."

"I believe," said Valentin after a moment, "that you'd be as good a prince as another."

"I should be as good a husband."

"And that's what you want me to tell my sister?"

"That's what I want you to tell her."

The young man laid his hand on his companion's arm, looked at him critically, from head to foot, and then, with a loud laugh and shaking the other hand in the air, turned away. He walked again the length

of the room and again he came back and stationed
himself in front of Newman. "All this is very interesting and very curious. In what I said just now
I was speaking not for myself, but for my traditions
and my superstitions. For myself really your idea stirs
me up. It startled me at first, but the more I think
of it the more I see in it. It's no use attempting to
explain anything; you would n't, I think, follow me.
After all, I don't see why you need; it's no great
loss."

"Oh, if there's anything more to explain try me
with it. I guess I've had to understand some queerer
things than any you're likely to tell."

"No," said Valentin, "we'll do without them;
we'll let them go. I took you for somebody — God
knows whom or what — the first time I saw you, and
I'll abide by that. It would be quite odious for me
to come talking to you as if I could patronise you.
I've told you before that I envy you; *vous m'im-
posez*, as we say — I did n't know you much till these
last five minutes. So we'll let things go, and I'll
say nothing to you that, with our positions reversed,
you would n't say to me."

I know not whether in renouncing the mysterious
opportunity to which he alluded Valentin felt himself do something very generous. If so he was not
rewarded; his generosity was not appreciated. Newman failed to recognise any power to disconcert or
to wound him, and he had now no sense of coming
off easily. He had not at his command the gratitude
even of a glance; and he was in truth occupied with
a particular fear, which he presently expressed. "Do

you think she may be by chance determined not to marry at all ?"

"Oh, I quite think it! But that's not necessarily too much against you. Such a determination never yet spoiled a right opportunity."

"But suppose I don't seem a right one. I'm afraid it will be hard," Newman said with a gravity that appeared to signify at the same time a sort of lucid respect for the fact.

"I don't think it will be easy. In a general way I don't see why a widow should ever marry again. She has gained the benefits of matrimony — freedom and consideration — and she has got rid of the drawbacks. Why should she put her head back into the noose ? Her usual motive is ambition — if a man can offer her a great position, make her a princess or an ambassadress."

"And — in that way — is Madame de Cintré ambitious ?"

"Who knows ?" her brother asked with slightly depressing detachment. "I don't pretend to say all she is or all she is n't. I think she might be touched by the prospect of becoming the wife of a great man. But in a certain way, I believe, whatever she does will be the *improbable*. Don't be too confident, but don't absolutely doubt. Your best chance for success will be precisely in affecting her as unusual, unexpected, original. Don't try to be any one else; be simply yourself as hard as ever you can, and harder perhaps indeed (if you understand) than you've ever been before. Something or other can't fail to come of *that*. I'm very curious to see what."

"I'm much obliged to you for your curiosity," Newman said — "if I may take it as your advice I'm glad for your sake at least that I'm likely to prove so amusing."

His friend, who had been staring at the fire a minute, looked up. "It's a pity you don't fully understand me, that you don't know just what I'm doing."

"Oh," laughed Newman, "don't do anything wrong! Leave me to myself rather, or defy me out and out to try it. I wouldn't lay any load on your conscience."

Valentin sprang up again, evidently quite inflamed. "You'll never understand — you'll never know; and if you succeed and I turn out to have helped you you'll never be grateful, not as I shall deserve you should be. You'll be an excellent fellow always, but you'll not be grateful. But it does n't matter, for I shall get my own fun out of it." And he broke into an extravagant laugh. "You look worried," he added; "you look almost alarmed."

"It's a pity," said Newman, "that I don't wholly catch on. I shall lose some very good sport."

"I told you, you remember, that we're very strange people," his visitor pursued. "Well, I give you warning again. We're fit for a museum or a Balzac novel. My mother's strange, my brother's strange, and I verily believe I'm stranger than either. You'll even find my sister a little strange. Old trees have crooked branches, old houses have queer cracks, old races have odd secrets. Remember that we're eight hundred years old!"

"Very good," said Newman; "that's the sort of

thing I came to Europe for. You're *made* for me to work right in."

"*Touchez-là* then," Bellegarde returned, putting out his hand. "It's a bargain; I accept you, I espouse your cause. It's because I like you, in a great measure; but that's not the only reason." And he stood holding Newman's hand and looking at him askance.

"What's the other one?"

"Well, I'm in the Opposition. I've a positive aversion —!"

"To your brother?" asked Newman in his unmodulated voice.

Valentin laid a finger on his lips with a whispered *hush!* "Old races have strange secrets! Put yourself into motion. Come and see my sister and be assured of my sympathy!" With which he took leave while his host dropped into a chair before the fire. Newman stared long and late into the blaze

IX

HE called on Madame de Cintré the very next day, and learnt from the servant that she was at home. He passed as usual up the large cold staircase and through a spacious vestibule above, where the walls seemed all composed of small door-panels touched with long-faded gilding; whence he was ushered into the sitting-room in which he had already been received. It was empty, but the footman told him that Madame la Comtesse would presently appear. He had time, while he waited, to wonder if Bellegarde had seen his sister since the evening before and if in this case he had spoken to her of their talk. In that event Madame de Cintré's receiving him was not, as he would have said, a bucket of cold water. He felt a certain trepidation as he reflected that she might come in with the knowledge of his supreme admiration and of the project he had built on it in her eyes; but the apprehension conveyed no chill. Her face could wear no look that would make it less beautiful, and he was sure beforehand that, however she might take the proposal he had in reserve, she would n't make him pay for it in the least to his ruin. He had a belief that if she could only look at the bottom of his heart and see it all bared to the quick for her she would be entirely kind.

She came in at last, after so long an interval that he wondered if she had been hesitating. She smiled

at him, as usual, without constraint, and her great
mild eyes, while she held out her hand, seemed to
shine at him perhaps even straighter than before.
She then remarkably observed, without a tremor in
her voice, that she was glad to see him and that she
hoped he was well. He found in her what he had
found before — that faint perfume of a personal
diffidence worn away by contact with the world, but
the more perceptible the more closely she was approached. This subtle shyness gave a peculiar value
to what was definite and assured in her manner,
making it an acquired accomplishment, a beautiful
talent, something that one might compare to an
exquisite touch in a pianist. It was, in fact, her
"authority," as they say of artists, that especially
impressed and fascinated him; he always came back
to the feeling that, when he should have rounded out
his "success" by the right big marriage, this was the
way he should like his wife to express the size of it
to the world. The only trouble indeed was that when
the instrument was so perfect it seemed to interpose
too much between the audience and the composer.
She gave him, the charming woman, the sense of an
elaborate education, of her having passed through
mysterious ceremonies and processes of culture in
her youth, of her having been fashioned and made
flexible to certain deep social needs. All this, as
I have noted, made her seem rare and precious —
a very expensive article, as he would have said, and
one which a man with an ambition to have everything about him of the best would taste of triumph
in possessing. Yet looking at the matter with an eye

to private felicity he asked himself where, in so exquisite a compound, nature and art showed their dividing-line. Where did the special intention separate from the habit of good manners? Where did fine urbanity end and fine sincerity begin? He indulged in these questions even while he stood ready to accept the admired object in all its complexity; he felt indeed he could do so in profound security, examining its mechanism afterwards and at leisure. "I'm very glad to find you alone. You know I've never had such good luck before."

"But you've seemed before very well contented with your luck," said Madame de Cintré. "You've sat and watched my visitors as comfortably as from a box at the opera. What have you thought of our poor performance?"

"Oh, I've thought the ladies very bright and very graceful, wonderfully quick at repartee. But what I've chiefly thought has been that they only help me to admire *you*." This was not the habit of the pretty speech on Newman's part, the art of the pretty speech never having attained great perfection with him. It was simply the instinct of the practical man who had made up his mind to what he wanted and was now beginning to take active steps to obtain it.

She started slightly and raised her eyebrows; she had evidently not expected so straight an advance. "Oh, in that case," she none the less gaily said, "your finding me alone is n't good luck for me. I hope some one will come in quickly."

"I hope not," Newman returned. "I've something particular to say to you. Have you seen your brother Valentine?"

"Yes, I saw him an hour ago."

"Did he tell you that he had seen me last night?"

"I think he spoke of it."

"And did he tell you what we had talked about?"

She visibly hesitated. While Newman made these enquiries she had grown a little pale, as if taking what might impend for inevitable rather than convenient. "Did you give him a message to me?"

"It was not exactly a message. I asked him to render me a service."

"The service was to sing your praises, was it not?" She had been clearly careful to utter this question in the tone of trifling.

"Yes, that is what it really amounts to," said Newman. "*Did* he therefore sing my praises?"

"He spoke very well of you. But when I know that it was by special request I must of course take his eulogy with a grain of salt."

"Ah, that makes no difference," Newman went on. "Your brother wouldn't have spoken well of me unless he believed what he was saying. He's too honest for that."

"Are you a great diplomatist?" she answered. "Are you trying to please me by praising my brother? I confess it's a good way."

"For me any way that succeeds will be good. I'll praise your brother all day if that will help me. I just love him, you know, and I regard him as perfectly straight. He has made me feel, in promising to do what he can to help me, that I can depend upon him."

"Don't make too much of that," said Madame de Cintré. "He can help you very little."

"Of course I must work my way myself. I know that very well; I only want a chance to. In consenting to see me, after what he told you, you almost seem to be giving me a chance."

"I'm seeing you," she slowly and gravely pronounced, "because I promised my brother I would."

"Blessings on your brother's head then!" Newman cried. "What I told him last evening was this: that I admired you more than any woman I had ever seen and that I should like extraordinarily to make you my wife." He spoke these words with great directness and firmness and without any sense of confusion. He was full of his idea, he had completely mastered it, and he seemed to look down on the woman he addressed, and on all her gathered graces, from the height of his bracing good conscience. It is probable that this particular tone and manner were the very best he could have adopted; yet the light, just visibly forced smile with which she had listened to him died away and she sat looking at him with her lips parted and her face almost as portentous as a tragic mask. There was evidently an inconvenience amounting to pain for her in this extravagant issue; her impatience of it, however, found no angry voice. Newman wondered if he were hurting her; he could n't imagine why the liberal devotion he meant to express should be offensive. He got up and stood before her, leaning one hand on the chimney-piece. "I know I've seen you very little to say this, so little that it may make what I say seem disrespectful. But that s my misfortune. I could have said it at the first time I saw you. Really I had seen you before; I had seen you in imagination; you seemed almost an old friend. So what I say, you can at least believe, is not mere grand talk in the air, an exaggerated compliment. I can't talk for any effect but one I want very much to bring about, and I would n't to you if I could. What I say is as serious as such words can be. I feel as if I knew you and knew how fine and rare and true you are. I shall know better perhaps some day, but I have a general notion now. You're just the woman I've been look-ing for, except that you're far more perfect. I won't make any protestations and vows, but you can trust me. It's very soon, I know, to say all this; it may almost shock you. But why not gain time if one can? And if you want time to reflect — as of course you'd do — the sooner you begin the better for me. I don't know what you think of me; but there's no great mystery, nor anything at all difficult to tell, about me — nor difficult to understand. Your brother told me that my antecedents and occupations will be against me; that your family has a social standing so high that I can't be taken as coming up to it. Well, I don't know about coming 'up' — I don't think you can very well keep me *down*, anywhere. You can't make a man feel low unless you can make him feel base; and if you may fit yourself into any class you see your way to, you can't fit *him* where he won't go. But I don't believe you care anything about that. I can assure you there's quite enough of me to last, and that if I give my mind to it I can arrange things so that in a very few years I shall not need to waste time in explaining who I am and how much I matter. You'll decide for yourself if you like me or not. I honestly believe I've no hidden vices nor nasty tricks. I'm kind, kind, kind! Everything that a man can give a woman I'll give you. I've a large fortune, a very large fortune; some day, if you'll allow me, I'll go into details. If you want grandeur, everything in the way of grandeur that money can give you, why you shall have it. And as regards anything you may give up, don't take for granted too much that its place can't be filled. Leave that to me — I've filled some places. I'll take care of you; I shall know what you need. I would n't talk if I did n't believe I knew how. I want you to feel I'm strong, because if you do that will be enough. There; I have said what I had on my heart. It was better to get it off. I'm very sorry if it worries you; but the air's clearer — don't you already see? If I've made a mistake we had better not have met at all; and I can't think *that*, Madame de Cintré, can *you?*" Newman asked. "Don't answer me now, if you don't wish it. Think about it; think about it only a little at a time, if you want. Of course I have n't said, I can't say, half I mean, especially about my admiration for you. But take a favourable view of me; it will only be just."

During this speech, the longest personal plea, of any kind, that he had ever uttered in his life, she kept her gaze fixed on him, and it expanded at the last into a sort of fascinated stare. When he ceased speaking she lowered it and sat for some moments looking

down and straight before her. Then she slowly rose
to her feet, and a pair of exceptionally keen eyes
would have made out in her an extraordinarily fine
tremor. She still looked extremely serious. "I'm
very much obliged to you for your offer. It seems
to me very strange, but I'm glad you spoke without
waiting any longer. It's better the subject should
be dismissed between us. I appreciate immensely
all you say; you do me great honour. But I've decided not to marry."

"Oh, don't say that!" cried Newman with the
very innocence of pleading desire. She had turned
away, and it made her stop a moment with her back
to him. "Think better of that. You're too young,
too beautiful, too much made to be happy and to
make others happy. If you're afraid of losing your
freedom I can assure you that this freedom here,
the life you now lead, is a dreary bondage to what
I'll offer you. You shall do things that I don't think
you've ever thought of. I'll take you to live anywhere
in the wide world you may want. Are you unhappy?
You give me a feeling that you *are* unhappy. You've
no right to be, or to be made so. Let me come in
and put an end to it."

The young woman waited, but looking again all
away from him. If she was touched by the way he
spoke the thing was conceivable. His voice, always
very mild, almost flatly soft and candidly interrogative for so full an organ, had become as edgeless
and as tenderly argumentative as if he had been talking to a much-loved child. He stood watching her,
and she presently turned again, but with her face

not really meeting his own; and she spoke with a
quietness in which there was a visible trace of effort.
"There are a great many reasons why I should n't
marry — more, I beg you to believe, than I can explain to you. As for my happiness, I 'm perfectly
content. If I call your proposal 'strange' it 's also
for more reasons than I can say. Of course you 've
a perfect right to make it. But I can't accept it —
that 's impossible. Please never speak of the matter
again. If you can't promise me this I must ask you
not to come back."

"Why is it impossible?" he demanded with an
insistence that came easily to him now. "You may
think it is at first without its really being so. I did n't
expect you to be pleased at first, but I do believe that
if you 'll think of it a good while you may finally be
satisfied."

"I don't know you," she returned after a moment.
"Think how little I know you!"

"Very little of course, and therefore I don't ask
for your ultimatum on the spot. I only ask you not
simply to put me off. I only ask you to let me 'stay
round,' and by so doing to let me hope. I 'll wait as
long as ever you want. Meanwhile you can see more
of me and know me better, look at me in the light —
well, of my presumption, yes, but of other things too.
You can make up your mind."

Something was going on, rapidly, in her spirit;
she was weighing a question there beneath his eyes,
weighing it and deciding it. "From the moment
I don't very respectfully beg you to leave the house
and never return I listen to you — I seem to give

you hope. I *have* listened to you — against my judgement. It's because, you see, you're eloquent. Yes," she almost panted, "you touch me. If I had been told this morning that I should consent to consider you as a person wishing to come so very near me I should have thought my informant a little crazy. I *am* listening to you, you see!" And she threw her arms up for a moment and let them drop with a gesture in which there was just an expression of surrendering weakness.

"Well, as far as saying goes, I've said everything," Newman replied. "I believe in you without restriction, and I think all the good of you it's possible to think of a human creature. I firmly believe that in marrying me you'll be *safe*. As I said just now," he went on with his smile as of hard experience, "I've no bad ways. I can really *do* so much for you! And if you're afraid that I'm not what you've been accustomed to, not as refined and cultivated, or even as pleasant all round, as your standard requires, you may easily carry that too far. I *am* refined — I *am* pleasant. Just you try me!"

Claire de Cintré got still further away and paused before a great plant, an azalea, which flourished in a porcelain tub before her window. She plucked off one of the flowers and, twisting it in her fingers, retraced her steps. Then she sat down in silence, and her attitude seemed a consent that he should say more. She might almost be liking it.

"Why should you say it's impossible you should marry?" he therefore continued. "The only thing that could make it really impossible would be your being already subject to that tie! — which must be awful, I admit, when it's only a grind. Is it because you've been unhappy in marriage? That's all the more reason. Is it because your family exert a pressure on you, interfere with you or worry you? That's still another reason: you ought to be perfectly free, and marriage will make you so. I don't say anything against your family — understand that!" added Newman with an eagerness which might have made a perspicacious witness smile. "Whatever way you feel about them is the right way, and anything you should wish me to do to make myself agreeable to them I'll do as well as I know how. They may put me through what they like — I guess I shall hold out!"

She rose again and came to the fire near which he had hovered. The expression of pain and embarrassment had passed out of her face, and it had submitted itself with a kind of grace in which there might have been indeed a kind of art. She had the air of a woman who had stepped across the frontier of friendship and looks round her a little bewildered to find the spaces larger than those marked in her customary chart. A certain checked and controlled exaltation played through the charm of her dignity. "I won't refuse to see you again, because much of what you've said has given me pleasure. But I will see you only on this condition: that you say nothing more in the same way for a long long time."

"What do you mean by 'long long' — ?"

"Well, I mean six months. It must be a solemn promise."

"Very good; I promise."

"Good-bye then." And she put out her hand.

He held it a moment as if to say more. But he only looked at her — "long, long"; then he took his departure.

That evening, on the Boulevard, he met Valentin de Bellegarde. After they had exchanged greetings he told him he had seen his sister a few hours before.

"I know it, pardieu!" said Valentin. "I dined *là-bas*." With which, for some moments, both men were silent. Newman wished to ask what visible impression his visit had made, but the Count had a question of his own and he ended by speaking first. "It's none of my business, but what the deuce did you say to Claire?"

"I'm quite willing to tell you I made her an offer of marriage."

"Already!" And the young man gave a whistle. "'Time is money!' Is that what you say in America? And my sister — ?" he discreetly added.

"She did n't close with me."

"She could n't, you know, in that way."

"But I'm to see her again," said Newman.

"Oh, the strangeness of *ces dames!*" Then he stopped and held Newman off at arm's length. "I look at you with respect! You've achieved what we call a personal success! Immediately, now, I must present you to my brother."

"Whenever you like!" said Newman.

X

NEWMAN continued to see his other good friends with scarce-diminished frequency, though if you had listened to Mrs. Tristram's account of the matter you would have supposed they had been cynically repudiated for the sake of grander acquaintance. "We were all very well so long as we had no rivals — we were better than nothing. But now that you 've become the fashion and have your pick every day of three invitations to dinner, we 're tossed into the corner. I 'm sure it is very good of you to come and see us once a month; I wonder you don't send us your cards in an envelope. When you do, pray have them with black edges; it will be for the death of my last illusion." It was in this incisive strain she moralised over Newman's so-called neglect, which was in truth a most excellent constancy. Of course she was joking, but she embroidered with a sharp needle.

"I know no better proof that I 've treated you very well," Newman had said, "than the fact that you make so free with my character. I 've let you tweak my nose, I 've allowed you the run of the animal's cage. If I had a little proper pride I 'd stay away a while and, when you should ask me to dinner, say I 'm going to Princess Borealska's. But I have n't any pride where my pleasure's concerned, and to keep you in the humour to see me — if you must see me only to call me bad names — I 'll agree to any·

thing you choose; I'll admit I'm the biggest kind of a sneak." Newman in fact had declined an invitation personally given by the Princess Borealska, an enquiring Polish lady to whom he had been presented, on the ground that on that particular day he always dined at Mrs. Tristram's; and it was only a tenderly perverse theory of his hostess of the Avenue d'Iéna that he was faithless to his early friendships. She needed the theory to explain one of her fine exasperations. Having launched our hero on the current that was bearing him so rapidly along she felt but half-pleased at its swiftness. She had succeeded too well; she had played her game too cleverly and wished to mix up the cards. Newman had told her, in due season, that her friend was "quite satisfactory." The epithet was not romantic, but Mrs. Tristram had no difficulty in perceiving that in essentials the feeling which lay beneath it was. Indeed the mild expansive brevity with which it was uttered, and a certain look, at once appealing and inscrutable, that issued from her guest's half-closed eyes as he leaned his head against the back of his chair, seemed to her the most eloquent attestation of a mature sentiment that she had ever encountered. He was only abounding in her own sense, but his temperate raptures exerted a singular effect on that enthusiasm with which she had overflowed a few months before. She now seemed inclined to take a purely critical view of Madame de Cintré, and wished to have it understood that she did n't in the least pretend to have gone into a final analysis of her life, or in other words of her honesty. "No woman" — she played with this idea — "can be so good as that one seems. Remember what Shakespeare calls Desdemona: 'a supersubtle Venetian.' Claire de Cintré's a supersubtle Parisian. She's a charming creature and has five hundred merits; but you had better keep her supersubtlety in mind." Was Mrs. Tristram simply finding herself jealous of her special favourite on the other side of the Seine, so that in undertaking to provide Newman with an ideal wife she had counted too much on the lapse of her own passions and her immunity from wild yearnings? We may be permitted to doubt it. The inconsistent little lady of the Avenue d'Iéna had an insuperable need of intellectual movement, of critical, of ironic exercise. She had a lively imagination, and was capable at times of holding views, of entertaining be'iefs, directly opposed to her most cherished opinions and convictions. She got tired of thinking right, but there was no serious harm in it, as she got equally tired of thinking wrong. In the midst of her mysterious perversities she had admirable flashes of justice. One of these occurred when Newman mentioned to her that he had made their beautiful friend a formal offer of his hand. He repeated in a few words what he had said, and in a great many what she had answered, and Mrs. Tristram listened with extreme interest.

"But after all," he admitted, "there's nothing to congratulate me upon. It is not much of a triumph."

"I beg your pardon; it's a great triumph. It's really dazzling that she didn't silence you at the first word and request you never to come near her again."

"Well, she would n't have got much by that," he made answer.

She looked at him a moment. "No one, I think, gets as much by anything as you. When I told you to go your own way and do what came into your head I had no idea you 'd go over the ground so fast. I never dreamed you 'd propose after five or six morning calls. What had you done as yet to make her like you ? You had simply sat — not very straight — and stared at her. But she does like you."

"That remains to be seen."

"No, it only remains to be criticised. What will come of it remains to be seen. That you should make but a mouthful of her marrying you without more ado could never have come into her head. You can form very little idea of what passed through her mind as you spoke; if she ever really takes you the affair will be marked by the usual justice of all human judgements of women. You 'll think you take generous views of her, but you 'll never begin to know through what a strange sea of feeling she 'll have passed before accepting you. As she stood there in front of you the other day she plunged into it. She said ' Well, why not ? ' to something that a few hours earlier had been inconceivable. She turned about on a thousand gathered prejudices and traditions as on a pivot and looked where she had never looked till that instant. When I think of it, when I think of Claire de Cintré and all that she represents, there seems to me something very fine in it. When I recommended you to try your fortune with her I of course thought well of you, and in spite of your base ingratitude I think so still. But I confess I don't see quite what you are and what you've done to make such a woman go these extravagant lengths for you."

"Oh, there's something very fine in it!" — Newman laughed as he repeated her words. He took an extreme satisfaction in hearing that there was something very fine in it. He had not the least doubt of this himself, but he had already begun to value the world's view of his possible prize as adding to the prospective glory of possession.

It was immediately after this passage that Valentin de Bellegarde came to conduct his friend to the Rue de l'Université and present him to the other members of his family. "You're already introduced and you've begun to be talked about. My sister has mentioned your successive visits to my mother, and it was an accident that my mother was present at none of them. I've spoken of you as an American of immense wealth, and the best fellow in the world, who's looking for something quite superior in the way of a wife."

"Do you suppose," asked Newman, "that Madame de Cintré has reported to your mother the last conversation I had with her?"

"I'm very certain she hasn't; she'll keep her own counsel. Meanwhile," Valentin said, "you must make your way with the rest of the family. Thus much is known about you — that you've made a great fortune in trade, that you're a frank outsider and an honest eccentric, and that you furiously admire our charming Claire. My sister-in-law, whom you remember seeing in Claire's sitting-room, took, it appears, a marked fancy to you; she has described you as having *beaucoup de cachet*. My mother is therefore curious to see you."

"She expects to laugh at me, eh?" said Newman.

"She never laughs — or at least never expects to. If she does n't like you don't hope to purchase favour by being funny. I 'm funny — take warning by *me!*"

This conversation took place in the evening, and half an hour later Valentin ushered his companion into an apartment of the house of the Rue de l'Université into which he had not yet penetrated, the salon of the dowager Marquise. It was a vast high room, with elaborate and ponderous mouldings, painted a whiteish grey, along the upper portion of the walls and the ceiling; with a great deal of faded and carefully-repaired tapestry in the doorways and chair-backs; with a Turkey carpet, in light colours, still soft and rich despite great antiquity, on the floor; and with portraits of each of Madame de Bellegarde's children at the age of ten suspended against an old screen of red silk. The dimness was diminished, exactly enough for conversation, by half a dozen candles placed in odd corners and at a great distance apart. In a deep armchair near the fire sat an old lady in black; at the other end of the room another person was seated at the piano and playing a very expressive waltz. In this latter person Newman recognised the younger Marquise.

Valentin presented his friend, and Newman came sufficiently near to the old lady by the fire to take in that she would offer him no handshake — so that he knew he had the air of waiting, and a little like a customer in a shop, to see what she *would* offer. He received a rapid impression of a white, delicate, aged face, with a high forehead, a small mouth and a pair of cold blue eyes which had kept much of the clearness of youth. Madame de Bellegarde looked hard at him and refused what she did refuse with a sort of British positiveness which reminded him that she was the daughter of the Earl of Saint Dunstans. Her daughter-in-law stopped playing and gave him an agreeable smile. He sat down and looked about him while Valentin went and kissed the hand of the young Marquise.

"I ought to have seen you before," said Madame de Bellegarde. "You've paid several visits to my daughter."

"Oh yes," Newman liberally smiled; "Madame de Cintré and I are old friends by this time."

"You've gone very fast," she went on.

"Not so fast as I should like."

"Ah, you're very ambitious," the old woman returned.

"Well, if I don't know what I want by this time I suppose I never shall."

Madame de Bellegarde looked at him with her cold fine eyes, and he returned her gaze, reflecting that she was a possible adversary and trying to take her measure. Their eyes remained for some moments engaged; then she looked away and, without smiling, "I'm very ambitious too," she said.

Newman felt that taking her measure was not easy; she was a formidable, inscrutable little woman. She resembled her daughter as an insect might resemble a flower. The colouring in Madame de Cintré was the same, and the high delicacy of her brow and nose was hereditary. But her face was a larger and freer copy, and her mouth in especial a happy divergence from that conservative orifice, a small pair of lips at once plump and pinched, that suggested, when closed, that they could scarce open wider than to swallow a gooseberry or to emit an "Oh dear no!" and which had probably been thought to give the finishing touch to the aristocratic prettiness of the Lady Emmeline Atheling as represented, half a century before, in several Books of Beauty. Madame de Cintré's face had, to Newman's eye, a range of expression as delightfully vast as the wind-streaked, cloud-flecked distance on a Western prairie; but her mother's white, intense, respectable countenance, with its formal gaze and its circumscribed smile, figured a document signed and sealed, a thing of parchment, ink and ruled lines. "She's a woman of conventions and proprieties," he said to himself as he considered her; "her world's the world of things immutably decreed. But how she's at home in it and what a paradise she finds it! She walks about in it as if it were a blooming park, a Garden of Eden; and when she sees 'This is genteel' or 'This is improper' written on a milestone she stops as ecstatically as if she were listening to a nightingale or smelling a rose." Madame de Bellegarde wore a little black velvet hood tied under her chin and was wrapped in an old black cashmere shawl. "You're an American?" she went on presently. "I've seen several Americans."

"There are several in Paris," Newman jocosely said.

"Oh, really? It was in England I saw these, or somewhere else; not in Paris. I think it must have been in the Pyrenees many years ago. I'm told your ladies are very pretty. One of these ladies was very pretty — with such a wonderful complexion. She presented me a note of introduction from some one — I forget whom — and she sent with it a note of her own. I kept her letter a long time afterwards, it was so strangely expressed. I used to know some of the phrases by heart. But I've forgotten them now — it's so many years ago. Since then I've seen no more Americans. I think my daughter-in-law has; she's a great gadabout; she sees every one."

At this the younger lady came rustling forward, pinching in a very slender waist and casting idly preoccupied glances over the front of her dress, which was apparently designed for a ball. She was, in a singular way, at once ugly and pretty; she had protuberant eyes and lips that were strangely red. She reminded Newman of his friend Mademoiselle Nioche; this was what that much-hindered young lady would have liked to be. Valentin de Bellegarde walked behind her at a distance, hopping about to keep off the far-spreading train of her dress. "You ought to show more of the small of your back," he said very gravely. "You might as well wear a standing ruff as such a dress as that."

The young woman turned to the mirror over the chimney-piece the part of her person so designated, and glanced behind her to verify this judgement.

The mirror descended low and yet reflected nothing but a large unclad flesh-surface. Its possessor put her hands behind her and gave a downward pull to the waist of her dress. "Like that, you mean?"

"That's a little better," said Valentin in the same tone, "but it leaves a good deal to be desired."

"Oh, I never go to extremes." And then turning to Madame de Bellegarde, "What were you calling me just now, madame?" her daughter-in-law enquired.

"I called you a gadabout. But I might call you something else too."

"A gadabout? What an ugly word! What does it mean?"

"A very beautiful lady," Newman ventured to say, seeing that it was in French.

"That's a pretty compliment but a bad translation," the young Marquise returned. After which, looking at him a moment: "Do you dance?"

"Not a step."

"You lose a great deal," she said simply. And with another look at her back in the mirror she turned away.

"Do you like Paris?" asked the old lady, who was apparently wondering what was the proper way to talk to an American.

"I think that must be the matter with me," he smiled. And then he added with a friendly intonation: "Don't *you* like it?"

"I can't say I know it. I know my house — I know my friends — I don't know Paris."

"You lose a great deal, as your daughter-in-law says," Newman replied.

Madame de Bellegarde stared; it was presumably the first time she had been condoled with on her losses. "I'm content, I think, with what I have," she said with dignity. Her visitor's eyes were at this moment wandering round the room, which struck him as rather sad and shabby; passing from the high casements, with their small thickly-framed panes, to the sallow tints of two or three portraits in pastel, of the last century, which hung between them. He ought obviously to have answered that the contentment of his hostess was quite natural — she had so much; but the idea didn't occur to him during the pause of some moments which followed.

"Well, my dear mother," said Valentin while he came and leaned against the chimney-piece, "what do you think of my good friend? Isn't he the remarkably fine man I told you of?"

"My acquaintance with Mr. Newman has not gone very far," Madame de Bellegarde replied. "I can as yet only appreciate his great politeness."

"My mother's a great judge of these matters," Valentin went on to Newman. "If you've satisfied her it's a triumph."

"I hope I shall satisfy you some day," said Newman to the old lady. "I've done nothing yet."

"You mustn't listen to my son; he'll bring you into trouble. He's a sad scatterbrain," she declared.

Newman took it genially. "Oh, I've got to like him so that I can't do without him."

"He amuses you, eh?"

"I think it must be that."

"Do you hear that, Valentin?" said his mother "You exist for the amusement of Mr. Newman."

"Perhaps we shall all come to that!" Valentin exclaimed.

"You must see my other son," she pursued. "He's much better than this one. But he'll not amuse you."

"I don't know — I don't know!" Valentin thoughtfully objected. "But we shall very soon see. Here comes *monsieur mon frère*." The door had just opened to give ingress to a gentleman who stepped forward and whose face Newman remembered as that of the author of his discomfiture the first time of his calling. Valentin went to meet his brother, looked at him a moment and then, taking him by the arm, led him up to their guest. "This is my excellent friend Mr. Newman," he said very blandly. "You must know him if you can."

"I'm delighted to know Mr. Newman," said the Marquis with an unaccompanied salutation.

"He's the old woman at second-hand," Newman reflected with the sense of having his health drunk from an empty glass. And this was the starting-point of a speculative theory, in his mind, that the late head of this noble family had been a very amiable foreigner with an inclination to take life easily and a sense that it was difficult for the husband of the stilted little lady by the fire to do so. But if he had found small comfort in his wife he had found much in his two younger children, who were after his own heart, while Madame de Bellegarde had paired with her eldest-born.

"My brother has spoken to me of you," said M. de Bellegarde, "and as you are also acquainted with my sister it was time we should meet." He turned to his mother and gallantly bent over her hand, touching it with his lips; after which he assumed a position before the chimney-piece. With his long lean face, his high-bridged nose and small opaque eyes he favoured, in the old phrase, the English strain in his blood. His whiskers were fair and glossy and he had a large dimple, of unmistakeable British origin, in the middle of his handsome chin. He was "distinguished" to the tips of his polished nails, and there was not a movement of his fine perpendicular person that was not noble and majestic. Newman had never yet been confronted with such an incarnation of the maintained attitude; he felt himself in presence of something high and unusual.

"Urbain," said young Madame de Bellegarde, who had apparently been waiting for her husband to take her to her ball, "I call your attention to the fact that I'm dressed."

"That's a good idea — to show what you claim for it," Valentin commented.

"I'm at your orders, dear friend," said M. de Bellegarde. "Only you must allow me first the pleasure of a little conversation with Mr. Newman."

"Oh, if you're going to a party don't let me keep you; I'm so sure we shall meet again. Indeed if you'd like to meet me I'll gladly name an hour." He was eager to make it known that he would readily answer all questions and satisfy all exactions.

M. de Bellegarde stood in a well-balanced position

before the fire, caressing one of his fair whiskers with one of his white hands and looking at our friend, half-askance, with eyes from which a particular ray of observation made its way through a general meaningless smile. "It's very kind of you to make such an offer. If I'm not mistaken your occupations are such as to make your time precious. You're in — a — as we say — a — *dans les affaires?*"

"In business, you mean? Oh no, I've thrown business overboard for the present. I'm regularly 'loafing,' as *we* say. My time's quite my own."

"Ah, you're taking a holiday," rejoined M. de Bellegarde. "'Loafing.' Yes, I've heard that expression."

"Mr. Newman's a distinguished American," Madame de Bellegarde observed.

"My brother's a great ethnologist," said Valentin.

"An ethnologist?" — and Newman groped for gaiety. "You collect negroes' skulls and that sort of thing?"

The Marquis looked hard at his brother and began to caress his other whisker. Then turning to their new acquaintance with sustained urbanity: "You're travelling for pure recreation?"

"Well, I'm visiting your country, sir," Newman replied with a certain conscious patience — a patience he felt he on his side too could push, should need be, to stiffness; "and I confess I'm having a good time in it. Of course I get a good deal of pleasure out of it."

"What more especially interests you?" the Marquis benevolently pursued.

"Well," our friend continued, "the life of the people, for one thing, interests me. Your people are very taking. But economically, technically, as it were, manufactures are what I care most about."

"Those — a — products have been your speciality?"

"I can't say I have had any speciality. My speciality has been to accumulate the largest convenient competency in the shortest possible time." Newman made this last remark very designedly and deliberately; he wished to open the way, should it be necessary, to an authoritative statement of his means.

M. de Bellegarde laughed agreeably. "I hope you enjoy the sense of that success."

"Oh, one has still, at my age, the sense also of what's left to do. I'm not so very old," our hero candidly explained.

"Well, Paris is a very good place to spend a fortune. I wish you all the advantages of yours." And M. de Bellegarde drew forth his gloves and began to put them on.

Newman for a few moments watched him sliding his fair, fat hands into the pearly kid, and as he did so his feelings took a singular turn. M. de Bellegarde's good wishes seemed to flutter down on him from the cold upper air with the soft, scattered movement of a shower of snowflakes. Yet he was not irritated; he didn't feel that he was being patronised; he was conscious of no especial impulse to introduce a discord into so noble a harmony. Only he felt himself suddenly in personal contact with the forces with which his so valued backer had told him that ne would have to contend, and he became sensible of their intensity. He wished to make some answering manifestation, to stretch himself out at his own length, to sound a note at the uttermost end of *his* scale. It must be added that if this impulse was neither vicious nor malicious, it was yet by no means unattended by the play in him of his occasional disposition to ironic adventure. He hated the idea of shocking people, he respected the liability to be shocked. But there were impressions that threw him back, after all, on his own measures of proportion "Paris," he presently remarked, "is a very good place for people who take a great deal of stock, as we say, *in* their location, and want to be very much aware of it all the time; or it's a very good place if your family has been settled here for a long time and you've made acquaintances and got your relations round you; or if you've got a big house like this and a wife and children and mother and sister — everything right there. I don't like that way that prevails in many of your districts of people's living all in rooms door to door with each other. But I'm not, as I may put it, a *natural*, a real inspired loafer. I'm a poor imitation and it goes against the grain. My business habits are too deep-seated. Then I have n't any house to call my own or anything in the way of a family. My sisters are five thousand miles away, my mother died when I was pretty small, and I have n't what a man has when he has taken the regular way to get it — if I express myself clearly; and I often miss *that* pleasantness very much. So you see I'm sometimes rather conscious of a void. I'm not proficient in literature, as you are, sir, and I get tired of dining out and going to the opera. I miss my business activity. You see I began to earn my living when I was almost a baby, and until a few months ago I've never had my hand off the plough. I miss the regular call on my attention."

This speech was followed by a profound silence of some moments on the part of Newman's entertainers. Valentin stood looking at him fixedly, hands in pockets, and then slowly, with a half-sidling motion, went out of the room. The Marquis continued to draw on his gloves and to smile benignantly. "You began to earn your living in the cradle?" said the old Marquise, who appeared to wish to encourage, a little grimly, yet not wholly without an effect of pleasantry, her guest's autobiographic strain.

"Well, madam, I'm not absolutely convinced I *had* a cradle!"

"You say you're not proficient in literature," M. de Bellegarde resumed; "but you must do yourself the justice to remember that your studies were interrupted early."

"That's very true; on my tenth birthday my schooling stopped short. I thought that a grand way to keep it. Still, I *have* picked up knowledge," Newman smiled.

"You have some sisters?" Madame de Bellegarde enquired.

"Yes, two splendid sisters. I wish you knew *them!*"

"I hope that for *ces dames* the hardships of life commenced less early."

"They married very early indeed, if you call that a hardship — as girls do in our Western country. The husband of one of them is the owner of the largest india-rubber house in the West."

"Ah, you make houses also of india-rubber?" the Marquise asked.

"You can stretch them as your family increases," said her daughter-in-law, now enveloped in a soft shining cape. Newman indulged at this in a burst of hilarity and explained that the house in which his relatives lived was a large wooden structure, but that they manufactured and sold india-rubber on a colossal scale. "My children have some little india-rubber shoes which they put on when they go to play in the Tuileries in damp weather," the young Marquise accordingly pursued. "I wonder if your brother-in-law made them."

"I guess he did, — and *if* he did you may be very sure you've got a good article."

"Well, you mustn't be too much discouraged," said M. de Bellegarde with vague benevolence.

"Oh, I don't mean to be. I've a project — really a grand one — which gives me plenty to think about, and that's an occupation." And then Newman waited, hesitating yet debating rapidly; he wished again to get near his point, though to do so forced him to depart still further from the form of not asking favours. He *had* to ask that of their attention. "Nevertheless," he continued, addressing himself to old Madame de Bellegarde, "I'll tell you my great idea; perhaps you can help me. I want not only to marry, but to marry remarkably well."

"It's a very good project, but I never made a match in all my life," said his hostess with her odd mincing plainness.

Newman looked at her an instant and then all sincerely, "I should have thought you a great hand," he declared.

Madame de Bellegarde might well have thought him too sincere. She murmured something sharply in French and fixed her eyes on her son. At this moment the door of the room was thrown open, and with a rapid step Valentin reappeared. "I've a message for you," he said to his sister-in-law. "Claire bids me ask you not to start for your ball. If you'll wait a minute she'll go with you."

"Claire will go with us?" cried the young Marquise. "*En voilà du nouveau!*"

"She has changed her mind; she decided half an hour ago and is sticking the last diamond into her hair!" said Valentin.

"What on earth has taken possession of my daughter?" Madame de Bellegarde asked with a coldness of amazement. "She has not been this age where any candle was lighted. Does she take such a step at half an hour's notice and without consulting me?"

"She consulted me, dear mother, five minutes since," said Valentin, "and I told her that such a beautiful woman — she's more beautiful than ever, you'll see — has no right to bury herself alive."

"You should have referred Claire to her mother

my brother," said M. de Bellegarde in French.
"This is not the way —!"

"I refer her to the whole company!" Valentin
broke in. "Here she comes!" — and he went to the
open door, met Madame de Cintré on the threshold,
took her by the hand and led her into the room.
She was dressed in white, but a cloak of dark blue,
which hung almost to her feet, was fastened across
her shoulders by a silver clasp. She had tossed it
back, however, and her long white arms were uncovered. In her dense fair hair there glittered a dozen
diamonds. She looked serious and, Newman thought,
rather pale; but she glanced round her and, when
she saw him, smiled and put out her hand. He
thought her at this moment far and away the handsomest woman he had ever seen. He had a chance
to look her full in the face, for she stood a little in
the centre of the room, where she seemed to consider what she should do, without meeting his eyes.
Then she went up to her mother, who sat in the deep
chair by the fire with an air of immeasurable detachment. Her back turned to the others, Madame de
Cintré held her cloak apart to show her dress.

"What do you think of me?"

"I think you seem to have lost your head. It was
but three days ago, when I asked you as a particular
favour to myself to go to the Duchesse de Lusig-
nan's, that you told me you were going nowhere and
that one must be consistent. Is this your consistency? Why should you distinguish Madame Robin-
eau? Who is it you wish to please to-night?"

"I wish to please myself, dear mother," said

Madame de Cintré. And she bent over and kissed the old lady.

"I don't like violent surprises, my sister," said Urbain de Bellegarde; "especially when one's on the point of entering a drawing-room."

Newman at this juncture felt inspired to speak. "Oh, if you're going anywhere with this lady you need n't be afraid of being noticed yourself!"

M. de Bellegarde turned to his sister with an intense little glare. "I hope you appreciate a compliment that's paid at your brother's expense. *Venez donc*, madame." And offering Madame de Cintré his arm he led her rapidly out of the room. Valentin rendered the same service to young Madame de Bellegarde, who had apparently been reflecting on the fact that the ball-dress of her sister-in-law was much less brilliant than her own, and yet had failed to derive absolute comfort from the reflexion. With a leave-taking smile she sought the complement of her consolation in the eyes of the American visitor, and, perceiving in them an almost unnatural glitter, not improbably may have flattered herself she had found it.

Newman, left alone with his hostess, if she might so be called, stood before her a few moments in silence. "Your daughter's very beautiful," he said at last.

"She's very perverse," the old woman returned.

"I'm glad to hear it," he smiled. "It makes me hope."

"Hope what?"

"That she'll consent some day to marry me."

She slowly got up. "That really is your 'great idea'?"

"Yes. Will you give it any countenance?"

Madame de Bellegarde looked at him hard and shook her head. Then her so peculiarly little mouth rounded itself to a "No!" which she seemed to blow at him as for a mortal chill.

"Will you then just let me alone with my chance?"

"You don't know what you ask. I'm a very proud and meddlesome old person."

"Well, I'm very rich," he returned with a world of desperate intention.

She fixed her eyes on the floor, and he thought it probable she was weighing the reasons in favour of resenting his so calculated directness. But at last looking up, "How rich?" she simply articulated.

He gave her, at this, the figure of his income — gave it in a round number which had the magnificent sound that large aggregations of dollars put on when translated into francs. He added to the enunciation of mere brute quantity certain financial particulars which completed a sufficiently striking presentment of his resources.

Madame de Bellegarde had let him enjoy her undisguised attention. "You're very frank," she finally said, "and I'll be the same. I would rather, on the whole, get all the good of you there is — rather, I mean, than, as you call it, let you alone. I would rather," she coldly smiled, "take you in our way than in your way. I think it will be easier."

"I'm thankful for any terms," Newman quite radiantly answered. "It's enough for me to feel

I'm taken. But it need n't be, for you," he at the same time rather grimly laughed, "in too big doses to begin with. Good-night!" — and he rapidly quitted her.

XI

HE had not, on his return to Paris, resumed the study of French conversation with M. Nioche; he had been conscious of too many other uses for his time. That amiable man, however, came to see him very promptly, having ascertained his whereabouts by some art of curiosity too subtle to be challenged. He repeated his visit more than once; he seemed oppressed by an humiliating sense of having been overpaid, and wished apparently to redeem his debt by the offer of grammatical and statistical information in small instalments. He exhaled the same decent melancholy as a few months before; a few months more or less of brushing could make little difference in the antique lustre of his coat and hat. But his spirit itself was a trifle more threadbare; it had clearly received some hard rubs during the summer. Newman asked with interest about Mademoiselle Noémie, and M. Nioche at first, for answer, simply looked at him in lachrymose silence.

"Don't press me on that subject, sir. I sit and watch her, but I can do nothing."

"Do you mean she gives you serious cause — ?"

"I don't know, sir, *what* I mean! I can't follow her. I don't understand her. She has something in her head; who can say what's in the head of a little person so independent, so dreadful — and so pleasing? She's too deep for her poor papa."

"Does she continue to go to the Musée? Has she made any of those copies for me?" Newman continued.

"She goes to the Musée, but I see nothing of the copies. She has something on her easel; I suppose it's one of the pictures you ordered. Such a splendid commission ought to give her fairy fingers. But she's not in earnest. I can't say anything to her; I'm afraid of her, if you must know. One evening last summer when I took her to walk in the Champs Elysées she said to me things that made me turn cold."

"And what things?"

"Excuse an unhappy father from telling you," said M. Nioche while he unfolded his calico pocket-handkerchief.

Newman promised himself to pay Mademoiselle Noémie another visit at the Louvre. He was curious of the progress of his copies, but it must be added that he was still more curious of the personal progress of the copyist. He went one afternoon to the great museum, but wandered through several of the rooms without finding her; after which, on his way to the long hall of the Italian masters, he stopped face to face with Valentin de Bellegarde. The young Frenchman eagerly greeted him, assuring him he was a godsend. He himself was in the worst of humours and wanted some one to contradict. "In a bad humour among all these beautiful things? I thought you were so fond of pictures, especially the grand old black ones," Newman said. "There are two or three here that ought to keep you in spirits."

"Oh, to-day," Valentin returned, "I'm not in a mood for gimcracks, and the more remarkable they are the less I like them. The great staring eyes and fixed positions of all these dolls and mannikins irritate me. I feel as if I were at some big dull party, a roomful of people I should n't wish to speak to. What should I care for their beauty? It's a bore and, worse still, it's a reproach. I've a *tas d'ennuis*. I feel damnably vicious."

"If this grand sight works you up so why do you expose yourself?" Newman asked with his quiet play of reason.

"That's one of my worries. I came to meet my cousin — a dreadful English cousin, a member of my mother's family — who's in Paris for a week with her husband and who wishes me to point out the 'principal beauties.' Imagine a woman who wears a green crape bonnet in December and has straps sticking out of the ankles of her interminable boots! My mother begged I would do something to oblige them. I've undertaken to play *valet de place* this afternoon. They were to have met me here at two o'clock, and I've been waiting for them twenty minutes. Why does n't she arrive? She has at least a pair of feet to carry her. I don't know whether to be furious at their playing me false or to toss up my hat for the joy of escaping them."

"I think in your place I'd be furious," said Newman, "because they may arrive yet, and then your fury will still be of use to you. Whereas if you were delighted and they were afterwards to turn up, you might n't know what to do — well, with your hat"

"You give me excellent advice, and I already feel better. I'll be furious; I'll let them go to the deuce and I myself will go with *you* — unless by chance you too have a rendezvous."

"It's not exactly a rendezvous," Newman returned. "But I've in fact come to see a person, not a picture."

"A woman, presumably?"

"A young lady."

"Well," said Valentin, "I hope for you, with all my heart, that she's not clothed in green tulle and that her feet are not too much out of focus."

"I don't know much about her feet, but she has very pretty hands."

The young man breathed all his sadness. "And on that assurance I must part with you?"

"I'm not certain of finding my young lady," said Newman, "and I'm not quite prepared to lose your company on the chance. It does n't strike me quite as good business to introduce you to her, and yet I should rather like to have your opinion of her."

"Is she formed to please?"

"Well, I guess you'll think so."

Valentin passed his arm into that of his companion. "Conduct me to her on the instant! I should be ashamed to make a pretty woman wait for my verdict"

Newman suffered himself to be gently propelled in the direction in which he had been walking, but his step was not rapid. He was turning something over in his mind. The two men passed into the long gallery of the Italian masters, and our friend, after having scanned for a moment its brilliant vista, turned aside into the smaller apartment devoted to the same school on the left. It contained very few persons, but at the further end of it Mademoiselle Nioche sat before her easel. She was not at work; her palette and brushes had been laid down beside her, her hands were folded in her lap and she had relapsed into her seat to look intently at two ladies on the other side of the hall, who, with their backs turned to her, had stopped before one of the pictures. These ladies were apparently persons of high fashion, they were dressed with great splendour and their long silken trains and furbelows were spread over the polished floor. It was on their dresses the young woman had fixed her eyes, though what she was thinking of I am unable to say. I hazard the hypothesis of her mutely remarking that to carry about such a mass of ponderable pleasure would surely be one of the highest uses of freedom. Her reflections, at any rate, were disturbed by the advent of her unannounced visitors, whom, as she rose and stood before her easel, she greeted with a precipitation of eye and lip that was like the glad clap of a pair of hands.

"I came here on purpose to see you — *seulement vous*, expray, expray," Newman said in his fairest, squarest, distinctest French. And then, like a good American, he introduced Valentin formally: "Allow me to make you acquainted with Comte Valentin de Bellegarde."

Valentin made a bow which must have seemed to her quite in harmony with the impressiveness of his title, but the graceful brevity of her response was a negation of underbred surprise. She turned to her generous patron, putting up her hands to her hair and smoothing its delicately-felt roughness. Then, rapidly, she turned the canvas that graced her easel over on its face. "You've not forgotten me?"

"I shall never forget you. You may be sure of that."

"Oh," she protested, "there are a great many different ways of remembering a person." And she looked straight at the Comte de Bellegarde, who was looking at her as a gentleman may when a verdict is expected of him.

"Have you painted me a pretty picture?" Newman went on. "Have you shown *beaucoup d'industrie?*"

"No, I've done nothing." And, taking up her palette, she began to mix her colours at random.

"But your father tells me your attendance has been regular."

"I've nowhere else to go! Where do you suppose, cher monsieur — ? Here, all summer, one could breathe at least."

"Being here then," said Newman, "don't you think you might have tried something?"

"I told you before," she sweetly answered, "that I haven't the advantage of knowing how to paint."

"But you've something of interest on your easel now," Valentin gaily objected, "if you'd only let me see it."

She spread out her two hands, with the fingers expanded, over the back of the canvas — those hands which Newman had called pretty and which, in spite of several little smudges of colour, Valentin could now admire. "My painting is n't of interest."

"It 's the only thing about you that is not, then, mademoiselle," the young man gallantly returned.

She took up her shamefaced study and silently passed it to him. He looked at it, and in a moment she said: "I 'm sure you 're a great judge."

"Yes," he admitted; "I recognise merit."

"Only when it 's there, I hope! I 've given up," she bravely declared, "trying to have it."

He faced her, with a smile, over her demoralised little daub. "If one has n't one sort one can always have another."

She considered with downcast eyes — which, how-ever, she presently raised. "We 're talking of the sort of which you 're a judge." Then, as to antici-pate too obvious a rejoinder, she turned, for more urgent good manners, to Newman. "Where have you been all these months? You took those great jour-neys, you amused yourself well?"

"Oh yes," our hero returned — "always beau-coup, beaucoup!"

"Ah, so much the better." She spoke with charm-ing unction and, having taken back her canvas from Valentin, who meanwhile had looked at his friend with eyes of rich meaning, began again to dabble in her colours. She was singularly pretty, with the look of serious sympathy she threw into her face. "Tell me," she continued, "a little of all you 've done."

"Oh, I went to Switzerland — to Geneva and Zermatt and Zürich and all those places, you know; and down to Venice, and all through Germany, and down the Rhine, and into Holland and Belgium — the regular round. How do you say that in French — the regular round?" Newman asked of Valentin.

Mademoiselle Nioche fixed her eyes an instant on their companion, and then with all the candour of her appeal: "I don't understand monsieur when he says so much at once. Would you be so good as to translate?"

"I'd rather talk to you out of my own head," Valentin boldly declared.

"No," said Newman gravely, still in his formal French, "you must n't talk to Mademoiselle Nioche, because you say discouraging things. You ought to tell her to work, to persevere."

"And we Parisians, mademoiselle," the young man exclaimed, "are accused of paying hollow compliments and of being false flatterers!"

"Ah, I don't want any compliments," the girl protested, "I want only the cruel truth. But if I did n't know it by this time —!"

"I utter no truth more cruel," Valentin returned, "than that there are probably many things you *can* do very well."

"Oh, I can at least do *this!*" And dipping a brush into a clot of red paint she drew a great horizontal daub across her unfinished picture.

"What are you making that mark for?" Newman asked with his impartial interest.

Without answering, she drew another long crimson daub, in a vertical direction, down the middle of her canvas and so in a moment completed the rough indication of a cross. "It's the sign of the cruel truth."

The two men looked at each other, Valentin as with vivid intelligence. "You've spoiled my picture," said his friend.

"I know that very well. It was the only thing to do with it. I had sat looking at it all day without touching it. I had begun to hate it. It seemed to me something was going to happen."

"I like it better that way than as it was before," said Valentin. "Now it's more interesting. It tells a little story now. Is it for sale, mademoiselle?"

"Everything I have is for sale," she promptly replied.

"How much then is this object?"

"Ten thousand francs — and very cheap!"

"Everything mademoiselle may do at present is mine in advance," Newman interposed. "It makes part of an order I gave her some months ago. So you can't have that!"

"Monsieur will lose nothing by it," said mademoiselle with her charming eyes on Valentin. And she began to put up her utensils.

"I shall have gained an ineffaceable memory," Valentin smiled. "You're going away? your day's over?"

"My father comes to fetch me," the young lady replied.

She had hardly spoken when, through the door behind her, which opens on one of the great white stone staircases of the Louvre, M. Nioche made his appearance. He came in with his usual patient shuffle, indulging in a low salute to the gentlemen who had done him the honour to gather about his daugh-

ter. Newman shook his hand with muscular friend-
liness and Valentin returned his greeting with high
consideration. While the old man stood waiting for
Noémie to make a parcel of her implements he let his
mild oblique gaze play over this new acquaintance,
who was watching her put on her bonnet and mantle
Valentin was at no pains to disguise the benevolence
of his own interest. He looked at a pretty person as
he would have listened to a good piece of music. Intelligent participation was in such a case simple good
manners. M. Nioche at last took his daughter's paint-
box in one hand and the bedaubed canvas, after giving it a solemn puzzled stare, in the other, and led the
way to the door. Noémie followed him after making
her late interlocutors the formal obeisance of the per-
fectly-educated female young.

"Well," said Newman, "what do you think of
her?"

"She's very remarkable. *Diable, diable, diable!*"
his friend reflectively repeated; "she's the perfection
of the type."

"I'm afraid she's a sad little trifler," Newman
conscientiously remarked.

"Not a little one — rather an immense one. She
has all the material." And Valentin began to walk
slowly off, looking vaguely, though with eyes now so
opened, at the pictures on the walls. Nothing could
have appealed to his imagination more than the possible futility of a young lady so equipped for futility.
"She's very interesting," he went on. "Yes, the type
shines out in her."

"'The type'? The type of what?"

"Well, of soaring, of almost sublime ambition! She's a very bad little copyist, but, endowed with the artistic sense in another line, I suspect her none the less of a strong feeling for her great originals."

Newman wondered, but presently followed. "Surely her great originals will have had more beauty."

"Not always. She has enough to look as if she had more, and that's always plenty. It's a face and figure in which everything tells. If she were prettier she would be less intelligent, and her intelligence is half her charm."

"In what way does her intelligence strike you as so remarkable?" asked Newman, at once puzzled impressed and vaguely scandalised by his friend's investment of such a subject with so much of the dignity of demonstration.

"She has taken the measure of life, and she has determined to *be* something — to succeed at any cost. Her smearing of colours is of course a mere trick to gain time. She's waiting for her chance; she wishes to launch herself, and to do it *right*. Nobody, my dear man, can ever have *had* such a love of the right. She knows her Paris. She's one of fifty thousand, so far as her impatiences and appetites go, but I'm sure she has an exceptional number of ideas."

Newman raised his strong eyebrows. "Are you also sure they're really good ones?"

"Ah, 'good, good'!" cried Valentin: "you people are too wonderful with your goodness. Good for what, please — ? They'll be excellent, I warrant, for some things! They'll be much better than the hopeless game she has just given up. They'll be good enough to make her, I dare say, one of the celebrities of the future."

"Lord o' mercy, you *have* sized her up! But don't — I must really ask it of you — let her quite run away with you," Newman went on. "I shall owe it to her good old father not to have upset her balance. For he's a real nice man."

"Oh, oh, oh, her good old father!" Valentin incorrigibly mocked. And then as his companion looked grave: "He expects her to assure his future."

"I thought he rather expected *me!* And don't you judge him, as a friend of mine," Newman asked, "too cruelly? He's as poor as a rat, but very high-toned."

"Why, mon cher, I should adore his tone, and you're right to do the same: it's much better than mine, and he'll do you more good as a companion, he'll protect your innocence better, than ever I shall. I don't mean," Valentin explained, "that he would n't much rather his daughter were a good girl, that she remained as 'nice' — as worthy, that is, say, of your particular use — as he may himself remain. But all the same he won't, if the worst comes to the worst — well, he won't do what Virginius did. He does n't want her to be a failure — as why should he? — and if she is n't a failure it's plain she'll be a success. On the whole he has confidence."

"He has touching fears, sir — I admit he has betrayed *them* to me." Newman felt himself loyally concerned to defend a character that had struck him as pleasingly complete — though completeness was, after all, what Valentin also claimed for it. The difference was in their view of that picturesque grace, and Newman would, to an appreciable degree, have sentimentally suffered from not being able to keep Monsieur Nioche before him as he had first seen him. He was, to an extent he never fully revealed, a collector of impressions as romantically concrete, even when profane, as the blest images and sanctified relics of one of the systematically devout, and he at bottom liked as little to hear anything he had picked up with the hand of the spirit pronounced unauthentic. "I don't quite remember what Virginius did," he presently pursued, "and I don't say for certain that my old friend would shoot. He does n't affect me — no — as a shooting man. But I guess he would n't want to *make* very much out of anything"

"Then he'll be very different," Valentin laughed, "from any of the rest of his species! Why, my dear fellow, we all here in Paris want to make as much as possible out of everything. That's how we differ, I conceive, from the people of *your* country: the objects of your exploitation appear to be fewer, and above all of fewer kinds. I don't mind telling you," he declared in the same tone, "that I don't see the end of what I might be capable of making out of *this*."

"Of 'this' — ?"

"Of the relation of Monsieur Nioche to his daughter, and of the relation of his daughter to — well, to as many other persons as you like!"

"I shan't at all like *you* to be one of them," Newman still gravely returned. "I did n't ask you to come round with me just to set you after her."

The young man appeared for an instant embarrassed. "Do you object then to her having engaged my enlightened curiosity?"

Newman considered. "Well, no — since, from the moment I recognise she'll never deliver my goods I don't quite see where I stand or how I can improve her."

"Oh, you certainly can't improve her!" Valentin gaily cried.

Newman looked at him a moment. "I should like then to improve *you*. I guess at any rate you had better leave her alone."

"Oh, oh, oh!" his companion exclaimed, at this, with an accent that made him pull up. "Do you mean, my dear fellow, that you warn me off?" They had stopped a minute before, and he stood there staring. "Hanged if I don't believe you suppose I'm afraid of you!"

Valentin had given a cock to his moustache, and he stroked it an instant, meeting this exclamation with a glance of some ambiguity and a smile just slightly strained. "Oh, I should n't put it that way: you don't even yet know me enough to fear me! Which gives you the advantage — for you've yourself attitudes that, I confess, make me tremble. I think you're afraid, at most," he continued, "of my bad example."

Newman had again — for he had had it before — a strange fine sense of something he would have called, in relation to this brilliant friend, the waste of anim-adversion. It was somehow one with the accepted economic need of keeping him pleasantly in view. Even to argue with him was somehow to misuse a

luxury, and to think of him as perverse was somehow to miss an occasion. No one had ever given him
that impression, which he might have compared to
the absolute pleasure, for the palate, of wine of the
highest savour. One did n't put anything "into"
such a vintage and there was a way of handling the
very bottle. The grace of him, of Valentin, was all
precious, the growth of him all fortunate, the quantity of him elsewhere all doubtless limited. "I *might*
perhaps have been a factor in that young lady's
moral future," Newman presently said — "but I don't
come in now. And evidently," he added "you've
no room for me in yours."

The young man gave a laugh, and the next moment, arm in arm, they had resumed their walk. "Oh,
on the contrary," Valentin then replied; "since what
I want, precisely, is to keep it spacious and capacious
— at least on the scale, if you please, of my moral
past; which indeed seems to me, when I look back
on it, as boundless as the desert. It's a prospect that,
at all events, such figures as you and your wonderful
friends help to people. And I may say about *them*,"
he went on, "that I should like really — in the interest of the impression that I confess the young lady
makes on me — to propose to you a fair agreement."

On which, amusedly enough, Newman debated as
they went. "That I shall shut my eyes to what you
want to do?"

"Well, yes — say I may expect you'll shut them
to me as soon as I shall find you've opened them to
the grand manner in which your old gentleman *is* a
man of the world. You'll be obliged, I'm convinced,

to recognise it, and I only ask you to let me know, in all honesty, when you've done so."

"So that *you*, in all honesty — ?"

"Well, call it in all delicacy!" Valentin suggested.

Newman continued to wonder. "May have a free hand — ?"

"Without your being shocked," the young man gracefully said.

But it only made our friend rather quaintly groan. "I think it's your delicacies, all round, that shock me most!"

"Ah, don't say," Valentin pleaded, "that I'm not at the worst a man of duty! See for yourself!" His English cousins had come into view, and he advanced gallantly to meet the lady in the green crape bonnet.

XII

Coming in toward evening, three days after his introduction to the family of Madame de Cintré, Newman found on his table the card of the Marquis de Bellegarde. On the following day he received a note informing him that this gentleman's mother requested the pleasure of his company at dinner. He went of course, though he had first to disengage himself from appeals that struck him as in comparison the babble of vain things. He was ushered into the room in which Madame de Bellegarde had received him before, and here he found his venerable hostess surrounded by her entire family. The room was lighted only by the crackling fire, which illumined the very small pink shoes of a lady who, from a low chair, stretched out her toes to it. This lady was the younger Madame de Bellegarde, always less effectively present, somehow, than perceptibly posted. Madame de Cintré, not posted at all, but oh so present, was seated at the other end of the room, holding a little girl against her knee, the child of her brother Urbain, to whom she was apparently relating a wonderful story. Valentin had perched on a puff close to his sister-in-law, into whose ear he was certainly distilling the finest nonsense. The Marquis was stationed before the chimney, his head erect and his hands behind him in an attitude of formal expectancy.

The old Marquise stood up to give Newman her greeting, and there was that in the way she did so which seemed to measure narrowly the quantity of importance such a demonstration might appear to attach to him. "We're all alone, you see; we've asked no one else," she said austerely.

"I'm very glad you did n't; this is much more sociable. I wish you good-evening, sir" — and Newman offered his hand to the Marquis.

M. de Bellegarde was affable, yet in spite of his dignity was restless. He changed his place, fidgeted about, looked out of the long windows, took up books and laid them down again. Young Madame de Bellegarde gave their guest her hand without moving and without looking at him.

"You may think that's coldness," Valentin freely explained; "but it's not, it's the last confidence, and you'll grow up to it. It shows she's treating you as an intimate. Now she detests me, and yet she's always looking at me."

"No wonder I detest you if I'm always looking at you!" cried the lady. "If Mr. Newman does n't like my way of shaking hands I'll do it for him again."

But this charming privilege was lost on our hero who was already making his way over to Madame de Cintré. She raised her eyes to him as she accepted from him the customary form, but she went on with the story she was telling her little niece. She had only two or three phrases to add, but they were apparently of great moment. She deepened her voice, smiling as she did so, and the little girl immensely gazed at her. "But in the end the young prince married the beautiful Florabella, and carried her off to live with him in the Land of the Pink Sky. There she was so happy that she forgot all her troubles and went out to drive every day of her life in an ivory coach drawn by five hundred white mice. Poor Florabella," she mentioned to Newman, "had suffered terribly."

"She had had nothing to eat for six months," said little Blanche.

"Yes, but when the six months were over she had a plum-cake as big as that ottoman," Madame de Cintré insisted. "That quite set her up again."

"What a strong constitution and what a chequered career!" said Newman. "Are you very fond of children?" He was certain she must be, but wished to make her say it.

"I like to talk with them; we can talk with them so much more seriously than with grown persons. That's great nonsense I've been telling Blanche, but it has much more value than most of what we say in society."

"I wish you would talk to me then as if I were Blanche's age," Newman laughed. "Were you happy at your ball the other night?"

"Extravagantly!"

"Now you're talking the nonsense that we talk in society," said Newman. "I don't believe that."

"It was my own fault if I wasn't happy. The ball was very pretty and every one very amiable."

"It was on your conscience," he presently risked, "that you had annoyed your mother and your brother."

She looked at him a moment in silence. "That's possible — I had undertaken more than I could carry out. I've very little courage; I'm not a heroine." She said this, he could feel, to be very true with him; and it touched him as if she had pressed into his hand, for reminder, some note she had scrawled or some ribbon or ring she had worn. Then changing her tone, "I could never have gone through the sufferings of the beautiful Florabella," she added, "not even for her prospective rewards."

Dinner was announced and he betook himself to the side of old Madame de Bellegarde. The dining-room, at the end of a cold corridor, was vast and sombre; the dinner was simple and delicately excellent. Newman wondered if the daughter of the house had had to do with ordering the repast, and, with a fine applied power of remote projection, hoped this might have been. Once seated at table, with the various members of so rigidly closed a circle round him, he asked himself the meaning of his position. Was the old lady responding to his advances? Did the fact that he was a solitary guest augment his credit or diminish it? Were they ashamed to show him to other people or did they wish to give him a sign of sudden adoption into their last reserve of favour? He was on his guard; he was watchful and conjectural, yet at the same time he was vaguely indifferent. Whether they gave him a long rope or a short he was there now, and Madame de Cintré was opposite him. She had a tall candlestick on each side of her; she would sit there for the next hour, and that was enough. The dinner was extremely solemn and measured; he won-

dered if this was always the state of things in old families. Madame de Bellegarde held her head very high
and fixed her eyes, which looked peculiarly sharp in
her little finely-wrinkled white face, very intently on
the table-service. The Marquis appeared to have
decided that the fine arts offered a safe subject of
conversation, as not leading to uncouth personal revelations. Every now and then, having learned from
Newman that he had been through the museums of
Europe, he uttered some polished aphorism on the
flesh-tints of Rubens or the good taste of Sansovino.
He struck his guest as precautionary, as apprehen-
sive; his manner seemed to indicate a fine nervous
dread that something disagreeable might happen if
the atmosphere were not kept clear of stray currents
from windows opened at hazard. "What under the
sun is he afraid of?" Newman asked himself. "Does
he think I'm going to offer to swap jack-knives with
him?" It was useless to shut his eyes to the fact that
the Marquis was as disagreeable to him as some
queer, rare, possibly dangerous biped, perturbingly
akin to humanity, in one of the cages of a "show."
He had never been a man of strong personal aver-
sions; his nerves had not been at the mercy of the
mystical qualities of his neighbours. But here was
a figure in respect to which he was irresistibly in opposition; a figure of forms and phrases and postures;
a figure of possible impertinences and treacheries.
M. de Bellegarde made him feel as if he were standing barefooted on a marble floor; and yet to gain his
desire, he felt perfectly able to stand. He asked himself what Madame de Cintré thought of his being

accepted — if it was acceptance that was thus conveyed to him. There was no judging from her face,
which expressed simply the desire to show kindness
in a manner requiring as little explicit recognition as
possible. Young Madame de Bellegarde had always
the same manner; preoccupied, distracted, listening
to everything and hearing nothing, looking at her
dress, her rings, her finger-nails and seeming inef-
fably bored, she yet defied you to pronounce on her
ideal of social diversion. Newman was enlightened
on this point later. Even Valentin failed quite to
seem master of his wits; his vivacity was fitful and
forced, but his friend felt his firm eyes shine through
the lapses of the talk very much as to the effect of
one's being pinched by him very hard in the dark.
Newman himself, for the first time in his life, was *not*
himself; he measured his motions and counted his
words; he had the sense of sitting in a boat that required inordinate trimming and that a wrong move
ment might cause to overturn.

After dinner M. de Bellegarde proposed the smoking-room and led the way to a small and somewhat
musty apartment, the walls of which were orna-
mented with old hangings of stamped leather and
trophies of rusty arms. Newman refused a cigar, but
established himself on one of the divans while the
Marquis puffed his own weed before the fireplace
and Valentin sat looking through the light fumes of
a cigarette from one to the other. "I can't keep quiet
any longer," this member of the family broke out at
last. "I must tell you the news and congratulate you.
My brother seems unable to come to the point; he

revolves round his announcement even as the priest round the altar. You're accepted as a candidate for the hand of our sister."

"Valentin, be a little proper!" murmured the Marquis, the bridge of whose high nose yielded to a fold of fine irritation.

"There has been a family council," his brother nevertheless continued; "my mother and he have put their heads together, and even my testimony has not been altogether excluded. My mother and Urbain sat at a table covered with green cloth; my sister-in-law and I were on a bench against the wall. It was like a committee at the Corps Législatif. We were called up one after the other to testify. We spoke of you very handsomely. Madame de Bellegarde said that if she had not been told who you were she'd have taken you for a duke — an American duke, the Duke of California. I said I could warrant you grateful for the smallest favours — modest, humble, unassuming. I was sure you'd know your own place always and never give us occasion to remind you of certain differences. You couldn't help it, after all, if you had not come in for a dukedom. There were none in your country; but if there had been it was certain that with your energy and ability you'd have got the pick of the honours. At this point I was ordered to sit down, but I think I made an impression in your favour."

M. de Bellegarde looked at his brother as Newman had seen those unfortunates looked at who have told, before waiting auditors, stories of no effect. Then he removed a spark of cigar-ashes from the

sleeve of his coat; he fixed his eyes for a while on
the cornice of the room, and at last he inserted one
of his white hands into the breast of his waistcoat.
"I must apologise to you for Valentin's inveterate
bad taste, as well as notify you that this is probably
not the last time that his want of tact will cause you
serious embarrassment."

"No, I confess, I've no tact," said Valentin. "Is
your embarrassment really serious, Newman? Urbain
will put you right again; he'll know just how you
feel."

"My brother, I'm sorry to say," the Marquis
pursued, "has never had the real sense of his duties
or his opportunities —of what one must after all call
his position. It has been a great pain to his mother,
who's very fond of the old traditions. But you must
remember that he speaks for no one but himself."

"Oh, I don't mind him, sir" — Newman was all
good-humour. "I know what the Valentines of this
world amount to."

"In the good old times," the young man said.
"marquises and counts used to have their appointed
buffoons and jesters to crack jokes for them. Nowadays we see a great strapping democrat keeping
one of 'us,' as Urbain would say, about him to play
the fool. It's a good situation, but I certainly am very
degenerate."

The Marquis fixed his eyes for some time on the
floor. "My mother has let me know," he presently
resumed, "of the announcement that you made her
the other evening."

"That I want so much to marry your sister?"

"That you desire to approach the Comtesse de Cintré with that idea, and ask of us therefore your facility for so doing. The proposal gave my mother — you can perhaps even yourself imagine — a great deal to think about. She naturally took me into her counsels, and the subject has had my most careful attention. There was a great deal to be considered; more than you perhaps appear to conceive. We have viewed the question on all its faces, we have weighed one thing against another. Our conclusion has been that we see no reason to oppose your pretension — though of course the matter, the question of your success, rests mainly with yourself. My mother has wished me to inform you then of our favourable attitude. She'll have the honour of saying a few words to you on the subject herself. Meanwhile you have our sanction, as heads of the family."

Newman got up and came nearer. "You personally will do all you can to back me up, eh?"

"I engage to you to throw my weight into the scale of your success."

Newman passed his hand over his face and pressed it for a moment upon his eyes. This promise had a great sound, and yet the pleasure he took in it was embittered by his having to stand there so and receive, as he might say, this prodigious person's damned permission. The idea of having the elder M. de Bellegarde mixed up with his wooing and wedding was more and more unpleasant to him. But he had resolved to go through the mill, as he had imaged it, and he would n't cry out at the first turn of the wheel. He was silent a while and then said with a certain dryness which Valentin told him afterwards had a very grand air: "I'm much obliged to you."

"I take note of the promise," said Valentin; "I register the vow."

M. de Bellegarde began to gaze at the cornice again; he apparently had more to say. "I must do my mother the justice, I must do myself the justice, to make the point that our decision was not easy. Such an arrangement was not what we had expected. The idea that my sister should marry a gentleman so intimately involved in — a — business, was something of a novelty."

"So I told you, you know!" Valentin recalled to Newman with a fine admonitory finger.

"The incongruity has not quite worn off, I confess," the Marquis went on; "perhaps it never will entirely. But possibly that's not altogether to be regretted"; and he went through that odd dim form of a smile that affected his guest as the scraping of a match that doesn't light. "It may be that the time has come when we should make some concession to the spirit of the day. There had been no such positive sacrifice in our house for a great many years. I made the remark to my mother, and she did me the honour to admit that it was worthy of attention."

"My dear brother," interrupted Valentin, "is not your memory just here leading you the least bit astray? Our mother is, I may say, distinguished by her small respect for abstract reasoning. Are you very sure she replied to your striking proposition in the gracious manner you describe? You know how,

when it suits her, she goes straight to the point —
au pas de charge! Did n't she rather do you the
honour to say: 'A fiddlestick for your fine phrases!
There are better reasons than that'?"

"Other reasons were discussed," said the Marquis
without looking at Valentin, but with a slightly more
nasal pitch; "some of them possibly were better.
We're highly conservative, Mr. Newman, but we
have never, I trust, been stupidly narrow. We're
judging this so interesting question on its merits only.
We've no doubt we shall be fully justified. We've
no doubt everything will be comfortable."

Newman had stood listening to these remarks
with his arms folded and his eyes fastened on the
speaker. "Justified?" he echoed with his way of
putting rather less than more sense into words he
repeated. "Why should n't we be? I assure you
I've no fear for myself. Why should n't we be comfortable? If you're not it will be your own fault.
I've everything to make *me* so."

"My brother means that with the lapse of time
you may get used to the difference." And Valentin
paused to light another cigarette.

"What difference?" Newman unimaginatively
asked.

"Urbain," said Valentin very gravely, "I'm afraid
that Mr. Newman does n't quite realise the difference
We ought to insist on that."

"My brother goes too far," M. de Bellegarde
observed to Newman. "He has no nice sense of
what should n't be said. It's my mother's wish and
mine that no comparisons should be made Pray

never make them yourself. We prefer to assume that the person accepted as the possible husband of my sister is one of ourselves, and that he should feel no explanations necessary. With a little tact on both sides everything ought to be easy. That's exactly what I wished to say — that we quite understand what we've undertaken and that you may depend on our not breaking down."

Valentin shook his hands in the air and then buried his face in them. "I don't quite steer clear myself, no doubt, but oh, my brother, if you knew what *you* are saying!" And he went off into a sound that combined a long laugh with a long wail.

M. de Bellegarde's face flushed a little, but he held his head higher, as if to repudiate this concession to vulgar perturbability. "I'm sure you quite know what I mean," he said to Newman.

"Oh no, not quite — or perhaps not at all," Newman answered. "But you need n't mind that. I don't care whether I know — or even, really, care, I think, what you say; for if I did there might be things I should n't like, should in fact, quite *dis*like, and that would n't suit me at all, you know. I want, very originally, no doubt, but very obstinately, to marry your sister and nobody other whomsoever — that's all; to do it as quickly as possible and to do as little else among you besides. I don't care therefore *how* I do it — as regards the rest of you! And that's all I have to say."

"You had better, nevertheless, receive the last word from my mother," said the Marquis, who had n't blanched.

"Very good; I'll go and get it." And Newman prepared to return to the drawing-room.

M. de Bellegarde made a motion for him to pass first, and on his doing so shut himself into the room with Valentin. Newman had been a trifle bewildered by the free play of his friend's wit and had not needed its aid to feel the limits of the elder brother's. That was what he had heard of as patronage — a great historic and traditionary force that he now personally encountered for the first time in his life. Did n't it consist in calling your attention to the impertinences it spared you? But he had recognised all the bravery of Valentin's backing that underlay Valentin's comedy, and he was unwilling so fine a comedian should pay a tax on it. He paused a moment in the corridor, after he had gone a few steps, expecting to hear the resonance of M. de Bellegarde's displeasure; but he detected only a perfect stillness. The stillness itself seemed a trifle portentous; he reflected, however, that he had no right to stand listening and made his way back to the salon. In his absence several persons had come in. They were scattered about the room in groups, two or three of them having passed into a small boudoir, next to the drawing-room, which had now been lighted and opened. Madame de Bellegarde was in her place by the fire, talking to an antique gentleman in a wig and a profuse white neckcloth of the fashion of 1820. Madame de Cintré had bent a listening head to the historic confidences of an old lady who was presumably the wife of this personage, an old lady in a red satin dress and an ermine cape, whose forehead was adorned with a topaz set in a velvet band. The young Marquise, when he came in, left some people among whom she was sitting and took the place she had occupied before dinner. Then she gave a little push to the puff that stood near her and seemed to indicate by a glance that she had placed it in position for him. He went and took possession of it; the young Marquise amused and puzzled him.

"I know your secret," she said in her bad but charming English; "you need make no mystery of it. You wish to marry my sister-in-law. *C'est un beau choix.* A man like you ought in effect to marry a very tall and very thin woman. You must know that I 've spoken in your favour, I'm really on your side and in your interest. You owe me a famous taper!"

"You 've spoken well of me to Madame de Cintré?" Newman asked

"Oh no, not that. You may think it strange, but my sister-in-law and I are not so intimate as that. Taking my courage in my hands, I put in my word for you to my husband and to my mother-in-law. I said I was sure we could do what we choose with you."

"I'm much obliged to you," laughed Newman, "but I guess you 'll find you can't."

"I know that very well; I did n't believe a word of it. But I wanted you to come into the house; I thought we should be friends."

"I'm very sure of it," said Newman.

"Don't be too sure. If you like the Comtesse so much perhaps you won't like me. We're as different -- well, as this fan and that poker. But you and

I have something in common. I've come into this
family by marriage; you want to come into it in the
same way.'

"Oh no, I don't want to come into it at all," he
interrupted — 'not a wee mite! I only want to take
Madame de Cintré out of it."

"Well, to cast your nets you have to go into the
water. Our positions are alike; we shall be able to
compare notes. What do you think of my husband?
It's a strange question, is n't it? But I shall ask you
some stranger ones yet."

"Perhaps a stranger one will be easier to answer,"
Newman said. "You might try me."

"Oh, you get off very well; the old Comte de la
Rochefidèle, yonder, could n't do it better. I told
them that if we only gave you a chance you'd be one
of our *plus fins causeurs*. I know something about
men. Besides, you and I belong to the same camp.
I'm a ferocious modern. I'm more modern than
you, you know — because I've been *through* this
and come out, very far out; which you have n't.
Oh, you don't know what this is. *Vous allez bien
voir.* By birth I'm *vielle roche;* a good little bit of
the history of France is the history of my family.
Oh, you never heard of us, of course! *Ce que c'est
que la gloire de race.* We're much better than the
Bellegardes at any rate. But I don't care a pin for
my pedigree — I only want to belong to my time.
So, being a reactionary — from the reaction — I'm
sure I go beyond you. That's what you look, you
know — that you're not reactionary enough. But
I like clever people, wherever they come from, and

I take my amusement wherever I find it. I don't pout at the Empire; here all the world pouts at the Empire. Of course I've to mind what I say, but I expect to take my revenge with *you*." The little lady discoursed for some time longer in this sympathetic strain, with an eager abundance indicating that her opportunities for revealing her esoteric philosophy were indeed rare. She hoped Newman would never be afraid of her, however he might be with the others, for really she went very far indeed. "Strong people" — *les gens forts* — were in her opinion equal all the world over. Newman listened to her with an attention at once beguiled and irritated. He wondered what the deuce she too was driving at, with her hope he would n't be afraid of her and her protestations of equality. In so far as he could understand her she was wrong — he did n't admit her equality; a silly rattling woman was never on a level with a sensible man, a man preoccupied with an ambitious passion. The young Marquise stopped suddenly and looked at him sharply, shaking her fan. "I see you don't believe me, you're too much on your guard. You won't form an alliance, offensive or defensive? You're very wrong; I could really help you."

Newman answered that he was very grateful and that he would certainly ask for help; she should see. "But first of all," he said, "I must help myself." And he went to join Madame de Cintré.

"I've been telling Madame de la Rochefidèle that you're an American," she said as he came up. "It interests her greatly. Her favourite uncle went over with the French troops to help you in your battles in the last century, and she has always, in consequence, wanted greatly to see one of your people. But she has never succeeded till to-night. You 're the first — to her knowledge — that she has ever looked at."

Madame de la Rochefidèle had an aged cadaverous face, with a falling of the lower jaw which prevented her bringing her lips together and reduced her conversation to a series of impressive but inarticulate gutturals. She raised an antique eye-glass, elaborately mounted in chased silver, and looked at Newman from head to foot. Then she said something to which he listened deferentially but which conveyed to him no idea whatever

"Madame de la Rochefidèle says she 's convinced she must have seen Americans without knowing it," Madame de Cintré explained. Newman thought it probable she had seen a great many things without knowing it· and the old lady, again addressing herself to utterance, declared -- as interpreted by Madame de Cintré — that she wished she *had* known it.

At this moment the old gentleman who had been talking to their hostess drew near, leading that lady on his arm. His wife pointed out Newman to him, apparently explaining his remarkable origin. M. de la Rochefidèle, whose old age was as rosy and round and polished as an imitation apple, spoke very neatly and cheerily; almost as prettily, Newman thought, as M. Nioche, and much more hopefully. When he had been enlightened he turned to Newman with an inimitable elderly grace. "Monsieur is by no means the first American I have seen. Almost the first person I *ever* saw — to notice him — was an American."

"Ah!" said Newman sympathetically.

"The great Dr. Franklin. Of course I was very very young. I believe I had but just come into the world. He was received very well *dans le nôtre*."

"Not better than Mr. Newman," said Madame de Bellegarde. "I beg he 'll offer me his arm into the other room. I could have offered no higher privilege to Dr. Franklin." Newman, complying with her request, perceived that her two sons had returned to the drawing-room. He scanned their faces an instant for traces of the scene that had followed his separation from them, but if the Marquis had been ruffled he stepped all the more like some high-crested though distinctly domestic fowl who had always the alternative of the perch. Valentin, on his side, was kissing ladies' hands as much as ever as if there were nothing else in the world but these and sundry other invitations to the moustachioed lip. Madame de Bellegarde gave a glance at her elder son, and by the time she had crossed the threshold of her boudoir he was at her side. The room was now empty and offered a sufficient privacy. She disengaged herself from Newman's arm and rested her hand on that of their companion; and in this position she stood a moment bridling, almost quivering, causing her ornaments, her earrings and brooches and buckles, somehow doubly to twinkle, and pursing, as from simple force of character, her portentous little mouth. I am afraid the picture was lost on Newman, but she was in fact at this moment a striking image of the dignity which — even in the case of a small time-shrunken old lady — may reside in the habit of unquestioned authority and the absoluteness of a social theory favourable to the person holding it. "My son has spoken to you as I desired, and you'll understand that you've nothing to fear from our opposition. The rest will lie with yourself."

"M. de Bellegarde told me several things I did n't understand," said Newman, "but I made out that you'll let me stand on my merits. I'm much obliged."

"I wish nevertheless to add a word that my son probably did n't feel at liberty to say," the Marquise pursued. "I must say it for my own peace of mind. We've stretched a point; we've gone very far to meet you."

"Oh, your son said it very well; did n't you, Marquis?" Newman asked.

"Not so well as my mother," the Marquis declared.

"Well," Newman returned, "I don't know what I can do but make a note of it and try to profit by it."

"It's proper I should tell you," Madame de Bellegarde went on as if to relieve an insistent inward need, "that I'm a very stiff old person and that I don't pretend not to be. I may be wrong to feel certain things as I do, but it's too late for me to change. At least I know it — as I know also why. Don't flatter yourself that my daughter also is n't proud. She's proud in her own way — a somewhat different way from mine. You'll have to make your terms with that. Even Valentin's proud, if you touch the right spot — or the wrong one. Urbain's proud — that you see for yourself. Sometimes I think he's a little too proud; but I would n't change him. He 's the best of my children; he cleaves to his old mother. I 've said, in any case, enough to show you that we are all very much aware of ourselves and very absurd and rather impossible together. It 's well you should know the sort of people you have come among."

"Well," said Newman, "I can only say that I hope I 'm as little like you then as may be. But though I don't think I 'm easy to scare, you speak as if you quite intended to be as disagreeable as you know how."

His hostess fixed him a moment. "I shall not enjoy it if my daughter decides to marry you, and I shall not pretend to enjoy it. If you don't mind that, so much the better."

"If you stick to your own side of the contract we shall not quarrel; that 's all I ask of you," Newman replied. "Keep your hands off — I shall mind my own business. I 'm very much in earnest and there 's not the slightest danger of my getting discouraged or backing out You 'll have me constantly before your eyes, so that if you don't like it I 'm sorry for you. I 'll do for your daughter, if she 'll accept me, everything that a man can do for a woman I 'm happy to tell you that, as a promise — a pledge. I consider that on your side you take an equally definite engagement. You 'll not back out, eh ?"

"I don't know what you mean by 'backing out,'" said the Marquise with no small majesty. "It suggests a movement of which I think no Bellegarde has ever been guilty."

"Our word's our word," Urbain pronounced. "We recognise that we've given it."

"Well then," said Newman, "I'm very glad of your pride and your pretensions. You'll have to keep your word to keep *them* up."

The Marquise was silent a little; after which, suddenly, "I shall always be polite to you, Mr. Newman," she declared, "but decidedly I shall never like you."

"Don't be too sure, madam!" her visitor laughed.

"I'm so sure that I shall ask you to take me back to my armchair without the least fear of having my sentiments modified by the service you render me." And Madame de Bellegarde took his arm and returned to the salon and to her customary place.

M. de la Rochefidèle and his wife were preparing to take their leave, and Madame de Cintré's interview with the mumbling old lady was at an end. She stood looking about her, asking herself apparently to whom she should next speak, when Newman approached. "Your mother has given me leave — very solemnly — to come here often. I intend to come often."

"I shall be glad to see you," she answered simply. And then in a moment: "You probably think it very strange that there should be such a solemnity — as you say — about your coming."

"Well yes; I do, rather."

"Do you remember what my brother Valentin said the first day you came to see me? — that we're a strange, strange family."

"It was n't the first day I came, but the second," Newman amended.

"Very true. Valentin annoyed me at the time, but now I know you better I may tell you he was right If you come often you 'll see!" And Madame de Cintré turned away.

He watched her a while as she talked with other people and then took his leave. It was practically indeed to Valentin alone that he so addressed himself, and his friend followed him to the top of the staircase. "Well, you 've taken out your passport," said that young man. "I hope you liked the process and that you admire our red tape."

"I like your sister better than ever. But don't worry your poor brother any more for my sweet sake," Newman added. "There must be something the matter with him."

"There 's a good deal!"

"Well, I don't seem to mind him — I don't seem to mind anything!" Newman just a bit musingly acknowledged. "I was only afraid he came down on you in the smoking-room after I went out."

"When my brother comes down on me," said Valentin, "he drops hard. I 've a particular way of receiving him. I must say," he continued, "that they 've fallen into line — for it has been a muster of all our forefathers too! — sooner than I expected. I don't understand it; they must really have put forward their clock! It 's a tribute to your solidity."

"Well, if my solidity 's all they want —!" Newman again rather pensively breathed.

"You can cut them a daily slice of it and let them

have it with their morning coffee?" But he was turning away when Valentin more effectually stopped him. "I should like to know whether, within a few days, you've seen your venerable friend M. Nioche."

"He was yesterday at my rooms."

"What had he to tell you?"

"Nothing particular."

"You did n't see the weapon of Virginius sticking out of his pocket?"

"What are you driving at?" Newman demanded. "I thought he seemed rather cheerful, for him."

Valentin broke into a laugh. "I'm delighted to hear of his high spirits — they make me so beautifully right and so innocently happy. For what they mean, you see, must be that his charming child is favourably placed, at last, for the real exercise of her talents, and that the pair are relieved, almost equally, from the awkwardness of a false position. And M. Nioche is rather cheerful — *for him!* Don't brandish your tomahawk at that rate," the young man went on; "I've not seen her nor communicated with her since that day at the Louvre. Andromeda has found another Perseus than I. My information's exact; on such matters it always is. I suppose," he wound up, "that I may now cease so elaborately to neglect her?"

Newman, struggling up out of intenser inward visions, listened as he could, and then, having listened, remained with his eyes on his friend's face. "It would do you good to fall in love. You want it badly," he at last remarked.

"Well, that's perhaps exactly what, according to

my perpetual happy instinct, I'm now trying to do!"

"Oh hell!" said our hero impatiently as he broke away again.

XIII

HE kept his promise, or his menace, of presenting himself often in the Rue de l'Université, and during the next six weeks saw Madame de Cintré more times than he could have numbered. He flattered himself *he* had not fallen, and had n't needed to fall, after the fashion enjoined by him on Valentin, in love, but his biographer may be supposed to know better what, as he would have said, was the matter with him. He claimed certainly none of the exemptions and emoluments of the merely infatuated state. That state, he considered, was too consistent with asininity, and he had never had a firmer control of his reason or a higher opinion of his judgement. What he was conscious of, none the less, was an intense all-consuming tenderness, which had for its object an extraordinarily graceful and harmonious, yet at the same time insidiously agitating woman who lived in a grand grey house on the left bank of the Seine. His theory of his relation to her was that he had become conscious of how beautifully she might, for the question of his future, come to his aid; but this left unexplained the fact that his confidence had somehow turned to a strange, muffled heartache. He was in truth infinitely anxious, and, when he questioned his anxiety, knew it was not all for himself. If she might come to his aid he might come to hers; and he had the imagination — more than he had ever had in his life about anything — of fantastic straits or splendid miseries in the midst of which, standing before her with wide arms out, he would have seen her let herself, even if still just desperately and blindly, make for his close embrace as for a refuge.

He really would n't have minded if some harsh need for mere money had most driven her; the creak of that hinge would have been sweet to him had it meant the giving way of the door of separation. What he wanted was to *take* her, and that her feeling herself taken should come back to him for their common relief. The full surrender, so long as she did n't make it, left the full assurance an unrest and a yearning — from which all his own refuge was in the fine ingenuity, the almost grim extravagance, of the prospective provision he was allowing to accumulate. She gave him the sense of "suiting" him so, exactly as she was, that his desire to interpose for her and close about her had something of the quality of that solicitude with which a fond mother might watch from the window even the restricted garden-play of a child recovering from an accident. But he was above all simply charmed, and the more for feeling wonderstruck, as the days went on, at the proved rightness both of the instinct and of the calculation that had originally moved him. It was as if there took place for him, each day, such a revelation of the possible number of forms of the "personal" appeal as he could otherwise never have enjoyed, and as made him yet ask himself how, *how*, all unaided (save as Mrs. Tristram, subtle woman, had aided him!) he could have known. For he *had*, amazingly, known.

And the impression must now thereby have been for him, he thought, very much that of the wistful critic or artist who studies "style" in some exquisite work or some quiet genius, and who sees it come and come and come, and still never fail, like the truth of a perfect voice or the safety of a perfect temper. Just as such a student might say to himself, "How could I have got on without this particular research?" so Christopher Newman could only say, "Fancy this being to be had and — with my general need — my not having it!"

He made no violent love and, as he would have said, no obvious statements; he just attended regularly, as he would also have said, in the manner of the "interested party" present at some great liquidation where he must keep his eye on what concerns him. He never trespassed on ground she had made him regard, ruefully enough, as forbidden; but he had none the less a sustaining sense that she knew better from day to day all the good he thought of her. Though in general no great talker, and almost incapable, on any occasion, of pitching his voice for the gallery, he now had his advances as well as his retreats, and felt that he often succeeded in bringing her, as he might again have called it, into the open. He determined early not to care if he should bore her, whether by speech or by silence — since he certainly meant she should so suffer, at need, before he had done; and he seemed at least to know that even if she actually suffered she liked him better, on the whole, with too few fears than with too many. Her visitors, coming in often while he sat there, found a tall, lean, slightly flushed and considerably silent man, with a lounging, permanent-looking seat, who laughed out sometimes when no one had meant to be droll, and yet remained grave in presence of those calculated witticisms and those initiated gaieties for the appreciation of which he apparently lacked the proper culture and the right acquaintances. It had to be confessed that the number of the subjects upon which he was without ideas was only equalled by the number of the families to which he was not allied; and it might have been added more gravely still that as regards those subjects upon which he was without ideas he was also quite without professions. He had little of the small change of conversation and rarely rose to reach down one of those ready-made forms and phrases that drape, whether fresh or frayed, the hooks and pegs of the general wardrobe of talk — that repository in which alone so many persons qualify for the discipline of society, as supernumerary actors prepare, amid a like provision, for the ordeal of the footlights. He was able on the other hand, at need, to make from where he sat one of the long arms that stretch quite out of the place — to the effect, as might mostly be felt, of coming back with some proposition as odd as a single shoe.

Bent, at any rate, on possession, he had at his command treasures of attention and never measured the possibilities of interest in a topic by his own power of contribution to it: he liked topics to grow at least big enough for him to walk round them and see. This made, for his advantage, to his being little acquainted with satiety either of sound or of sense; he

was not himself more often bored than he was often
alarmed, and there was no man with whom it would
have been a greater mistake than to take his inter-
missions always for absences or his absences always
for holidays. What it was that entertained or that
occupied him during some of his speechless sessions
I shall not, however, undertake fully to say. The
Marquise Urbain had once found occasion to declare
to him that he reminded her, in company, of a swim-
ming-master she had once had who would never
himself go into the water and who yet, at the baths,
en costume de ville, managed to control and direct the
floundering scene without so much as getting splashed.
He had so made her angry, she professed, when he
turned her awkwardness to ridicule. Newman affected her in like manner as keeping much too dry:
it was urgent for her that *he* should be splashed —
otherwise what was he doing at the baths ? — and
she even hoped to get him into the water. We know
in a general way that many things which were old
stories to those about him had for him the sharp high
note, but we should probably find a complete list of
his new impressions surprising enough. He told Madame de Cintré stories, sometimes not brief, from
his own repertory; he was full of reference to his own
great country, over the greatness of which it seldom
occurred to him that every one might n't, on occasion
offered, more or less insatiably yearn; and he explained to her, in so discoursing, the play of a hundred of its institutions and the ingenuity of almost
all its arrangements. Judging by the sequel, judging
even by the manner in which she suffered his good

faith to lay an apparent spell upon her attitude she was mildly — oh mildly and inscrutably! — beguiled; but one would n't have been sure beforehand of the shade of her submission. As regards any communication she herself meanwhile made him he could n't nevertheless but guess that on the whole she "wanted" to make it. This was in so far an amendment to the portrait Mrs. Tristram had drawn of her.

He had been right at first in feeling her a little — or more than a little — proudly shy; her shyness, in a woman whose circumstances and tranquil beauty afforded every facility for sublime self-possession, was only a charm the more. For Newman it had lasted some time and had, even when it went, left something behind it that for a while performed the same office. Was this the uneasy secret of which Mrs. Tristram had had a glimpse, and of which, as of her friend's reserve, her high breeding and her profundity, she had given a sketch marked by outlines perhaps rather too emphatic? He supposed so, yet to find himself, as a result, wondering rather less what Madame de Cintré's secrets might consist of, and convinced rather more that secrets would be in themselves hateful and inconvenient things, things as depressing and detestable as inferior securities, for such a woman to have to lug, as he inwardly put it, round with her. She was a creature for the sun and the air, for no sort of hereditary shade or equivocal gloom; and her natural line was neither imposed reserve nor mysterious melancholy, but positive life, the life of the great world — *his* great world, not the *grand monde* as there understood if he was n't mistaken, which seemed squeezeable into a couple of rooms of that inconvenient and ill-warmed house: all with nothing worse to brood about, when necessary, than the mystery perhaps of the happiness that would so queerly have come to her. To some perception of his view and his judgement, and of the patience with which he was prepared to insist on them, he fondly believed himself to be day by day bringing her round. She might n't, she could n't yet, no doubt, wholly fall in with them, but she saw, he made out, that he had built a bridge which would bear the very greatest weight she should throw on it, and it was for him often, all charmingly, as if she were admiring from this side and that the bold span of arch and the high line of the parapet — as if indeed on occasion she stood straight there at the spring, just watching him at *his* extremity and with nothing, when the hour should strike, to prevent her crossing with a rush.

He often spent an evening's end, when she had so appointed — her motives and her method and her logic being meanwhile something of her own, though something thus beautifully *between them*, even if never named, and which he would n't for the world have asked her to name — he often passed a stiff succession of minutes at the somewhat chill fireside of Madame de Bellegarde; contenting himself there for the most part with looking across the room, through narrowed eyelids, at his mistress, who always made a point, before her family, of talking to some one else. Her mother, on that scene, would sit by the fire conversing neatly and coldly with whomsoever approached her and yet detaching for his own especial benefit a glance that seemed to say: "See how completely I'm interested, how agreeably I'm occupied, how deeply I'm absorbed." He often wondered what those supposedly honoured by this intensity of participation thought of her at such moments, and he sometimes answered her look by looking at *them;* but no one, for all the fine community of taste, that air in the place as of bitter convictions dissolved in iced indifference and partaken of for refreshment with small rare old "family" spoons, appeared to meet him on any such particular question any more intimately than on any other — and all by direct default of ability; which would have made him again ask himself, but for his constant anxious ache, what he was doing in so deadly a hole at all. To ache very hard at one point, he found, was practically to be unconscious of punctures at any other. When he at all events made his bow to the old lady by the fire he always asked her with a laugh whether she could "stand him" another evening, and she replied without a laugh, that, thank God, she had always been able to do her duty. Talking of her once to Mrs. Tristram he had remarked that, after all, it was very easy to get on with her; it always was easy to get on with out-and-out rascals.

"And is it by that elegant term that you designate the Marquise?"

"Well, she's a bad, bold woman. She's a wicked old sinner."

"What then has been her sin?"

He thought a little. "I should n't wonder if she

had done some one to death — all of course from a high sense of duty."

"How can you be so dreadful?" Mrs. Tristram had luxuriously sighed.

"I'm not dreadful. I am speaking of her favourably."

"Pray what will you say then when you want to be severe?"

"I shall keep my severity for some one else — say for that prize donkey of a Marquis. There's a man I can't swallow, mix the drink as I will."

"And what has *he* done?"

"I can't quite make out, but it's something very nice of its kind — I mean of a kind elegantly sneaking and fastidiously base; not redeemed as in his mother's case by a fine little rage of passion at some part of the business. If he has never committed murder he has at least turned his back and looked the other way while some one else was committing it."

In spite of this free fancy, which indeed struck his friend as, for a specimen of American humour, exceptionally sardonic, Newman did his best to maintain an easy and friendly style of communication with M. de Bellegarde. So long as he was in personal contact with people he disliked extremely to have anything to forgive them, and was capable of a good deal of unsuspected imaginative effort (for the working of the relation) to assume them to be of a human substance and a social elasticity not alien to his own. He did his best to treat the Marquis as practically akin to him; he believed honestly, moreover, that he couldn't in reason be such a confounded fool as he seemed. Newman's assumptions, none the less, were never importunate; his habit of sinking differences and supposing equalities was not an aggressive taste nor an æsthetic theory, but something as natural and organic as a physical appetite which had never been put on a scant allowance and had consequently never turned rabid. His air as of not having to account for his own place in the social scale was probably irritating to Urbain, for whom it could but represent a failure to conceive of other places either, and who thus saw himself reflected in the mind of his potential brother-in-law in a crude and colourless form, unpleasantly dissimilar to the impressive image thrown upon his own intellectual mirror. He never forgot himself an instant, and replied with mechanical politeness to the large bright vaguenesses that he was apparently justified in regarding as this visitor's wanton advances. Newman, who was constantly forgetting himself and indulging in an unlimited amount of irresponsible enquiry and conjecture, now and then found himself confronted by these obscure abysses of criticism. What in the world M. de Belle-garde was falling back either from or on he was at a loss to divine. M. de Bellegarde's general orderly retreat may meanwhile be supposed to have been, for himself, a compromise between a great many emotions. So long as he ambiguously smiled — and what could make more for order? — he was polite, and it was proper he should be polite. A smile more-over committed him to nothing more than politeness; it left the degree of politeness agreeably vague. Civil ambiguity too — and it was perfectly civil —

was neither dissent, which was too serious, nor agreement, which might have brought on terrible complications. And then it covered his own personal dignity, which at such a crisis he was resolved to keep immaculate: it was quite enough that the glory of his house should pass into eclipse. Between him and Newman, his whole manner seemed to declare, there could be no interchange of opinion; he could but hold his breath so as not to inhale the strong smell — since who liked such *very* strong smells ? — of a democracy so gregarious as to be unable *not* to engender heat and perspiration.

Newman was far from being versed in "European" issues, as he liked to call them; but he was now on the very basis of aspiring to light, and it had more than once occurred to him that he might here both arrive at it and give this acquaintance the pleasure of his treating him as an oracle. Interrogated, however, as to what he thought of public affairs, M. de Belle-garde answered on each occasion, and quite indeed as if thanking him for the opportunity, that he thought as ill of them as possible, that they were going from bad to worse, though there was always at least the comfort of their being too dreadful to touch. This gave our friend, momentarily, almost an indulgence for a spirit so depressed; he pitied the man who had to look at him in such a fashion when he ventured to insist, particularly about their great shining France, "Why, don't you see anything anywhere ?" — and he was brought by it to an attempt, possibly indiscreet, to call attention to some of the great features of the world's progress. This had presently led the Marquis to observe, once for all, that he entertained but a single political conviction — dearer to him, however, than all the others, put together, that other people might entertain: he believed, namely, in the divine right of Henry of Bourbon, Fifth of his name, to the throne of France. This had in truth, upon Newman, as many successive distinct effects as the speaker could conceivably have desired. It made him in the first place look at the latter very hard, harder than he had ever done before; which had the appearance somehow of affording M. de Bellegarde another of the occasions he personally appreciated. It was as if he had never yet shown how he could return such a look; whereby, producing that weapon of his armoury, he made the demonstration brilliant. Then he reduced his guest, further, just to staring with a conscious, foolish failure of every resource, at one of the old portraits on the wall, out of which some dim light for him might in fact have presently glimmered. Lastly it determined on Newman's part a wise silence as to matters he did n't understand. He relapsed, to his own sense, into silence very much as he would have laid down, on consulting it by mistake, some flat-looking back-number or some superseded time-table. It might do for the "collection" craze but would n't do for use.

One afternoon, on his presenting himself, he was requested by the servant to be so good as to wait, a very few minutes, till Madame la Comtesse should be at liberty. He moved about the room a little, taking up a book here and there as with a vibration of tact in his long and strong fingers; he hovered, with a bent head, before flowers that he recognised as of a "lot" he himself must have sent; he raised his eyes to old framed prints and grouped miniatures and disposed photographs, ten times as many of which she should some day possess; and at last he heard the opening of a door to which his back was turned. On the threshold stood an old woman whom he remembered to have met more than once in entering and leaving the house. She was tall and straight and dressed in black, and she wore a cap which, if Newman had been initiated into such mysteries, would have sufficiently assured him she was not a Frenchwoman; a cap of pure British composition. She had a pale, decent, depressed-looking face and a clear, dull English eye. She looked at Newman a moment, both intently and timidly, and then she dropped a short, straight English curtsey. "The Countess begs you'll kindly wait, sir. She has just come in; she'll soon have finished dressing."

"Oh, I'll wait as long as she wants," said Newman. "Pray tell her not to hurry."

"Thank you, sir," said the woman softly, and then instead of retiring with the message advanced into the room. She looked about her a moment and presently went to a table and began to dispose again several small articles. Newman was struck with the high respectability of her appearance; he was afraid to address her as a servant. She busied herself with ordering various trifles, with patting out cushions and pulling curtains straight, while our hero rather attentively hovered. He perceived at last, from her reflexion in the mirror as he was passing, that her hands were idle and her eyes fixed on him. She evidently wished to say something, and, now aware of it, he helped her to begin.

"I guess you're English, ain't you?"

"Oh dear, yes," she answered, quickly and softly. "I was born in Wiltshire, sir."

"And what do you think of Paris?"

"Oh, I don't think of Paris, sir," she said in the same tone. "It's so long that I've been here."

"Ah, you have been here very long?"

"More than forty years, sir. I came over with Lady Emmeline."

"You mean with old Madame de Bellegarde?"

"Yes, sir. I came with her when she married. I was my lady's own woman."

"And you've been with her ever since?"

"I've been in the house ever since. My lady has taken a younger person. You see I'm very old. I do nothing regular now. But I keep about."

"You keep about remarkably well," said Newman, observing the erectness of her figure and a certain venerable pink in her cheek. "I like," he genially added, "to *see* you about."

"Very good of you, sir. Thank God I'm not ill. I hope I know my duty too well to go panting and coughing over the house. But I'm an old woman, sir, and it's as an old woman that I venture to speak to you."

"Oh, speak, if you like, as you never spoke!" said Newman curiously. "You need n't be afraid of me."

"Yes, sir, I think you're kind. I've seen you before."

"On the stairs, you mean?"

"Yes, sir. When you've been coming to see the Countess. I've taken the liberty of noticing that you come often."

"Oh yes; I come very often," he laughed. "You need n't have been very much emancipated to notice that."

"I've noticed it with pleasure, sir," said this interesting member of the family. And she stood looking at him with a strange expression of face. The old instinct of deference and humility was there; the habit of decent self-effacement and the knowledge of her appointed orbit. But there mingled with it an impulse born of the occasion and of a sense, probably, of this free stranger's unprecedented affability; and, beyond this, a vague indifference to the old proprieties, as if my lady's own woman had at last begun to reflect that, since my lady had taken another person, she had a slight reversionary property in herself.

"You take a great interest in our friends?" he asked.

She looked at him as if she admired that expression and had never heard anything quite like it. "A deep interest, sir. Especially in the Countess."

"I'm glad of that," said Newman. And he smilingly followed it up. "You can't take more than I do!"

"So I supposed, sir. We can't help noticing these things and having our ideas; can we, sir?"

"You mean as an old employee?"

"Ah, there it is, sir. I'm afraid that when I let my thoughts meddle with such matters I rather step

out of my place. But I'm so devoted to the Countess
if she were my own child I could n't love her more.
That's how I come to be so bold, sir." Her boldness
failed her a moment, but she brought it round with
a turn. "They say in the house, sir, that you want
to marry her."

Newman eyed his interlocutress, and, as if something had suddenly begun to depend on it, made up
his mind about her. Something at least passed between them with his exchange of distinct truths, and
at the end of a minute he felt almost like a lost child
kindly taken by the hand. He gave the hand a re-
sponsive grasp. He looked quite up into the deep mild
face. "I want to marry Madame de Cintré more
than I ever wanted anything in my life."

"And to take her away to America?"

"I'll take her wherever she wants to go."

"The further away the better, sir!" exclaimed the
old woman with sudden intensity. But she checked
herself and, taking up a paper-weight in mosaic,
began to polish it with her black apron. "I don't
mean anything about the house or the family, sir.
But I think a great change would do the poor Countess
good. There's no very grand life here."

"Oh, grand life —!" he quite sarcastically sighed.
"But Madame de Cintré," he added, "has great
courage in her heart."

"She has everything in her heart that's good.
You'll not be vexed to hear that she has been more
her natural self these two months past than she had
been for many a day before."

Newman was delighted to gather this testimony

to the progress of his suit, but he kept his expression within bounds. "Had she been *very* long as you did n't want to see her?"

"Well, sir, she had good reason not to be gay. The Count was no natural husband for a young lady like that. And it is n't as if, in this house, there were other great pleasures — to make up, I mean, for anything so sad. It's better, in my humble opinion, that she should leave it altogether. So if you'll pardon my saying such a thing, I hope very much she'll see her blessed way —!"

"You can't hope it as much as I do!" Newman returned.

"But you must n't lose courage, sir, if she does n't make up her mind at once. That's what I wanted to beg of you," his friend proceeded. "Don't give it up, sir. You'll not take it ill if I say it's a great risk for any lady at any time; all the more when she has got rid of one bad bargain. But if she can take advantage of a good, kind, respectable gentleman I think she had better make up her mind. They speak very well of you, sir, in the house — I mean in my part of it; and, if you'll allow me to say so, there's everything in your appearance — ! You've a very different one to the late Count; he was n't, really sir, much more than five feet high. And they say your fortune's beyond everything. There's no harm in that. So I entreat you to be patient, sir, and to bide your time. If I don't say it to you perhaps no one will. Of course it's not for me to make any promises. I can answer for nothing. But I believe in your chance because I believe in your spirit I'm nothing but a weary old woman in my quiet corner, but one of us poor things here may understand another, and I don't think I could ever mistake the Countess. I received her in my arms when she came into the world, and her first wedding-day was the saddest of my life. She owes it to me to show me another and a brighter. If you'll but hold on fast, sir — and you look as if you would — I think we may see it."

Newman had listened to this slow, plain, deliberate speech, the first evidently of much waiting and wishing, with as hushed and grateful a pleasure as he had ever had for some grand passage at the opera. "Why, my dear madam, I just love you for your encouragement. One can't have too much, and I mean to hold on fast — you may bet your life on that. And if Madame de Cintré does see her way you must just come and live with her."

The old woman looked at him with grave lifeless eyes. "It may seem a heartless thing to say, sir, when one has been forty years in a house, but I promise you I should like to leave this place."

"Why, it's just the *time* to promise," said Newman with ingenuity. "After forty years one wants a big change. That's what *I'm* going in for," he smiled.

"You're very kind indeed, sir," — and this faithful servant dropped another curtsey and seemed disposed to retire. She moved slowly, however, and gave while she lingered a dim joyless smile. Newman was disappointed, and his fingers stole so impatiently to his waistcoat-pocket that his informant noticed the gesture. "Ah, thank God I'm not a mercenary French person! If I were I would tell you with a brazen simper, old as I am, that if you please, monsieur, my information is worth something. Yet let me tell you so after all in my own decent English way. It *is* worth something."

"How much, please?"

"Simply this, sir: your solemn promise not to hint by a single word to the Countess that I've gone so far."

"Oh, I promise all right," said Newman. "And when I promise —!"

"I do believe you keep, sir! That's all, sir. Thank you, sir. Good-day, sir." And having once more slid down telescope-wise into her scant petticoats, his visitor departed. At the same moment Madame de Cintré came in by an opposite door. She noticed the movement of the other *portière* and asked Newman who had been entertaining him.

"The British female — in her most venerable form. An old lady in a black dress and a cap, who bobs up and down and expresses herself ever so well."

"An old lady who bobs and expresses herself? Ah, you mean poor Mrs. Bread. I happen to know you've made a conquest of her."

"Mrs. Cake, she ought to be called," Newman declared. "She's very sweet. She's a delicious old woman."

His friend looked at him a moment. "What can she have said to you? She's an excellent creature, but we think her rather dismal."

"I suppose," he presently answered, "that I like her so much because she has lived near you so long. Since your birth, she told me."

"Yes — such an age as that makes! She's very faithful," Madame de Cintré went on simply. "I can absolutely trust her."

Newman, however that might be, had never made a reflexion to this lady on her mother and her brother Urbain — he had given no hint of the impression they made on him. But, as if she could perfectly guess his feeling and subtly spare his nerves, she had markedly avoided any occasion for making him speak of them. She never alluded to her mother's domestic decrees; she never quoted the opinions of the Marquis. They had talked, it was true, of Valentin, and she had made no secret of her extreme affection for her younger brother. Newman listened sometimes with a vague, irrepressible pang; if he could only have caught in his own cup a few drops of that overflow! She once spoke to him with candid elation of something Valentin had done which she thought very much to his honour. It was a service he had rendered to an old friend of the family — something more "serious" and useful than he was usually supposed capable of achieving. Newman said he was glad to hear of it, and then began to talk of a matter more personal to himself. His companion listened, but after a while she said: "I don't like the way you speak of poor Valentin." At which, rather surprised, he protested he had never spoken of him save in kindness.

"Well, it's just the sort of kindness," she smiled,

"the kindness that costs nothing, the kindness you show to a child. It's as if you rather looked down on him. It's as if you did n't respect him."

"Respect him? Why, respect's a big feeling. But I guess I do."

"You guess? If you're not sure, it's no respect."

"Do *you* respect him?" Newman asked. "If you do then I do."

"If one loves a person, that's a question one's not bound to answer," said Madame de Cintré.

"You should n't have asked it of me then. I'm very fond of your brother."

"He amuses you. But you would n't like to resemble him."

"I should n't like to resemble any one. It's hard enough work resembling one's self."

"What do you mean," she demanded, "by resembling one's self?"

"Why, doing what's expected of one. Doing one's duty."

"But that's hard — or at any rate it's urgent — only when one's very good."

"Well, a great many people are good enough — so long as they insist on being so!" he optimistically laughed. "Valentine, at all events, is good enough for *me*."

She was silent a little, and then, with inconsequence, "Ah, I could wish him rather better!" she declared. "I could wish he would do something."

Her companion considered: after which, candidly: "What in the world can Valentine 'do'?"

"Well, he's very clever."

"But I guess it's a proof of power," Newman reasoned, "to be so happy without doing anything."

"Ah, but I don't think Valentin's really so happy. He's intelligent, generous, brave — but what is there to show for it? To me there's something sad in his life, and sometimes I have a sort of foreboding about him. I don't know why, but it seems to come to me that he may have some great trouble — perhaps a really unhappy end."

"Oh, leave him to me," Newman cheerfully returned. "I guess I can keep him all right."

One evening, however, in spite of such passages as these, the conversation in Madame de Bellegarde's own apartment had flagged most sensibly. The Marquis walked up and down in silence, like a sentinel at the door of some menaced citadel of the proprieties; his mother sat staring at the fire; his wife worked at an enormous band of tapestry. Usually there were three or four visitors, but on this occasion a violent storm sufficiently accounted for the absence even of the most assiduous. In the long silences the howling of the wind and the beating of the rain were distinctly audible. Newman sat perfectly still, watching the clock, determined to stay till the stroke of eleven and not a moment longer. Madame de Cintré had turned her back to the circle and had been standing for some time within the uplifted curtain of a window, her forehead against the pane and her eyes reaching out to the deluged darkness. Suddenly she turned round to her sister-in-law. "For heaven's sake," she said with peculiar eagerness, "go to the piano and play something."

The young Marquise held up her tapestry and pointed to a little white flower. "Don't ask me to leave this. I'm in the midst of a masterpiece. My little flower's going to smell very sweet; I'm putting in the smell with this gold-coloured silk. I'm holding my breath; I can't leave off. Play something yourself."

"It's absurd for me to play when you're present," Claire returned; yet the next moment she had plunged, as it were, into the source of music, had begun to strike the keys with vehemence. She sounded them for some time, to a great, and almost startling effect; when she stopped Newman went over and asked her to begin again. She shook her head and, on his insisting, said: "I've not been playing for you, I've been playing for myself." She went back to the window again and looked out, and shortly afterwards she left the room.

When he took leave Urbain de Bellegarde accompanied him, as always, just three steps down the staircase. At the bottom stood a servant with his overcoat. He had just put it on when he saw Madame de Cintré come to him across the vestibule. "Shall you be at home on Friday?" he asked.

She looked at him a moment before answering, and the servant moved away to the great house-door. "You don't like my mother and my brother. Ah, but not the least little bit!"

He hesitated a moment and then said ever so mildly, "Well, since you mention it —!"

She laid her hand on the balustrade and prepared to ascend the stairs, fixing her eyes on the first step

"I shall be at home on Friday," she brought out; and she passed up while he watched her. But on the Friday, as soon as he came in, she asked him to be so good as to tell her why he had such an aversion to her family.

"Such an aversion? Did I call it that? Don't think I make too much of it. See how easily I work it."

"I wish you would tell me what you think of them," she simply said.

"I don't think of any of them but you."

"That's because you dislike them too much. Speak the truth; you can't offend me."

"Well, I could live at a pinch without the Marquis," Newman confessed. "It comes to me now, if you mention it. But what's the use of our bringing it up? I don't think of him."

"You're too good-natured," Madame de Cintré gravely said. Then, as if to avoid the appearance of inviting him to speak ill of her brother, she turned away, motioning him to sit down.

But he remained there before her. "What's of much more importance is that they can scarcely stand me."

"Scarcely," she said with the gentlest, oddest distinctness.

"And don't you think they're wrong? I don't strike myself as a man to hate."

"I suppose a man who may inspire strong feelings," she thoughtfully opined, "must take his chance of what they are. But have my brother and my mother made you hate *them?*"

"Oh, I don't sling my passions about — I've put

all my capital into one good thing," he smiled. "Yet I may have spent about ten cents on the luxury of rage."

"You 've never then let me see you doing it."

"Ah, I don't do it here," he still sturdily smiled.

She dropped her eyes, and it somehow held him a minute in suspense. But "They think they 've treated you rather handsomely" was, however, all she said at last.

"Well, I 've no doubt they could have been much worse. They must have let me off pretty easily," he went on; "for see how little I feel damaged. And I think I show you everything. Honestly."

She faced him again, at this, as if really to take the measure, more than she had done yet, of what he showed her. "You 're very generous. It 's a painful position."

"For them, you mean. Not for me."

"For me," said Madame de Cintré.

"Not when their sins are forgiven!" Newman laughed. "They don't think I 'm as good as themselves. I do, you see. What should I be — well, even for you — if I did n't? But we shan't quarrel about it."

"I can't even agree with you without saying something that has a sound I dislike. The presumption, if I may put it so, was against you. That you probably don't understand."

He sat down before her, all carefully and considerately, as he might have placed himself at the feet of a teacher. "I don't think I really understand it. But when you say it I believe it."

She gave, still with her charming eyes on him, the slowest, gentlest headshake. "That's a poor reason."

"No, it's a very good one. I believe everything you say, and I know why — if you'll let me tell you. You've a high spirit, a high standard; but with you it's all natural and unaffected: you don't seem to have stuck your head into a vise, as if you were sitting for the photograph of propriety. Yet you do also think of me, I guess, as a sort of animal that has had no idea in life but to make money and drive sharp bargains. Well, that's a fair description," he pursued, "but it's not the whole. A man ought to care for something else — I'm alive to that and always was, even if I don't know exactly for what. I cared for money-making, but I never cared so very terribly for the money. There was nothing else to do, and I take it you don't see me *always* on the loaf. I've been very easy to others, and I've tried always to know where I was myself. I've done most of the things that people have asked me — I don't mean scoundrels. I guess no one has suffered by me very badly. As regards your mother and your brother," he added, "there's only one point on which I feel that I might quarrel with them. I don't ask them to sing my praises to you, but I ask them to let you alone. If I thought they talked against me to you at all badly" — and he just paused — "why I'd have to come in somewhere on *that*."

She reassured him. "They've let me alone, as you say. They haven't talked against you to me at all badly."

It gave him, and for the first time, the exquisite pleasure of her apparently liking to use and adopt his words. "Well then I'm ready to declare them only too good for this world!"

This brought something into her face that — as it seemingly was n't relief — he did n't quite understand, and she might have spoken in a sense to explain it if the door at the moment had not been thrown open and Urbain de Bellegarde had not stepped across the threshold. He appeared surprised at finding Newman; but his surprise was but a momentary shadow across the surface of an unwonted cheer. His guest had never seen him so exhilarated; he produced the effect of an old faded portrait that had suddenly undergone restoration. He held open the door for some one else to enter, and was presently followed by the old Marquise, supported on the arm of a gentleman whom Newman saw for the first time. He was already on his feet, and Madame de Cintré rose, as she always did before her mother. The Marquis, who had greeted him almost genially, stood apart and slowly rubbed his hands ; his mother came forward with her companion. She gave Newman a majestic little nod and then released the other visitor, that he might make his bow to her daughter. "I've brought you an unknown relative, Lord Deepmere, Lord Deepmere who's our cousin, but who has done only to-day what he ought to have done long ago, come to make our acquaintance."

Madame de Cintré dropped her soft but steady light on this personage, who had advanced to take her hand. "It's very extraordinary," he ingenuously

265

remarked, "but this is the first time in my life I've
been in Paris for more than three or four weeks."

"And how long have you been here now?" she
enquired with a certain detachment.

"Oh, for the last two months." The young man —
he was still a young man — showed no hesitation.
His artless observations might have constituted an
impertinence; but a glance at his face would have
satisfied you, as it apparently satisfied Madame de
Cintré, that nothing about him could well be explained
save in the light of his simplicity. When their group
was seated Newman, who was out of the conversation,
reflected, observing him, that unless he had the
benefit of that he had n't the benefit of very much.
His other advantages — beyond his three or four
and thirty years — were a scant stature and an odd
figure, a bald head, a short nose, round clear blue
eyes and a frank and natural smile, which made the
loss of a couple of front teeth by some rude misad-
venture constantly conspicuous. Perceptibly embarrassed, by more than one sign, he laughed as if
he were bold and free, catching his breath with a
loud startling sound. He admitted that Paris was
charming, but pleaded that he was a wild, bog-
trotting Paddy who preferred his Dublin even to his
London and who would never be caught where they
had caught him save for his taste for light music. He
came over for the new Offenbach things, since, though
they always brought them out in Dublin, it was perhaps with a whiff too much of the brogue. He had
been nine times to hear "La Pomme de Paris." Had
Madame de Cintré ever been to Dublin? They must

all come over some day and he'd show them some grand old Irish sport. His younger kinswoman, leaning back with her arms folded and her eyes set in a certain dimness of wonder, might have been drifting away from him, conveniently and resignedly, on some deep slow current. Her mother's face, on the other hand, was lighted as if in honour of the hour, and Newman felt himself make out in it a queer prehistoric prettiness. The Marquis noted that among light operas his favourite was "La Gazza Ladra." The Marquise, however, began a series of enquiries about the duke and the cardinal, the old duchess and Lady Barbara, after listening to which and to Lord Deepmere's somewhat irreverent responses for a quarter of an hour, our friend rose to take his leave. The Marquis went with him their three usual steps into the hall.

"He *is* a real Paddy!" — and Newman nodded in the direction of the visitor.

His companion took it coldly. "His mother was the daughter of Lord Finucane; he has great Irish estates. Lady Bridget, in the complete absence of male heirs, either direct or collateral — a most extraordinary circumstance — came in for no end of things. Lord Deepmere takes his principal title, however, from his English property, which is immense. He's a charming young man."

Newman answered nothing, but he detained the Marquis as the latter was beginning gracefully to recede. "It's a good time for me to thank you for sticking so punctiliously to our bargain — for doing so much to help me with your sister."

The Marquis stared. "Really, I've done nothing that I can boast of."

"Oh, don't be modest," Newman genially urged. "I can't flatter myself I'm doing so well — so well, that is, as I hope and pray -- simply by my own merit. Please tell your mother too, won't you? how thoroughly I feel it." And, turning away with a sense of the fair thing done now, after all, all round, he left M. de Bellegarde looking after him more ambiguously than he knew.

XIV

THE next time Newman came to the Rue de l'Université he had the good fortune to find Madame de Cintré alone. He arrived with a definite intention and lost no time in applying it, for she wore even to his impatience an expectant, waiting look. "I've been coming to see you for six months now and have never spoken to you a second time of marriage. That was what you asked me — I obeyed. Could any man have done better?"

"You've acted with great delicacy," she said.

"Well, I'm going to change now. I don't mean I'm going to risk offending, but I'm going to go back to where I began. I *am* back there. I've been all round the circle. Or rather I've never been away from there. I've never ceased to want what I wanted then. Only now I'm more sure of it, if possible; I'm more sure of myself and more sure of you. I know you better, though I don't know anything I didn't believe three months ago. You're everything, you're beyond everything, I can imagine or desire. You know me now—you *must* know me. I won't say you've seen the best, but you've seen the worst. I hope you've been thinking all this while. You must have seen I was only waiting; you can't suppose I was changing. What will you say to me now? Say that everything is clear and reasonable and that I've been very patient and considerate and deserve my reward. And then give me your hand. Madame de Cintré, do that. Do it."

"I knew you were only waiting," she answered, "and I was sure this day would come. I've thought about it a great deal. At first I was half afraid of it. But I'm not afraid of it now." She paused a moment and then added: "It's a relief."

She sat on a low chair and Newman on an ottoman near her; he leaned a little and took her hand, which for an instant she let him keep "That means that I've not waited for nothing." She looked at him a moment, and he saw her eyes fill with tears. "With me," he went on, "you'll be as safe — as safe" — and even in his ardour he hesitated for a comparison — "as safe," he said with a kind of simple solemnity, "as in your father's arms."

Still she looked at him and her tears flowed; then she buried her face on the cushioned arm of the sofa beside her chair and broke into noiseless sobs. "I'm weak — I'm weak," it made him fairly tremble to hear her say.

"All the more reason why you should give yourself up to me," he pleaded. "Why are you troubled? There's nothing here that should trouble you. I offer you nothing but happiness. Is that so hard to believe?"

"To you everything seems so simple," she said as she raised her head. "But things are not so. I like you — oh, I like you. I liked you six months ago and now I'm sure of it, as you say *you're* sure. But it's not easy, simply for that, to decide for what you ask. There are so many things to think about."

"There ought to be only one thing -- that we love each other." And as she remained silent he quickly added: "Very good; if you can't accept that, don't tell me."

"I should be very glad to think of nothing," she returned at last; "not to think at all — only to shut both my eyes and give myself up. But I can't. I'm cold, I'm old, I'm a coward. I never supposed I should ever marry again," she continued, "and it seems to me too strange I should ever have listened to you. When I used to think, as a girl, of what I should do if I were to marry freely, by my own choice, I thought of a very different man from you."

"That's nothing against me," said Newman with an immense smile. "Your taste was n't formed."

His smile lighted her own face. "Have you formed it?" And then she said in a different tone: "Where do you wish to live?"

"Anywhere in the wide world you like. We can easily settle that."

"I don't know why I ask you," she presently went on — "I care so very little. I think that if I were to marry you I could live almost anywhere. You've some false ideas about me, you think I need a great many things — that I must have a brilliant worldly life. I'm sure you're prepared to take a great deal of trouble to give me such things. But that's very arbitrary; I've done nothing to show that." She paused again, looking at him, and her mingled sound and silence were so sweet to him that he had no more wish to hurry her than he would have had to hurry the slow flushing of the east at dawn. "Your being so different, which at first seemed a difficulty, a danger, began one day to seem to me a pleasure, a great pleasure. I was glad you were different. And yet if I had said so no one would have understood me. And I don't mean simply my family."

"*They* at least would have said I was a queer monster, eh?" he asked.

"They would have said I could never be happy with you — you were too different ; and I would have said it was just *because* you were so different that I might be happy. But they would have given better reasons than I. My only reason—!" And she paused again.

But this time, before his golden sunrise, he felt the impulse to grasp at a rosy cloud. "Your only reason is that you love me!" he almost groaned for deep insistence; and he laid his two hands on her with a persuasion that she rose to meet. He let her feel as he drew her close, bending his face to her, the fullest force of his imposition; and she took it from him with a silent, fragrant, flexible surrender which — since she seemed to keep back nothing — affected him as sufficiently prolonged to pledge her to everything.

He came back the next day and in the vestibule, as he entered the house, encountered his friend Mrs. Bread. She was wandering about in honourable idleness and when his eyes fell upon her delivered to him straight one of her Wiltshire curtsies; then turning to the servant who had admitted him she said with a cognate respectability to which evidently a proper pronunciation of French had never had anything to add: "You may retire ; I'll have the honour of con-

ducting monsieur." In spite of this clean consciousness, however, it appeared to Newman that her
voice had a queer quaver, as if the tone of uncontested
authority were not habitual to it. The man gave her
an impertinent stare, but he walked slowly away,
and she led Newman upstairs. At half its course the
staircase put forth two arms with an ample rest
between. In a niche of this landing stood an indifferent statue of an eighteenth-century nymph, sim-
pering with studied elegance. Here Mrs. Bread stopped
and looked with shy kindness at her companion. " I
know the good news, sir."

"You've a good right to be first to know it; you've
taken such a friendly interest." And then as she
turned away and began to blow the dust off the image
as if this might but be free pleasantry, "I suppose
you want to congratulate me," Newman went on, "and
I'm greatly obliged." To which he added: "You
gave me much pleasure the other day."

She turned round, apparently reassured. "You're
not to think I've been told anything — I've only
guessed. But when I looked at you as you came in
I was sure I had guessed right."

"You're really a grand judge," said Newman.
" I'm sure that what you don't see isn't worth seeing."

"I'm not a fool, sir, thank God. I've guessed
something else beside," said Mrs. Bread.

"What's that?"

"I need n't tell you, sir; I don't think you'd
believe it. At any rate it would n't please you."

"Oh, tell me nothing but what *will* please me,"
he laughed. "That's the way you began."

"Well, sir," she went on, "I suppose you won't be vexed to hear that the sooner everything's over the better."

"The sooner we're married, you mean? The better for me, certainly."

"The better for every one."

"The better for you perhaps. You know you're coming to live with us," said Newman.

"I'm extremely obliged to you, sir, but it's not of my poor self I was thinking. I only wanted, if I might take the liberty, to recommend you to lose no time."

"Who are you afraid of?"

Mrs. Bread looked up the staircase and then down, and then looked at the undusted nymph as if she possibly had sentient ears. "I'm afraid of every one."

"What an uncomfortable state of mind!" said Newman. "Does 'every one' wish to prevent my marriage?"

"I'm afraid of already having said too much," Mrs. Bread replied. "I won't take it back, but I won't say any more." And she kept her course up the staircase again and led him into her mistress's salon

Newman indulged in a brief and silent imprecation when he found this lady not alone. With her sat her mother, and toward the middle of the room stood young Madame de Bellegarde in bonnet and mantle. The old Marquise, who leant back in her chair clasping the knob of each arm, looked at him hard and without moving. She seemed barely conscious of his greeting; she might have had too much else to think

of. Newman said to himself that her daughter had
been announcing their engagement and that she found
the morsel hard to swallow. But Madame de Cintré,
as she gave him her hand, gave him also a look by
which she appeared to mean that he should understand something. Was it a warning or a request?
Did she wish to enjoin speech or silence? He was
puzzled, and young Madame de Bellegarde's pretty
grin gave him no information.

"I've not told my mother," said Madame de
Cintré abruptly and with her eyes on him.

"Told me what?" the Marquise demanded. "You
tell me too little. You should tell me everything."

"That's what I do," laughed Madame Urbain with
all her bravery.

"Let *me* tell your mother," said Newman.

The old woman stared at him again and then
turned to her daughter. "You're going to marry
him?" she brought out.

"Oui, ma mère," said Madame de Cintré.

"Your daughter has consented, to my very great
happiness," Newman announced.

"And when was this arrangement made?" asked
Madame de Bellegarde. "I seem to be picking up
the news by chance!"

"My suspense came to an end yesterday," said
Newman.

"And how long was mine to have lasted?" the
Marquise further enquired of her daughter. She
spoke without irritation, with cold, noble displeasure.

Madame de Cintré stood silent and with her eyes
on the ground "It's over at all events now."

"Where's my son — where's Urbain?" asked the Marquise. "Send for your brother and let him know."

Young Madame de Bellegarde laid her hand on the bell-rope. "He was to make some visits with me, and I was to go and knock — very softly, very softly —at the door of his study. But he can come to *me!*" She pulled the bell and in a few moments Mrs. Bread appeared with a face of calm enquiry.

"Send for your brother," the old lady went on to Claire.

But Newman felt an irresistible impulse to speak — and to speak in a certain way. "Please tell the Marquis we want him immediately," he said to Mrs. Bread, who quietly retired.

Young Madame de Bellegarde approached her sister-in-law and embraced her, and then she turned, intensely smiling, to Newman. "She's as charming as you like. I congratulate you."

"I do the same, Mr. Newman," said Madame de Bellegarde with extreme solemnity. "My daughter's an extraordinarily good woman. She may have faults, but I don't know them."

"My mother doesn't often make jokes," Madame de Cintré observed; "but when she does they're terrible."

"She's a pearl, she's adorable," the Marquise Urbain resumed, looking at her sister-in-law with her head on one side. "Yes, I congratulate you."

Madame de Cintré turned away and, taking up a piece of tapestry, began to ply the needle. Some minutes of silence elapsed, which were interrupted by the arrival of M. de Bellegarde. He came in with

hat in hand and irreproachably gloved, and was
followed by his brother Valentin, who appeared to
have just entered the house. The Marquis looked
round the circle and administered to Newman his
due little measure of recognition. Valentin saluted
his mother and sisters and, as he shook hands with
his friend, appeared to put him a sharp mute question.

"*Arrivez donc, messieurs!*" cried the young
Marquise. "We've great news for you."

"Speak to your brother, my daughter," said the
old woman to Claire.

Madame de Cintré had been looking at her tapestry, but on this she raised her eyes. "I've accepted
Mr. Newman, Urbain."

"Yes, sir, your sister has nobly consented," said
Newman. "You see after all I knew what I was
about."

"I beg you to believe I'm charmed!" M. de Bellegarde replied with superior benignity.

"So am I, my dear man," said Valentin to Newman. "The Marquis and I are charmed. I can't
marry myself, but I can understand it in others when
the inducements to it are overwhelming. I can't stand
on my head, but I can applaud a clever acrobat when
he brings down the house. My dear sister, I bless
your union with this delightful gentleman."

The Marquis stood looking for a while into the
crown of his hat. "We've been prepared," he said
at last, "but it's inevitable that in the face of the
event we should *éprouver* a certain emotion." And
he gave the oddest smile his visitor had ever be-
held.

"I feel no emotion that I was not perfectly prepared for," his mother, upon this, remarked.

"I can't say that for myself," said Newman, who felt in his face a different light from that of the Marquis. "I'm distinctly happier than I expected to be. I suppose it's the sight of all your happiness!"

"Don't exaggerate that," said Madame de Bellegarde as she got up and laid her hand on her daughter's arm. "You can't expect an honest old woman to thank you for taking away her beautiful only daughter."

"You forget *me*, dear madame," the young Marquise demurely interposed.

"Yes, she's very, very beautiful," Newman agreed while he covered Claire with his bright still protection.

"And when is the wedding, pray?" asked young Madame de Bellegarde. "I must have a month to think over the question of my falbalas."

"Ah, the time must be particularly discussed," said the Marquise.

"Oh, we'll discuss it thoroughly, and we'll promptly let you know!" Newman gaily declared.

"I make very little doubt we shall agree," said Urbain.

"If you don't agree with Madame de Cintré you'll be very unreasonable," his visitor went on.

"Come, come, Urbain," said young Madame de Bellegarde, "I must go straight to my tailor's."

The old lady had been standing with her hand on her daughter's arm and her eyes on her face. Madame de Cintré had got up; she seemed inscrutably to wait. Her mother exhaled a long heavy breath. "No, I can't say I had been sure of you. You're a very lucky gentleman," she added with a rather grand turn to their guest.

"Oh, I know that!" he answered. "I feel tremendously proud. I feel like crying it on the housetops — like stopping people in the street to tell them."

Madame de Bellegarde narrowed her lips. "Pray do nothing of the sort."

"Oh, the more people who know it the better," Newman roundly returned. "I haven't yet announced it here, but I cabled it this morning to America."

"'Cabled' it?" She spoke as if — what indeed well might be — she had never heard the expression.

"To New York, to Saint Louis and to San Francisco; those are the principal cities you know. To-morrow I shall tell my friends here."

"Have you so many?" asked Madame de Bellegarde in a tone of which he perhaps but partly measured the impertinence.

"Enough to bring me a great many hand-shakes and congratulations. To say nothing," he added in a moment, "of those I shall receive from your own friends."

"Our own won't use the telegraph," said the Marquise as she took her departure.

M. de Bellegarde, whose wife, her imagination having apparently taken flight to the tailor's, was fluttering her silken wings in emulation, shook hands with Newman very pertinently and said with a more persuasive accent than the latter had ever heard him

use: "I beg you to count on me for everything."
Then his wife led him away.

Valentin, on this, stood looking from his sister to
his friend. "I hope you've both reflected very
seriously."

Madame de Cintré smiled. "We've neither your
powers of reflexion nor your depth of seriousness, but
we've done our best."

"Well, I've a great regard for each of you," the
young man continued. "You're charming, innocent,
beautiful creatures. But I'm not satisfied, on the
whole, that you belong to that small and superior
class — that exquisite group — composed of persons
who are worthy to remain unmarried. These are
rare souls, they're the salt of the earth. But I don't
mean to be invidious; the marrying people are often
very *gentils*."

"Valentin holds that women should marry and that
men should n't," said Madame de Cintré. "I don't
know how he arranges it."

"I arrange it by adoring you, my sister," he
ardently answered.

"You had better adore some one you can marry,
by my example," Newman laughed. "I'll arrange
that for you some day. I foresee I'm going to turn
apostle."

Valentin was on the threshold; he looked back a
moment with a face that had grown grave. "I adore
some one I *can't* marry!" And he dropped the
portière and departed.

"They don't really like it, you know," Newman
said as he stood there before his mistress.

"No," she returned after a moment, "they don't really like it."

"Well now, do you mind that?" he asked.

"Yes!" she said after another interval.

"But is n't that a mistake?"

"It may be, but I can't help it. I should prefer that my mother were pleased."

"Why the dickens then," he yearningly enquired, "*is n't* she pleased? She gave you leave to accept me."

"Very true; I don't understand it. And yet I do 'mind' it, as you say. You'll call that superstitious."

"That will depend on how much you let it worry you. Then I shall call it an awful bore."

"I'll keep it to myself," said Madame de Cintré. "It shall not, I promise, worry *you*." And they then talked of their marriage-day, and she assented unreservedly to his desire to have it fixed for an early date.

His messages by cable were answered promptly and with interest. Having despatched in reality but three of these, he received, for fruit of his investment, as he called it, no less than eight electrical outpourings, all concisely humorous, which he put into his pocketbook and, the next time he encountered Madame de Bellegarde, drew forth and displayed to her. This, it must be confessed, was a slightly malicious stroke; the reader will judge in what degree the offence was venial. He knew she would dislike his barbaric trophies, but he was himself possessed by a certain hardness of triumph. Madame de Cintré, on the other hand, quite artlessly, quite touchingly admired them, and, most of them being of a wit quainter than any she had ever encountered, laughed at them immoderately and enquired into the character of their authors. Newman, now that his prize was gained, felt a peculiar desire that his triumph should be manifest. He more than suspected the Bellegardes of keeping quiet about it and allowing it, in their select circle, but a limited resonance; and it pleased him to think that if he were to take the trouble he might, as he phrased it, break all their windows. No honest man ever enjoys any sign of his not being acknowledged in his totality, and yet our friend, with his lucid vision, was not conscious of humiliation. He had not this good excuse for his somewhat aggressive impulse to promulgate his felicity; his sentiment was of another degree. He wanted for once to make the heads of the house of Bellegarde simply feel the weight of his hand; for when should he have another chance? He had had for the past six months a sense of the old woman's and her elder son's looking straight over *his* head, and he was now resolved that they should toe a mark which he would give himself the satisfaction of drawing.

"It's like seeing a bottle emptied when the wine's poured too slowly," he said to Mrs. Tristram. "They make me want to joggle their elbows and force them to spill their wine."

To this Mrs. Tristram answered that he had better leave them alone and let them do things in their own way. "You must make allowances for them — it's natural enough they should hang fire a little. They thought they accepted you when you made your application: but they're not people of imagination, they could n't project themselves into the future, and now they 'll have to begin again. But they *are* people of honour and they 'll do whatever 's necessary."

Newman spent a few moments in narrow-eyed meditation. "I 'm not hard on them," he presently said, "and to prove it I 'll invite them all to a festival."

"A festival — ?"

"You 've been laughing at my great gilded rooms all winter; I 'll show you they 're good for something. I 'll give a party. What 's the grandest thing one can do here ? I 'll hire all the great singers from the opera and all the first people from the Théâtre Français, and I 'll hold an entertainment — the biggest kind of show."

"And who will you invite ?"

"You two, first of all. And the old woman, damn her, and her son and her son's wife. And Valentin of course — for the fun of him. And then every one of their friends whom I have met at their house or elsewhere, every one who has shown me the minimum of politeness, every duke of them, such as they are, every doddering old duchess, every 'great name' in the place. And then all my friends, without exception — Miss Kitty Upjohn, Miss Dora Finch, General Packard, C. P. Hatch, every pet horror even of yours. And every one shall know what it 's about — to celebrate my engagement to the Countess de Cintré, who shall sit, through it all, on a golden chair above their heads and look as beautiful — and perhaps, poor dear, as bored — as a saint in paradise. What do you think of the idea ?"

"I think it odious!" said Mrs. Tristram. And then in a moment: "I think it delicious!"

The very next evening Newman repaired to Madame de Bellegarde's own drawing-room, where he found her surrounded by her children and invited her to honour his poor dwelling by her presence on a certain evening a fortnight distant.

The Marquise stared a moment. "My dear sir," she cried, "what on earth do you want to do to me?"

"To make you acquainted with a few people and then to place you in a very easy chair and ask you to listen to Madame Frezzolini's singing."

"You mean to give a concert?"

"Something of that sort."

"And to have a crowd of people?"

"All my friends, and I hope some of yours and your daughter's. I want to celebrate my engagement."

It seemed to him she had turned perceptibly pale. She opened her fan, a fine old painted fan of the last century, and looked at the picture, which represented a *fête champêtre* — a lady singing to a guitar and a group of dancers round a garlanded Hermes. "We go out so little," her elder son murmured, "since my poor father's death."

"But *my* poor father's still alive, my friend," said his wife. "I'm only waiting for my invitation to accept it;" and she glanced with amiable confidence at Newman. "It will be magnificent, I'm sure of that."

I am sorry to say, to the discredit of Newman's gallantry, that this lady's invitation was not then and there bestowed; he was giving all his attention to her mother-in-law. Madame de Bellegarde looked up at last with a prodigious extemporised grace. "I can't think of letting you offer me a fête until I've offered you one. We want to present you to our friends; we'll invite them all. We have it very much at heart. We must do things in order. Come to me about the twenty-fifth; I'll let you know the exact day immediately. We shall not have any one so fine as Madame Frezzolini, but we shall have some very good people. After that you may talk of your own party." She spoke with a certain quick eagerness, smiling more agreeably as she went on.

It seemed to Newman a handsome proposal, and such proposals always touched the sources of his good-nature. He replied after a little discussion that he would be glad to come on the twenty-fifth or any other day, and that it mattered very little whether he met his friends at her house or his own. We have noted him for observant, yet on this occasion he failed to catch a thin sharp eyebeam, as cold as a flash of steel, which passed between Madame de Bellegarde and the Marquis and which we may presume to have been a commentary on the innocence displayed in that latter clause of his speech.

Count Valentin walked away with him that evening and, when they had left the scene of so many anxieties well behind them, said reflectively: "My mother's very strong — ah, but uncommonly strong." Then in answer to an interrogative movement of Newman's: "She was driven to the wall, but you'd never have thought it. Her party on the twenty-fifth was an invention of the moment. She had no idea whatever of giving one, but, finding it tne only issue from your proposal, she looked straight at the dose — pardon the expression — and bolted it, as you saw, without winking. She's really rather grand, you know."

"Well, I wonder!" said Newman, divided, this time, rather whimsically, quite appreciatively, between the sense of his own force and the sense of hers. "I don't care a straw for her fiddles and ices; I'm willing to take the will for the deed."

"No, no!" — and Valentin showed an inconsequent touch of family pride. "The thing will be done now, and I dare say it will be quite *folichon!*"

XV

VALENTIN'S ironic forecast of the secession of Mademoiselle Nioche from her father's domicile and his irreverent reflexion on the attitude of this anxious parent in so grave a catastrophe received a practical commentary in the fact that M. Nioche was slow to seek another interview with his late pupil. It had cost Newman some disgust to be forced to assent to his friend's expert analysis of the old man's philosophy, and, though circumstances seemed to indicate that he had not given himself up to a noble despair, our hero thought it possible he might be suffering more keenly than he allowed to become flagrant. M. Nioche had been in the habit of paying him a respectful little visit every two or three weeks, and his absence might be a proof quite as much of extreme depression as of a desire to conceal the success with which he had patched up his sorrow. Newman presently gathered in the bright garden of Valentin's talk several of the flowers of the young woman's recent history.

"I told you she was remarkable," this consistent reasoner declared, "and it's proved by the way she has managed this most important of all her steps. She has had other chances, but she was resolved to take none but the best. She did you the honour to think for a while that you might be such a chance. You were not; so she gathered up her patience and waited a little longer. At last her occasion arrived, and she made her move with her eyes open. I'm very sure she had no innocence to lose, but she had all her respectability. Dubious little damsel as you thought her she had kept a firm hold of that; nothing could be proved against her, and she was determined not to let her reputation go till she had got her equivalent. About her equivalent she had high ideas. Apparently her requirements have been met. Well, they've been met in a superior form. The form's fifty years old, baldheaded and deaf, but he's very easy about money."

"And where in the world," asked Newman, "did you pick up this valuable information?"

"In animated conversation. Remember my frivolous habits. Conversation — and this time not criminal! — with a young woman engaged in the humble trade of glove-cleaner who keeps a small shop in the Rue Saint-Roch. M. Nioche lives in the same house, up six pairs of stairs, across the court in and out of whose ill-swept doorway Miss Noémie has been flitting for the last five years. The little glove-cleaner was an old acquaintance; she used to be the friend of a friend of mine — the foolish friend of a foolish friend — who has married and given up friendship. I often saw her in his society. As soon as I made her out behind her clear little window-pane I recollected her. I had on a spotlessly fresh pair of gloves, but I went in and held up my hands and said to her: 'Dear mademoiselle, what will you ask me for cleaning these?' 'Dear Count,' she answered immediately, 'I'll clean them for *you* for nothing.'

She had instantly recognised me and I had to hear her history from ever so far back. But after that I put her on that of her neighbours. She knows and admires Noémie, and she told me what I've just repeated."

A month elapsed without any reappearance of M. Nioche, and Newman, who every morning read, for practice, about the suicides of the day in a newspaper, began to suspect that, mortification proving stubborn, he had sought a balm for his wounded pride in the waters of the Seine. He had a note of the poor gentleman's address in his pocket-book, and, finding himself one day in the *quartier*, determined, so far as he might, to clear up his doubts. He repaired to the house in the Rue Saint-Roch which bore the recorded number, and observed in a neighbouring basement, behind a dangling row of neatly inflated gloves, the unmistakeable face of Valentin's informant — a sallow person in a dressing-gown — peering into the street as if in expectation that this amiable nobleman would pass again. But it was not to her that Newman applied; he simply enquired of the portress if M. Nioche were at home. The portress replied, as the portress invariably replies, that her lodger had gone out barely three minutes before, but then, through the little square hole of her lodge-window, taking the measure of Newman's resources and seeing them, by an unspecified process, refresh the dry places of servitude to occupants of fifth floors on courts, she added that M. Nioche would have had just time to reach the Café de la Patrie, round the second turning to the left, at which establishment he regularly spent his afternoons. Newman thanked her for the information, took the second turning to the left and arrived at the Café de la Patrie. He felt a momentary hesitation to go in; was it not rather mean to press so hard on humiliated dignity? There passed across his vision an image of a haggard little septuagenarian taking measured sips of a glass of sugar and water and finding them quite impotent to sweeten his desolation. But he opened the door and entered, perceiving nothing at first but a dense cloud of tobacco-smoke. Across this, however, in a corner, he presently descried the figure of M. Nioche, stirring the contents of a deep glass and with a lady seated in front of him. The lady's back was presented, but her companion promptly perceived and recognised his visitor. Newman had gone forward, and the old man rose slowly, gazing at him with a more blighted expression even than usual.

"If you're drinking hot punch," Newman said, "I suppose you're not dead. That's all right. You need n't move to show it."

M. Nioche stood staring with a fallen jaw, not risking any confidence. The lady who faced him turned round in her place and glanced up with a spirited toss of her head, displaying the agreeable features of his daughter. She looked at Newman hard, to see how he was looking at her, then — I don't know what she discovered — she said graciously: "How d'ye do, monsieur? won't you come into our little corner?"

"Did you come — did you come after *me*, monsieur?" asked M. Nioche very softly.

"I went to your house to see what had become of you. I thought you might be sick," monsieur said mildly enough.

"It's very good of you, as always," the old man returned. "No, I'm not well. Yes, I'm *seek.*"

"Ask monsieur to sit down," said Mademoiselle Nioche. "Garçon, bring a chair for monsieur."

"Will you do us the honour to *seat?*" M. Nioche enquired timorously and with a double foreignness of accent.

Newman said to himself that he had better see the thing out, and he took a place at the end of the table with the brilliant girl on his left and the dingy old man on the other side. "You'll take something of course," said Miss Noémie, who was sipping a brown *madère.* Newman said he guessed not, and then she turned to her parent with a smile. "What an honour, eh? — he has only come for us." M. Nioche drained his pungent glass at a long draught and looked out from eyes more lachrymose in consequence. "But you did n't come for *me,* eh?" Noémie went on. "You did n't expect to find me here?"

He observed the change in her appearance and that she was very elegant, really prettier than before; she looked a year or two older, and it was noticeable that, to the eye, she had only added a sharp accent to her appearance of "propriety," only taken a longer step toward distinction. She was dressed in quiet colours and wore her expensively unobtrusive gear with a grace that might have come from years of practice. Her presence of mind, her perfect equilibrium, struck Newman as portentous, and he inclined to agree with Valentin that the young lady was very remarkable. "No, to tell the truth, I did n't come for you," he said, "and I did n't expect to find you. I was told," he added in a moment, "that you had left your good father."

"*Quelle horreur!*" she cried with the brightest of all her smiles. "Does one *ever* leave one's good father? You 've the happy proof of the contrary."

"Yes, convincing proof," said Newman with his almost embarrassed eyes on M. Nioche. The old man caught his glance obliquely, with his faded deprecation, and then, lifting his empty glass, pretended to drink again.

"Who told you that?" Noémie demanded. "But I know very well. It was M. de Bellegarde. Why don't you say yes? You 're not polite."

"I 'm so shy and simple and stupid," Newman said with a certain fond good faith.

"I set you a better example. I know M. de Bellegarde told you. He knows a great deal about me — or he thinks he does. He has taken a great deal of trouble to find out, but half of it is n't true. In the first place I have n t left my father, any more than he has left me. I 'm much too fond of him, and never so fond as now, when he has been *gentil, mais gentil* —! Is n't it so, little father? Have n't you been *gentil, mais gentil?* M. de Bellegarde 's a charming young man; it 's impossible to *mieux causer.* I know a good deal about *him* too; you can tell him that when you next see him."

"No," said Newman with a sturdy grin; "I won't carry any messages from you."

"Just as you please," his young friend placidly returned. "I don't depend on you, nor does M. de Bellegarde either. He's very much interested in me, he can be left to his own devices. He's a contrast to *you*, monsieur," Noémie went on with a fine little flight of dignity.

"Oh, he's a great contrast to me, I've no doubt," said Newman. "But I don't exactly know how you mean it."

"I mean it in this way. First of all he never offered to help me to a *dot* and a husband." And Mademoiselle Nioche expressively paused. "I won't say that's in his favour, for I do you justice. What led you, by the way, to make me such a monstrous offer? You did n't care for me."

"Oh yes — I did," said Newman.

"Well, how much?"

"It would have given me real pleasure to see you married to a respectable young fellow."

"With six thousand francs of income!" Noémie cried. "Do you call that caring for me? I'm afraid you know little about women. You were not *galant;* you were not what you might have been."

Newman flushed a trifle fiercely. "I say!" he exclaimed, "that's rather strong. I had no idea I had been so shabby."

She laughed out as she took up her muff — it was almost her only hint of vulgarity. "It's something at any rate to have made you angry."

Her father had leaned both his elbows on the table, and his head, bent forward, was supported on his hands, the thin white fingers of which were pressed over his ears. In this position he stared fixedly at the bottom of his empty glass, and Newman supposed he was not hearing. Noémie buttoned her furred jacket and pushed back her chair, casting a glance charged with the consciousness of an expensive appearance first down over her flounces and then up at Newman.

"You had better have remained an honest girl," his obstinate sense of his old friend's painful situation prompted him at last to remark.

M. Nioche continued to stare at the bottom of his glass, and his daughter got up, still bravely smiling. "You mean that I look so much like one? That's more than most women do nowadays. Don't judge me yet a while," she added. "I mean to succeed; that's what I mean to do. I leave you; I don't mean to be seen in such places as this, for one thing. I can't think what you want of my poor father; he's very comfortable now. It isn't his fault either. *Au revoir*, little father." And she tapped the old man on the head with her muff. Then she stopped a minute, looking again at their visitor. "Tell M. de Bellegarde, when he wants news of me, to come and get it from *me!*" And she turned and departed, the white-aproned waiter, with a bow, holding the door wide open for her.

M. Nioche sat motionless, and Newman hardly knew what to say to him. The old man looked dismally foolish. "So you determined not to shoot her, after all," Newman said presently.

M. Nioche, without moving, raised his eyes and let all their confession quite dismally and abjectly come. They did n't somehow presume to ask for pity, yet they doubtless pretended even less to a rugged ability to do without it. They might have expressed the state of mind of an innocuous insect, flat in shape, conscious of the impending pressure of a boot-sole and reflecting that he was perhaps too flat to be crushed. M. Nioche's gaze was a profession of moral flatness. "You despise me terribly," he said in the weakest possible voice.

"Oh no; it's not your own affair. And hanged if I understand your institutions anyway!"

"I made you too many fine speeches," M. Nioche added. "I meant them at the time."

"I'm sure I'm very glad you did n't shoot her," Newman went on. "I was afraid you might have shot yourself. That's why I came to look you up." And he began to button his coat.

"Neither, *hélas!* You despise me and I can't explain to you. I hoped I should n't see you again."

"Why, that's pretty mean," said Newman. "You should n't drop your friends that way. Besides, the last time you came to see me I thought you felt rather fine."

"Yes, I remember" — M. Nioche musingly recalled it. "I must have been, I *was*, in a fever. I did n't know what I said, what I did. I spoke, no doubt, wild words."

"Ah well, you're quieter now."

M. Nioche bethought himself. "As quiet as the grave," he then struck off.

"Are you very unhappy?" Newman more ingenuously asked.

M. Nioche rubbed his forehead slowly and even pushed back his wig a little, looking askance at his empty glass. "Yes — yes. But that's an old story. I've always been unhappy. My daughter does what she will with me. I take what she gives me — I make a face, but I take it. I've no pluck, and when you've no pluck you must keep quiet: you can't go about telling people. I shan't trouble you any more."

"Well," said Newman, rather disgusted at the smooth operation of the old man's philosophy, "that's as you please."

M. Nioche seemed to have been prepared to be despised, but he nevertheless appealed feebly from his patron's faint praise. "After all she's my daughter and I can still look after her. If she has her bad idea, why she has it and she won't let go of it. And then *now*," he pointed out — "it's fine talking! But there are many different paths, there are degrees. I can place at her disposal the benefit, the benefit" — and he paused, staring vaguely at his friend, who began to suspect his mind of really giving way — "the benefit of my experience."

"Your experience?" Newman inquired, both amused and amazed.

"My experience of business," said M. Nioche gravely.

"Ah yes," Newman laughed, "that will be a great advantage to her!" And then he said good-bye and offered the poor foolish old man his hand.

M. Nioche took it and leaned back against the wall, holding it a moment and looking up at him. "I suppose you think my wits are going. Very likely; I've always a pain in my head. That's why I can't explain, I can't present the case. And she's so strong, she makes me walk as she will — anywhere! But there's this — there's this." And he stopped, still staring up at his visitor. His little white eyes expanded and glittered for a moment like those of a cat in the dark. "It's not as it seems. I have n't forgiven her. Oh, *par exemple*, no!"

"That's right, don't let up on it. If you should, you don't know what she still *might* do!"

"It's horrible, it's terrible," said M. Nioche; "but do you want to know the truth? I hate her! I take what she gives me, and I hate her more. To-day she brought me three hundred francs; they're here in my waistcoat-pocket. Now I hate her almost cruelly. No, I have n't forgiven her."

Newman had a return of his candour. "Why then did you accept the money?"

"If I had n't I should have hated her still more. That, you see, is the nature of misery. No, I have n't forgiven her."

"Well, take care you don't hurt her!" Newman laughed again. And with this he took his leave. As he passed along the glazed side of the café, on reaching the street, he saw the old man motion the waiter, with a melancholy gesture, to replenish his glass.

A week after his visit to the Café de la Patrie he called one morning on Valentin de Bellegarde and by good fortune found him at home. He spoke of his interview with M. Nioche and his daughter, and said he was afraid Valentin had judged the old man correctly. He had found the couple hobnobbing together in amity; the old gentleman's rigour was purely theoretic. Newman confessed he was disappointed; he should have expected to see his venerable friend take high ground.

"High ground, my dear fellow!" Valentin returned; "there's no high ground for him to take. The only perceptible eminence in M. Nioche's horizon is Montmartre, which isn't an edifying quarter. You can't go mountaineering in a flat country."

"He remarked indeed," said Newman, "that he had not forgiven her. But she'll never find it out."

"We must do him the justice to suppose he intensely disapproves. His gifted child," Valentin added, "is like one of the great artists whose biographies we read, those who at the beginning of their career suffered opposition in the domestic circle. Their vocation was not recognised by their families, but the world has done it justice. Noémie has a vocation."

"Damn her vocation! Oh," added Newman impatiently, "you're a cold-blooded crew!"

Valentin sounded him a moment with curious eyes. "You must be very fond of boiled beef and cabbage to have such a suspicion of ripe peaches and plums."

But Newman sturdily met his look. "I should n't think I'd have to tell *you* what fruit I gather!"

The young man, at this, closed his eyes an instant and then, with a motion of his hand, shook his head. After which he gravely said: "I back you more than ever!"

"Let me then," his companion returned, "do

what I suppose you'd call the fair thing by you.
Miss Noémie desired me to tell you — but hanged
if I know what!"

"Bless your quiet imagination," said Valentin,
"do you suppose I've been waiting for you? I've
been to see her for myself — no less than three times
these five days. She's a charming hostess; we attack
the noblest subjects of discussion. She's really very
clever and a rare and remarkable type; not at all
low nor wanting to be low — determined not to be.
She means to take very good care of herself. She's
as perfect as you please, and as hard and clear-cut
as some little figure of a sea-nymph on an antique
intaglio; and I warrant she hasn't a grain more
true sensibility than if she were scooped out of a big
amethyst. You can't scratch her even with a diamond. Extremely pretty — really, when you know
her, she's wonderfully pretty — intelligent, determined, ambitious, unscrupulous, capable of seeing
a man strangled without changing colour, she's, upon
my honour, remarkably agreeable."

"Well," said Newman after reflexion, "I once
saw in a needle-factory a gentleman from the city,
who had stopped too near a machine that struck
him as curious, picked up as clean as if he had been
removed by a silver fork from a china plate, and
swallowed down and ground to small pieces!"

Re-entering his rooms late in the evening, three
days after Madame de Bellegarde had struck her
bargain with him, as he might feel, over the entertainment at which she was to present him to the
world, he found on his table a goodly card of an-

nouncement to the effect that she would be at home on the twenty-seventh of the month and at ten o'clock in the evening. He stuck it into the frame of his mirror and eyed it with some complacency; it seemed to him a document of importance and an emblem of triumph. Stretched out in a chair he looked at it lovingly, and while he so revelled Valentin was shown into the place. The young man's glance presently followed the direction of Newman's and he perceived his mother's invitation.

"And what have they put into the corner? Not the customary 'music,' 'dancing,' or '*tableaux vivants*'? They ought at least to put 'An American of Americans.'"

"Oh, there are to be several of us," Newman said. "Mrs. Tristram told me to-day she had received a card and sent an acceptance."

"Ah then, with Mrs. Tristram and her husband you'll have support. My mother might have put on her card 'Three Americans in a Row'—which you can pronounce in either way you like, though I know the way I should suppose most American. I dare say at least you'll not lack amusement. You'll see a great many of the best people in France—I mean of the long pedigrees, and the *beaux noms*, and the great fidelities, and the rare stupidities, and the faces and figures that, after all, sometimes, I suppose God did make. We've already shown you specimens in numbers—you know by which end to take them."

"Oh, they have n't hurt me yet," said Newman, "and I guess they would, by this time, if they were

going to. I seem to want to like people, these days
— seem regularly to *like* liking them, and almost
any one will do. I feel so good that if I was n't sure
I 'm going to be married I might think I 'm going to
lie."

"Do you make," the young man enquired, "so
much of a distinction?" But he dropped rather
wearily into a chair and went on before his host
could answer. "Happy man, only remember that
there are poor devils whom the flaunted happiness
of others sometimes irritates."

"Do you call a person a poor devil," demanded
Newman, "who 's as good as my brother-in-law?"

"Your brother-in-law?" his friend a trifle musingly
echoed.

"Say then my brother," Newman kindly returned
— "and leave the other description for yours."

It made Valentin after an instant rise to him.
"You 're really very charming You have your own
way for it — which must have been your way of
making love. Well," he sighed with a dimmer smile
than usual, "I don't wonder and I don't question!
Only you *are*, I understand" — he immediately
took himself up — "'really and truly' in love?"

"Yes, sir!" said Newman after a pause.

"And do you hold that *she* is?"

"You had better ask her," Newman answered
"Not for me, but for yourself."

"I never ask anything for myself. Have n't you
noticed that? Besides, she would n't tell me, and
it 's after all none of my business."

Newman hesitated, but "She does n't know!" he

the next thing brought out. "However, she *will* know."

"Ah then, *you* will — which I see you don't yet But what you'll know will be what you want, for that's the way things turn out for you." And Valentin's grave fine eyes, as if under some impression oddly quickened, measured him again a moment up and down. "The way you cover the ground! However, being as you are a giant, you move naturally in seven-league boots." With which again he turned restlessly off.

Newman's attention, from before the fire, followed him a little. "There's something the matter with you to-night: you're kind of perverse — you're almost kind of vicious. But wait till I'm through with my business — to which I wish to give just now my undivided attention — and then we'll talk. By which I mean I'll fix you somehow."

"Ah, there will be plenty of me for you, such as I am—for you always. Only when, then," Valentin asked, "*is* the event?"

"About five weeks hence — on a day not quite yet settled."

He accepted this answer with interest, in spite of which, however, "You feel very confident of the future?" he next attentively demanded.

"Confident," said Newman with the large accent from which semitones were more than ever absent. "I knew what I wanted exactly, and now I know what I've got."

"You're sure then you're going to be happy?"

"Sure?" — Newman competently weighed it. "So

foolish a question deserves a foolish answer. Yes
— I'll be hanged if I ain't sure!"

Well, if Valentin was to pass for perverse it would
not be, he seemed to wish to show, for nothing.
"You're not afraid of anything?"

"What should I be afraid of? You can't hurt
me unless you kill me by some violent means. That
I should indeed regard as a tremendous sell. I want
to live and I mean to live: I mean to have a good
time. I can't die of sickness, because I'm naturally
healthy, and the time for dying of old age won't
come round yet a while. I can't lose my wife, I shall
take too good care of her. I can't lose my money,
or much of it — I've fixed it so on purpose. So what
have I to be afraid of?"

"You're not afraid it may be rather a mistake
for such an infuriated modern to marry — well, such
an old-fashioned rococo product; a daughter, as one
may say, of the Crusaders, almost of the Patriarchs?"

Newman, who had been moving about as they
talked, stopped before his visitor. "Does that mean
you're worried for her?"

Valentin met his eyes. "I'm worried for everything."

"Ah, if that's all — !" And then: "Trust me —
because I'm modern and can compare all round —
to know where I stand!" With which, as from the
impulse to celebrate his happy certitude by a bonfire,
he turned to throw a couple of logs on the already
blazing hearth. Valentin watched a few moments
the quickened flame; after which, with his elbow
supported on the chimney and his head on his hand,

he gave an expressive sigh. "Got a headache?" Newman asked.

"*Je suis triste*," he answered with Gallic simplicity.

Newman stared at the remark as if it had been scrawled on a slate by a school-boy — a weakling whom he would n't wish, however, too harshly to snub. "You 've got a sentimental stomach-ache, eh? Have you caught it from the lady you told me the other night you adored and could n't marry?"

"Did I really speak of her?" Valentin asked as if a little struck. "I was afraid afterwards I had made some low allusion — for I don't as a general thing (and it 's a rare scruple I have!) drag in *ces dames* before Claire. But I was feeling the bitterness of life, as who should say, when I spoke; and -- yes, if you want to know — I 've my mouth full of it still. Why did you ever introduce me to that girl?"

"Oh, it 's Noémie, is it? Lord deliver us! You don't mean to say you 're lovesick about *her*?"

"Lovesick, no; it 's not a grand passion. But the cold-blooded little demon sticks in my thoughts; she has bitten me with those even little teeth of hers; I feel as if I might turn rabid and do something crazy in consequence. It 's very low, it 's disgustingly low. She 's the most mercenary little jade in Europe. Yet she really affects my peace of mind; she 's always running in my head. It 's a striking and a vile contrast to your noble and virtuous attachment. It 's rather pitiful that it should be the best I 'm able to do for myself at my present respectable age. I 'm a nice young man, eh, *en somme?* You can't warrant my future as you do your own."

"Drop the creature right here," said Newman; "don't go near her again, and your future will be all right. Come over to America and I'll get you a place in a bank."

"It's easy to say drop her" — Valentin spoke with a certain gravity in his lucidity. "You might as well drop a pretty panther who has every one of her claws in your flesh and who's in the act of biting your heart out. One *has* to keep up the acquaintance, if only to show one isn't afraid."

"You've better things to keep up, it seems to me, than such acquaintances. Remember too," Newman went on, "that I didn't want to introduce you to her; you insisted. I had a sort of creepy feeling about it even at the time."

"Oh, I no more reproach you with misleading my innocence than I reproach myself with practising on hers. She's really extraordinary. The way she has already spread her wings is amazing. I don't know when a woman has amused me more. But pardon me," he added in an instant; "she doesn't amuse *you*, at second-hand; your interest appears to flag just where that of many men would wake up. Let us talk of something else." Valentin introduced another topic, but he had within five minutes reverted by a bold transition to Mademoiselle Nioche and was throwing off pictures of her "home" and quoting specimens of her *mots*. These latter were very droll and, for a young woman who six months before had been dabbling in sacred subjects, remarkably profane. But at last, abruptly, he stopped, became thoughtful and for some time afterwards said nothing When he rose to go it was evident that his thoughts were still running on his rare young friend. "Yes," he wound up, "she's a beautiful little monster!"

XVI

THE next ten days were to be the happiest Newman had ever known. He saw Madame de Cintré every day, and never saw either her mother or the elder of his prospective brothers-in-law. The woman of his choice at last seemed to think it becoming to apologise for their never being present. "They're much taken up," she said, "with doing the honours of Paris to Lord Deepmere." Her gravity as she made this declaration was almost prodigious, and it even deepened as she added: "He's our seventh cousin, you know, and blood's thicker than water. And then he's so interesting!" And with this she strangely smiled.

He met young Madame de Bellegarde two or three times, always roaming about with graceful vagueness and as if in search of an unattainable ideal of diversion. She reminded him of some elegant painted phial, cracked and fragrantly exhaling; but he felt he owed indulgence to a lady who on her side owed submission to Urbain de Bellegarde. He pitied that nobleman's wife the more, also, that she was a silly, thirstily-smiling little brunette with a suggestion of the unregulated heart. The small Marquise sometimes looked at him with an intensity too marked not to be innocent, since vicious advances, he conceived, were usually much less direct. She apparently wanted to ask him something; he wondered what it might be. But he was shy of giving her an opportunity, because, if her communication bore upon the aridity of her matrimonial lot, he was at a loss to see how he could help her. He had a fancy, however, of her coming up to him some day and saying (after looking round behind her) with a little passionate hiss: "I know you detest my husband; let me have the pleasure of promising you that you're right. Pity a poor woman who's married to a clock-image in *papier-mâché!*" Possessing, at any rate, in default of a competent knowledge of the principles of etiquette, a very downright sense of the "meanness" of certain actions, it seemed to him to belong to his proper position to keep on his guard; he was not going to put it into the power of these people to say he had done in their house anything not absolutely straight. As it was, Madame de Bellegarde used to give him news of the dress she meant to wear at his wedding, and which had not yet, in her creative imagination, in spite of many interviews with the tailor, resolved itself into its composite totality. "I told you pale blue bows on the sleeves, at the elbow," she would say. "But to-day I don't see my blue bows at all. I don't know what has become of them. To-day I see pink — a tender sort of *cuisse de nymphe* pink. And then I pass through strange desolate phases in which neither blue nor pink says anything to me. And yet I must have the bows."

"Have them green or yellow," Newman sometimes suggested.

"*Malheureux!*" the little Marquise would then piercingly cry. "I hope you're not going to pretend to dress your wife. Claire's an angel, yes, but her bows, already, are -- well, quite of another world!"

Madame de Cintré was calmly content before society, but her lover had the felicity of feeling that before him, when society was absent, her sense of security overflowed. She said charming and tender things. "I take no pleasure in you. You never give me a chance to scold you, to correct you. I bargained for that; I expected to enjoy it. But you won't do anything wrong or queer or dreadful, and yet you won't even look as if you were trying to do right. You're easier than we are, you're easier than I am, and I quite see that you've reasons, of some sort, that are as good as ours. It's dull for me therefore," she smiled, "and it's rather disappointing, not to have anything to show you or to tell you or to teach you, anything that you don't seem already quite capable of knowing and doing and feeling. What's left of all the good one was going to do you? It's very stupid, there's no excitement for me; I might as well be marrying some one — well, some one *not* impossible."

"I'm afraid I'm as impossible as I know how to be, and that it's all the worst I can do in the time," Newman would say in answer to this. "Kindly make the best of *any* inconvenience." He assured her that he would never visit on her any sense of her own deficiencies; he would treat her at least as if she were perfectly satisfactory. "Oh," he then broke out, "if you only knew how exactly you're what I coveted! I'm beginning to understand why I wanted it; the having it makes all the difference that I expected.

Never was a man so pleased with his good fortune.
You've been holding your head for a week past just
as I wanted my wife to hold hers. You say just
the things I want her to say. You walk about the
room just as I want her to walk. You've just
the taste in dress I want her to have. In short you
come up to the mark, and, I can tell you, my mark
was high."

These assurances tended to make his friend more
grave. At last she said: "Depend on it I don't
come up to the mark at all; your mark's much too
high. I'm not all you suppose; I'm a much smaller
affair. She's a magnificent person, the person you
imagine. Pray how did she come to such perfection?"

"She was never anything *but* perfection," Newman replied.

"I really believe," his companion went on, "that
she's better than any fond flight of my own ambition.
Do you know that's a very handsome compliment?
Well, sir, I'll *make* her my ambition!"

Mrs. Tristram came to see her dear Claire after
Newman had announced his engagement, and she
observed to our hero the next day that his fortune
was simply absurd. "For the ridiculous part of it is
that you're evidently going to be as happy as if you
were marrying Miss Smith or Miss Brown. I call
it a brilliant match for you, but you get brilliancy
without paying any tax on it. Those things are usually
a compromise, but here you've everything, and
nothing crowds anything else out. You'll be brilliantly happy — with the rest of the brilliancy. I
consider really that I've done it for you, but it's

almost more than I can myself bear." Newman
thanked her for her pleasant encouraging way of
saying things; no woman could encourage or dis-
courage better. Tristram's way was different; he had
been taken by his wife to call on Madame de Cintré
and he gave an account of the expedition.

"You don't catch me risking a personal estimate
this time, I guess, do you? I put my foot in it for you
once. That's a jolly underhand thing to do, by the
way — coming round to sound a fellow on the woman you're going to marry. You deserve anything
you get. Then of course you rush and tell her, and
she takes care to make it pleasant for the spiteful
wretch the first time he calls. I'll do you the justice
to say, however, that you don't seem to have told
your present friend — or if you did she let me down
easy. She was very nice; she was tremendously
polite. She and Lizzie sat on the sofa pressing each
other's hands and calling each other *chère belle*, and
Madame de Cintré sent me every third word a magnificent smile, as if to give me to understand that
I too was a beauty and a darling. She made up for
past neglect, I assure you; she was very pleasant
and sociable. Only in an evil hour it came into her
head to say that she must present us to her mother
— her mother wished to know any good friends of
yours. I did n't want to know her mother, and I was
on the point of telling Lizzie to go in alone and let
me wait for her outside. But Lizzie, with her usual
infernal ingenuity, guessed my purpose and looked
me into obedience. So they marched off arm-in-arm
and I followed as I could. We found the old lady

in her armchair twiddling her aristocratic thumbs. She eyed Lizzie hard, from head to foot; but at that game Lizzie, to do her justice, was a match for her. My wife told her we were great friends of Mr. Newman. The Marquise stared a moment and then said: 'Oh, Mr. Newman? My daughter has made up her mind to marry a Mr. Newman.' Then Madame de Cintré began to fondle Lizzie again and said it was this dear lady who had had the idea and brought them together. 'Oh, it's you I have to thank for my American son-in-law?' Madame de Bellegarde said to Mrs. Tristram. 'It was a very clever thought of yours. Be sure of my high appreciation.' With which she began to look at me too, and presently said: 'Pray, are you engaged in some species of manufacture?' I wanted to say that I manufactured broomsticks for old witches to ride on, but Lizzie got in ahead of me. 'My husband, madame la Marquise, belongs to that unfortunate class of persons who have no profession and no occupation, and who thereby do very little good in the world.' To get her poke at the old woman she didn't care where she shoved *me*. 'Dear me,' said the Marquise, 'we all have our duties.' 'I'm sorry mine compel me to take leave of you,' said Lizzie. And we bundled out again. But you have a mother-in-law in all the force of the time-honoured term."

"Oh," Newman made answer, "my mother-in-law desires nothing better than to let me alone!"

Betimes, on the evening of the twenty-seventh, he went to Madame de Bellegarde's ball. The old house in the Rue de l'Université shone strangely in his eyes

In the circle of light projected from the outer gate
a detachment of the populace stood watching the carriages roll in; the court was illumined with flaring
torches and the portico draped and carpeted. When
Newman arrived there were but few persons present.
The Marquise and her two daughters were on the top
landing of the staircase, where the ancient marble
nymph peeped out from a bower of plants. Madame
de Bellegarde, in purple and pearls and fine laces,
resembled some historic figure painted by Vandyke;
she made her daughter, in comparative vaguenesses
of white, splendid and pale, seem, for his joy of
possession, infinitely modern and near. His hostess
greeted him with a fine hard urbanity and, looking
round, called to several of the persons standing at
hand. They were elderly gentlemen with faces as
marked and featured and filled-in, for some science
of social topography, as, to Newman's whimsical
sense, any of the little towered and battered old
towns, on high eminences, that his tour of several
countries during the previous summer had shown
him; they were adorned with strange insignia. cor-
dons and ribbons and orders, as if the old cities were
flying flags and streamers and hanging out shields
for a celebration, and they approached with measured alertness while the Marquise presented them
the good friend of the family who was to marry her
daughter. The good friend heard a confused enumeration of titles and names that matched, to his
fancy, the rest of the paraphernalia; the gentlemen
bowed and smiled and murmured without reserve,
and he indulged in a series of impartial hand-shakes.

accompanied in each case by a "Very happy to meet you, sir." He looked at Madame de Cintré, but her attention was absent. If his personal self-consciousness had been of a nature to make him constantly refer to her as to the critic before whom in company he played his part, he might have found it a flattering proof of her confidence that he never caught her eyes resting on him. It is a reflexion he did n't make, but we may nevertheless risk it, that in spite of this circumstance she probably saw every movement of his little finger. The Marquise Urbain was wondrously dressed in crimson crape bestrewn with huge silver moons — full discs and fine crescents, half the features of the firmament.

"You don't say anything about my *toilette*," she impatiently observed to him.

"Well, I feel as if I were looking at you through a telescope. You put me in mind of some lurid comet, something grand and wild."

"Ah, if I'm grand and wild I match the occasion! But I'm not a heavenly body."

"I never saw the sky at midnight that particular shade of crimson," Newman said.

"That's just my originality: any fool could have chosen blue. My sister-in-law would have chosen a lovely shade of that colour, with a dozen little delicate moons. But I think crimson much more amusing. And I give my idea, which is moonshine."

"Moonshine and bloodshed," said Newman.

"A murder by moonlight," the young woman laughed. "What a delicious idea for a toilet! To make it complete there's a dagger of diamonds, you

see, stuck into my hair. But here comes Lord Deepmere," she added in a moment; "I must find out
what he thinks of it." Lord Deepmere came up very
red in the face and very light, apparently, at heart;
at once very much amused and very little committed.
"My Lord Deepmere can't decide which he prefers,
my sister-in-law or me," Madame Urbain went on.
"He likes Claire because she's his cousin, and me
because I'm not. But he has no right to make love
to Claire, whereas I'm perfectly *disponible*. It's very
wrong to make love to a woman who's engaged, but
it's very wrong *not* to make love to a woman who's
married."

"Oh, it's very jolly making love to married women," the young man said, "because they can't ask
you to marry them."

"Is that what the others do — the spinsters?"
Newman enquired.

"Oh dear, yes — in England all the girls ask a
fellow to marry them."

"And a fellow brutally refuses," Madame Urbain
commented.

"Why, really, you know, a fellow can't marry any
girl that asks him," said his lordship.

"Your cousin won't ask you. She's going to
marry Mr. Newman."

"Oh, that's a very different thing!" Lord Deepmere readily agreed.

"You'd have accepted *her*, I suppose. That makes
me hope that, after all, you prefer me."

"Oh, when things are nice I never prefer one to
the other," said the young man. "I take them all."

"Ah, what a horror! I won't be taken in that way, especially as a 'thing,'" cried his interlocutress. "Mr. Newman's much better; he knows how to choose. Oh, he chooses as if he were threading a needle. He prefers the Comtesse to any rival attraction, however brilliant."

"Well, you can't help my being her cousin," said Lord Deepmere to Newman with candid hilarity.

"Oh no, I can't help that," Newman laughed back. "Neither can she!"

"And you can't help my dancing with her," said Lord Deepmere with sturdy simplicity.

"I could prevent that only by dancing with her myself," Newman returned. "But unfortunately I don't know how to dance."

"Oh, you may dance without knowing how; may you not, milord?" Madame Urbain asked. But to this Lord Deepmere replied that a fellow ought to know how to dance if he did n't want to make an ass of himself; and at this same moment the Marquis joined the group, slow-stepping and with his hands behind him.

"This is a very splendid entertainment," Newman cheerfully observed. "The old house looks very pleasant and bright."

"If you 're pleased we 're content." And the Marquis lifted his shoulders and bent them forward.

"Oh, I suspect every one 's pleased," said Newman. "How can they help being pleased when the first thing they see as they come in is your sister standing there as beautiful as an angel of light and of charity?"

"Yes, she's very beautiful," the Marquis a little distantly admitted. "But that's not so great a source of satisfaction to other people, naturally, as to you."

"Well, I *am* satisfied and suited, Marquis — there's no doubt but what I *am*," said Newman with his protracted enunciation. "And now tell me," he added, taking in more of the scene, "who some of these pleasant folks are."

M. de Bellegarde looked about him in silence, with his head bent and his hand raised to his lower lip, which he slowly rubbed. A stream of people had been pouring into the salon in which Newman stood with his host, the rooms were filling up and the place, all light and colour and fine resonance, looked rich and congressional. It borrowed its splendour largely from the shining shoulders and profuse jewels of the women, and from the rest of their festal array. There were uniforms, but not many, as Madame de Bellegarde's door was inexorably closed against the mere myrmidons of the upstart power which then flourished on the soil of France, and the great company of smiling and chattering faces was not, as to line and feature, a collection of gold or silver medals. It was a pity for our friend, nevertheless, that he had not been a physiognomist, for these mobile masks, much more a matter of wax than of bronze, were the picture of a world and the vivid translation, as might have seemed to him, of a text that had had otherwise its obscurities. If the occasion had been different they would hardly have pleased him; he would have found in the women too little beauty and in the men too many smirks; but he was now in a humour to receive none but fair impressions, and it sufficed him to note that every one was charged with some vivacity or some solemnity and to feel that the whole great sum of character and confidence was part of his credit. "I'll present you to some people," said M. de Bellegarde after a while. "I'll make a point of it in fact. You'll allow me?—if I may exercise my judgement."

"Oh, I'll shake hands with any one you want," Newman returned. "Your mother just introduced me to half a dozen old gentlemen. Take care you don't pick out the same parties again."

"Who are the gentlemen to whom my mother presented you?"

"Upon my word I forget them," Newman had to confess. "I'm afraid I've got them rather mixed; and don't all Chinamen—even great mandarins'—look very much the same to Occidentals?"

"I suspect they've not forgotten you," said the Marquis; and he began to walk through the rooms. Newman, to keep near him in the crowd, took his arm; after which, for some time, the Marquis walked straight on in silence. At last, reaching the further end of the apartments, Newman found himself in the presence of a lady of monstrous proportions seated in a very capacious armchair and with several persons standing in a semicircle round her. This little group had divided as the Marquis came up, and he stepped forward and stood for an instant silent and obsequious, his flattened hat raised to his lips as Newman had seen gentlemen stand in churches as soon as they entered their pews. The lady indeed bore a very fair likeness to a revered effigy in some idolatrous shrine. She was monumentally stout and imperturbably serene. Her aspect was to Newman almost formidable; he had a troubled consciousness of a triple chin, a pair of eyes that twinkled in her face like a pair of polished pin-heads in a cushion, a vast expanse of uncovered bosom, a nodding and twinkling tiara of plumes and gems, an immense circumference of satin petticoat. With her little circle of beholders this remarkable woman reminded him of the Fat Lady at a fair. She fixed her small unwinking gaze at the newcomers.

"Dear Duchess," said the Marquis, "let me present you our good friend Mr. Newman, of whom you've heard us speak. Wishing to make Mr. Newman known to those who are dear to us, I couldn't possibly fail to begin with you."

"Charmed, dear friend; charmed, monsieur," said the Duchess in a voice which, though small and shrill, was not disagreeable, while Newman performed with all his length his liberal obeisance. He always made his bow, as he wrote his name, very distinctly. "I came on purpose to see monsieur. I hope he appreciates the compliment. You've only to look at me to do so, sir," she continued, sweeping her person with a much-encompassing glance. Newman hardly knew what to say, though it seemed that to a duchess who joked about her corpulence one might say almost anything. On hearing she had come on purpose to see this object of interest the gentlemen who surrounded her turned a little and looked at him with grave, with almost overdone consideration. The Marquis, with supernatural gravity, mentioned to him the name of each, while the gentleman who bore it bowed; and these pronouncements again affected Newman as some enumeration of the titles of books, of the performers on playbills, of the items of indexes. "I wanted extremely to see you," the Duchess went on. "*C'est positif.* In the first place I'm very fond of the person you're going to marry; she's the most charming creature in France. Mind you treat her well or you'll have news of me. But *vous avez l'air bien honnête,* and I'm told you're very remarkable. I've heard all sorts of extraordinary things about you. *Voyons.* are they true?"

"I don't know what you can have heard," Newman promptly pleaded.

"Oh, you've had your *légende.* You've had a career the most chequered, the most *bizarre.* What's that about your having founded a city some ten years ago in the great West, a city which contains to-day half a million of inhabitants? Isn't it half a million, messieurs? You're exclusive proprietor of the wonderful place and are consequently fabulously rich, and you'd be richer still if you didn't grant lands and houses free of rent to all newcomers who'll pledge themselves never to smoke cigars. At this game, in three years, we're told, you're going to become President of all the Americas."

The Duchess recited this quaint fable with a smooth self-possession which gave it to Newman's ear the sound of an amusing passage in a play interpreted by a veteran comic actress. Before she had ceased speaking he had relieved himself, applausively, by laughter as frank as clapping or stamping. "Dear Duchess, dear Duchess!" the Marquis began to murmur soothingly. Two or three persons came to the door of the room to see who was laughing at the Duchess. But the lady continued with the soft, serene assurance of a person who, as a great lady, was certain of being listened to, and, as a garrulous woman, was independent of the pulse of her auditors. "But I know you're very remarkable. You must be, to have endeared yourself to our good Urbain and to his admirable mother. They don't scatter their approval about. They're very exacting. I myself am not very sure at this hour of really enjoying their esteem — eh, Marquis? But your real triumph, cher monsieur, is in pleasing the Comtesse; she's as difficult as a princess in a fairy-tale. Your success is a miracle. What's your secret? I don't ask you to reveal it before all these gentlemen, but you must come and see me some day and show me how you proceed."

"The secret is with Madame de Cintré," Newman found a face to answer. "You must ask her for it. It consists in her having a great deal of charity."

"Very pretty!" the Duchess pronounced. "That, to begin with, is a nice specimen of your system. What, Marquis, are you already taking monsieur away?"

"I've a duty to perform, dear friend," said Urbain, pointing to the other groups.

"Ah, for you I know what that means! Well, I've seen monsieur; that's what I wanted. He can't

persuade me he has n't something wonder-working
Au revoir, monsieur."

As Newman passed on with his host he asked who
the Duchess might be. "The greatest lady in France!"
the Marquis hereupon reservedly replied. He then
presented his prospective brother-in-law to some
twenty other persons of both sexes, selected apparently for some recognised value of name or fame or
attitude. In some cases their honours were written in
a good round hand on the countenance of the wearer;
in others Newman was thankful for such help as his
companion's impressively brief intimation, measured
as to his scant capacity, contributed to the discovery
of them. There were large, heavy imperturbable
gentlemen and small insinuating extravagant ones;
there were ugly ladies in yellow lace and quaint
jewels, and pretty ladies with reaches of white de-
nudation that even their wealth of precious stones
scarce availed to overtake. Every one gave Newman
extreme attention, every one lighted up for him re-
gardless, as he would have said, of expense, every one
was enchanted to make his acquaintance, every
one looked at him with that fraudulent intensity of
good society which puts out its bountiful hand but
keeps the fingers closed over the coin. If the Marquis
was going about as a bear-leader, if the fiction of
Beauty and the Beast was supposed to show thus its
companion-piece, the general impression appeared
that the bear was a very fair imitation of humanity.
Newman found his reception in the charmed circle
very handsome — he liked, handsomely, himself, not
to say less than that for it. It was handsome to be

treated with so much explicit politeness; it was handsome to meet civilities as pointed as witticisms, and to hear them so syllabled and articulated that they suggested handfuls of crisp counted notes pushed over by a banker's clerk; it was handsome of clever Frenchwomen — they all seemed clever — to turn their backs to their partners for a good look at the slightly gaunt outsider whom Claire de Cintré was to marry, and then shine on the subject as if they quite understood. At last as he turned away from a battery of vivid grimaces and other amenities, Newman caught the eye of the Marquis fixed on him inscrutably, and thereupon, for a single instant, he checked himself. "Am I behaving like a blamed fool?" he wondered. "Am I stepping about like a terrier on his hind legs?" At this moment he perceived Mrs. Tristram at the other side of the room and waved his hand in farewell to M. de Bellegarde in order to make his way toward her.

"Am I holding my head too high and opening my mouth too wide?" he demanded. "Do I look as if they were saying 'Catch' and I were snapping down what they throw me and licking my lips?"

"You look like all very successful men — fatuous without knowing it. Women triumph with more tact, just as they suffer with more grace. Therefore it's the usual thing for such situations — neither better nor worse. I've been watching you for the last ten minutes, and I've been watching M. de Bellegarde. He doesn't like what he has to do."

"The more credit to him for putting it through," Newman returned. "But I shall be generous. I

shan't trouble him any more. Only I'm very happy.
I can't stand still here. Please take my arm and
we'll go for a walk."

He led Mrs. Tristram from one room to another,
where, scattering wide glances and soft, sharp comments, she reminded him of the pausing wayfarer
who studies the contents of the confectioner's window, with platonic discriminations, through a firm
plate of glass. But he made vague answers; he
scarcely heard her; his thoughts were elsewhere.
They were lost in the vastness of this attested truth
of his having come out where he wanted. His momentary consciousness of perhaps too broad a grin
passed away, and he felt, the next thing, almost
solemnly quiet. Yes, he had "got there," and now
it was, all-powerfully, to stay. These prodigies of
gain were in a general way familiar to him, but the
sense of what he had "made" by an anxious operation had never been so deep and sweet. The lights,
the flowers, the music, the "associations," vague
and confused to him, yet hovering like some odour
of dried spices, something far-away and, as he had
hinted to the Marquis, Mongolian; the splendid
women, the splendid jewels, the strangeness even of
the universal sense of a tongue that seemed the
language of society as Italian was the language of
opera: these things were all a gage of his having
worked, from the old first years, under some better
star than he knew. Yet if he showed again and again
so many of his fine strong teeth, it was not tickled
vanity that pulled the exhibition-string: he had no
wish to be pointed at with the finger or to be con-

sidered by these people for himself. If he could have looked down at the scene invisibly, as from a hole in the roof, he would have enjoyed it quite as much. It would have spoken to him of his energy and prosperity and deepened that view of his effective "handling" of life to which, sooner or later, he made all experience contribute. Just now the cup seemed full.

"It's all very fine and very funny, I mean very special and quite thrilling and almost interesting," said Mrs. Tristram while they circulated. "I've seen nothing objectionable except my husband leaning against that adorably faded strawberry damask of the other room and talking to an individual whom I suppose he takes for a prince, but whom I more than suspect to be the functionary taking care of the lamps. Do you think you could separate them? Do knock over a lamp!"

I doubt whether Newman, who saw no harm in Tristram's conversing with an ingenious mechanic, would have complied with this request; but at this moment Valentin de Bellegarde drew near. Newman, some weeks previously, had presented Madame de Cintré's youngest brother to Mrs. Tristram, for whose rather shy and subtle merit the young man promptly professed an intelligent relish and to whom he had paid several visits.

"Did you ever read," she asked, "Keats's 'Belle Dame sans Merci'? You remind me of the hero of the ballad:

> "'Oh, what can ail thee, knight-at-arms,
> Alone and palely loitering?'"

"If I'm alone it's because I've been deprived of your society," Valentin returned. "Besides, it's good manners for no man except Newman to look happy. This is all to his address. It's not for you and me to go before the curtain."

"You prophesied to me last spring," said Newman to Mrs. Tristram, "that six months from that time I should get into a tearing rage. It seems to me the time's up, and yet the nearest I can now come to doing anything rough is to offer you a café glacé."

"I promised you we should do things grandly," Valentin observed. "I don't allude to the cafés glacés. But every one's here, and my sister told me just now that Urbain has been adorable."

"He's a real nice man — all the way through. If I don't look out," Newman went on — "or if *he* does n't — I shall begin to love him as a brother. That reminds me that I ought to go and say something enthusiastic to your mother."

"Let it be something very enthusiastic indeed," said Valentin. "It may be the last time you'll feel so much in the vein."

Newman walked away almost disposed to clasp Madame de Bellegarde round the waist. He passed through several rooms and at last found her in the first saloon, seated on a sofa with her young kinsman Lord Deepmere beside her. The young man unmistakeably felt the strain; his hands were thrust into his pockets and his eyes fixed on the toes of his shoes, his feet being thrust out in front of him. His hostess appeared to have been addressing him with some intensity and to be now waiting for an answer to what she had said or for some other sign of the effect of her words. Her hands were folded in her lap and she considered his lordship's simple physiognomy as she might have studied some brief but baffling sentence in an obscure text. He looked up as Newman approached, met his eyes and changed colour. On which the latter said: "I'm afraid I disturb an interesting interview."

Madame de Bellegarde rose, and, her companion rising at the same time, she put her hand into his arm. She answered nothing for an instant, and then as he remained silent brought out with a smile: "It would be amiable for Lord Deepmere to say it was very interesting."

"Oh, I'm not amiable!" cried his lordship. "But it was all right."

"Madame de Bellegarde was giving you some good advice, eh?" Newman asked: "preaching you, with her high authority, the way you should go? In your place I'd go it then — blind!"

"I was giving him some excellent advice," said the Marquise, fixing her fresh cold eyes on our hero. "It's for him to take it."

"Take it, sir, take it!" Newman exclaimed. "Any advice she gives you to-night must be good; for to-night, Marquise, you must speak from a cheerful, comfortable spirit, and that makes for good ideas. You see everything going on so brightly and successfully round you. Your party's magnificent; it was a very happy thought. It's a much better show than that feeble effort of mine would have been."

"If you're pleased I'm satisfied," she answered

with rare accommodation. "My desire was to please you."

"Do you want to please me a little more then?" Newman went on. "Just let Lord Deepmere digest your wisdom and take care of himself a little; and then take my arm and walk through the rooms."

"My desire was to please you," the Marquise rather stiffly repeated; and as she liberated her companion our friend wondered at her docility. "If this young man is wise," she added, "he'll go and find my daughter and ask her to dance."

"I've been endorsing your advice," said Newman, bending over her and laughing; "I suppose therefore I must let him cut in where I can neither lead nor follow."

Lord Deepmere wiped his forehead and departed, and Madame de Bellegarde took Newman's arm. "Yes, it has been a real friendly, hearty, jolly idea," he declared as they proceeded on their circuit. "Every one seems to know every one and to be glad to see every one. The Marquis has made me acquainted with ever so many people, and I feel quite like one of the family. It's an occasion," Newman continued, wanting still more to express appreciation without an afterthought, "that I shall always remember, and remember very pleasantly."

"I think it's an occasion that we shall none of us ever forget," said the Marquise with her pure, neat enunciation.

People made way for her as she passed, others turned round and looked at her, and she received a great many greetings and pressings of the hand, all of which she accepted with a smooth good grace. But though she smiled on every one she said nothing till she reached the last of the rooms, where she found her elder son. Then "This is enough, sir," she observed with her dignity of distinctness, turning at the same time from Newman to Urbain. He put out both his hands and took both hers, drawing her to a seat with an air of the tenderest veneration. It appeared to attest between them the need of more intimate communion, and Newman discreetly retired. He moved through the rooms for some time longer, circulating freely, overtopping most people by his great height, renewing acquaintance with some of the groups to which the Marquis had presented him, and expending generally the surplus of his equanimity. He continued to find it all a regular celebration, but even the Fourth of July of his childhood used to have an end, and the revelry on this occasion began to deepen to a close. The music was sounding its last strains and people about to take their leave were looking for their hostess. There seemed to be some difficulty in finding her, and he caught a report that she had left the ball in an access of fatigue or of faintness. "She has succumbed to the emotions of the evening," he heard a voluble lady say. "Poor dear Marquise; I can imagine all they may have been for her!"

But he learned immediately afterwards that she had recovered herself and was seated in an armchair near the doorway, receiving final honours from members of her own sex who insisted upon her not rising. He himself had set out in quest of Madame de Cintré, whom he had seen move past him many times in the rapid circles of a waltz, but with whom, also, conforming to her explicit instructions, he had exchanged no word since the beginning of the evening. The whole house having been thrown open the apartments of the rez-de-chaussée were also accessible, though a smaller number of persons had gathered there. Newman wandered through them, observing a few scattered couples to whom this comparative seclusion appeared grateful, and reached a small conservatory which opened into the garden. The end of the conservatory was formed by a clear sheet of glass, unmasked by plants and admitting the winter starlight so directly that a person standing there would seem to have passed into the open air. Two persons stood there now, a lady and a gentleman; the lady Newman, from within the room and although she had turned her back to it, immediately recognised as his friend. He hesitated as to whether he should advance, but as he did so she looked round, feeling apparently that he was there. She rested her eyes on him a moment and then turned again to her companion.

"It's almost a pity not to tell Mr. Newman," she said with restraint, but in a tone Newman could hear.

"Tell him if you like!" the gentleman answered in the voice of Lord Deepmere.

"Oh, tell me by all means!" — and our hero came straight forward.

Lord Deepmere, he observed, was very red in the face and had twisted his gloves into as tight a cord as if squeezing them dry. These, presumably, were tokens of violent emotion, and it struck him that the traces of a corresponding agitation were visible in Madame de Cintré. The two had been talking with extreme animation. "What I should tell you is only to milord's credit," said Madame de Cintré, however, with a clear enough smile.

"It would n't please him any better for that!" cried milord with his awkward laugh.

"Come; what's the mystery?" Newman demanded. "Clear it up. I don't like what I don't understand."

"We must have some things we don't like, and go without some we do," said the ruddy young nobleman, still almost unnaturally exhilarated.

"It's to Lord Deepmere's credit, but it's not to every one's," Madame de Cintré imperfectly explained. "So I shall say nothing about it. You may be sure," she added; and she put out her hand to the Englishman, who took it with more force than grace. "And now go and dance hard!" she said.

"Oh yes, I feel awfully like dancing hard! I shall go and drink champagne — as hard as I can!" And he walked away with a gloomy guffaw.

"What has happened between you?" Newman asked.

"I can't tell you — now," she said. "Nothing that need make you unhappy."

"Has that weak brother been trying to make love to you?"

She hesitated, then uttered a grave "No! — He's a perfectly honest young man."

"But you've been somehow upset and are still worried. Something's the matter."

"Nothing, I repeat, that need make you unhappy. I've completely recovered my balance — if I had lost it: which I had n't! Some day I'll tell you what it was; not now. I can't now," she insisted.

"Well, I confess," Newman returned, "I don't want to hear anything out of key. I'm satisfied with everything — most of all with you. I've seen all the ladies and talked with a great many of them; but I'm really satisfied with you." The charming woman covered him for a moment with her bright mildness, and then turned her eyes away into the starry night. So they stood silent a moment, side by side. "Say you're really satisfied with *me*," Newman said.

He had to wait a moment for the answer; but it came at last, low yet distinct. "I'm very very happy."

It was presently followed by a few words from another source which made them both turn round. "I'm sadly afraid Madame la Comtesse will take a chill. I've ventured to bring a shawl." Mrs. Bread stood there softly solicitous, holding a white drapery in her hand.

"Thank you, *ma bonne*," said Madame de Cintré; "the sight of those cold stars gives one a sense of frost. I won't take your shawl, but we'll go back into the house."

She passed back and Newman followed her, Mrs. Bread standing respectfully aside to make way for them. Newman paused an instant before the old woman and she glanced up at him with a silent greeting. "Oh yes," he said, "you must come and live with us."

"Well then, sir, if you will," she answered, "you've not seen the last of me

XVII

NEWMAN was fond of music, and went often to the opera, where, a couple of evenings after Madame de Bellegarde's ball, he sat listening to "Don Giovanni"; having in honour of this work, which he had never yet seen represented, come to occupy his orchestra-chair before the rising of the curtain. Frequently he took a large box and invited a group of his compatriots; this was a mode of recreation to which he was much addicted. He liked making up parties of his friends and conducting them to the theatre or taking them to drive on mail-coaches and dine at restaurants renowned, by what he could a trifle artlessly ascertain, for special and incomparable dishes. He liked doing things that involved his paying for people; the vulgar truth is he enjoyed "treating" them. This was not because he was what is called purse-proud; handling money in public was, on the contrary, positively disagreeable to him; he had a sort of personal modesty about it akin to what he would have felt about making a toilet before spectators. But just as it was a gratification to him to be nobly dressed, just so it was a private satisfaction (for he kept the full flavour of it quite delicately to himself) to see people occupied and amused at his pecuniary expense and by his profuse interposition. To set a large body of them in motion and transport them to a distance, to have special conveyances, to charter railway-carriages

334

and steamboats, harmonised with his relish for bold
processes and made hospitality the potent thing it
should ideally be. A few evenings before the occasion of which I speak he had invited several ladies
and gentlemen to the opera to listen to the young and
wondrous Adelina Patti — a party which included
Miss Dora Finch. It befell, however, that Miss Dora
Finch, sitting near him in the box, discoursed brilliantly, not only during the entr'actes but during
many of the finest portions of the performance, so
that he had really come away with an irritated sense
that the new rare diva had a thin, shrill voice and
that her roulades resembled giggles. After this he
promised himself to go for a while to the opera alone.

When the curtain had fallen on the first act of
"Don Giovanni" he turned round in his place to
observe the audience. Presently, in one of the boxes,
he perceived Urbain de Bellegarde and his wife.
The little Marquise swept the house very busily with
a glass, and Newman, supposing she saw him, determined to go and bid her good-evening. M. de Bellegarde leaned against a column, motionless, looking
straight in front of him, one hand in the breast of his
white waistcoat and the other resting his hat on his
thigh. Newman was about to leave his place when
he noticed in that obscure region devoted to the small
boxes which in French are called, not inaptly, bath-
tubs, from their promoting at least immersion through
the action of the pores, a face which even the dim
light and the distance could not make wholly indistinct. It was the face of a young and pretty woman,
crowned with an arrangement of pink roses and dia-

monds. This person looked round the house while her fan moved with practised grace; when she lowered it Newman perceived a pair of plump white shoulders and the edge of a rose-coloured dress. Beside her, very close to the shoulders and talking, apparently with an earnestness which it suited her scantly to heed, sat a young man with a red face and a very low shirt-collar. A moment's consideration left Newman no doubts; the pretty young woman was Noémie Nioche. He looked hard into the depths of the box, thinking her father might perhaps be in attendance, but from what he could see the young man's eloquence had no other auditor. Newman at last made his way out, and in doing so passed beneath the *baignoire* of his former client. She saw him as he approached, giving him a nod and smile which seemed meant as a hint that her enviable rise in the world had not made her inhuman. He passed into the *foyer* and walked through it, but suddenly to pause before a gentleman seated on one of the divans. The gentleman's elbows were on his knees; he leaned forward and stared at the pavement, lost apparently in meditations of a gloomy cast. But in spite of his bent head Newman recognised him and in a moment had sat down beside him. Then the gentleman looked up and displayed the expressive countenance of Valentin de Bellegarde. "What in the world are you thinking of so hard?"

"A subject that requires hard thinking to do it justice," Valentin promptly replied. "My immeasurable idiocy."

"What's the matter now?"

"The matter now is that. as I'm a madman with lucid intervals, I'm having one of them now. But I came within an ace of entertaining a sentiment —!"

"For the young lady below stairs, in a *baignoire*, in a pink dress?"

"Did you notice what a rare kind of pink it was?" Valentin enquired by way of answer. "It makes her look as white as new milk."

Newman had a stare of some wonderment, and then: "Is *she* what you call *crème de la crème?*" But as Valentin's face pronounced this a witticism below the Parisian standard he went on: "You've stopped then, at any rate, going to see her?"

"Oh bless you, no. Why should I stop? I've changed, but she has n't," said Valentin. "The more I see her the more sure I am — well, that I see her right. She has awfully pretty arms, and several other things, but she's not really a bit *gentille*. The other day she had the bad taste to begin to abuse her father, to his face, in my presence. I should n't have expected it of her; it was a disappointment. Heigho!"

"Why, she cares no more for her father than for her door-mat," Newman declared. "I discovered that the first time I saw her."

"Oh, that's another affair; she may think of the poor old beggar what she pleases. But it was base in her to call him bad names; it spoiled my reckoning and quite threw me off. It was about a frilled petticoat that he was to have fetched from the washerwoman's; he appeared to have forgotten the frilled petticoat. She almost boxed his ears. He stood there staring at her with his little blank eyes and smoothing his old hat with his coat-tail. At last he turned round and went out without a word. Then I told her it was in very bad taste to speak so even to an unnatural father. She said she should be so thankful to me if I would mention it to her whenever her taste was at fault; she had immense confidence in mine. I told her I could n't have the inconvenience of forming her manners; I had had an idea they were already formed, after the best models. She had quite put me out. But I shall get over it," said Valentin gaily.

"Oh, time 's a great consoler!" Newman answered with humorous sobriety. He was silent a moment and then added in another tone: "I wish you 'd think of what I said to you the other day. Come over to America with us and I 'll put you in the way of doing some business. You 've got a very fine mind if you 'd only give it a chance."

Valentin made a genial grimace. "My mind 's much obliged to you: you make it feel finer than ever. Would the 'chance' be that place in a bank ?"

"There are several places, but I suppose you 'd consider the bank the most aristocratic."

Valentin burst into a laugh. "My dear fellow, at night all cats are grey! When one falls from such a height there are no degrees!"

Newman answered nothing for a minute. Then, "I think you 'll find there are degrees in success," he said with his most exemplary mild distinctness.

Valentin had leaned forward again with his elbows on his knees and was scratching the pavement with his stick. At last, looking up, "Do you really think I ought to do something ?" he asked.

Newman laid his hand on his companion's arm and eyed him a moment through measuring lids "Try it and see. I 'm not sure you 're not too bright to live; but why not find out how bright a man can *afford* to be?"

"Do you really think I can make some money? Once when I was a small boy I found a silver piece under a door-mat. I should like awfully to see how it feels to find a gold one."

"Well, do what I tell you and you shall find salvation," said Newman. "Think of it well." And he looked at his watch and prepared to resume his way to Madame de Bellegarde's box.

"Upon my honour I *will* think of it," Valentin returned. "I 'll go and listen to Mozart another half-hour — I can always think better to music — and profoundly meditate on it."

The Marquis was with his wife when Newman entered their box; he was as remotely bland as usual, but the great demonstration in which he had lately played his part appeared to have been a drawbridge lowered and lifted again. Newman was once more outside the castle and its master perched on the battlements. "What do you think of the opera?" our hero none the less artlessly demanded. "What do you think of the cool old Don?"

"He does n't remain so very cool," the Marquis amusedly replied. "But we all know what Mozart is; our impressions don't date from this evening. Mozart is youth, freshness, brilliancy, facility — facility perhaps a little too unbroken. But the execution is here and there deplorably rough."

"I 'm very curious to see how it ends," Newman less critically continued.

"You speak as if it were a feuilleton in the *Figaro*," observed the Marquis. "You 've surely seen the opera before?"

"Never — I 'm sure I should have remembered it. Donna Elvira reminds me of Madame de Cintré; I don't mean in her situation, but in her lovely tone."

"It 's a very nice distinction," the Marquis neatly conceded. "There 's no possibility, I imagine, of my sister's being forsaken."

"That 's right, sir," Newman said. "But what becomes of the Don?"

"The Devil comes down — or comes up — and carries him off," Madame Urbain replied. "I suppose Zerlina reminds you of me."

"I 'll go to the *foyer* for a few moments," said her husband, "and give you a chance to say that I 'm like the Commander — the man of stone." With which he passed out of the box.

The little Marquise stared an instant at the velvet ledge of the balcony and then murmured: "Not a man of stone, a man of wood!" Newman had taken her husband's empty chair; she made no protest, but turned suddenly and laid her closed fan on his arm. "I 'm very glad you came in; I want to ask you a favour. I wanted to do so on Thursday, at my mother-in-law's ball, but you would give me no chance. You were in such very good spirits that I thought you might grant my little prayer then; not that you look particularly doleful now. It 's something you must promise me; now 's the time to take

you; after you 're married you 'll be good for nothing.
Allons, promise!"

"I never sign a paper without reading it first,"
said Newman. "Show me your document."

"No, you must sign with your eyes shut; I 'll hold
your hand. *Voyons*, before you put your head into
the noose you ought to be thankful for me giving
you a chance to do something amusing."

"If it 's so amusing," said Newman, "it will be in
even better season after I 'm married."

"In other words," she cried, "you 'll not do it at
all, for then you 'll be afraid of your wife."

"Oh, if the thing violates the moral law — pardon
my strong language! — I won't go into it. If it
does n't I shall be quite as ready for it after my
marriage."

"Oh, you people, with your moral law — I wonder
that with such big words in your mouth you don't all
die of choking!" Madame Urbain declared. "You
talk like a treatise on logic, and English logic into
the bargain. Promise then after you 're married," she
went on. "After all, I shall enjoy keeping you to it."

"Well, then after I 'm married," said Newman
serenely.

She hesitated a moment, looking at him, and he
wondered what was coming. "I suppose you know
what my life is," she presently said. "I 've no pleasure, I see nothing, I do nothing. I live in Paris as
I might live at Poitiers. My mother-in-law calls
me — what is the pretty word? — a gadabout;
accuses me of going to unheard-of places and thinks
it ought to be joy enough for me to sit at home and

count over **my** ancestors on my fingers. But why should I bother about my ancestors? I 'm sure they never bothered about me. I don't propose to live with a green shade over my eyes; I hold that the only thing you can do with things arranged in a row before you is see them. My husband, you know, has principles, and the first on the list is that the Tuileries are dreadfully vulgar. If the Tuileries are vulgar his principles are imbecile. If I chose I might have principles quite as well as he. If they grew on one's family tree I should only have to give mine a shake to bring down a shower of the finest. At any rate I prefer clever Bonapartes to stupid Bourbons."

"Oh, I see; you want to go to court," said Newman, fantastically wondering if she might n't wish him to smooth her way to the imperial halls through some ingenious use of the American Legation.

The Marquise gave a little sharp laugh. "You 're a thousand miles away. I 'll take care of the Tuileries myself; the day I decide to go they 'll be glad enough to have me. Sooner or later I shall dance in an imperial quadrille. I know what you 're going to say: 'How will you dare?' But I *shall* dare. I 'm afraid of my husband; he 's soft, smooth, irreproachable, everything you know; but I 'm afraid of him — horribly afraid of him. And yet I shall arrive at the Tuileries. But that will not be this winter, nor perhaps next, and meantime I must live. For the moment I want to go somewhere else; it 's my dream. I want to go to the Bal Bullier."

"To the Bal Bullier?" repeated Newman, for whom the words at first meant nothing.

"The ball in the Latin Quartei, where the students dance with their mistresses. Don't tell me you 've not heard of it."

"Oh yes," said Newman; "I 've heard of it; I remember now. I 've even been there. And you want to go there?"

"It 's *bête*, it 's low, it 's anything you please. But I want to go. Some of my friends have been, and they say it 's very curious. My friends go every-where; it 's only I who sit moping at home."

"It seems to me you 're not at home now," said Newman, "and I should n't exactly say you were moping."

"I 'm bored to death. I 've been to the opera twice a week for the last eight years. Whenever I ask for anything my mouth is stopped with that: Pray, madame, have n't you your *loge aux Italiens?* Could a woman of taste want more? In the first place my box was down in my *contrat;* they have to give it to me. To-night, for instance, I should have preferred a thousand times to go to the Palais Royal. But my husband won't go to the Palais Royal because the ladies of the court go there so much. You may imagine then whether he would take me to Bullier's; he says it is a mere imitation — and a bad one — of what they do in the imperial *intimité*. But as I 'm not yet for a little in the imperial *intimité* — which must be charming — why should n't I look in where you can get the nearest notion of it? It 's my dream at any rate; it 's a fixed idea. All I ask of you is to give me your arm; you 're less compromising than any one else. I don't know why, but you are. I can arrange it. I shall risk something, but that's my own affair. Besides, fortune favours the bold. Don't refuse me; it is my dream!"

Newman gave a loud laugh. It seemed to him hardly worth while to be the wife of the Marquis de Bellegarde, a daughter of the crusaders, heiress of six centuries of glories and traditions, only to have centred one's aspirations upon the sight of fifty young ladies kicking off the hats of a hundred young men. It struck him as a theme for the moralist, but he had no time to moralise. The curtain rose again; M. de Bellegarde returned and he went back to his seat

He observed that Valentin had taken his place in the *baignoire* of Mademoiselle Nioche, behind this young lady and her companion, where he was visible only if one carefully looked for him. In the next act Newman met him in the lobby and asked him if he had reflected upon possible emigration. "If you really meant to meditate," he said, "you might have chosen a better place for it."

"Oh, the place was n't bad," Valentin replied. "I was n't thinking of that girl. I listened to the music and, heedless of the play and without looking at the stage, turned over your handsome proposal. At first it seemed quite fantastic. And then a certain fiddle in the orchestra — I could distinguish it — began to say as it scraped away: 'Why not, why not, why not?' And then in that rapid movement all the fiddles took it up and the conductor's stick seemed to beat it in the air: 'Why not, why not, why not?' I'm sure I can't say! I don't see why not. I don't see why I should n't do something. It appears to me a really very bright idea. This sort of thing is certainly very stale. And then I should come back with a trunk full of dollars. Besides, I might possibly find it amusing. They call me an extravagant *raffiné;* who knows but that I might discover an unsuspected charm in shopkeeping? It would really have a certain rare and romantic side; it would look well in my biography. It would look as if I were a strong man, an *homme de premier ordre*, a man who dominated circumstances."

"I guess you had better not mind how it would look," said Newman. "It always looks well to have half a million of dollars. There's no reason why you should n't have them if you 'll mind what I tell you — I alone — and not fool round with other parties." He passed his arm into that of his friend, and the two walked for some time up and down one of the less frequented corridors. Newman's imagination began to glow with the idea of converting this irresistible idler into a first-class man of business. He felt for the moment a spiritual zeal, the zeal of the propagandist. Its ardour was in part the result of that general discomfort which the sight of all uninvested capital produced in him; so charming an intelligence ought to be dedicated to fine uses. The finest uses known to Newman's experience were transcendent operations in ferocious markets. And then his zeal was quickened by personal kindness; he entertained a form of pity which he was well aware he never could have made the Comte de Bellegarde understand. He never lost a sense of its being pitiable that so bright a figure should think it a large life to revolve in varnished boots between the Rue d'Anjou and the Rue de l'Université, taking the Boulevard des Italiens on the way, when over there in America one's promenade was a continent and one's boulevard stretched from one world-sea to another. It mortified him moreover to have to understand that Valentin wanted for money; it was n't business, that was what was the matter with it, he would have said; it was unpractical, unsuitable, unsightly — very much as if he had n't known how to spell or to ride. There was something almost ridiculously anomalous to Newman in the sight of lively pretensions unaccompanied by a considerable control of Western railroads; though I may add that he would not have maintained that such advantages were in themselves a proper ground for pretensions. "I'll put you into something," he said at any rate; "I'll see you through. I know half a dozen things in which we can make a place for you. You'll find it a big rush and you'll see some high jumps; it will take you a little while to get used to the scale. But you'll work in before long and at the end of six months — after you've tasted blood, after you've done a thing or two on your own account — you'll have some good times. And then it will be very pleasant for you having your sister over there. It will be pleasant for her to have you too. Yes, Valentine," he continued, pressing his comrade's arm genially, "I think I see just the opening for you. Keep quiet, and I'll find something nice — I'll fix you all right."

Newman pursued this favouring strain over a wide stretch of prospect; the two men strolled about for

a quarter of an hour. Valentin listened and questioned, making his friend laugh at his ignorance of
the very alphabet of affairs, smiling himself too, half
ironical and half curious. And yet he was serious
and nearly convinced, fascinated as by the biggest,
plainest map of the great land of El Dorado ever
spread before him. It is true, withal, that if it might
be bold, original and even amusing to surrender his
faded escutcheon to the process, the smart patent
transatlantic process, of heavy regilding, he did n't
quite relish the freedom with which it might be
handled, and yet suddenly felt eager to know the
worst that might await him. So that when the bell
rang to indicate the close of the entr'acte there was
a certain mock-heroism in his saying all gaily: "Well
then, put me through; locate me and fix me! I make
myself over to you. Dip me into the pot and turn
me into gold."

They had passed into the corridor which encircled
the row of *baignoires*, and Valentin stopped in front
of the dusky little box in which Mademoiselle
Nioche had bestowed herself, laying his hand on the
door-knob. "Oh come, are you going back there?"
Newman hereupon asked.

"*Mon Dieu, oui*," said Valentin.

"Have n't you another place?"

"Yes, I 've my usual place in the stalls."

"You had better go then and occupy it."

"I see her very well from there too," Valentin went
on serenely; "and to-night she 's worth seeing. But,"
he added in a moment, "I 've a particular reason for
going back just now."

"Oh, I give you up," said Newman. "You're sunk in depravity and don't know the light when you see it."

"No, it's only this. There's a young man in the box whom I shall worry by going in, and I really want to worry him."

"Why, you cold-blooded calculating wretch!" Newman cried. "Can't you give the poor devil a chance?"

"No, he has trod with all his weight on my toes. The box is not his; Noémie came alone and installed herself. I went and spoke to her, and in a few moments she asked me to go and get her fan from the pocket of her cloak, which the greedy *ouvreuse* had carried off, with her eye to a fee, instead of hanging it up on a peg. In my absence a gentleman came in and took the chair beside her in which I had been sitting. My reappearance put him out, and he had the grossness to show it. He came within an ace of being impertinent. I don't know who he is — a big hard-breathing red-faced animal. I can't think where she picks up such acquaintances. He has been drinking too, but he knows what he's about. Just now, in the second act, the brute did unmistakeably betray an intention. I shall put in another appearance for ten minutes — time enough to give him an opportunity to commit himself if he feels inclined. I really can't let him suppose he's keeping me out of the box."

"My poor dear boy," said Newman remonstrantly, "why shouldn't he have his good time? You're not going to pick a quarrel about such an article as that, I hope."

"The nature of the article — if you mean of the young lady — has nothing to do with it, and I 've no intention of picking a quarrel. I 'm not a bully nor a fire-eater, I simply wish to make a point that a gentleman must."

"Oh, damn your point!" Newman impatiently returned. "That 's the trouble with you Frenchmen; you must be always making points. Well," he added, "be lively, or I shall pack you off first to a country where you 'll find half your points already made and the other half quite unnoticed."

"Very good," Valentin answered, "whenever you like. But if I go to America I must n't let the fellow suppose it 's to run away from him."

And they separated. At the end of the act Newman observed that Valentin was still in the *baignoire.* He strolled into the corridor again, expecting to meet him, and when he was within a few yards of Noémie's retreat saw his friend pass out accompanied by the young man who had been seated beside its more interesting occupant. The two walked with some quickness of step to a distant part of the lobby, where Newman perceived them stop and stand talking. The manner of each was quiet enough, but the stranger, who was strikingly flushed, had begun to wipe his face very emphatically with his pocket-handkerchief. By this time Newman was abreast of the *baignoire;* the door had been left ajar and he could see a pink dress inside. He immediately went in. Noémie turned on him a glitter of interest.

"Ah, if you 've at last decided to come and see me you but just save your politeness. You find me in a fine moment. Sit down." She looked, it had to be owned, exceedingly pretty and perverse and animated and elegant, and quite as if she had had some very good news.

"Something has happened here!" Newman said while he kept his feet.

"You find me in a very fine moment," she repeated. "Two gentlemen — one of them 's M. de Bellegarde, the pleasure of whose acquaintance I owe to you — have just had words about your humble servant. Very sharp words too. They can't come off without its going further. A meeting and a big noise — that will give me a push!" said Noémie, clapping with a soft thud her little pearl-coloured hands. "*C'est ça qui pose une femme!*"

"You don't mean to say Bellegarde's going to fight about *you!*" Newman disgustedly cried.

"Nothing less!" — and she looked at him with a hard little smile. "No, no, you're not *galant!* And if you prevent this affair I shall owe you a grudge — and pay my debt!"

Newman uttered one of the least attenuated imprecations that had ever passed his lips, and then, turning his back without more ceremony on the pink dress, went out of the box. In the corridor he found Valentin and his companion walking toward him. The latter had apparently just thrust a card into his waistcoat pocket. Noémie's jealous votary was an immense, robust young man with a candid, excited glare, a thick nose and a thick mouth, the certainty of a thick articulation; also with a pair of very large white gloves and a very massive, voluminous watch-chain. When they reached the box Valentin, over whom he towered, made with an emphasised bow way for him to pass in first. Newman touched his friend's arm as a sign he wished to speak with him, and Valentin answered that he would be with him in an instant. Valentin entered the box after the robust young man, but a couple of minutes later reappeared in a state of aggravated gaiety. "She's immensely set up — she says we'll make her fortune. I don't want to be fatuous, but I think it very possible."

"So you're going to fight?" Newman asked.

"My dear fellow, don't look at me as if I had told you I'm *not!* It was not my own choice. The thing's perfectly settled."

"I told you so!" groaned Newman.

"I told *him* so," smiled Valentin.

"What the hell did he ever do to you?"

"My good friend, it does n't matter what. It seems to me you don't understand these things. He used an expression — I took it up."

"But I insist on knowing; I can't, as your elder brother, let you give way to public tantrums — !"

"I'm, as your younger brother, very much obliged to you," said Valentin. "I've nothing to conceal, but I can't go into particulars now and here."

"We'll leave this place then. You can tell me outside."

"Oh no, I can't leave this place; why should I hurry away? I'll go to my stall and sit out the opera."

"You'll not enjoy it."

Valentin looked at him a moment, coloured a little,

smiled and patted his arm. "You'd have been an ornament to the Golden Age. Before an affair a man's quiet. The quietest thing I can do is to go straight to my place."

"Ah," said Newman, "you want her to see you there — you and your quietness. Your quietness will drown the orchestra. I'm not so undeveloped. It's the damnedest foolery."

Valentin remained, and the two men, in their respective places, sat out the rest of the performance, which was also enjoyed by Mademoiselle Nioche and her truculent admirer. At the end Newman joined his friend again, and they went out into the street together. The young man shook his head at the proposal that he should get into Newman's own vehicle and stopped on the edge of the pavement. "I must go off alone; must look up a couple of friends who'll be so good as to act for me."

"I'll be so good as to act for you," Newman declared. "Put the case into my hands."

"You're very kind, but that's hardly possible. In the first place you're, as you said just now, almost my brother; you're going to marry my sister. That alone disqualifies you; it casts doubts on your impartiality. And if it did n't it would be enough for me that you have n't, as I say, God forgive you, the sentiment of certain shades. You'd only try to prevent a meeting."

"Of course I should," said Newman. "Whoever your friends are they'll be ruffians if they don't do that."

"Unquestionably then they'll do it. They'll urge

that excuses be made, the most proper excuses. But you'd be much too *coulant*. You won't do."

Newman was silent a moment. He was in presence, it seemed to him, of a vain and grotesque parade, poor, restricted, indirect as a salve to an insult or a righting of a wrong, and yet pretentious and pompous as an accommodation. But he saw it useless to attempt interference. "When is this precious performance to come off?" he could only ask.

"The sooner the better. The day after to-morrow I hope."

"Well," Newman went on, "I've certainly a claim to know the facts. I can't consent to shut my eyes to a single one of them."

"I shall be most happy to tell you them all then. They're very simple and it will be quickly done. But now everything depends on my putting my hands on my friends without delay. I'll jump into a cab; you had better drive to my rooms and wait for me there. I'll turn up at the end of an hour."

Newman assented protestingly, let him go, and then betook himself to the encumbered little apartment in the Rue d'Anjou. It was more than an hour before Valentin returned, but when he did so he was able to announce that he had found one of his accessories and that this gentleman had taken upon himself the care of securing the other. Newman had been sitting without lights by the faded fire, on which he had thrown a log; the blaze played over the rich multifarious properties of the place and produced fantastic gleams and shadows. He listened in silence to Valentin's account of what had passed between him

and the gentleman whose card he had in his pocket —
M. Stanislas Kapp of Strasbourg — after his return
to the society of their common hostess. This acute
young woman had espied an acquaintance on the
other side of the house and had expressed her displeasure at his not having the civility to come and
pay her a visit. "Oh, let him alone," M. Stanislas
Kapp had hereupon exclaimed; "there are too
many people in the box already!" And he had
fixed his eyes on his fellow-guest with the utmost
ferocity. Valentin had promptly retorted that if there
were too many people in the box it was easy for M.
Kapp to diminish the number. "I shall be most
happy to open the door for *you!*" M. Kapp had
exclaimed: "And I shall be delighted to fling you into
the pit!" Valentin had as promptly retorted. "Oh
do make a rumpus and get into the papers!" Miss
Noémie had gleefully ejaculated. "M. Kapp, turn
him out; or, M. de Bellegarde, pitch him into the pit,
into the orchestra — anywhere! I don't care who
does which, so long as you make a scene." Valentin
had answered that they would make no scene, but
that the gentleman would be so good as to step into
the corridor with him. In the corridor, after a brief
further exchange of words, there had been an exchange of cards. M. Stanislas Kapp had pressed on
his intention, the flat-faced imbecile, with all his
weight; and there were fifty tons, at the least, of that.

"Well, say there *are!* If you had n't gone back
into the box the thing would n't have happened."

"Why, don't you see," Valentin replied, "that the
event proves the extreme propriety of my going back

into the box? M. Kapp wished to provoke me; he was awaiting his chance. In such a case — that is, when he has been, so to speak, notified — a man must be on hand to receive the provocation. My not returning would simply have been tantamount to my saying to M. Stanislas Kapp: 'Oh, if you 're going to be offensive —!'"

"'You must manage it by yourself; damned if I 'll help you!' That would have been a thoroughly sensible thing to say. The only attraction for you seems to have been the idea that you *could* help him," Newman went on. "You told me you were not going back for that minx herself."

"Oh, don't mention her ever, ever any more!" Valentin almost plaintively sighed. "She 's really quite a bad bore."

"With all my heart. But if that 's the way you feel about her, why could n't you let her alone?"

Valentin shook his head with a fine smile. "I don't think you quite understand, and I don't believe I can make you. She understood the situation; she knew what was in the air; she was watching us."

"Then you *are* doing it for *her*?" Newman railed.

"I 'm doing it for myself, and you must leave me judge of what concerns my honour."

"Well, I 'll leave you judge if you 'll leave me to quite impartially, kick somebody!"

"It 's vain talking," Valentin replied to this. "Words have passed and the thing 's settled."

Newman turned away, taking his hat. Then pausing as if with interest, his hand on the door: "You 're going to use knives?"

"That's for M. Stanislas Kapp, as the challenged party, to decide. My own choice would be a short, light sword. I handle it well. I'm an indifferent shot."

Newman had put on his hat; he pushed it back, gently scratching his forehead high up. "I wish it were guns," he said. "I could show you how to hold one."

Valentin gave him a hard look and then broke into a laugh. "Murderer!" he cried with some intensity, but agreeing to see him again on the morrow, after the details of the meeting with M. Stanislas Kapp should have been arranged.

In the course of the day Newman received three lines from him to the effect that it had been decided he should cross the frontier with his adversary, and that he was accordingly to take the night express to Geneva. They should have time, however, to dine together. In the afternoon Newman called on Madame de Cintré for the single daily hour of rein-voked and reasserted confidence — a solemnity but the more exquisite with repetition — to which she had, a little strangely, given him to understand it was convenient, important, in fact vital to her, that their communion, for their strained interval, should be restricted, even though this reduced him for so many other recurrent hours, the hours of evening in par-ticular, the worst of the probation, to the state of a restless, prowling, time-keeping ghost, a taker of long night-walks through streets that affected him at moments as the alleys of a great darkened bankrupt bazaar. But his visit to-day had a worry to reckon with — all the more that it had as well so much of one to conceal. She shone upon him, as always, with that light of her gentleness which might have been figured, in the heat-thickened air, by a sultry harvest moon; but she was visibly bedimmed, and she confessed, on his charging her with her red eyes, that she had been, for a vague vain reason, crying them half out. Valentin had been with her a couple of hours before and had somehow troubled her without in the least intending it. He had laughed and gossiped, had brought her no bad news, had only been, in taking leave of her, rather "dearer," poor boy, than usual. A certain extravagance of tenderness in him had in fact touched her to positive pain, so that on his departure she had burst into miserable tears. She had felt as if something strange and wrong were hanging about them — ah, she had had that feeling in other connexions too; nervous, always nervous, she had tried to reason away the fear, but the effort had only given her a headache. Newman was of course tongue-tied on what he himself knew, and, his power of simulation and his general art of optimism breaking down on this occasion as if some long needle-point had suddenly passed, to make him wince, through the sole crevice of his armour, he could, to his high chagrin, but cut his call short. Before he retreated, however, he asked if Valentin had seen his mother.

"Yes; but he did n't make *her* cry!"

It was in Newman's own apartments that the young man dined, having sent his servant and his effects to await him at the railway M. Stanislas Kapp had positively declined to make excuses, and he on his side had obviously none to offer. Valentin had found out with whom he was dealing, and that his adversary was the son and heir of a rich brewer of Strasbourg, a youth sanguineous, brawny, bullheaded, and lately much occupied in making ducks and drakes of the paternal brewery. Though passing in a general way for a good companion, he had already been noted as apt to quarrel after dinner and to be disposed then to charge with his head down. "Que voulez-vous?" said Valentin: "brought up on beer how could he stand such champagne as Noémie, cup-bearer to the infernal gods, had poured out for him?" He had chosen the weapon known to Newman as the gun. Valentin had an excellent appetite: he made a point, in view of his long journey, of eating more than usual: one of the points, no doubt, that his friend had accused him of always needing to make. He took the liberty of suggesting to the latter the difference of the suspicion of a shade in the composition of a fish-sauce; he thought it worth hinting, with precautions, to the cook. But Newman had no mind for sauces; there was more in the dish itself, the mixture now presented to him, than he could swallow; he was in short "nervous" to a tune of which he felt almost ashamed as he watched his inimitable friend go through their superior meal without skipping a step or missing a savour; the exposure, the possible sacrifice, of so charming a life on the altar of a stupid tradition struck him as intolerably wrong. He exaggerated the perversity of Noémie, the ferocity of M. Kapp, the grimness of M. Kapp's friends, and only knew that he did yearn now as a brother.

"This sort of thing may be all very well," he broke out at last, "but I'll be blamed if I see it. I can't stop you perhaps, but at least I can swear at you handsomely. Take me as doing so in the most awful terms."

"My dear fellow, don't make a scene"— Valentin was almost sententious. "Scenes in these cases are in very bad taste."

"Your duel itself is a scene," Newman said; "a scene of the most flagrant description. It's a wretched theatrical affair. Why don't you take a band of music with you outright? It's G— d— barbarous, and yet it's G— d— effete."

"Oh, I can't begin at this time of day to defend the theory of duelling," the young man blandly reasoned. "It's our only resource at given moments, and I hold it a good thing. Quite apart from the merit of the cause in which a meeting may take place, it strikes a romantic note that seems to me in this age of vile prose greatly to recommend it. It's a remnant of a higher-tempered time; one ought to cling to it. It's a way of more decently testifying. Testify when you can!"

"I don't know what you mean by a higher-tempered time," Newman retorted. "Because your great-grandfather liked to prance, is that any reason for you, who have got beyond it? For my part I think we had better let our temper take care of itself; it generally seems to me quite high enough; I'm not more of a fire-eater than most, but I'm not afraid of being too mild. If your great-grandfather were to make himself unpleasant to me I think I could tackle him yet."

"My dear friend"—Valentin was perfectly patient with him—"you can't invent anything that will take the place of satisfaction for an insult. To demand it and to give it are equally excellent arrangements."

"Do you call this sort of thing satisfaction?" Newman groaned. "Does it satisfy you to put yourself at the disposal of a bigger fool even than yourself? I'd see him somewhere first! Does it satisfy you that he should set up this ridiculous relation with *you*? I'd like to see him try anything of the sort with *me*! If a man has a bad intention on you it's his own affair till it takes effect; but when it does, give him one in the eye. If you don't know *how* to do that — straight — you're not fit to go round alone. But I'm talking of those who claim they *are*, and that they don't require some one to take care of them."

"Well," Valentin smiled, "it would be interesting truly to go round with *you*. But to get the full good of that, alas, I should have begun earlier!"

Newman could scarcely bear even the possible pertinence of his "alas." "See here," he said at the last; "if any one ever hurts you again —!"

"Well, *mon bon?*" — and Valentin, with his eyes on his friend's, might now have been much moved.

"Come straight to me about it. *I'll* go for him."

"*Matamore!*" the young man laughed as they parted.

XVIII

It was the next morning that, by exception, Newman went to see Madame de Cintré, timing his visit so as to arrive after the noonday breakfast. In the court of the hôtel, before the portico, stood Madame de Bellegarde's old square heavy carriage. The servant who opened the door answered his enquiry with a slightly embarrassed and hesitating murmur, and at the same moment Mrs. Bread appeared in the background, dim-visaged as usual and wearing a large black bonnet and shawl.

"What's the matter?" he asked. "Is Madame la Comtesse at home or not?"

Mrs. Bread advanced, fixing her eyes on him; he observed that she held a sealed letter, very delicately, in her fingers. "The Countess has left a message for you, sir; she has left this." And the good woman held out the missive, which he took.

"Left it? Is she out? Is she gone away?"

"She's going away, sir; she's leaving town," said Mrs. Bread.

"Leaving town!" he exclaimed. "What in the world has happened?"

"It is not for me to say, sir." And Mrs. Bread cast her eyes to the ground. "But I thought it would come."

"What would come, pray?" Newman demanded. He had broken the seal of the letter, but he

361

still questioned. "She's in the house? She's visible?"

"I don't think she expected you this morning," his venerable friend replied. "She was to leave immediately."

"Where is she going?"

"To Fleurières."

"Away off there? But surely I can see her?"

Mrs. Bread hesitated, but then, clasping together her black-gloved hands, "I'll take you!" she rather desperately said. And she led the way upstairs. At the top of the staircase, however, she paused and fixed her dry sad eyes on him. "Be very easy with her. Nobody else is." Then she went on to Madame de Cintré's apartment. Newman, perplexed and alarmed, followed her fast. She threw open the door and he pushed back the curtain at the further side of its deep embrasure. In the middle of the room stood Madame de Cintré; her face was flushed and marked and she was dressed for travelling. Behind her, before the fireplace, stood Urbain de Bellegarde and looked at his finger-nails; near the Marquis sat his mother, buried in an armchair and with her eyes immediately fixing themselves on the invader, as he felt them pronounce him. He knew himself, as he entered, in the presence of something evil; he was as startled and pained as he would have been by a threatening cry in the stillness of the night. He walked straight to Madame de Cintré and seized her by the hand.

"What's the matter?" he asked commandingly; "what's happening?"

Urbain de Bellegarde stared, then left his place and came and leaned on the back of his mother's chair. Newman's sudden irruption had evidently discomposed them both. Madame de Cintré stood silent and with her eyes resting on her friend's. She had often looked at him with all her soul, as it seemed to him; but in this present gaze there was a bottomless depth. She was in distress, and — monstrously — was somehow to her own sense helpless. It would have been the most touching thing he had ever seen if it had n't been the most absurd. His heart rose into his throat and he was on the point of turning to her companions with an angry challenge; but she checked him, pressing the hand of which she had possessed herself.

"Something very grave has happened," she brought out. "I can't marry you."

Newman dropped her hand — as if, suddenly and unnaturally acting with the others, she had planted a knife in his side: he stood staring, first at her and then at them. "Why not?" he asked as quietly as his quick gasp permitted.

Madame de Cintré almost smiled, but the attempt was strange. "You must ask my mother. You must ask my brother."

"Why can't she marry me?" — and he looked all at them.

Madame de Bellegarde never moved in her seat, but her consciousness had paled her face. The Marquis hovered protectingly. She said nothing for some moments, but she kept her keen clear eyes on their visitor. The Marquis drew himself up and con·

sidered the ceiling. "It's impossible!" he finely articulated.

"It's improper," said Madame de Bellegarde.

Newman began to laugh. "Oh, you're fooling!" he exclaimed.

"My sister, you've no time; you're losing your train," the Marquis went on.

"Come, is he mad?" Newman asked.

"No; don't think that," said Madame de Cintré. 'But I'm going away."

"Where are you going?"

"To the country; to Fleurières; to be alone."

"To leave *me* alone?" Newman put it.

"I can't see you now," she simply answered.

"'Now' — why not?"

"I'm ashamed," she still more simply confessed.

Newman turned to the Marquis. "What have you done to her — what does it mean?" he asked with the same effort at calmness, the fruit of his constant practice in taking things easily. He was excited, but excitement with him was only an intenser deliberateness; it was the plunger stripped.

"It means that I've given you up," said Madame de Cintré. "It means that."

Her appearance was too charged with tragic expression not fully to confirm her words. Newman was profoundly shocked, but he felt as yet no resentment against her. He was amazed, bewildered, and the presence of the Marquise and her son seemed to smite his eyes like the glare of a watchman's lantern. "Can't I see you alone?" he asked.

"It would be only more painful. I hoped I should n't see you — that I should escape. I wrote to you, but only three words. Good-bye." And she put out her hand again.

Newman put both his own into his pockets. "I 'll simply go with you."

She laid her two hands on his arm. "Will you grant me a last request?" — and as she looked at him, urging this, her eyes filled with tears. "Let me go alone—let me go in peace. Peace I say—though it 's really death. But let me bury myself. So — good-bye."

Newman passed his hand into his hair and stood slowly rubbing his head and looking through his keenly-narrowed eyes from one to the other of the three persons before him. His lips were compressed, and the two strong lines formed beside his mouth and riding hard, as it were, his restive moustache, might have at first suggested a wide grimace. I have said that his excitement was an intenser deliberateness, and now his deliberation was grim. "It seems very much as if you had interfered, Marquis," he said slowly. "I thought you said you would n't interfere. I know you did n't like me; but that does n't make any difference. I thought you promised me you would n't interfere. I thought you swore on your honour that you would n't interfere. Don't you remember, Marquis?"

The Marquis lifted his eyebrows, but he was apparently determined to be even more urbane than usual. He rested his two hands upon the back of his mother's chair and bent forward as if he were lean-

ing over the edge of a pulpit or a lecture-desk. He
did n't smile, but he looked softly grave. "Pardon
me, sir — what I assured you was that I would n't
influence my sister's decision. I adhered to the letter
to my engagement. Did I not, my sister?"

"Don't appeal, my son," said the Marquise.
"Your word 's all sufficient."

"Yes — she accepted me," said Newman.
"That 's very true; I can't deny that. At least," he
added in a different tone while he turned to Madame
de Cintré, "you *did* accept me?" The effect of deep
irony in it — even if there had been nothing else —
appeared to move her strongly, and she turned away,
burying her face in her hands. "But you 've interfered now, have n't you?" he went on to the Marquis.

"Neither then nor now have I attempted to influence my sister. I used no persuasion then — I 've
used no persuasion to-day."

"And what have you used?"

"We 've used authority," said Madame de Bellegarde in a rich, bell-like voice.

"Ah, you 've used authority!" Newman wonderfully echoed. 'They 've used authority —" He
turned to Madame de Cintré. "What in the world is
their authority and how do they apply it?"

"My mother addressed me her command," Madame de Cintré said with a sound that was the
strangest yet.

"Her command that you should give me up —
I see. And you obey — I see. But *why* do you
obey?" Newman pursued.

Madame de Cintré looked across at the old Marquise, measuring her from head to foot. Then she spoke again with simplicity. "I'm afraid of my mother."

Madame de Bellegarde rose with a certain quickness. "This is a most indecent scene!"

"I've no wish to prolong it," said Madame de Cintré; and, turning to the door, she put out her hand again. "If you can pity me a little, let me go alone."

Newman held her quietly and firmly. "I'll come right down there." The portière dropped behind her, and he sank with a long breath into the nearest chair. He leaned back in it, resting his hands on the knobs of the arms and looking at Madame de Bellegarde and Urbain. There was a long silence. They stood side by side, their heads high and their handsome eyebrows arched. "So you make a distinction?" he went on at last. "You make a distinction between persuading and commanding? It's very neat. But the distinction's in favour of commanding. That rather spoils it."

"We've not the least objection to defining our position," said M. de Bellegarde. "We quite understand that it should n't at first appear to you altogether clear. We rather expect indeed that you'll not do us justice."

"Oh, I'll do you justice," said Newman. "Don't be afraid. Only give me a chance!"

The Marquise laid her hand on her son's arm as if to deprecate the attempt to marshal reasons or to meet their friend again, on any ground, too intimately. "It's quite useless," she opined, "to try and arrange this matter so as to make it agreeable to you. It's a disappointment, and disappointments are — I grant it — sometimes odious things. I thought our necessity over — that of letting you know that we don't after all see our way! I considered carefully and tried to arrange it better; but I only gave myself bad headaches and lost my sleep. Say what we will you'll think yourself ill-treated and will publish your wrong among your friends. But we're not afraid of that. Besides, your friends are not our friends, and it will matter by so much the less. Think of us as you like — you don't really know us. I only beg you not to be violent. I've never in my life been present at any sort of roughness, and I think my age should now protect me."

"Is *that* all you have to say?" asked Newman, slowly rising from his chair. "That's a poor show for a clever lady like you, Marquise. Come, try again."

"My mother goes to the point with her usual honesty and intrepidity," said the Marquis, toying with his watchguard. "But it's perhaps right I should add another word. We of course quite repudiate the charge of having broken faith with you. We left you entirely at liberty to make yourself agreeable to my sister. We left her quite at liberty to entertain your proposal. When she accepted you we said nothing. We therefore wholly observed our promise. It was only at a later stage of the affair, and on quite a different basis, as it were, that we determined to speak. It would have been better perhaps if we had spoken before. But really, you see, nothing has yet been done."

"Nothing has yet been done?" — Newman repeated the words as if unconscious of their comical effect. He had lost the sense of what the Marquis was saying; M. de Bellegarde's superior style was a mere humming in his ears. All he understood, in his deep and simple wrath, was that the matter was not a violent joke and that the people before him were perfectly serious. "Do you suppose I can take this from you?" he wonderingly asked. "Do you suppose it can matter to me what you say? Do you suppose I'm an idiot that you can so put off?"

Madame de Bellegarde gave a rattle of her fan in the hollow of her hand. "If you don't take it you can leave it, sir. It matters very little what you do. The simple fact is that my daughter has given you up."

"She does n't mean it," Newman declared after a moment.

"I think I can assure you that she does," the Marquis fluted.

"Poor stricken woman, poor bleeding heart, what damnable thing have you done to her?" Newman demanded.

"Gently, gently!" murmured M. de Bellegarde as ne rocked on his neat foundations.

"She told you," his mother said. "I expressed my final wish."

Newman shook his head heavily. "This sort of thing can't be, you know. A man can't be used in this fashion. You not only have nc right that is n't a preposterous pretence, but you have n't a pennyworth of power."

"My power," Madame de Bellegarde observed, "is in my children's obedience."

"In their fear, your daughter said. There's something very strange in it. Why should any one be afraid of you?" added Newman after looking at her a moment. "There has been something at play I don't know and can't guess."

She met his gaze without flinching and as if neither hearing nor heeding. "I did my best," she said quietly. "I could bear it no longer."

"It was a bold experiment!" the Marquis pursued.

Newman felt disposed to walk to him and clutch his neck with irresistible firm fingers and a prolongation of thumb-pressure on the windpipe. "I need n't tell you how you strike me," he said, however, instead of this; "of course you know that. But I should think you 'd be afraid of your friends — all those people you introduced me to the other night. There were some decent people apparently among them; you may depend upon it there were some good, honest men and women."

"Our friends approve us," said M. de Bellegarde; "there 's not a responsible *chef de famille* among them who would have acted otherwise. And however that may be we take the cue from no one. We 've been much more used — since one really has to tell you — to setting the example than to waiting for it."

"You 'd have waited long before any one would have set you such an example as this, I guess!" Newman cried. "Have I done anything wrong or mean or base?" he rang out. "Have I given you any reason to change your opinion? Have you found out anything against me? Hanged if I can imagine!"

"Our opinion," said Madame de Bellegarde, "is quite the same as at first — exactly. We've no ill-will towards yourself; we're very far from accusing you of misconduct. Since your relations with us began you've been, I frankly confess, less eccentric than I expected. It's not your personal character that we object to, it's your professional — it's your antecedents. We really can't reconcile ourselves to a commercial person. We tried to believe in an evil hour it was possible, and that effort was our great misfortune. We determined to persevere to the end and to give you every advantage. I was resolved you should have no reason to accuse me of a want of loyalty. We let the thing certainly go very far — we introduced you to our friends. To tell the truth it was that, I think, that broke me down. I succumbed to the scene that took place the other night in these rooms. You must pardon me if what I say is disagreeable to you, but you've insisted, with violence, on an explanation."

"There's no better proof of our good faith," the Marquis superadded, "than our committing ourselves to you in the eyes of the world three evenings since. We endeavoured to bind ourselves — to tie our hands and cut off our retreat. Could we have done more?"

"But it was that," his mother subjoined, "that opened our eyes and broke our bonds. We should have been deeply uncomfortable with any such continuance. You know," she wound up in a moment, "that you were forewarned as to our high, stiff way of carrying ourselves. Oh, I grant you that we're as proud and odious as you please! But we did n't seek your acquaintance. You sought ours."

Newman took up his hat and began mechanically to smooth it; the very fierceness of his scorn kept him from speaking. "You're certainly odious enough," he cried at last, "but it strikes me your pride falls short altogether."

"In the whole matter," said the Marquis, still as with a fine note of cool reason, "I really see nothing but our humility."

"Let us have no more painful discussion than is necessary," his mother resumed. "My daughter told you everything when she said she gives you up."

"I'm not in the least satisfied about your daughter," Newman insisted: "I want to know what you did to her. It's all very easy talking about authority and saying she likes your orders. She did n't accept me blindly and she would n't give me up blindly. Not that I believe yet she has really done it after what has passed between us; she 'll talk it over with me. But you've frightened her, you've bullied her, you've *hurt* her. What was it you did to her?"

"I had very little to do," said Madame de Belle-garde in a tone which gave him a chill when he afterwards remembered it.

"Let me remind you that we offered you this amount of consideration," the Marquis observed, "with the express understanding that you should abstain from intemperance."

"I'm not intemperate," Newman answered; "it's you who are intemperate. You stab me in the back and I turn on you; is it *I* who am offensive? But I don't know that I've much more to say to you. What you expect of me, apparently, is to go on my way — in the manner most convenient to you — thanking you for favours received and promising never to trouble you again."

"We expect of you to act like an *homme d'esprit*," said Madame de Bellegarde. "You've shown yourself remarkably that, already, and what we've done is altogether based upon your being so. When one must recognise a situation — well, one must. That's all that we've done. Since my daughter absolutely withdraws, what do you gain by making a noise under our windows? You proclaim, at the best, your discomfiture."

"It remains to be seen if your daughter absolutely withdraws. Your daughter and I are still very good friends; nothing's changed in that. As I say, there has been that between us that must make her recognise at least my claim to some light of mercy from her."

"I recommend you in your own interest not to expect more than you'll get," the Marquis returned with firmness. "I know her well enough to know that a meaning signified as she just now signified hers to you is final. Besides, she has given me her word."

"I've no doubt her word's worth a great deal more than your own," said Newman. "Nevertheless I don't give her up."

"There's nothing of course to prevent your saying so! But if she won't even see you — and she won't — your constancy must remain very much on your hands."

Newman feigned in truth a greater confidence than he felt. Madame de Cintré's strange intensity had really struck a chill to his heart; her face, still impressed on his vision, had been a terrible image of deep renunciation. He felt sick and suddenly helpless. He turned away and stood a moment with his hand on the door; then he faced about and, after the briefest hesitation, broke out with another accent. "Come, think of what this must be to me, and leave her to herself and to the man whom, before God I believe, she loves! Why should you object to me — what's the matter with me? I can't hurt you, I wouldn't if I could. I'm the most unobjectionable man in the world. What if I *am* a commercial person? What under the sun do you mean? A commercial person? I'll be any sort of person you want. I never talked to you about business — where on earth does it come in? Let her go and I'll ask no questions. I'll take her away and you shall never see me or hear of me again. I'll stay in America if you like. I'll sign a paper promising never to come back to Europe. All I want is not to lose her!"

His companions exchanged a glance of mutual re-enforcement, and Urbain said: "My dear sir, what you propose is hardly an improvement. We've not the slightest objection to seeing you, as an amiable foreigner, and we've every reason for not wishing to be eternally separated from my sister. We object to her marriage; and in that way" — M. de Belle-garde gave a small, thin laugh — "she'd be more married than ever."

"Well then," Newman presently broke out again, "where's this interesting place of yours — Fleurières? I know it's near some old city on a hill."

"Precisely. Poitiers is on a hill," the Marquise admitted. "I don't know exactly how old it is. We're not afraid to tell you."

"It's Poitiers, is it? Very good," said Newman. "I shall immediately follow Madame de Cintré."

"The trains after this hour won't serve you," Urbain appeared to judge it his duty to mention.

"I shall then hire a special train."

"That will be a very foolish waste of money," said Madame de Bellegarde.

"It will be time enough to talk about waste three days hence," Newman answered; with which, clapping his hat on his head, he departed.

He didn't immediately start for Fleurières; he was too stunned and wounded for consecutive action. He simply walked; he walked straight before him, following the river till he got out of the stony circle of Paris. He had a burning, tingling sense of personal outrage. He had never in his life received so absolute a check; he had never been pulled up, or, as he would have said, "let down," so short, and he found the sensation intolerable as he strode along tapping the trees and lamp-posts fiercely with his stick and inwardly raging. To lose such a woman after taking such jubilant and triumphant possession of her was as great an affront to his pride as it was an injury to his happiness. And to lose her by the interference and the dictation of others, by an impudent old hag's and a pretentious coxcomb's stepping in with their "authority"! It was too preposterous, it was too pitiful. Upon what he deemed the unblushing treachery of the Bellegardes he wasted little thought; he consigned it once for all to eternal perdition. But the treachery of Madame de Cintré herself amazed and confounded him; there was a key to the mystery, of course, but he groped for it in vain. Only three days had elapsed since she stood beside him in the starlight, beautiful and tranquil as the trust with which he had inspired her, and told him she was happy in the prospect of their marriage. What was the meaning of the change? of what infernal potion had she tasted? He had, however, a terrible apprehension that she had really changed. His very admiration for her attached the idea of force and weight to her rupture. But he did n't rail at her as false, for he was sure she was unhappy. In his walk he had crossed one of the bridges of the Seine, and he still followed unheedingly the long and unbroken quay. He had left Paris behind and was almost in the country; he was in the pleasant suburb of Auteuil. He stopped at last, looked about at it without seeing or caring for its pleasantness, and then slowly turned round and at a slower pace retraced his steps. When he came abreast of the fantastic embankment known as the Trocadéro he reflected, through his throbbing pain, that he was near Mrs. Tristram's dwelling and that Mrs. Tristram, on particular occasions, had much of a woman's kindness in her chords. He felt he needed to pour out his ire, and he took the road to her house. She was at home and alone, and as soon as she had looked at him, on his entering the room, she told him she knew what he had come for. He sat down heavily, in silence, with his eyes on her.

"They've backed out!" she said without his even needing to tell her. "Well, you may think it strange, but I felt something the other night in the air." Presently he gave her his account; she listened while her whole face took it in. When he had finished she said quietly: "They want her to marry Lord Deepmere." Newman stared — he did n't know she knew anything about Lord Deepmere. "But I don't think she will," Mrs. Tristram added.

"*She* marry that poor little cub!" cried Newman. "Oh Lord save us! And yet why else can she have so horribly treated me?"

"But that is n't the only thing," said Mrs. Tristram. "They really could n't *live* with you any longer. They had overrated their courage. I must say, to give the devil his due, that there's something rather fine in that. It was your commercial quality in the abstract, and the mere historic facts of your washtubs and other lucrative wares, that they could n't swallow. That's really consistent — the inconsistency had been the other way. They wanted your money, but they've given you up for an idea."

Newman frowned most ruefully and took up his hat again. "I thought you'd encourage me!" he brought out with almost juvenile sadness.

"Pardon my trying to understand — of course it does n't concern *you* to understand," she answered very gently. "I feel none the less sorry for you, especially as I'm at the bottom of your troubles. I've not forgotten that I suggested the marriage to you. I don't believe Claire has any intention of consenting to marry Lord Deepmere. It's true he's not younger than she, as he might pass for being. He's thirty-three years old; I looked in the Peerage. But no — I can't believe her so hideously, cruelly false."

"Please say nothing against her!" Newman strangely cried.

"Poor woman," she none the less continued, "she *is* cruel. But of course you'll go after her and you'll plead powerfully. Do you know that as you are now," Mrs. Tristram added with characteristic audacity of comment, "you're extremely eloquent, even without speaking? To resist you a woman must have a very fixed idea or a very bad conscience. I wish I had done you a wrong — that you might come to me and make me so feel it; and feel *you*, dear man, just you." She looked at him an instant, then had one of her odd little outbreaks. "You're lamentable — you're splendid! Go to Madame de Cintré, at any rate, and tell her that she's a puzzle even to one of the intelligent, like me, who so greatly admires her. I'm very curious to see how far family discipline in a fine case like this does go."

Newman sat a while longer, leaning his elbows on his knees and his head in his hands, and Mrs. Tristram continued to temper charity with reason and compassion with criticism. At last she inquired· "And what does Count Valentin say to it?" New-

man started; he had not thought of Valentin and his
errand on the Swiss frontier since the morning.
The reflexion made him restless again, and he broke
away on a promise that his hostess should have without delay his next news. He went straight to his
apartment, where, on the table in the vestibule, he
found a waiting telegram. "I'm seriously ill and
should be glad to see you as soon as possible.— VAL-
ENTIN." He had a savage groan for this miserable
news and for the interruption of his journey to Fleurières. But he addressed to Madame de Cintré a
brief, the briefest, statement of these things; it formed
a response as well to the ten words of the note that
had come to him by Mrs. Bread, and was now all
the time allowed him.

"I don't give you up and don't really believe you
speak your own intention. I don't understand it, but
ım sure we shall clear it up together. I can't follow
you to-day, as I'm called to see a friend at a distance
who's very ill, perhaps dying. Why should n't I tell
you he's your brother? —C. N."

XIX

HE had a rare gift for sitting still when nothing else would serve, and rare was his opportunity to use it on his journey to Switzerland. The successive hours of the night brought him no sleep; but he kept motionless in his corner of the railway-carriage, his eyes closed, and the most observant of his fellow-travellers might have envied him his apparent rest. Toward morning rest really came, as an effect of mental rather than of physical fatigue. He slept for a couple of hours, and at last, waking, found his eyes attach themselves to one of the snow-powdered peaks of the Jura, behind which the sky was just reddening with the dawn. But he took in neither the cold mountain nor the warm light: his consciousness began to throb again, on the very instant, with a sense of his wrong. He got out of the train half an hour before it reached Geneva — alighted in the pale early glow and at the station indicated in Valentin's telegram. A drowsy station-master was on the platform with a lantern and the hood of his overcoat over his head, and near him stood a gentleman who advanced to meet Newman. This personage, a man of about forty, showed a tall lean figure, a long brown face, marked eyebrows, high moustaches and fresh light gloves. He took off his hat, looking very grave, and articulated, "Monsieur!" To which our hero replied: "You've been acting, in this tragedy, for the Count?"

"I unite with you in having been chosen for that sad honour," said the gentleman. "I had placed myself at M. de Bellegarde's service in this melancholy affair, together with M. de Grosjoyaux, who is now at his bedside. M. de Grosjoyaux, I believe, has had the honour of meeting you in Paris, but as he is a better nurse than I, he remained with our poor friend. Bellegarde has been eagerly expecting you."

"And how *is* the rascal?" said Newman. "He was badly hit?"

"The doctor has condemned him; we brought a surgeon with us. But he will die in the best sentiments. I sent last evening for the curé of the nearest French village, who spent an hour with him. The curé was quite satisfied."

"Heaven forgive us!" groaned Newman. "I'd rather the surgeon were so! And can he see me — shall he know me?"

"When I left him, half an hour ago, he had fallen asleep — after a feverish, wakeful night. But we shall see." And this companion proceeded to lead the way out of the station to the village, explaining as he went that the little party was lodged in the humblest of Swiss inns, where, however, they had succeeded in making M. de Bellegarde much more comfortable than could at first have been expected. "We're old companions-in-arms," the personage said; "it's not the first time one of us has helped the other to lie easy. It's a very nasty wound, and the nastiest thing about it is that Valentin's adversary was no shot. He put his beastly bullet where he could. It entered, accursedly, our poor friend's left side, just below the heart."

As they picked their way, in the grey, deceptive dawn, between the manure-heaps of the village street, Newman's new acquaintance narrated the particulars of the meeting. The conditions had been that if the first exchange of shots should fail to satisfy one of the parties a second should take place. Valentin's first bullet had done exactly what Newman's companion was convinced he had intended it to do; it had grazed the arm of M. Stanislas Kapp, just scratching the flesh. M. Kapp's own projectile, meanwhile, had passed at ten good inches from the person of Valentin. The representatives of M. Stanislas had demanded another shot, which was then, on Valentin's absolute insistence, granted. But Valentin had fired into space, and the young Alsatian had done effective execution. "I saw, when we met him on the ground," said Newman's informant, "that he was not going to be *commode*. A mixture of the donkey and the buffalo — with no sense whatever of proportion." Valentin had immediately been installed at the inn, while M. Stanislas and his friends had withdrawn to regions unknown. The police authorities of the canton had waited upon the others, had placed them under technical arrest and had drawn up a long *procès-verbal;* but as the wine had been drawn — alas! — the powers would have to drink it. Newman asked if a message had not been sent to the family, and learned that up to a late hour of the previous night Valentin had opposed it. He had refused to believe his wound dangerous.

After his interview with the curé, however, he had consented, and a telegram had been despatched to his mother. "But the Marquise will scarcely have time —!" So judged Newman's conductor.

"Well, it's a wicked, wanton, infernal affair!" So judged Newman himself.

"Ah, you don't approve?" his friend gravely questioned, while he himself remained passionately careless of the involved reflexion on this gentleman's control of the encounter.

"Approve?" cried Newman. "I wish that when I had him there night before last I had locked him up in my *cabinet de toilette!*"

Valentin's supporter opened his eyes and shook his head up and down two or three times, portentously, with a little flute-like whistle. But he had evidently been prepared, in respect to this outer barbarian, for some oddity of emotion and expression. They had in any case reached the inn, where a stout maid-servant in a nightcap was on the threshold, with a lantern, to take the traveller's bag from the porter who trudged behind him. Valentin was lodged on the ground floor at the back of the house, and Newman's companion went along a stone-faced passage and softly opened a door. Then he beckoned to the visitor, who advanced and looked into the room, lighted by a single shaded candle. Beside the fire sat M. de Grosjoyaux asleep in his dressing-gown — a short stout fair man, with an air of gay surprise, whom Newman had seen several times in Valentin's company. On the bed lay Valentin, pale and still, his eyes closed — a figure very shocking to Newman,

who had known it hitherto awake to its finger-tips.
M. de Grosjoyaux's colleague pointed to an open
door beyond and whispered that the doctor was within,
where he kept guard. So long as Valentin slept, or
seemed to sleep, of course he was not to be
approached; so our hero withdrew for the present,
committing himself to the care of the half-waked
bonne. She took him to a room above-stairs and introduced him to a bed on which a magnified bolster,
in yellow calico, figured as a counterpane. He lay
down and, in spite of his counterpane and most other
things, slept for three or four hours. When he awoke
the morning was advanced and the sun filling his
window, outside of which he heard the clucking of
hens.

While he was dressing there came to his door
a message from M. de Grosjoyaux and his companion, who amiably proposed he should breakfast
with them. Presently he went downstairs to the little
stone-paved dining-room, where the maid-servant,
who had taken off her nightcap, was serving the
repast. M. de Grosjoyaux was there, surprisingly
fresh for a gentleman who had been playing sick-
nurse half the night; he now rubbed his hands very
constantly and very hard and watched the breakfast-
table attentively. Newman renewed acquaintance
with him and learned that Valentin was still in a doze;
the doctor, who had had a fairly tranquil night, was
at present sitting with him. Before M. de Grosjoyaux's associate reappeared Newman learned that
his name was M. Ledoux and that Bellegarde's
acquaintance with him dated from the days when

they served together in the Pontifical Zouaves. M
Ledoux was the nephew of a distinguished Ultramontane bishop. At last he came in with an effect
of dress in which an ingenious attempt at adjustment
at once to a confirmed style and to the peculiar situation was visible, and with a gravity tempered by
a decent deference to the best breakfast the Croix
Helvétique had ever set forth. Valentin's servant,
who was allowed but with restrictions the honour of
attending his master, had been lending a light Parisian hand in the kitchen. The two Frenchmen did
their best to prove that if circumstances might over-
shadow they could n't really obscure the national
gift for good talk, and M. Ledoux delivered a neat
little eulogy on poor Bellegarde, whom he pronounced the most charming Englishman he had ever
known.

"Do you call him an Englishman?" Newman
asked.

M. Ledoux smiled a moment and then just fell
short of an epigram: "*C'est plus qu'un Anglais, le
cher homme — c'est un Anglomane !*" Newman returned, sturdily and handsomely, that any country
might have been proud to claim him, and M. de
Grosjoyaux remarked that it was really too soon to
deliver a funeral oration on poor Bellegarde. "Evidently," said M. Ledoux. "But I could n't help
observing this morning to Mr. Newman that when
a man has taken such excellent measures for his salvation as our dear friend did last evening, it seems
almost a pity he should put it in peril again by coming back to the world." M. Ledoux was a great

Catholic, and Newman thought him a queer mixture.
His countenance, by daylight, had an amiably satur-
nine cast; he had a large lean nose and looked like an
old Spanish picture. He appeared to think the use of
pistols at thirty paces a very perfect arrangement, pro-
vided, should one get hit, one might promptly see the
priest. He took, clearly, a great satisfaction in Valentin's interview with that functionary, and yet his general tone was far from indicating a sanctimonious
habit of mind. M. Ledoux had evidently a high
sense of propriety and was furnished, in respect to
everything, with an explanation and a grave grin that
combined together to push his moustache up under
his nose. *Savoir-vivre* — knowing how to live — was
his strong point, in which he included knowing how
to die; but, as Newman reflected with a good deal of
dumb irritation, he seemed disposed to delegate to
others the application of his mastery of this latter
resource. M. de Grosjoyaux was quite of another
complexion and could but have regarded his friend's
theological unction as the sign of an inaccessibly
superior spirit. His surprise was so bright that it
made him look amused; as if, under the impression
of M. Kapp's mere mass, he could n't recover from
the oddity of these hazards, that of the translation of
so much large looseness into a thing so fine as a
direction — even, as it were, a dreadfully wrong one.
He could have understood the *coup* if it had been his
own indeed, and he kept looking through the window,
over the shoulder of M. Ledoux, at a slender tree by
the end of a lane opposite the inn, as if measuring its
distance from his extended arm and secretly wishing

that, since the association of ideas was so close, he might indulge in a little speculative practice.

Newman found his company depressing, almost irritating. He himself could neither eat nor talk; his soul was sore with grief and anger and the weight of his double sorrow intolerable. He sat with his eyes on his plate, counting the minutes, wishing at one moment that Valentin would see him and leave him free to go in quest of Madame de Cintré and his lost happiness, and mentally calling himself a vile brute the next, for the egotism of his impatience. He at least was poor enough company, and even his acute preoccupation and his general lack of the habit, determined by all his need, of pondering the impression he produced, did n't prevent his guessing the others to be puzzled at poor Bellegarde's taking such a fancy to a dull barbarian as to desire him at his deathbed. After breakfast he strolled forth alone into the village and looked at the fountain, the geese, the open barn-doors, the brown, bent old women who showed their hugely-darned stocking-heels at the end of their slowly-clicking sabots, as well as at the beautiful view of snowy Alp and purple Jura hanging across either end of the rude street. The day was brilliant; early spring was in the air and the sunshine, and the winter's damp trickled out of the cottage eaves. It was birth and brightness for all nature, even for chirping chickens and other feathered waddling particles, and it was to be death and burial for poor foolish, generous, precious Valentin. Newman walked as far as the village church and went into the small graveyard beside it, where he sat down and looked at the awkward tablets planted about. They were all sordid and hideous, and he could feel only the hardness and coldness of death. He got up and came back to the inn, where he found M. Ledoux having coffee and a cigarette at a little green table which he had caused to be carried into the small garden. Newman, learning that the doctor was still sitting with Valentin, asked if he might n't be allowed to relieve him; he had a great desire to be useful to their patient. This was, through M. Ledoux, easily arranged; the doctor was very glad to go to bed. He was a youthful and rather jaunty practitioner, but he had a clever face and the ribbon of the Legion of Honour in his buttonhole; Newman listened attentively to his instructions and took mechanically from his hand an old book that had lain on the window-seat of the inn, recommended by him as a help to wakefulness and which proved an odd volume of "Les Liaisons Dangereuses."

Valentin still lay with his eyes closed and without visible change of condition. Newman sat down near him and for a long time narrowly watched him. Then he let his vision stray with his consciousness of his own situation — range away and rest on the chain of the Alps disclosed by the drawing of the scant white cotton curtain of the window, through which the sunshine passed and lay in squares on the red-tiled floor. He tried to interweave his gloom with strains of hope, but only half succeeded. What had happened to him was violent and insolent, like all great strokes of evil, unnatural and monstrous, it showed the hard hand of the Fate that rejoices in the groans and the blood of men, in the tears and the terrors of women, and he had no arms against it. At last a sound struck on the stillness and he heard Valentin's voice.

"It can't be about *me* you're pulling that long face!" He found when he turned that his patient lay in the same position, but with eyes now open and showing the glimmer of a smile. It was with a very slender strength that he felt the pressure of his hand answered. "I've been watching you for a quarter of an hour," Valentin went on; "you've been looking as if you too had had to swallow some vile drug. You're greatly disgusted with me, I see. Well, of course! So am I!"

'Oh, I shan't abuse you," said Newman. "I feel too badly. And how are you getting on?"

"Oh, I'm getting *off!* They've quite settled that. Aren't you here to *see* me off?"

"That's for you to settle; you can get well if you try," Newman declared with a queer strained quaver.

"My dear fellow, how can I try? Trying's violent exercise, and that sort of thing isn't in order for a man with a hole in his side as big as your hat, which begins to bleed if he moves a hair's breadth. I knew you'd come," he continued; "I knew I should wake up and find you here; so I'm not surprised. But last night I was very impatient. I didn't see how I could keep still without you. It was a matter of keeping still, just like this; as still as a mummy in his case. You talk about trying; I tried that! Well, here I am yet — these twenty hours. It's more like twenty days." Valentin's speech was slowly taken, with strange precautions and punctuations, but it had, however faint, the flicker of his gaiety, and he seemed almost to say what he wanted. It was visible, however, that he was in extreme pain, and at last he again closed his eyes. Newman begged him to make no effort — just, as he called it, to take his ease; the doctor had left urgent orders against worry. "Oh," returned Valentin, "let us eat and drink, for to-morrow — to-morrow —!" And he paused again. "No, not to-morrow, perhaps, but to-day. I can't eat and drink, but I can talk. What's to be gained, at this pass, by renun—renunciation? I must n't use such big words. I was always a chatterer; Lord, how I 've *bavardé* in my day!"

"That 's a reason for keeping quiet now," said Newman. "We know how beautifully you talk — it's all right about that."

But Valentin, without heeding him, went on with the same effect of trouble and of pluck. "I wanted to see you because you 've seen my sister. Does she know — will she come?"

Newman felt himself the poorest of deceivers. "Yes, by this time she must know."

"Did n't you tell her?" Valentin asked. And then, in a moment: "Did n't you bring me any message from her?" His eyes now covered his friend like lifted lamps.

"I did n't see her after I got your telegram. I wrote to her."

"And she sent you no answer?"

Newman managed to reply that Madame de Cintré had left Paris. "She went yesterday to Fleurières."

"Yesterday — to Fleurières? Why did she go to

Fleurières ? What day is this ? What day was yesterday ? Ah then, I shan't see her," Valentin moaned.
"Fleurières is too far!" And he became dark and
dumb again, only breathing a little harder. Newman
sat silent, invoking duplicity, but was relieved at
being able soon to believe him really too weak to be
curious. He did, however, at last break out again.
"And my mother — and my brother — will they
come ? Are they at Fleurières ?"

"They were in Paris, but I did n't see them either,"
Newman answered. "If they received your telegram
in time they 'll have started this morning. Otherwise
they 'll be obliged to wait for the night express and
change, and will arrive at the same hour I did."

"They won't thank me — they won't thank me,"
Valentin murmured. "They 'll pass an atrocious
night, and Urbain does n't like the early morning air.
I don't remember ever in my life to have seen him
before noon — before breakfast. No one ever saw
him. We don't know how he is then. Perhaps he 's
different. Who knows ? Posterity perhaps will know.
That 's the time he works in his *cabinet*, at the history
of the Princesses. But I had to send for them —
had n't I ? And then I want to see my mother sit
there where you sit and say good-bye to her — hear
her above all say hers to me. Perhaps, after all,
I don't know her — she may have some surprise for
me. Don't think you know her yet, yourself; perhaps
she may surprise *you*. But if I can't see Claire I don't
care — what do you call it ? — a red cent. Have you
then green *sous* or blue ones or any other colour ?
Ah vous, mon cher, vous en avez, vous, de toutes les

couleurs! But what's the matter — while I've been dreaming of her? Why did she go to Fleurières to-day? She never told me. What has happened? Ah, she ought to have guessed I'm here — in this bad way. It's the first time in her life she ever disappointed me. Poor, poor Claire!"

"You know we're not man and wife quite yet — your sister and I," said Newman. "She does n't yet account to me for all her actions." He tried to throw off this statement with grace, but felt how little the muscles of his face served him.

Valentin looked at him harder. "Have you two unimaginably quarrelled?"

"Never, never, never!" Newman exclaimed.

"How happily you say that!" said Valentin. "You're going to be happy — la-la!" In answer to this stroke of irony, none the less powerful for being so unconscious, all poor Newman could do was to give a helpless and ridiculous grin, for the conscious failure of which he then more ridiculously blushed. Valentin, still playing over him the fitful light of fever, presently said: "But something *is* the matter with you. I watched you just now; you have n't a bridegroom's face."

"My dear fellow," Newman desperately pleaded, 'how can I show *you* a bridegroom's face? If you think I enjoy seeing you lie here and not being able to help you —!"

"Why, you're just the man to be jolly and — what do you call it? — to crow; don't forfeit your right to it! I'm a proof of your wisdom. When was a man ever down when he could say 'I told you so!' You

told me so, you know. You did what you could about
it. You said some very good things; I 've thought
them carefully over. But, my dear friend, I was
right, all the same. This is the regular way."

"I did n't do what I ought," said Newman. "I
ought to have done something better"

"For instance?"

"Oh, something or other. I ought to have treated
you as a vicious small boy and have locked you up."

"Well, I 'm a very small boy now," Valentin softly
sighed, "and God knows I 've been vicious enough!
I 'm even rather less than an infant. An infant 's
helpless, but it 's generally voted promising. I 'm not
promising, eh? Society can't lose a less valuable
member." Newman was strongly moved. He got up
and turned his back on his friend and walked away to
the window, where he stood looking out but only
vaguely seeing. "No, I don't like the look of your
back," Valentin continued. "I 've always been an
observer of backs; yours is quite out of sorts."

Newman returned to his bedside and begged him
to be quiet. "Only rest and get well, give yourself
the very best chance. That 's what you want and
what you must do. Get well and help me."

"I told you you were in trouble! But how can
I 'help' you?" Valentin wailed.

"I 'll let you know when you 're better. You were
always awfully enquiring; there 's something to get
well *for!*" Newman answered with resolute animation.

Valentin relapsed once more and lay a long time
without speaking. He seemed even to have fallen

asleep. But at the end of half an hour he was again conversing. "I'm rather sorry about that place in the bank. Who knows but I might have become another Rothschild? But I was n't meant for a banker; bankers are not so easy to kill. Don't you think I've been very easy to kill? It's not like a serious man. It's really very mortifying. It's like telling your hostess you must go, when you count upon her begging you to stay, and then finding she does no such thing. 'Really — so soon? You've only just come!' This beastly underbred life of ours does n't make me any such polite little speech."

Newman for some time said nothing, but at last he broke out. "It's a bad case — it's a bad case — it's the worst case I ever met. I don't want to say anything unpleasant, but I can't help it. I've seen men dying before — and I've seen men shot. I've seen men in the worst kind of holes — worse even than yours. But it always seemed more natural; they were of no account compared to you — and at any rate I did n't care. But now — damnation, damnation! You might have done something more to the purpose. It's about the meanest wind-up of a man's legitimate business I can imagine!"

Valentin feebly waved his hand to and fro. "Don't insist — don't insist! It's taking a mean advantage. For you see at the bottom — down at the bottom in a little place as small as the end of a wine-funnel — I agree with you!" A few moments after this the doctor put his head through the half-opened door and, perceiving his charge was awake, came in to feel his pulse. He shook his head and declared he had talked too much — ten times too much. "Nonsense!" his patient protested; "a man sentenced to death is allowed to get in first all he can. He can't talk *after*, and if he was ever a talker —! Have you never read an account of an execution in a newspaper?" he went on. "Don't they always set a lot of people at the prisoner — lawyers, reporters, priests — to *make* him talk? But it's not Newman's fault; he sits there as mum as a death's-head."

The doctor observed that it was time the wound should be dressed again; MM. de Grosjoyaux and Ledoux, who had already witnessed this delicate operation, taking Newman's place as assistants. Newman withdrew, learning from his fellow-watchers in the other room that they had received a telegram from the Marquis to the effect that their message had been delivered in the Rue de l'Université too late to allow him to take the morning train, but that he would start with his mother in the evening. Our friend wandered away into the village again and walked about restlessly for two or three hours. The day had, in its regulated gloom, the length of some interminable classic tragedy. At dusk he came back and dined with the doctor and M. Ledoux. The dressing of Valentin's wound had been a very critical business; the question was definitely whether he could bear a repetition of it. He then declared that he must beg of Mr. Newman to deny himself for the present the satisfaction of sitting with M. de Bellegarde; more than any one else, apparently, he had the flattering but fatal gift of interesting him more than he could bear. M. Ledoux, at this, swallowed a glass of wine in silence; he must have been wondering what the deuce Bellegarde found so exciting in the American.

Newman, after dinner, went up to his room, where, flinging himself too on his bed at his grim length, he lay staring, for blank weariness, at the lighted candle and thinking that Valentin was dying downstairs. Late, when the candle had burnt low, came a soft tap at his door. The doctor stood there with another light and a motion of despair.

"He must *faire la fête toujours!* He insists on seeing you, and I 'm afraid you must come. I think that at this rate he 'll hardly outlast the night."

Newman went back to Valentin's room, which he found lighted by a taper on the hearth, but with its occupant begging for something brighter. "I want to see your face. They say you work me up," he went on as Newman complied with this request, "and I confess I 've felt worked up; but it is n't you — it 's my own great intelligence, that sacred spark, of which you 've such an opinion. Sit down there and let me look at you again." Newman seated himself, folded his arms and bent a heavy gaze on his friend. He felt as if he were now playing a part, mechanically, in the most lugubrious of comedies. Valentin faced him thus for some time. "Yes, this morning I was right; you 've something on your mind heavier than ever I 've had. Come, I 'm a dying man, and it 's indecent to deceive me. Something happened after I left Paris. It was n't for nothing that my sister started off at this season of the year for Fleurières. Why was it? It sticks in my crop. I 've been thinking it over, and if you don't tell me I shall guess."

"I had better not tell you," Newman mildly reasoned. "It won't do you any good."

" If you think it will do me any good not to tell me you 're very much mistaken. There 's trouble about your marriage."

"Yes. There 's trouble about my marriage."

"Good!" With which Valentin again waited a little. "They 've stopped it off."

"They 've stopped it off," Newman admitted Now that he had spoken out he found in it a relief that deepened as he went on. "Your mother and brother have broken faith. They 've decided that it can't take place. They 've decided I 'm not good enough — when they come to think of it. They 've taken back their word. Since you want to know, there it is!" Valentin uttered a strange sound, thrice lifting his hands and letting them drop. "I 'm sorry not to have anything better to tell you of them," Newman pursued. "But it 's not my fault. I was indeed bewildered enough when your telegram reached me; I was quite upside down. You may imagine whether I feel any better now."

Valentin gasped and moaned as if his wound were throbbing. "Broken faith, broken faith! And my sister — my sister ?"

"Your sister 's very unhappy; she has consented to give me up. I don't know why — I don't know what they 've done to her; it must be something pretty bad. In justice to her you ought to know. They 've made her suffer — what it is they must have put her through! I have n't seen her alone, but only before them We had an interview yesterday morning. They let me have it full in the face. They told me to go about my business. It seems to me a very bad case. I'm sorry to have such a report to make of them. I'm angry, I'm sore, I'm sick."

Valentin lay there staring, his eyes more brilliantly lighted, his lips soundlessly parted, a flush of colour in his pale face. Newman had never before uttered so many words in the plaintive key, but now, in speaking to his friend in that friend's extremity, he had a sense of making his lament somewhere within the presence of the power that men pray to in trouble; he felt his outgush of resentment as a spiritual act, an appeal to higher protection. "And Claire," the young man breathed; "Claire? She has given you up?"

"I don't really believe it."

"No, don't believe it, don't believe it. She's gaining time. Believe that."

"I immensely pity her!" said Newman.

"Poor, poor Claire!" Valentin sighed. "But they — but they —?" And he paused again. "You saw them; they dismissed you, face to face?"

"Face to face — rather!"

"What did they say?"

"They said they couldn't stand a commercial person."

Valentin put out his hand and laid it on Newman's arm. "And about their promise — their engagement with you?"

"They made a distinction. They said it was to hold good only until Madame de Cintré accepted me."

"But since she did —!"

"Well, since she did — *after* she did — they found, as I understand, that they could n't."

Valentin lay staring — his flush died away. "Don't tell me any more. I'm ashamed."

"You? You 're the soul of honour," said Newman very simply.

Valentin groaned and averted his head. For some time nothing more was said. Then he turned back again and found a certain force to press Newman's arm. "It's very bad — very bad. When my people — when my 'race' — come to that, it is time for me to pass away. I believe in my sister; she 'll explain. Pardon her, allow for her, be patient with her; wait for that. If she can't — if she can't make her conduct clear: well, forgive her somehow; at any rate don't curse her. She 'll pay — she *has* paid; with her one chance of happiness. But for the others it's very bad — very bad. You take it very hard? No, it's a shame to make you say so." He closed his eyes and again there was a silence. Newman felt almost awed; he had stirred his companion to depths down into which he now shrank from looking. Presently Valentin fixed him again, releasing his arm. "I apologise. Do you understand? Here on my death-bed. I apologise for my family. For my mother. For my brother. For the name I *was* proud of. Voilà!" he added softly.

Newman for all answer took his hand and kept it in his own. He remained quiet, and at the end of half an hour the doctor noiselessly returned. Behind him, through the half-open door, Newman saw the

two questioning faces of MM. de Grosjoyaux and
Ledoux. The doctor laid a hand on the patient's
wrist and sat looking at him. He gave no sign, and
the two gentlemen came in, M. Ledoux having first
beckoned to some one outside. This was M. le curé,
who carried in his hand an object unknown to Newman and covered with a white napkin. M. le curé
was short, round and red: he advanced, pulling off
his little black cap to Newman, and deposited his
burden on the table; and then he sat down in the
best armchair, folding his hands across his person.
The other gentlemen had exchanged glances which
expressed unanimity as to the timeliness of their
presence. But for a long time Valentin neither spoke
nor moved. It was Newman's belief afterwards
that M. le curé had gone to sleep. At last, abruptly,
their friend pronounced Newman's name. This
visitor went to him and he said in French: "You're
not alone. I want to speak to you alone." Newman
looked at the doctor and the doctor looked at the
curé, who looked back at him; and then the
doctor and the curé together gave a shrug. "Alone
— for five minutes," Valentin repeated. "Please
leave us." The curé took up his burden again
and led the way out, followed by his companions.
Newman closed the door behind them and came
back to Valentin, who had watched all this intently.

"It's very bad, it's very bad," he said after Newman had seated himself close. "The more I think
of it the worse it is."

"Oh, don't think of it!" Newman groaned.

But his friend went on without heeding him
"Even if they should come round again the shame —
the baseness — is there."

"Oh, they won't come round!" said Newman

"Well, you can make them."

"Make them?"

"I can tell you something — a great secret — an
immense secret. You can use it against them —
frighten them, coerce them."

"A secret!" Newman repeated. The idea of letting Valentin, on his deathbed, confide to him any
matter sacredly intimate, shocked him, for the moment, and made him draw back. It seemed an
illicit way of arriving at information and even had
a vague analogy with listening at a keyhole. Then
suddenly the thought of reducing Madame de Bellegarde and her son to the forms of submission became
attractive, and, as to lose in any case no last breath
of the spirit for which he had felt such a kindness,
he brought his head nearer For some time, however,
nothing more came. Valentin but covered him with
kindled, expanded, troubled eyes, and he began to
believe he had spoken in delirium. But at last he
spoke again.

"There was something done — something done
at Fleurières. It was some wrong, some violence,
I believe some cruelty. It may have been — God
forgive me *now* — some crime. My father — something happened to him: I don't know what; I've
been ashamed, afraid, to know. But a bad business
— a worse even than yours — there was *that*. My
mother knows — Urbain knows."

"Something happened to your father?" Newman permitted himself to ask.

Valentin looked at him still more wide-eyed. "He didn't get well. They didn't let him."

"'Let' him?" — Newman stared back. "Get well of what?"

But the immense effort he had made, first to decide to utter these words and then to bring them out, appeared to have taken his last strength. He lapsed again into silence and Newman sat watching him. "Do you understand?" he began again presently. "At Fleurières. You can find out. Mrs. Bread knows. Tell her I made this point — at this hour — of your asking her. She'll give you the truth itself — and then you'll show them you know it. It may do something for you. It may make the difference. If it doesn't, tell every one. It will — it will" — here Valentin's voice sank to the feeblest murmur — "it will pay them."

"Pay them?" — Newman wondered.

"What you owe them!"

The words died away in a long vague wail. Newman stood up, deeply impressed, not knowing what to say; his heart was beating as never. "Thank you," he said at last. "I'm much obliged." But Valentin seemed not to hear him; he remained silent and his silence continued. At last Newman went and opened the door. M. le curé re-entered, bearing his sacred vessel and followed by a young ministrant at his altar in a white stole, by the three gentlemen and by Valentin's servant. It was quite processional.

XX

VALENTIN DE BELLEGARDE died tranquilly, just as the cold faint March dawn began to clear the grave faces of the little knot of friends gathered about his bedside. An hour later Newman left the inn and drove to Geneva; he was naturally unwilling to be present at the arrival of Madame de Bellegarde and her first-born. At Geneva, for the moment, he remained. He was like a man who has had a fall and wants to sit still and count his bruises. He instantly wrote to Madame de Cintré, detailing to her the circumstances of her brother's death — with certain exceptions — and asking her what was the earliest moment at which he might hope she would consent to see him. M. Ledoux had told him he had reason to know that Valentin's will — he had had a great deal of light but pleasant personal property to dispose of — contained a request that he should be buried near his father in the churchyard of Fleurières, and Newman intended that the state of his own relations with the family should not deprive him of the satisfaction of helping to pay the last earthly honours to the best fellow in the world. He reflected that Valentin's friendship was older than Urbain's enmity, and that at a funeral it was easy to escape notice. Madame de Cintré's answer to his letter enabled him to time his arrival at Fleurières. This answer was very brief; it ran as follows·

"I thank you for your letter and for your being with Valentin. It is the most inexpressible sorrow to me that I was not. To see you will be only anguish; there's no need therefore to wait for what you call brighter days. It is all one now, and I shall have no brighter days. Come when you please; only notify me first. My brother is to be buried here on Friday, and my family is to remain. — C. DE C."

On receipt of this Newman had gone straight to Paris and to Poitiers. The journey had taken him far southward, through green Touraine and across the far-shining Loire, into a country where the early spring deepened divinely about him, but he had never made one during which he had heeded less the lay of the land. He alighted at an hotel in respect to which he scarce knew whether the wealth of its provincial note more graced or compromised it, and the next morning drove in a couple of hours to the village of Fleurières. But here, for all his melancholy, he could n't resist the intensity of an impression. The *petit bourg* lay at the base of a huge mound, on the summit of which stood the crumbling ruins of a feudal castle, much of whose sturdy material, as well as that of the wall that dropped along the hill to enclose the clustered houses defensively, had been absorbed into the very substance of the village. The church was simply the former chapel of the castle, fronting upon its grass-grown court, which, however, was of generous enough width to have given up its quaintest corner to a small place of interment. Here the very headstones themselves seemed to sleep as they slanted into the grass; the patient elbow of the rampart held them together on one side, and in front, far beneath their mossy lids, the green plains and blue distances stretched away. The approach to the church, up the hill, defied all wheels. It was lined with peasants two or three rows deep, who stood watching old Madame de Bellegarde slowly ascend on the arm of her elder son and behind the pall-bearers of the other. Newman chose to lurk among the common mourners who murmured "Madame la Comtesse" as a particular tall slimness almost bowed beneath its ensigns of woe passed before them. He stood in the dusky little church while the service was going forward, but at the dismal tombside he turned away and walked down the hill. He went back to Poitiers and spent two days in which patience and revolt were confounded in a single ache. On the third day he sent Madame de Cintré a note to the effect that he would call on her in the afternoon, and in accordance with this he again took his way to Fleurières. He left his vehicle at the tavern in the village street and obeyed the simple instructions given him for finding the château.

"It's just beyond there," said the landlord, and pointed to the tree-tops of the *parc* above the opposite houses. Newman followed the first cross-road to the right — it was bordered with mouldy cottages — and in a few moments saw before him the peaked roofs of the towers. Advancing further he found himself before a vast iron gate, rusty and closed; here he paused a moment, looking through the bars. The residence was near the road, as if the very highway belonged to it; this gave it a fine old masterly air

Newman learned afterwards, from a guide-book of the province, that it dated from the reign of Henry III. It presented to the wide-paved area which preceded it, and which was edged with shabby farm-buildings, an immense façade of dark time-stained brick, flanked by two low wings, each of which terminated in a little Dutch-looking pavilion capped with a fantastic roof. Two towers rose behind, and behind the towers was a grand group of elms and beeches, now just faintly green. The great feature, however, was a wide green river, which washed the foundations of the pile. The whole mass rose from an island in the circling stream, so that this formed a perfect moat, spanned by a two-arched bridge without a parapet. The dull brick walls, which here and there made a grand straight sweep, the ugly little cupolas of the wings, the deep-set windows, the long steep pinnacles of mossy slate, all mirrored themselves in the quiet water.

Newman rang at the gate, and was almost frightened at the tone with which a big rusty bell above his head replied to him. An old woman came out from the gatehouse and opened the creaking portal just wide enough for him to pass, on which he went in and across the dry bare court and the little cracked white slabs of the causeway on the moat. At the door of the house he waited for some moments, and this gave him a chance to observe that Fleurières was not "kept up" and to reflect that it was a melancholy place of residence. "It looks," he said to himself — and I give the comparison for what it is worth — "like a Chinese penitentiary." At last the door was opened by a servant whom he remembered to have seen in the Rue de l'Université. The man's dull face brightened as he perceived our hero, the case always being that Newman, for indefinable reasons, enjoyed the confidence of the liveried gentry. The footman led the way across a great main vestibule, with a pyramid of plants at its centre and glass doors all around, to what appeared to be the principal saloon. The visitor crossed the threshold of a room of superb proportions, which made him feel at first like a tourist with a guide-book and a cicerone awaiting a fee. But when his guide had left him alone after observing that he would call Madame la Comtesse, he saw the place contained little that was remarkable beyond a dusky ceiling with curiously carved beams, a set of curtains of elaborate antiquated tapestry and a dark oaken floor polished like a mirror. He waited some minutes, walking up and down; then at last, as he turned at the end of the room, saw Madame de Cintré had come in by a distant door. She wore a black dress — she stood looking at him. As the length of the immense room lay between them he had time to take her well in before they met in the middle of it.

He was dismayed at the change in her appearance. Pale, heavy-browed, almost haggard, with a monastic rigidity in her dress, she had little but her pure features in common with the woman whose radiant good grace he had hitherto admired. She let her eyes rest on his own and surrendered to him her hand; but the eyes were like two rainy autumn moons and the touch portentously lifeless. "I was at your brother's funeral," he said. "Then I waited three days. But I could wait no longer."

"Nothing can be lost or gained by waiting," she answered. "But it was very considerate of you to wait, horribly wronged as you've been."

"I'm glad you think I've been horribly wronged," said Newman with that vague effect of whimsicality with which he often uttered words of the gravest meaning.

"Do I need to say so?" she asked. "I don't think I've wronged, seriously, many persons; certainly not consciously. To you, to whom I have done this hard and cruel thing, the only reparation I can make is to say that I know it, that I feel it. But such words are pitifully poor."

"Oh, they're a great step forward!" said Newman with a fixed and ah — as he even himself felt — such an anxious smile of encouragement. He pushed a chair toward her and held it, looking at her urgently. She sat down mechanically and he seated himself near her; but in a moment he got up and stood restlessly before her. She remained there like a troubled creature who had passed through the stage of restlessness.

"I say nothing's to be gained by my seeing you," she went on, "and yet I'm very glad you came. Now I can tell you what I feel. It's a selfish pleasure, but it's one of the last I shall have." And she paused with her great misty eyes on him. "I know how I've deceived and injured you; I know how cruel and cowardly I've been. I see it as vividly as you do — I feel it to the ends of my fingers." And she unclasped her hands, which were locked together in her lap, lifted them and dropped them at her side. "Anything that you may have said of me in your angriest passion is nothing to what I have said to myself."

"In my angriest passion," said Newman, "I 've said nothing hard of you. The very worst thing I 've said of you yet is that you 're the most perfect of women." And he seated himself before her again abruptly.

She flushed a little, but even her flush was dim. "That 's because you think I 'll come back. But I shall not come back. It 's in that hope you have come here, I know; I 'm very sorry for you. I 'd do almost anything for you. To say that, after what I have done, seems simply impudent; but what can I say that will not seem impudent? To wrong you and apologise — that 's easy enough. I should not, heaven forgive me, have wronged you." She stopped a moment, always with her tragic eyes on him, but motioned him to let her talk. "I ought never to have listened to you at first; that was the wrong. No good could come of it. I felt it, and yet I listened; that was your fault. I liked you too much; I believed in you."

"And don't you believe in me now?"

"More than ever. But now it does n't matter. I 've given you up."

Newman gave a great thump with his clenched fist upon his knee. "Why, why, why?" he cried. "Give me a reason — a decent reason. You 're not a child — you 're not a minor nor an idiot. You 're not obliged to drop me because your mother told you to. Such a reason is n't worthy of you."

"I know that; it 's not worthy of me. But it 's the only one I have to give. After all," said Madame de Cintré, throwing out vain hands, "think me an idiot and forget me! That will be the simplest way."

He got up and walked away with a crushing sense that his cause was lost and yet with an equal inability to give up fighting. He went to one of the great windows and looked out at the stiffly-embanked river and the formal gardens beyond it. When he turned round she had risen; she stood there silent and passive, so passive that it told terribly of her detachment. "You 're not frank," he began again; "you 're not really honest any more than you 're merciful. Instead of saying you 're imbecile you should say that other people are wicked. Your mother and your brother have been false and cruel; they have been so to me, and I 'm sure they have been so to you. Why do you try to shield them? Why do you sacrifice me to *them*? I 'm not false; I 'm not cruel. You don't know what you give up; I can tell you that -- you *don't*. They bully you and plot about you; and I — I —" And he paused, lifting the strong arms to which she would n't come. She but turned away and began to leave him. "You told me the other day that you were afraid of your mother," he followed her to say. "It must have meant something. What therefore *did* it mean?"

She shook her head. "I remember. I was sorry afterwards."

"You were sorry when she came down on you and used some atrocious advantage. In God's name, what *is* it she does to you?"

"Nothing. Nothing that you can understand. And now that I 've given you up I must n't complain of her to you."

"That 's no reasoning!" cried Newman. "Complain of her, on the contrary, for all you 're worth. To whom on God's earth *but* to me? Tell me all about it, frankly and trustfully, as you ought, and we 'll talk it over so satisfactorily that you 'll keep your plighted faith."

Madame de Cintré looked down some moments fixedly; at last she raised her eyes. "One good at least has come of this: I 've made you judge me more fairly. You thought of me in a way that did me great honour; I don't know why you had taken it into your head. But it left me no loophole for escape — no chance to be the common weak creature I am. It was not my fault; I warned you from the first. But I ought to have warned you more. I ought to have convinced you that I was doomed to disappoint you. But I *was*, in a way, too proud. You see what my superiority amounts to, I hope!" she went on, raising her voice with a tremor that even then and there he found all so inconsequently sweet. "I 'm too proud to be honest, I 'm not too proud to be faithless. I'm timid and cold and selfish. I'm afraid of being uncomfortable."

"And you call marrying me uncomfortable?" he stared.

She flushed as with the sense of being only shut up in her pain, and seemed to say that if begging his pardon in words had that effect of an easy condition for her she might at least thus mutely express her per-

fect comprehension of his finding her conduct odious.
"It's not marrying you; it's doing all that would go
with it. It's the rupture, the defiance, the insisting
upon being happy in my own way. What right have
I to be happy when — when — ?" Again she broke
down.

'When what?" he pressed.

"When others have so suffered."

"What others?" he demanded. "What have you
to do with any others but me? Besides, you said just
now that you wanted happiness and that you should
find it by obeying your mother. You strangely contradict yourself."

"Yes, I strangely contradict myself; that shows
you — strangely enough too — that I'm not even
intelligent."

"You're laughing at me!" he cried. "It's as if
you were horribly mocking!"

She looked at him intently, and an observer might
have believed her to be asking herself if she should n't
most quickly end their common pain by confessing to
some such monstrosity. Yet "No; I'm not," was
what she presently said.

"Granting that you're not intelligent," he went
on, "that you're weak, that you're common, that
you're nothing I've believed you to be — what I ask
of you is not an heroic effort, it's a very easy and
possible effort. There's a great deal on my side to
make it so. The simple truth is that you don't care
enough for me to make it.'

"I'm cold," said Madame de Cintré. "I'm as cold
as that flowing river."

Newman gave a great rap on the floor with his stick and a long grim laugh. "Ah, not you! You go altogether too far — you overshoot the mark. There is n't a woman in the world as bad as you would make yourself out. I see your game; it 's what I said. You 're blackening yourself to whiten others. You don't want to give me up at all; you like me — you like me, God help you! I know you do; you 've shown it, and I 've felt it and adored you for it! After that you may be as cold as you please! They 've bullied you, I say; they 've tortured you. It's an outrage, and I insist on saving you from the extravagance of your generosity. Would you chop off your hand if your mother required it?"

She gave at this the long sigh of a creature too hard pressed. "I spoke of my mother too blindly the other day. I'm my own mistress, by law and by her approval. She can do nothing to me; she has done nothing. She has never alluded to those hard words I used about her."

"She has made you feel them, I'll promise you!" said Newman.

"It's my conscience that makes me feel them."

"Your conscience then seems to me rather extraordinarily mixed!" he passionately returned

"It has been in great trouble, but now it's very clear. I don't give you up for any worldly advantage or for any worldly happiness."

"Oh, you don't give me up for Lord Deepmere, I know," he agreed. "I won't pretend, even to provoke you, that I think that. But that's what your mother and your brother wanted, and your mother at that villainous ball of hers — I liked it at the time, but the very thought of it now is a bath of fire! — tried to push him on to make up to you."

"Who told you this?" she asked with her strange, stricken mildness.

"Not Valentin. I observed it. I guessed it. I did n't know at the time that I was observing it, but it stuck in my memory. And afterwards, you recollect, I saw Lord Deepmere with you in the conservatory. You said then that you would tell me at another time what he had said to you."

"That was before — before *this*," she immediately pleaded.

"It does n't matter," said Newman; "and, besides, I think I know. He's an honest little Englishman. He came and told you what your mother was up to — that she wanted him to supplant me; not being a commercial person. If he would make you an offer she would undertake to bring you over and give me the slip — getting rid of me easily, or at least decently, somehow. Lord Deepmere is n't remarkably bright, so she had to spell it out to him. He said he admired you 'no end,' and that he wanted you to know it; but he did n't like being mixed up with that sort of treachery, and he came to you and told tales. That was about the size of it, was n't it? And then you said you were perfectly happy."

"I don't see why we should talk of Lord Deepmere," she returned. "It was n't for that you came here; and about my mother it does n't matter what you suspect and what you know. When once my mind has been made up, as it is now, I should n't discuss these things. Discussing anything now is very vain and only a fresh torment. We must try and live each as we can. I believe you'll be happy again; even, sometimes, when you think of *me*. When you do so, think this — that it was not easy and that I did the best I could. I've things to reckon with that you don't know. I mean I've feelings. I must do as they force me — I must, I must. They'd haunt me otherwise," she cried, with vehemence; "they'd give me no rest and would kill me!"

"I know what your feelings are: they're perversities and superstitions! They're the feeling that after all, though I *am* a good fellow, I've been in business; the feeling that your mother's looks are law and your brother's words are gospel; that you all hang together and that it's a part of the everlasting great order, *your* order, that they should have a hand in everything you do. It makes my blood boil. That *is* cold; you're right. And what I feel here," and Newman struck his heart and became more eloquent than he knew, "is a glowing fire!"

A spectator less preoccupied than Madame de Cintré's distracted wooer would have felt sure from the first that her appealing calm of manner was the result of violent effort, in spite of which the tide of agitation was rapidly rising. On these last words of Newman's it overflowed, though at first she spoke low, for fear her voice might betray her. "No, I was not right — I'm not cold! I believe that if I'm doing what seems so bad it's not mere weakness and falsity. My dear friend, my best of friends, it's like a religion.

I can't tell you — I can't! It's cruel of you to insist.
I don't see why I should n't ask you to believe me —
and pity me. It's like a religion. There's a curse
upon the house; I don't know what — I don't know
why — don't ask me. We must all bear it. I've been
too selfish; I wanted to escape from it. You offered
me a great chance — besides my liking you. I liked
you more than I ever liked any one," she insisted to
him with a beauty and purity of clearness, and yet
with the sad fallacy of thinking, apparently, that she
made the case less tragic for him by making it more
tragic for herself. "It seemed good to change completely, to break, to go away. And then I admired
you, I admired you," she so nobly and decently repeated. "But I can't — it has overtaken and come
back to me." Her self-control had now completely
abandoned her, and her words were broken with long
sobs. "Why do such dreadful things happen to us —
why is my brother Valentin killed, like a beast, in the
beauty of his youth and his gaiety and his brightness
and all that we loved him for? Why are there things
I can't ask about — that I'm afraid, for my life, to
know? Why are there places I can't look at, sounds
I can't hear? Why is it given to me to choose, to
decide, in a case so hard and so terrible as this? I'm
not meant for that — I'm not made for boldness and
defiance. I was made to be happy in a quiet natural
way." At this Newman gave a most expressive groan,
but she quavered heartbreakingly on: "I was made to
do gladly and gratefully what's expected of me. My
mother has always been very good to me; that's all
I can say. I must n't judge her; I must n't criticise

her. If I did it would come dreadfully back to me
I can't change!"

"No," said Newman bitterly; "*I* must change —
if I break in two in the effort!"

"You're different. You're a man; you'll get over
it. You'll live, you'll do things, you can't not do
good, therefore you can't not be happy: you'll find all
kinds of consolation. You were born — you were
trained — to changes. Besides, besides, I shall always think of you."

"I don't care for that!" he almost shouted.
"You're cruel — you're terribly cruel, God forgive
you! You may have the best reasons and the finest
feelings in the world; that makes no difference.
You're a mystery to me; I don't see how such hardness can go with anything so divine!"

Madame de Cintré fixed him a moment with her
swimming eyes. "You believe I'm hard then?"

He glared as if at her drowning beyond help; then
he broke out: "You're a perfect, faultless, priceless
creature! For God's sake, stay by me!"

"Of course I'm hard *in effect*," she pitifully reasoned; "though if ever a creature was innocent, in
intention — ! Whenever we give pain we're hard.
And we *must* give pain; that's the world — the hateful miserable world! Ah!" and she gave a sigh as
sharp as the shudder of an ague, "I can't even say
I'm glad to have known you — though I am. That
too is to wrong you. I can say nothing that's not
cruel. Therefore let us part without more of this
Good-bye!" And she put out her hand.

Newman stood and looked at it without taking it,

and then raised his eyes to her face. He felt in them the rising tears of rage. "What do you mean to do? Where are you going?"

"Where I shall give no more pain and suspect no more evil. I'm going out of the world."

"Out of the world?"

"I'm going into a convent."

"Into a convent!" He repeated the words with the deepest dismay; it was as if she had said she was going into an hospital for incurables. "Into a convent — *you!*"

"I told you that it was not for my worldly advantage or pleasure I was leaving you."

But still he hardly understood. "You're going to be a nun," he went on; "in a cell — for life — with a gown and a black veil?"

"A nun — a blest Carmelite nun," said Madame de Cintré. "For life, with God's leave and mercy."

The image rose there, at her words, too dark and horrible for belief, and affected him as if she had told him she was going to mutilate her beautiful face or drink some potion that would make her mad. He clasped his hands and began to tremble visibly. "Madame de Cintré, don't, don't, I beseech you! On my knees, if you like, I'll beseech you."

She laid her hand on his arm with a tender, pitying, almost reassuring gesture. "You don't understand, you've wrong ideas. It's nothing horrible. It's only peace and safety. It's to be out of the world, where such troubles as this come to the innocent, to the best. And for life — that's the blessing of it! They can't begin again."

He dropped into a chair and sat looking at her with a long inarticulate wail. That this superb woman, in whom he had seen all human grace, the rarest personal resource, should turn from him and all the brightness he offered her — him and his future and his fortune and his fidelity — to muffle herself in ascetic rags and entomb herself in a cell, was a confounding combination of the merciless and the impossible. As the vision spread before him the impossibility turned to the monstrous; it was a reduction to the absurd of the trial to which he was subjected. "You — you a nun; you with your beauty defaced and your nature wasted — you behind locks and bars! Never, never, if I can prevent it!" And he sprang to his feet in loud derision.

"You can't prevent it," she returned, "and it ought —a little—to satisfy you. Do you suppose I'll go on living in the world, still beside you, and yet not *with* you? It's all arranged. Good-bye, good-bye."

This time he took her hand, took it in both his own. "For ever?" he said. Her lips made an inaudible movement and his own sounded a deep imprecation. She closed her eyes as if with the pain of hearing it; then he drew her toward him and clasped her to his breast. He kissed her white face again and again, as to leave less of it for his loss; for an instant she resisted and for a minute she submitted; then, with a force that threw him back panting, she disengaged herself and hurried away over the long shining floor. The next moment the door closed behind her, and after another he had made his way out as he could.

XXI

THERE is a pretty public walk at Poitiers, laid out
upon the crest of the high hill around which the little
city clusters, planted with thick trees and looking
down on the fertile fields in which the old English
princes fought for their right and held it. Newman
paced up and down this retreat for the greater part of
the next day, letting his eyes wander over the historic
prospect; but he would have been sadly at a loss to
tell you afterwards if the latter was made up of coal-
fields or of vineyards. He was wholly possessed by
his pang, of which reflection by no means diminished
the ache. He feared the creature he had thus learned
to adore was irretrievably lost; and yet in what case
of straight violation of his right of property had he
ever merely sat down and groaned? In what case
had he not made some attempt at recovery? Wholly
unused to giving up in difficulties, he found it impossible to turn his back upon Fleurières and its
inhabitants; it seemed to him some germ of hope or
reparation must lurk there somewhere if he could only
stretch his arm out far enough to pluck it. It was as
if he had his hand on a door-knob and were closing his
clenched fist on it: he had thumped, he had called, he
had pressed the door with his powerful knee and
shaken it with all his strength, and dead, damning
silence had answered him. And yet something held
him there — something hardened the grasp of his

fingers. His satisfaction had been too intense, his whole plan too deliberate and mature, his prospect of happiness too rich and comprehensive, for this fine moral fabric to crumble at a stroke. The very foundation seemed fatally injured and yet he felt a stubborn desire still to try to save the edifice. He was filled with a sorer sense of wrong than he had ever known, or than he had supposed it possible he should know. To accept his injury and walk away without looking behind him was a stretch of accommodation of which he found himself incapable. He looked behind him intently and continually, and what he saw there did n't assuage his resentment. He saw himself trustful, generous, liberal, patient, easy, pocketing frequent irritation and furnishing unlimited modesty. To have eaten humble pie, to have been snubbed and patronised and satirised, and have consented to take it as one of the conditions of the bargain — to have done this, and done it all for nothing, surely gave one a right to protest.

And to be turned off because one was a commercial person! As if he had ever talked or dreamt of the commercial since his connexion with the Bellegardes began — as if he had made the least circumstance of the commercial — as if he would n't have consented to confound the commercial fifty times a day if it might have increased by a hair's breadth the chance of his not suffering this so much more than commercial treachery! Granted one's being commercial was fair ground for one's being cleverly " sold," how little they knew about the class so designated and its enterprising way of not standing on trifles! It was in the light of his injury that the weight of his past endurance seemed so heavy; his current irritation had not been so great, merged as it was in his vision of the cloudless blue that overarched his more intimate relation. But now his sense of outrage was deep, rancorous and ever-present; he felt himself as swindled as he had been confiding. As for his friend's spiritual position, it moved him but to dismal mystification; it struck him with a kind of awe, and the fact that he was powerless to understand it or feel the reality of its motives only made it a deadlier oppression. He had never let the fact of her religious faith trouble him; Catholicism was only a name to him, and to express a mistrust of her forms of worship would have implied that he had other and finer ones to offer: which was as little possible as might be. If such flawless white flowers as that could bloom in Catholic soil they but attested its richness. But it was one thing to be a Catholic and another to turn nun — on your hands! There was something lugubriously comical in the way Newman's thoroughly contemporaneous optimism was confronted with this dusky old-world expedient. To see a woman made for him and for motherhood to his children juggled away in this tragic travesty — it was a thing to rub one's eyes over, a nightmare, an extravagance, a hoax. But the hours passed without disproving anything, passed leaving him only the aftertaste of the vehemence with which he had held her to his heart. He remembered her words and her looks — he lived through again the sense of her short submission; he turned them over and tried to make them square with the saving of something from his

wreck. How had she meant that the force driving
her was, as a thing apart from the conventual ques
tion, a "religion"? It was the religion simply of the
family laws, the religion of which her implacable
mother was priestess. Twist the thing about as her
generosity would, the one certain fact was that they
had been able to determine her act. Her generosity
had tried to screen them, but Newman's heart rose
into his throat at the thought that they should go
scot-free.

The twenty-four hours spent themselves, and the
next morning he sprang to his feet with the resolution
to return to Fleurières and demand another interview
with Madame de Bellegarde and her son. He lost no
time in putting it into practice. As he rolled swiftly
over the excellent road in the little calèche furnished
him at the inn at Poitiers, he drew forth, as it were,
from the very safe place in his mind to which he had
consigned it, the last information given him by poor
Valentin. Valentin had told him he could do something with it, and Newman thought it would be well
to have it at hand. This was of course not the first
time, lately, that he had given it his attention. It was
information in the rough — it was formless and obscure; but he was neither helpless nor afraid. Valentin had clearly meant to put him in possession of
a weapon he could use, though he could n't be said
to have placed the handle very securely in his grasp.
But if he had told him nothing definite he had at
least given him a clue — a clue of which the decidedly remarkable Mrs. Bread held the other end.
Mrs. Bread had always looked to Newman as if she

held clues; and as he apparently enjoyed her esteem he suspected she might be induced to share with him her knowledge. So long as there was only Mrs. Bread to deal with he felt easy. As to what there was to find out, he had only one fear — that it might not be bad enough. Then, when the image of the Marquise and her son rose before him again, standing side by side, the old woman's hand in Urbain's arm and the same cold guarded glare in the eyes of each, he cried out to himself that the fear was groundless. There was crime in the air at the very least! He arrived at Fleurières almost in a state of elation; he had satisfied himself, logically, that in the presence of his threat of penetration they would, as he mentally phrased it, rattle down like loosened buckets. He remembered indeed that he must first catch his hare — first ascertain what there was to penetrate; but after that why should n't his happiness be as good as new? Mother and son, dropping in terror the tender victim they had mauled, would take to hiding, and Madame de Cintré, left to herself, would surely come back to him. Give her a chance and she would rise to the surface and return to the light How could she fail to perceive that his house would have all the security of a convent and none of the dampness?

Newman, as he had done before, left his conveyance at the inn and walked the short remaining distance to the château. When he reached the gate, however, a singular feeling took possession of him — a feeling which, strange as it may seem, had its source in his unfathomable good-nature. He stood there a while, looking through the bars at the large time-stained face beyond and wondering to what special misdeed it was that the dark old dwelling with the flowery name had given convenient occasion. It had given occasion, first and last, to tyrannies and sufferings enough, Newman said to himself; it was an evil-looking place to live in. Then suddenly came the reflexion: what a horrible rubbish-heap of iniquity to fumble through! The attitude of inquisitor turned its ignoble face, and with the same movement he declared that the Bellegardes should have another chance. He would appeal once more directly to their sense of fairness and not to their fear; and if they should be accessible to reason he need know nothing worse about them than what he already knew. That was bad enough.

The gate-keeper let him in through the same "mean" crevice of aperture — for so he qualified it — as before, and he passed through the court and over the rustic bridge of the moat. The door was opened before he had reached it, and, as if to put his clemency to rout with the suggestion of a richer opportunity, Mrs. Bread stood there awaiting him. Her face, as usual, looked hopelessly blank, like the tide-smoothed sea-sand, and her black garments hung as heavy as if soaked in salt tears. Newman had already learned how interesting she could make the expression of nothing at all, and he scarce knew whether she now struck him as almost dumb or as almost effusive. "I thought you would try again, sir. I was looking out for you."

"I'm glad to see you," he answered; "I think you're my friend."

Mrs. Bread looked at him opaquely. "I wish you well, sir; but it's vain wishing now."

"You know then how they've treated me?"

"Oh, sir," she dryly returned, "I know everything."

He frankly enough wondered. "Everything?"

Her eyes just visibly lighted. "I know at least too much."

"One can never know too much. I congratulate you on every scrap of it. I've come to see Madame de Bellegarde and her son," Newman added. "Are they at home? If they're not I'll wait."

"My lady's always at home," Mrs. Bread replied, "and the Marquis is mostly with her."

"Please then tell them — one or the other, or both — that I'm here and that I should like to see them."

Mrs. Bread hesitated. "May I take a great liberty, sir?"

"You've never taken a liberty but you've justified it," said Newman with diplomatic urbanity.

She dropped her wrinkled eyelids as if she were curtseying; but the curtsey stopped there: the occasion was too grave. "You've come to plead with them again, sir? Perhaps you don't know this — that the poor Countess returned this morning to Paris."

"Ah, she's gone!" And Newman, groaning, smote the pavement with his stick

"She's gone straight to the convent — the Carmelites, you know, is the miserable name. I see you do know, sir. My lady and the Marquis take it very ill. It was only last night she told them."

"Ah, she had kept it back then?" he cried. "Well, that's all right. And they're highly worked up?"

"They're certainly not pleased. But they may well dislike it. They tell me it's most dreadful, sir; of all the nuns in Christendom the Carmelites are the worst. They're so unnatural that you may say they're really not human; they make you give up everything in the world you have — for ever and for ever. And to think of *her* in that destitution! If I was one who sat down and cried, sir, I could give way at this moment."

Newman looked at her an instant. "We must n't cry, Mrs. Bread, and still less must we sit down. We must stand right up and act. Please let them know." And he took a forward step.

But she gently checked him. "May I take another liberty? I'm told you were with poor Count Valentin, heaven forgive him, in his last hours, and I should bless you, sir, if you could tell me a word about him. He was my own dear boy, sir; for the first year of his life he was hardly out of my arms; I taught him the first words he spoke — and he spoke so beautifully, did n't he, sir? He always spoke well to his poor old Bread. When he grew up and took his pleasure he always had a kind word for me. And to die in that wild wrong way! They've a story that he fought with a wine-merchant. I can't believe *that* of him, sir! And was he in great pain?"

"You're a wise, kind old woman, Mrs. Bread," said Newman. "I hoped I might see you with my

own children in your arms. Perhaps I shall yet."
And he put out his hand. She looked for a moment
at his open palm, and then, as if fascinated by the
novelty of the gesture, extended her own ladylike
member. Newman held it firmly and deliberately,
fixing his eyes on her. "You want to know all about
the Count?"

"It would be a terrible pleasure, sir."

"I can tell you everything. Can you sometimes
leave this place?"

"The château, sir? I really don't know. I've
never tried."

"Try then; try hard. Try this evening at dusk.
Come to me in the old ruin there on the hill, in the
court before the church. I'll wait for you on that
spot; I've something very important to tell you.
A grand old woman like you can do as she pleases."

She wondered with parted lips. "Is it from the
dear Count, sir?"

"From the dear Count — from his damnable
deathbed."

"I'll come, then. I'll be bold, for once, for
him."

She led Newman into the great drawing-room with
which he had already made acquaintance, and retired
to carry his message. He waited a long time; at last
he was on the point of ringing and repeating his request. He was looking round him for a bell when the
Marquis came in with his mother on his arm. It will
be seen he had a logical mind when I say that he
declared to himself, in perfect good faith, as a result
of Valentin's supreme communication, that his ad-

versaries looked grossly wicked and capable of the blackest evil. "There's no mistake about it now," he reflected as they advanced. "They're a bad, bad lot; they've pulled off the varnished mask." Madame de Bellegarde and her son certainly bore in their faces the signs of extreme perturbation; they were plainly people who had passed a sleepless night. Confronted, moreover, with an annoyance which they hoped they had disposed of, it was not natural they should meet their visitor with conciliatory looks. He stood before them, and of the coldest glare they could command he had the full benefit. He felt as if the door of a sepulchre had suddenly been opened and the damp darkness were exhaled.

"You see I've come back," he said, however, with a tentative freshness. "I've come to try again."

"It would be ridiculous," the Marquis returned, "to pretend that we're glad to see you or that we don't question the taste of your visit."

"Oh, don't talk about taste!" — and Newman permitted himself perhaps the harshest laugh into which he had ever broken; "that would bring us round to yours! If I consulted my taste I certainly would n't come to see you. Besides, I'll make as short work as you please. Give me a guarantee that you'll raise the blockade — that you'll set Madame de Cintré at liberty — and I'll retire on the spot."

"We hesitated as to whether we would see you," said Madame de Bellegarde; "and we were on the point of declining the honour. But it seemed to me we should act with civility, as we've always done, and I wished to have the satisfaction of informing you that there are certain weaknesses people of our way of feeling can be guilty of but once."

"You may be weak but once, but you'll be audacious many times, madam," Newman rang out. "I did n't come, however, for conversational purposes. I came to say this simply: that if you'll write immediately to your daughter that you withdraw your opposition to our marriage I'll take care of the rest. You don't want to make of her a cloistered nun — you know more about the horrors of it than I do. Marrying a commercial person is better than being buried alive. Give me a letter to her, signed and sealed, saying you give way and that she may take me with your blessing, and I'll take it to her at her place of retreat and bring that retreat to an instant end. There's your chance — and I call them easy terms."

"We look at the matter otherwise, you know. We call any terms that you can propose impossible," Urbain declared. They had all remained standing stiffly in the middle of the room. "I think my mother will tell you that she'd rather her daughter should become Sœur Catherine than Mrs. Christopher Newman."

But the old lady, with the serenity of supreme power, let her son make her epigrams for her. She only smiled, almost sweetly, shaking her head and repeating: "But once, Mr. Newman; but once!"

Nothing he had ever seen or heard gave him such a sense of polished marble hardness as this movement and the tone that accompanied it. "Is there anything that would weigh with you?" he asked

"Is there anything that would, as we say, squeeze you?" he continued.

"This language, sir," said the Marquis, "addressed to people in bereavement and grief, is beyond all qualification."

"In most cases," Newman answered, "your objection would have some force, even admitting that Madame de Cintré's present intentions make time precious. But I've thought of what you speak of, and I've come here to-day without superfluous scruples simply because I regard your brother and you as very different parties. I see no connexion between you. Your brother was mortally ashamed of you both. Lying there wounded and dying, lying there confounded and disgusted, he formally apologised to me for your conduct. He apologised to me for that of his mother."

For a moment the effect of these words was as if he had struck a physical blow. A quick flush leaped into the charged faces before him — it was like a jolt of full glasses, making them spill their wine. Urbain uttered two words which Newman but half heard, but of which the aftersense came to him in the reverberation of the sound. "*Le misérable!*"

"You show little respect for the afflicted living," said Madame de Bellegarde, "but you might at least respect the helpless dead. Don't profane — don't touch with your unholy hands — the memory of my innocent son."

"I speak the simple sacred truth," Newman now imperturbably proceeded, "and, speaking it for a purpose, I desire you shall have no genuine doubt of

it. You made Valentin's last hour an hour of anguish
and my friend's generous spirit repudiates your
abominable act."

Urbain de Bellegarde had, from whatever emotion,
turned so pale that it might have been at the evoked
spectre of his brother; but not for an appreciable
instant did his mother lower her crest. "You have
beau jeu, as we say, before the silence of the grave,
for every calumny and every insult. But I don't
know," she admirably wound up, "that it in the least
matters."

"Ah, I don't know that poor Valentin's apology
particularly does either," Newman reflectively conceded. "I pitied him certainly more for having to
utter it than I felicitate myself even now for your
having to hear it."

The Marquise wrapt herself for a minute in a high
aloofness so entire, so of her whole being, as he could
feel, that she fairly appeared rather to contract than
to expand with the intensity and dignity of it; and out
of the heart of this withdrawn extravagance her final
estimate of their case sounded clear. "To have
broken with you, sir, almost consoles me; and you
can judge how much that says! Urbain, open the
door." She turned away with an imperious motion
to her son and passed rapidly down the length of the
room. The Marquis went with her and held the
door open. Newman was left standing.

He lifted a finger as a sign to M. de Bellegarde, who
closed the door behind his mother and stood waiting.
Newman slowly advanced, more silent, for the moment, than life. The two men stood face to face.

Then our friend had a singular sensation; he felt his sense of wrong almost brim over into gaiety. "Come," he said, "you don't treat me well. At least admit that."

M. de Bellegarde looked at him from head to foot and then spoke in the most delicate, best-bred voice. "I execrate you personally."

"That's the way I feel to *you*, but for politeness' sake I don't say it. It's singular I should want so much to be your brother-in-law, but I can't give it up. Let me try once more." And Newman paused a moment. "You've something on your mind and on your conscience, your mother and you — something in your life that you've kept as much as possible in the dark because it would n't look well in the light of day. You've a skeleton, as they say, in your closet." M. de Bellegarde continued to look at him hard, but it was a question if his eyes betrayed anything; the expression of his eyes was always so strange. Newman paused again and then went on. "You've done, between you, somehow and at some time, something still more base — wonderful as that may seem — than what you've done to me." At this M. de Bellegarde's eyes certainly did change; they flickered like blown candles. Newman could feel him turn cold; but his form was still quite perfect.

"Continue," he encouragingly said.

Newman lifted a finger and made it waver a little in the air. "Need I continue? You know what I mean."

"Pray, where did you obtain this interesting information?" M de Bellegarde inordinately fluted.

"I shall be strictly accurate," said Newman. "I won't pretend to know more than I do. At present that's all I know. You've done something regularly nefarious, something that would ruin you if it were known, something that would disgrace the name you're so proud of. I don't know what it is, but I've reason to believe I can find out — though of course I had much rather not. Persist in your present course, however, and I *will* find out. Depart from that course, let your sister go in peace, and then fancy how I'll leave you alone. It's a bargain?"

Urbain's face looked to him now like a mirror, very smooth fine glass, breathed upon and blurred; but what he would have liked still better to see was a spreading, disfiguring crack. There was something of that, to be sure, in the grimace with which the Marquis brought out: "My brother regaled you with this infamy?"

Newman scantly hesitated. "Yes—it was a treat!"

The grimace, if anything, deepened. "He raved at the last then so horribly?"

"He raved if I find nothing out. If I find — what you know I *may* find — he was beautifully inspired."

M. de Bellegarde's shoulders declined even a shrug. "Eh, sir, find what you 'damn please'!"

"What I say has no weight with you?" Newman was thus reduced to asking.

"That's for you to judge."

"No, it's for *you* to judge — at your leisure. Think it over; feel yourself all round; I'll give you an hour or two. I can't give you more, for how do we know how tight they may n't be locking you sister up? Talk it over with your mother; let her judge what weight *she* attaches. She's constitutionally less accessible to pressure than you, I think; but *enfin*, as you say, you'll see. I'll go and wait in the village, at the inn, where I beg you to let me know as soon as possible. Say by three o'clock. A simple Yes or No on paper will do. That will refer to your attaching or not attaching what we call weight; or better still, to your consenting or refusing to take your hands off Madame de Cintré. Only you understand that if you do engage again I shall expect you this time to stick to your bargain." And with this Newman opened the door to let himself out. The Marquis made no motion, and his guest paused but for a last emphasis. "I can give you, let me add, no *more* than the time." Then Newman turned away altogether and passed out of the house.

He felt greatly uplifted by what he had been doing, as it was inevitable some emotion should proceed for him from the evocation of the spectre of dishonour for a family a thousand years old. But he went back to the inn and contrived to wait there, deliberately, for the next two hours. He thought it more than probable Urbain would give no sign; since an answer to his challenge, in either case, would be a recognition of his reference. What he most expected was silence — in other words defiance. He prayed, however, that, as he imaged it, his shot might bring them down. It did bring, by three o'clock, a note, delivered by a footman; a note addressed in Urbain's handsome English hand.

"I cannot deny myself the satisfaction of letting

you know that I return to Paris to-morrow, with my
mother, in order that we may see my sister and confirm her in the resolution which is the most effectual
reply to a delirium extravagant even as a result of
your injury. — Henri-Urbain de Bellegarde."

Newman put the letter into his pocket and continued his walk up and down the inn parlour. He
had spent most of his time, for the past week, in
walking up and down. He continued to measure the
length of the little *salle* of the Armes de France until
the day began to wane, when he went forth to keep
his rendezvous with Mrs. Bread. The path leading
up the hill to the ruin was easy to find, and he in
a short time had followed it to the top. He passed
beneath the rugged arch of the castle wall and looked
about him in the early dusk for an old woman in
black. The castle yard was empty, but the door of
the church was open. He went into the little nave
and of course found a deeper dusk than without.
A couple of tapers, however, twinkled on the altar
and just helped him to distinguish a figure seated by
one of the pillars. Closer inspection led him to recognise Mrs. Bread, in spite of the fact that she was
dressed with unwonted splendour. She wore a large
black silk bonnet with imposing bows of crape, while
an old black satin gown disposed itself in vaguely lus-
trous folds about her person. She had invoked for
the occasion the highest dignity of dress. She had
been sitting with her eyes fixed upon the ground, but
when he passed before her she looked up at him and
then rose.

"Are you of this awful faith, Mrs. Bread?"

"No, indeed, sir; I'm a good Church of England woman — very Low. But I thought I should be safer in here than outside. I was never out in the evening before, sir," she added.

"We shall be safer," he returned, "where no one can hear us." And he led the way back into the castle court and then followed a path beside the church, which he was sure must lead into another part of the ruin. He was not deceived. It wandered along the crest of the hill and terminated before a fragment of wall pierced by a rough aperture which had once been a door. Through this aperture Newman passed, to find himself in a nook peculiarly favourable to quiet conversation, as probably many an earnest couple, otherwise assorted than our friends, had assured themselves. The hill sloped abruptly away, and on the remnant of its crest were scattered two or three fragments of stone. Beneath, over the plain, lay the gathered twilight, through which, in the near distance, gleamed two or three lights from the Fleurières. Mrs. Bread rustled slowly after her guide, and Newman, satisfying himself that one of the fallen stones was steady, proposed to her to sit on it. She cautiously complied, and he placed himself near her on another.

XXII

"I'm very much obliged to you for coming," he began with observing. "I hope it won't get you into trouble."

"I don't think I shall be missed. My lady, in these days, is not fond of having me about her." This was said with a dry lucidity which added to his sense of having inspired his friend with confidence.

"From the first, you know," he rejoined, "you took an interest in my prospects. You were on my side. That gratified me, I assure you. And now that you know what they've done to me I'm sure you are with me all the more."

"They've not done well — I must say it. But you must n't blame the poor Countess; they pressed her cruelly hard."

"I'd give a million of dollars," he remarked, "to know the secret of such successful pressure as that."

Mrs. Bread sat with a dull, oblique gaze fixed on the Fleurières lights. "They worked on her sentiments, as they call 'em here; they knew that was the way. She's a delicate creature. They made her feel wicked. She's only too good."

"Ah, they made her feel wicked," said Newman, slowly; and then he repeated it. "They made her feel wicked — they made her feel wicked." The words represented to him for the moment, and quite as to the point of high interest, a wondrous triumph of infernal art.

"It was because she was so good that she gave up — poor sweet lady!" added Mrs. Bread.

"But she was better to them than to me."

"She was afraid," said Mrs. Bread very confidently; "she has always been afraid, or at least for a long time. Her fear was there — it was always like a pit that yawned for her. That was the real trouble, sir. She was just a fair peach, I may say, with but one little speck. She had one little sad spot. You pushed her into the sunshine, sir, and it almost disappeared. Then they pulled her back into the shade, and in a moment it began to spread. Before we knew it she was gone. She was a delicate creature."

This singular attestation of Madame de Cintré's delicacy, for all its singularity, set Newman's wound aching afresh. "I see. She knew something bad about her mother."

"No, sir, she knew nothing." And Mrs. Bread held her head very stiff and kept her watch on the glimmering windows of the residence.

"She guessed something then, or suspected it."

"She was afraid to know," said Mrs. Bread.

"But *you* know, at any rate."

She slowly turned her vague eyes on him, squeezing her hands together in her lap. "You're not quite faithful, sir. I thought it was to tell me about the Count you asked me to come."

"Oh, the more we talk of the Count the better," he declared. "That's exactly what I want. I was

with him, as I told you, in his last hour. He was in
a great deal of pain, but he was quite himself. You
know what that means; he was bright and charming
and clever."

"Oh, he'd always be clever, sir," said Mrs. Bread.
"And did he know of your trouble?"

"Yes, he guessed it of himself."

"And what did he say to it?"

"He said it was a disgrace to his name — but it
was not the first."

"Lord, Lord!" she murmured.

"He said his mother and his brother had once put
their heads together to some still more odious effect."

"You should n't have listened to that, sir."

"Perhaps not. But I *did* listen, and I don't forget
it. Now I want to know what it is they did."

Mrs. Bread gave a soft moan. "And you've enticed
me up into this strange place to tell you?"

"Don't be alarmed," said Newman. "I won't say
a word that shall be disagreeable to you. Tell me as
it suits you — and tell me *when* it suits you. Only
remember that it was the Count's dying wish that
you should."

"Did he say that?"

"He said it with his last breath: 'Tell Mrs. Bread
I told you to ask her.'"

"Why did n't he tell you himself?"

"It was too long a story for a dying man; he was
incapable of the effort and the pain. He could only
say that he wanted me to know — that, wronged as
I was, it was my right to know."

"But how will it help you, sir?" she asked.

"'That's for me to decide. The Count believed it would, and that's why he told me. Your name was almost the last word he spoke."

This statement produced in her a sharp checked convulsion; she shook her clasped hands slowly up and down. "Pardon me if I take a great liberty. Is it the solemn truth you're speaking? I *must* ask you that; don't you see that I must, sir?"

"There's no offence. It *is* the solemn truth; I solemnly swear it. The Count himself would certainly have told me more if he had been able."

"Oh, sir, if he had known more!"

"Don't you suppose he did know?"

"There's no saying what he knew about anything," she almost wailingly conceded. "He was clever to that grand extent. He could make you believe he knew things he did n't, and that he did n't know others he had better not have known."

"I suspect he knew something about his brother that made the Marquis mind his eye!" Newman propounded. "He made the Marquis feel him pretty badly. What he wanted now was to put me in his place; he wanted to give me a chance to make the Marquis feel *me*."

"Mercy on us," cried the old waiting-woman, "how malicious we all are, to be sure!"

"I don't know," said Newman; "some of us are malicious, certainly. I'm very angry, I'm very sore, and I'm very bitter, but I don't know that I'm malicious. I've been cruelly injured. They've hurt me and I want to hurt *them*. I don't deny that; on the contrary, I tell you plainly that that's the use I want to make of any information you're so good as to give me."

Mrs. Bread seemed to hold her breath. "You want to publish them — you want to shame them?"

"I want to bring them down — down, down, down! I want to turn the tables on them — I want to mortify them as they mortified me. They took me up into a high place and made me stand there for all the world to see me, and then they stole behind me and pushed me into this bottomless pit where I lie howling and gnashing my teeth! I made a fool of myself before all their friends; but I shall make something worse of them."

This passionate profession, which Newman uttered with the greater zeal that it was the first time he had felt the relief words at once as hard and as careful as hammer-taps could give his spirit, kindled two small sparks in Mrs. Bread's fixed eyes. "I suppose you've a right to your anger, sir; but think of the dishonour you'll draw down on the Countess."

"If the Countess is to be buried alive," he cried, "what's honour or dishonour to her ever again? The door of the living tomb is at this moment closing behind her."

"Yes, it's most awful," Mrs. Bread moaned.

"She has moved off, like her brother Valentin, to give me room to work. It's as if it were all done on purpose."

"Surely," said Mrs. Bread, who seemed impressed by the ingenuity of this reflection. She was silent some moments; then she added: "And would you bring my lady before the courts?"

"The courts care nothing for my lady," Newman replied. "If she has committed a crime she'll be nothing for the courts but a wicked old woman."

"And will they hang her, sir?"

"That depends upon what she has done." And Newman eyed his friend intently.

"It would break up the family most terribly, sir!"

"It's high time such a family *should* be broken up!" he outrageously declared.

"And me at my age out of place, sir!" sighed Mrs. Bread.

"Oh, I'll take care of you! You shall come and live with me. You shall be my housekeeper or anything you like. You shall sit and be waited on and twiddle your thumbs. I'll pension you for life."

"Dear, dear, sir, you think of everything." And she seemed to fall a-brooding.

He watched her a while; then he said suddenly "Ah, Mrs. Bread, you're too foolishly fond of my lady!"

She looked at him as quickly. "I would n't have you say that, sir. I don't think it any part of my duty to be fond of my lady. I've served her faithfully this many a year; but if she were to die tomorrow I believe before heaven I should n't shed a tear for her." Then after a pause, "I've no such great reason to love her!" Mrs. Bread added. "The most she has done for me has been not to turn me out of the house." Newman felt that decidedly his companion was more and more confidential — that, if luxury is corrupting, Mrs. Bread's conservative habits were already relaxed by the spiritual comfort

of this preconcerted interview, in an extraordinary
place, with a free-spoken millionaire All his native
shrewdness admonished him that his part was simply
to let her take her time — let the charm of the occasion work. So he said nothing; he only bent on her
his large benevolence while she nursed her lean
elbows. "My lady once did me a great wrong," she
went on at last. "She has a terrible tongue when
she's put out. It was many a year ago, but I've
never forgotten it. I've never mentioned it to a
human creature; I've kept my grudge to myself.
I dare say I've been wicked, but my grudge has
grown old with me. It has grown good for nothing
too, I dare say; but it has lived and lived, as I myself
have lived. It will die when I die — not before!"

"And what is your grudge, Mrs. Bread?" Newman blandly enquired.

Mrs. Bread dropped her eyes and hesitated. "If
I were a foreigner, sir, I should make less of telling
you; it comes harder to a decent Englishwoman.
But I sometimes think I've picked up too many
foreign ways. What I was telling you belongs to
a time when I was much younger and of a quite
different appearance altogether to what I am now.
I had a very high colour, sir, if you can believe it;
indeed I was a very smart lass. My lady was younger
too, and the late Marquis was youngest of all — I
mean in the way he went on, sir; he had a very high,
bold spirit; he was a very grand gentleman. He was
fond of his pleasure, like most foreigners, and it must
be owned he sometimes went rather below him to
take it. My lady was often jealous, and if you'll

believe it, sir, she did me the honour to have an eye on *me*. One day I had a red ribbon in my cap, and she flew out at me and ordered me to take it off. She accused me of putting it on to make the Marquis look at me — look in the way he should n't. I don't know that I was impertinent, but I spoke up like an honest girl and did n't count my words. A red ribbon indeed! As if it was my ribbons the Marquis looked at! My lady knew afterwards that I was perfectly respectable, yet she never said a word to show she believed it. But the Marquis did — *he* knew the rights of me," Mrs. Bread presently added; "and I took off my red ribbon and put it away in a drawer, where I have kept it to this day. It's faded now, it's a very pale pink; but there it lies. My grudge has faded too; the red has all gone out of it; but it lies here yet." And Mrs. Bread touched with old testifying knuckles her black satin bodice.

Newman listened with interest to this decent yet vivid narrative, which seemed to have opened up the deeps of memory to his companion. Then as she remained silent and seemed rather to lose herself in retrospective meditation on her perfect respectability, he ventured on a short cut to his goal. "So Madame de Bellegarde was jealous; I see. And the Marquis admired pretty women without distinction of class. I suppose one must n't be hard on him, for they probably did n't all behave so discreetly as you. But years afterwards it could hardly have been jealousy that turned his wife into a criminal."

Mrs. Bread gave a weary sigh. "We're using dreadful words, sir, but I don't care now. I see you've your idea, and I've no will of my own. My will was the will of my children, as I called them; but I've lost my children now. They're dead and gone — I may say it of both of them; and what should I care for the living? What's any one in the house to me now — what am I to *them*? My lady objects to me—has objected to me these thirty years. I should have been glad to be something to young Madame Urbain, though I never was nurse to the present Marquis. When he was a baby I was too young; they wouldn't trust me with him. But his wife told her own maid, Mamselle Clarisse, the opinion she had of me. Perhaps you'd like to hear it, sir."

"Oh, wouldn't I?" Newman almost panted.

"She said that if I'd sit in her children's schoolroom I should do very well for a penwiper! When things have come to that I don't think I need stand on ceremony."

"I never heard of anything so vicious!" Newman rejoicingly declared. "Go on, Mrs. Bread."

Mrs. Bread, however, relapsed again into troubled reserve, and all he could do was to fold his arms and wait. But at last she appeared to have set her memories in order. "It was when the late Marquis was an old man and his eldest son had been two years married. It was when the time came on for marrying Mademoiselle Claire; that's the way they talk of it here, you know, sir — as you might talk of sending a heifer to market. The Marquis's health was bad; he was sadly broken down. My lady had picked out M. de Cintré, for no good reason that I could see. But there are reasons, I very well know, that are beyond me, and you must be high in the world to catch all that's under and behind. Old M. de Cintré was very high, and my lady thought him almost as good as herself; that's saying as much as you please. Mr. Urbain took sides with his mother, as he always did. The trouble, I believe, was that my lady would give very little money — to go with the young lady; and all the other gentlemen wanted a bigger settlement. It was only M. de Cintré who was content. The Lord willed it he should have that one soft spot; it was the only one he had. He may have had very grand connexions, and he certainly made grand bows and speeches and flourishes; but that, I think, was all the measure of *his* honour. I think he was like what I've heard of comedians; not that I've ever seen one. But I know he painted his strange face. He might paint it all he would, he could never make me like it! The Marquis could n't abide him, and declared that sooner than take such a husband as that, his daughter, whom he was so fond of, should stop as she was. He and my lady had a great scene; it came even to our ears in the servants' hall. It was not their first quarrel, if the truth must be told. They were not a loving couple, but they did n't often come to words, because after a while neither had them to waste; they had too much use for them elsewhere and otherwise. My lady had long ago got over 'minding'—minding, I mean, the worst; for she had had plenty of assistance for throwing things off. In this, I must say, they were very well matched. The Marquis was one who would but too easily go as you please — he had the temper of the

perfect gentleman. He got angry once a year — he
kept to that; but then it was very bad. He always
took to bed directly afterwards. This time I speak
of he took to bed as usual, but he never got up again.
I'm afraid he was paying for the free life he had led;
is n't it true they mostly do, sir, when they get old
and sad? My lady and Mr. Urbain kept quiet, but
I know my lady wrote letters to M. de Cintré. The
Marquis got worse and the doctors gave him up.
My lady gave him up too, and if the truth must be
told she gave him up as I've seen her clap together
— with a sound to make you jump — the covers of
a book she has read enough of. When once he was
out of the way she could do what she wished with her
daughter, and it was all arranged that my poor child
and treasure should be handed over to M. de Cintré.
You don't know what Mademoiselle was in those
days, sir; she was the sweetest, gentlest, fairest! —
and guessed as little of what was going on around her
as the lamb can guess the butcher. I used to nurse
my unhappy master and was always in his room. It
was here at Fleurières, in the autumn. We had a
doctor from Paris, who came and stayed two or three
weeks in the house. Then there came two others,
and there was a consultation, and these two others,
as I said, declared the Marquis could n't come round.
After this they went off, pocketing their fees, but the
other one stopped over and did what he could. M. de
Bellegarde himself kept crying out that he refused to
be given up, that he insisted on getting better, that he
would live and look after his daughter. Mademoiselle
Claire and the Vicomte — that was Mr. Valentin, you

know — were both in the house. The doctor was a clever man — that I could see myself — and I think he believed the Marquis might recover with just the right things carefully done. We took good care of him, he and I, between us, and one day, when my lady had almost ordered her mourning, my patient suddenly began to mend. He took a better turn and came up so wonderfully that the doctor said he was out of danger. What was killing him was the dreadful fits of pain in his stomach. But little by little they stopped, and before I knew it he had begun again to have his joke at me. The doctor found something that gave him great comfort — some grand light-coloured mixture, a wonderful drug (I'm sure I forget the name) that we kept in a great bottle on the chimney-piece. I used to give it to him through a glass tube; it always made him easier. Presently the doctor went away, after telling me to keep on with the medicine whenever he was bad. After that there was a different sort of person from Poitiers — *he* came every day. So we were alone in the house — my lady and her poor husband and their three children. Madame Urbain had gone away, with her first small child, but a baby then, to her mother's. You know she's very lively, and her maid told me she didn't like to be where people were dying." Mrs. Bread had again a drop, but she went on soon and with the same quiet consistency: "I think you've guessed, sir, that when the Marquis began to give hopes again my lady was disappointed." And once more she paused, bending on Newman a face that seemed to grow whiter as the darkness settled down on them.

He had listened eagerly—with an eagerness greater even than that with which he had bent his ear to poor Valentin's weak lips. Every now and then, as his companion looked up at him, she reminded him of some old black cat, mild and sleek, protracting the enjoyment of a dish of rich milk. Even her triumph was measured and decorous; even her justice forbore to rattle the scales. "Late one night," she soon continued, "I was sitting by the Marquis in his room, the great red room in the west tower. He had been complaining a little and I had given him a spoonful of the remedy that so seldom failed to ease him. My lady had been there in the early part of the evening; she sat for more than an hour by his bed. Then she went away and left me alone. After midnight she came back and Mr. Urbain was with her. They went to the bed and looked at the Marquis, and my lady took hold of his hand. Then she turned to me and said he was not so well; I remember how the Marquis, without a word, lay staring at her. I can see his white face at this moment in the great black square between the bed-curtains. I said I did n't think he was very bad, and she told me to go to bed — she would sit a while with him. When he saw me going he gave a sound like a scared child and called out to me not to leave him; but Mr. Urbain opened the door for me and pointed the way out. The present Marquis — perhaps you 've noticed, sir — has a very high way of giving orders, and I was there to take orders. I went to my room, but I was n't easy; I could n't tell you why. I did n't undress; I sat there waiting and listening. For what would you have said, sir?

I could n't have told you, since surely a poor gentle
man, however helpless, might be in safety at such
a crisis with his wife and his son. It was as if I expected to hear his voice moan after me again. I listened, but I heard nothing. It was a very still night;
I never knew a night so still. At last the very stillness itself seemed to frighten me, and I came out of
my room and went very softly downstairs. In the
anteroom, outside of where his father was, I found
the Count, as he then was, walking up and down.
He asked me what I wanted, and I said I had returned to relieve my lady. He said *he* would relieve
my lady and ordered me back to bed; but as I stood
there, unwilling to turn away, the door of the room
opened and my lady herself came out. I noticed she
was very pale; she was altogether extraordinary. She
looked a moment at the Count and at me, and then
held out her arms to the Count. He went to her and
she fell upon him and hid her face. I brushed quickly
past her into the room and came to the Marquis's bed.
He was lying there very white and with his eyes shut;
you could have taken him for a corpse. I took hold of
his hand and spoke to him, but it was as if I had been
dealing with the dead. Then I turned round; my lady
and Mr. Urbain were there. 'My poor Bread,' said
my lady, 'M. le Marquis is gone.' Mr. Urbain knelt
down by the bed and said softly *'Mon père, mon père.'*
I thought it most prodigious, and asked my lady
what in the world had happened and why she had n't
called me. She said nothing had happened; that she
had only been sitting there with him in perfect stillness. She had closed her eyes, thinking she might

sleep, and she had slept she did n't know how long. When she woke up all was over. "It's surely death, my son, it's unmistakeably death,' she said to the Count. Mr. Urbain said they must have the doctor immediately from Poitiers, and that he would ride off and fetch him. He kissed his father's face — oh! — and then he kissed his mother and went away. My lady and I stood there at the bedside. As I looked at my poor master it came to me ever so sharply that he was n't dead, that he was only in a stupor of weakness. And then my lady repeated 'My poor Bread, it's death, it's just death'; and I said 'Yes, my lady, it's certainly death.' I said just the opposite to what I believed; it was my particular notion. Then my lady said we must wait for the doctor, and we sat there and waited. It was a long time; the poor Marquis neither stirred nor changed. 'I've seen death before,' said my lady, 'and it's terribly like this.' 'Yes, please, my lady,' said I; and I thought things I did n't say. The night wore away without the Count's coming back, and the Marquise began to be frightened. She was afraid he had had an accident in the dark or met with some prowling people. At last she got so restless that she went below to watch in the court for his return. I sat there alone and the Marquis never stirred."

Here Mrs. Bread paused again, and, for her listener, the most expert story-teller could n't have been more thrilling. Newman made almost the motion of turning the page of a "detective story." "So he *was* dead!" he exclaimed.

"Three days later he was in his grave," said Mrs

Bread sententiously. "In a little while I went away to the front of the house and looked out into the court, and there, before long, I saw Mr. Urbain ride in alone. I waited a bit to hear him come upstairs with his mother, but they stopped below and I returned to the other room. I went to the bed and held up the light to him, but I don't know why I did n't let the candlestick fall. The Marquis's eyes were open — open wide! they were staring at me. I knelt down beside him and took his hands and begged him to tell me, in the holy name of wonder, if he was truly alive or what or where he was. Still he looked at me a long time, and then made me a sign to put my ear close to him 'I'm dead, my dear,' he said, 'I'm dreadfully dead. The Marquise has killed me. Yes.' I was all in a tremble. I did n't understand him. I did n't know what had become of him: it was so as if the dead had been speaking. 'But you'll get well now, sir,' I said. And then he whimpered again, ever so weak: 'I would n't get well for a kingdom. I would n't be that woman's husband again.' And then he said more; he said she had murdered him. I asked him what she had done to him and I remember his very words: 'She has cruelly taken my life, as true as I lie here finished. And she'll do the same to my daughter,' he said; 'my poor unhappy child.' And he begged me to prevent that, and then he said he was dying, he was 'knowingly' dead. I was afraid to move or to leave him; I was almost as dead as himself. All of a sudden he asked me to get a pencil and write for him; and then I had to tell him I could n't manage that sort of thing. He asked me to hold him up in bed while he wrote himself, and I said he could never, never trace a line. But he seemed to have a kind of terror that gave him strength. I found a pencil in the room and a piece of paper and a book, and I put the paper on the book and the pencil into his hand, and I moved the candle near him. You'll think all this monstrous strange, sir — and I shall understand if you scarce believe me. But I must tell things as they happened to me — the rest is with Them that know all! Strangest of all was it, no doubt, that I believed it had somehow been done to him as he said and that I was eager to help him to write. I sat on the bed and put my arm round him and held him up. I felt very strong when it came to that; I believe I could have lifted him and carried him. It was a wonder how he wrote, but he did write, in a big scratching hand; he almost covered one side of the paper. It seemed a long time; I suppose it was three or four minutes. He was groaning terribly all the while, but at last he said it was ended, and I let him down upon his pillows, and he gave me the paper and told me to fold it and hide it, and to give it to those who'd act on it according to right. 'Who do you mean?' I said. 'Who are those who'll act on it?' But he made some sound for all answer; he could n't speak — he was spent. In a few minutes he told me to go and look at the bottle on the chimney-piece. I knew the bottle he meant, the remedy we were never without and that we felt to be regularly precious. I went and looked at it, but it was empty of every drop, as if it had been turned upside down. When I came back his eyes were open — oh so pitifully! — and he was staring at

me; but soon he closed them and he said no more
I hid the paper in my dress; I did n't look at what was
written on it, though I can read very well, sir, if I
have n't a hand for the pen. I sat down near the bed,
but it was nearly half an hour before my lady and the
Count came in. The Marquis looked as lost as when
they had left him, and I never said a word of his
having revived. Mr. Urbain said the doctor had been
called to a person in childbirth, but had promised to
set out for Fleurières immediately. In another half-
hour he arrived, and as soon as he had examined
his patient he said we had had a false alarm. The
poor gentleman was very low, but was still living.
I watched my lady and her son, on that, to see if they
looked at each other, and I'm obliged to admit they
did n't. The doctor said there was no reason he
should die; he had been going on so well. And then
he wanted to know how he had suddenly taken such
a turn; he had left him so quiet and natural. My
lady told her little story again — what she had told
Mr. Urbain and me — and the doctor looked at her
and said nothing. He stayed all the next day at the
château, and hardly left the Marquis. I was always
there, and I think I may assure you at least that I lost
nothing. Mademoiselle and the Vicomte came and
looked at their father, but he never stirred. It was
a strange deathly stupor. My lady was always
about; her face was as white as her husband's, and
she looked very proud and hard, as I had seen her
look when her orders or her wishes had been dis-
obeyed. It was as if the poor Marquis had gone
against her intention; and the way she took it from

him made me afraid of her. The local apothecary kept him along through the day, and we waited for the gentleman from Paris, who, as I tell you, had already stayed here. They had telegraphed for him early in the morning, and in the evening he arrived. He talked a bit outside with the other one, and then they came in to see their *malade* together. I was with him, and so was Mr. Urbain. My lady had been to receive the great man, and she did n't come back with him into the room. He sat down by the Marquis — I can see him there now with his hand on the Marquis's wrist and Mr. Urbain watching them with a little looking-glass in his hand. 'I'm sure he's better,' said our country doctor; 'I'm sure he'll come back.' A few moments after he had spoken the Marquis opened his eyes, as if he were waking up, and looked from one of us to the other. I saw him look at me from very, very far off, and yet very hard indeed, as you might say. At the same moment my lady came in on tiptoe; she came up to the bed and put in her head between me and the Count. The Marquis saw her and gave a sound like the wail of a lost soul. He said something we could n't understand and then a convulsion seemed to take him. He shook all over and closed his eyes, and the doctor jumped up and took hold of my lady. He held her for a moment harder than I've ever seen a gentleman hold a lady. The Marquis was stone dead — the sight of her had done for him. This time there were those there who knew."

Newman felt as if he had been reading by starlight the report of highly important evidence in a great murder case. "And the paper — the paper!" he said from a dry throat. "What was written on it?"

"I can't tell you, sir," Mrs. Bread replied. "I could n't read it. It was French."

"But could no one else read it?"

"I never asked a human creature."

"No one has ever seen it?"

"If you do you'll be the first."

Newman seized his companion's hand in both his own and pressed it almost with passion. "I thank you as I've never thanked any one for anything. I want to be the first; I want it to be mine as this closed fist is mine. You're the wisest old woman in Europe. And what did you do with the blest thing?" Her information had made him feel extraordinarily strong. "For God's sake, let me have it!"

Mrs. Bread got up with a certain majesty "It's not so easy as that, sir. When you want great things you must wait for great things."

"But waiting's horrible, you know," he candidly smiled.

"I'm sure I've waited; I've waited these many years," she quavered.

"That's very true. You have waited for *me*. I won't forget it. And yet how comes it you did n't do as M. de Bellegarde said — show the right people what you had got?"

"To whom should I show it and who were the right people?" she asked with high lucidity. "It was n't easy to know, and many's the night I have lain awake thinking of it. Six months afterwards, when they married Mademoiselle to the last person they ought to, I was very near bringing it out. I thought it my duty to do something with such a proof of what had happened, and yet I was terribly afraid. I did n't know what the Marquis had put there, nor how bad it might be, and there was no one I could trust enough to ask. And it seemed to me a cruel kindness to the person in the world I cared most for, letting her know her father had written her mother down so shamefully; for that's what he did, I suppose. I thought she would rather suffer from her husband than suffer from *them*. It was for her and for my dear Mr. Valentin I kept quiet. Quiet I call it, yet it was a queer enough quietness. It worried me and changed me altogether. But for others I held my tongue, and no one, to this hour, knows what had passed there between my poor prostrate master and his wife."

"But evidently there were suspicions," Newman urged. "Where did Count Valentin get his ideas?"

"From our little local man — who has yet never been in the house, as you may imagine, since. He was very ill-satisfied and he did n't care who knew it. He had a very good opinion of his own sharpness, as Frenchmen mostly have, and coming to the house, as he did, day after day, he had more ideas — as a consequence — than he had had, before, any call to put about. And indeed the way the poor Marquis went off as soon as his eyes fell on my lady was a most shocking sight for any kind person. The great man from Paris may have known, after he had taken things in, what to think, but he also knew what not to say, and he hushed it up. But for all he could do the Vicomte and Mademoiselle heard something; they knew their father's death was somehow against nature. Of course they could n't accuse their mother, and, as I tell you, I was as dumb as that stone. Mr. Valentin used to look at me sometimes, and his eyes seemed to shine as if he were thinking of some question he could ask me. I was dreadfully afraid he would speak, and always looked away and went about my business. If I were to tell him I was sure he would hate me afterwards, which was what I could never have borne. Once I went up to him and took a great liberty; I kissed him as I had kissed him when he was a child. 'You ought n't to look so sad, sir,' I said; 'believe your poor decent old Bread. Such a gallant, handsome young man can have nothing to be sad about.' And I think he understood me; he understood I was begging off and he made up his mind in his own way. He went about with his unasked question in his mind, as I did with my untold tale; we were both afraid of bringing disgrace on a great house. And it was the same with my dear young lady. She did n't know what had happened; she would n't hear of knowing. The Marquise and Mr. Urbain asked me no questions, because they had no reason. I was as still as a stopped clock. When I was younger her ladyship thought me false, and now she thought me *bête*, as they say. How should I have any ideas?"

Newman turned it all gravely over. "But you say that doctor made a talk. Did no one take it up?"

"I don't know how far they went. They're always talking scandal in these foreign countries — you may

have noticed — and they must have had their stories
about my lady. But after all what could they say?
The Marquis had been ill and the Marquis had died;
he had as good a right to die as any one. The doctor
could n't say he had n't come honestly by what he
suffered. The next year he left the place and bought
a practice at Bordeaux, and if there had been ugly
tales the worst of them were among ugly people.
There could n't have been any very bad ones that
those who were respectable believed. My lady herself is so very respectable."

Newman, at this last affirmation, broke into a re-
sounding laugh. Mrs. Bread had begun to move
away from the spot where they were sitting, and he
helped her through the aperture in the wall and along
the homeward path. "Yes, my lady's respectability's a treasure; I shall have a great deal of use for
my lady's respectability." They reached the empty
space in front of the church, where they stopped
a moment, looking at each other with something of
closer fellowship, like a pair of sociable conspirators.
"But what was it," Newman insisted, "what was it
she did to the miserable man? She did n't stab him
or throttle him or poison him."

"I don't know, sir. No one saw it."

"Unless it was Mr. Urbain," he thoughtfully
suggested. "You say he was walking up and down
outside the room. Perhaps he looked through the
keyhole. But no; I think that with his mother he'd
take it on trust."

"You may be sure I've often thought of it," Mrs.
Bread almost cheerfully returned. "I'm sure she

did n't touch him with her hands. I saw nothing on him anywhere. I believe it was in this way. He had a fit of his great pain, and he asked her for his medicine. Instead of giving it to him she went and poured it away, before his eyes, not speaking, only looking at him, so that he might have the scare and the shock and the horror of it. Then he saw what she meant and, weak and helpless, took fright, was terrified. 'You want to kill me,' he must have said — do you see? 'Yes, M. le Marquis, I want to kill you,' says my lady, and sits down and keeps her dreadful eyes on him. You know my lady's eyes, I think, sir; it was with that look of hers she killed him; it was with the terrible strong will and all the cruelty she put into it. It was as if she had pushed him out of her boat, fevered and sick, into the cold sea, and remained there to push him again should he try to scramble back; making him feel he was lost, by her intention, and watching him awfully sink and drown. It was enough indeed to take the heart out of him, and that, in his state, was enough for a death-stroke."

Newman rendered this vivid image, which in truth did great honour to the old woman's haunted sensibility, the tribute of a comprehensive gasp. "Well, you 've got right hold of it — you make me see it and hate it and want to go for it. But I 've got to keep tight hold of you too, you know."

They had begun to descend the hill, and she said nothing till they reached the foot. He moved beside her as on air, his hands in his pockets, his head thrown back while he gazed at the stars: he seemed to himself to be riding his vengeance along the Milky Way. "So you're serious about that?" she sighed.

"About your living with me? Why, you don't suppose I've turned you inside out this way not to want to get you into shape again. You're in no kind of shape for these people now — even if they were in any for you; after your seeing what they've done to me — and to *her*. You just give me the thing I'm after and then you move out."

"I never thought I should have lived to take a new place — unless," Mrs. Bread made moan, "I should have gone some day to Mr. Valentin or, in her own establishment, to my young lady."

"Come to me and you'll come to *her* establishment yet, I guess — you'll come at least to where both those names will be cherished and sacred."

She considered a little and then replied: "Oh, I shall like to pronounce them to *you*, sir! And if you're going to pull the house down," she added, "I had surely better be clear of it."

"Ah," said Newman almost with the gaiety of a dazzle of alternatives, "it won't be quite my idea to appeal — if that's what you mean — to the police. The meanest and the damnedest things are always beyond their ken and out of their hands. Which has the merit in this case, however, that it leaves the whole story in mine. And to mine," he declared, "you've given power!"

"Ah, you're bolder than I ever was!" she resignedly sighed; and he felt himself now, to whatever end, possessed of her. He walked back with her to the château; the curfew — it could n't have been

anything but the curfew, he was sure — had tolled
for the weary serfs and *villains* (as he could also quite
have believed) and the small street of Fleurières was
unlighted and empty. She promised he should have
what he was after, as he had called it, in half an
hour. Mrs. Bread choosing not to go in by the great
gate, they passed round by a winding lane to a door
in the wall of the park, of which she had the key and
which would enable her to re-enter the house from
behind. Newman arranged with her that he should
await outside the wall her return with his prize.

She went in, and his half-hour in the dusky lane
seemed very long. But he had plenty to think about.
At last the door in the wall opened and Mrs. Bread
stood there with one hand on the latch and the other
holding out a scrap of white paper folded small and
dearer to his sight than any love-token ever brought
of old by bribed duenna to lurking cavalier. In a
moment he was master of it and it had passed into
his waistcoat pocket. "Come and see me in Paris,"
he said; "we're to settle your future, you know; and
I'll translate poor M. de Bellegarde's French to you."
Never had he felt so grateful as at this moment for
M. Nioche's instructions.

Mrs. Bread's eyes had followed the disappearance
of her treasure, and she gave a heavy sigh. "Well,
you've done what you would with me, sir, and I suppose you'll do it again. You *must* take care of me
now. You're a terribly positive gentleman."

"Just now," said Newman. "I'm a terribly impatient one!" And he bade her good-night and walked
rapidly back to the inn. He ordered his vehicle to be

prepared for the return to Poitiers, and then he shut the door of the common *salle* and strode toward the solitary lamp on the chimney-piece. He pulled out the paper and quickly unfolded it. It was covered with pencil-marks, which at first, in the feeble light, seemed indistinct. But his fierce curiosity forced a meaning from the tremulous signs, the free English of which might have been, without the hopelessly obscure date:

"My wife has tried to kill me and has done it; I'm horribly, helplessly dying. It's in order to marry my beloved daughter to M. de Cintré and then go on herself all the same. With all my soul I protest — I forbid it. I'm not insane — ask the doctors, ask Mrs. B. It was alone with me here to-night; she attacked me and put me to death. It's murder if murder ever was. Ask the doctors, tell every one, show every one this.

"HENRI-URBAIN DE BELLEGARDE."

XXIII

NEWMAN returned to Paris the second day after his interview with Mrs. Bread. The morrow he had spent at Poitiers, reading over and over again the signed warrant he had lodged in his pocket-book, persuading himself more and more that it had, as he put it to himself, a social value, and thinking what he would now do and how he would do it. He would not have said that Poitiers had much to hold him, yet the day seemed very short. Domiciled once more in the Boulevard Haussmann he walked over to the Rue de l'Université and enquired of Madame de Bellegarde's portress whether the Marquise had come back. The portress answered that she had arrived with M. le Marquis on the preceding day, and further informed him that should he wish to see them they were both at home. As she said these words the little white-faced old woman who peered out of the dusky gate-house of the Hôtel de Bellegarde gave a small wicked smile — a smile that seemed to Newman to mean "Go in if you dare!" She was evidently versed in the current domestic history; she was placed where she could feel the pulse of the house. He stood a moment twisting his moustache and looking at her; then he abruptly turned away. But this was not because he was afraid to go in — though he doubted whether, for all his courage, he should be able to make his way unchallenged into the presence of his adversaries. Confidence, excessive confidence perhaps, quite as much as timidity, prompted his retreat. He was nursing his thunderbolt; he loved it; he was unwilling to part with it. He felt himself hold it aloft in the rumbling, vaguely-flashing air, directly over the heads of his victims, and he fancied he could see their pale upturned faces. Few specimens of the human countenance had ever given him such pleasure as these, lighted in the lurid fashion I have hinted at, and he took his ease while he harboured the vindictive vision. It must be added too that he was at a loss to see exactly how he could arrange to witness the operation of his thunder. To send in his card to Madame de Bellegarde would be a waste of ceremony; she would certainly decline to receive him. On the other hand he could n't force his way into her presence. He hated to see himself reduced to the blind satisfaction of writing her a letter; but he consoled himself in a measure with the thought that a letter might lead to an interview. He went home and, feeling rather tired — nursing a vengeance was, he had to confess, a fatiguing process; it took a good deal out of one — flung himself into one of his brocaded fauteuils, stretched his legs, thrust his hands into his pockets and, while he watched the reflected sunset fading from the ornate house-tops on the opposite side of the boulevard, began mentally to frame, as work for his pen, a few effective remarks. While he was so occupied his servant threw open the door and announced ceremoniously "Madame Brett!"

He roused himself expectantly and in a few

moments recognised on his threshold the worthy
woman with whom he had conversed to such good
purpose on the starlit hill-top of Fleurières. Mrs.
Bread had assumed for this visit the same dress as
for her other effort, and he was struck with her fine
antique appearance. His room was still lampless,
and as her large grave face gazed at him through the
clear dusk from under the shadow of her ample
bonnet he felt the incongruity of her pretending to
any servile stamp. He greeted her with high genial-
ity, and bade her come in and sit down and make herself comfortable. There was something that might
have touched the springs both of mirth and of melancholy in the spirit of formal accommodation with
which she endeavoured to meet this new conception
of her duty. She was not playing at being fluttered,
which would have been simply ridiculous; she was
doing her best to carry herself as a person so humble
that, for her, even embarrassment would have been
pretentious; but evidently she had never dreamed of
its being in her horoscope to pay a visit at nightfall
to a friendly single gentleman who lived in theatrical-
looking rooms on one of the new boulevards.

"I truly hope I'm not forgetting my place, sir," she
anxiously pleaded.

"Forgetting your place? Why, you're remember·
ing it as a good woman remembers her promise.
This is your place, you know. You're already in my
service; your wages as housekeeper began a fortnight
ago. I can tell you my house wants keeping! Why
don't you take off your bonnet and stay right now?"

"Take off my bonnet?" — she gave it her gravest

consideration. "Oh sir, I have n't my cap. And with your leave, sir, I could n't keep house in my best gown."

"Never mind your best gown," said Newman cheerfully. "You shall have a better gown than that."

She stared solemnly and then stretched her hands over her lustreless satin skirt as if the perilous side of her situation might be flushing into view. "Oh sir, I'm fond of my own clothes."

"I hope you've left those wicked people, at any rate," Newman went on.

"Well, sir, here I am! That's all I can tell you. Here I sit, poor Catherine Bread. It's a strange place for me to be. I don't know myself; I never supposed I was so bold. But indeed, sir, I've gone as far as my own strength will bear me."

"Oh, come, Mrs. Bread!" he returned almost caressingly; "don't make yourself uncomfortable. Why, you're going to have now the time of your life."

She began to speak again with a trembling voice "I think it would be more respectable if I could if I could — !" But she quavered to a pause.

"If you could give up this sort of thing altogether ?" said Newman kindly, trying to anticipate her meaning, which he supposed might be a wish to retire from service.

"If I could give up everything, sir! All I should ask is a decent Protestant burial."

"Burial!" he cried with a burst of laughter. "Why, to bury you now would be a sad piece of extravagance. It's only rascals who have to be buried to get respectable. Honest folks like you and me can live our time out — and live it together. Come! did you bring your baggage?"

"My two boxes are locked and corded; but I have n't yet spoken to my lady."

"Speak to her then and have done with it. I should like to have your chance!" cried Newman.

"I would gladly give it you, sir. I 've passed some weary hours in my lady's dressing-room; but this will be one of the longest. She 'll tax me with base ingratitude."

"Well," said Newman, "so long as you can tax her with murder —!"

"Oh sir, I can't; not I!" she pleaded.

"You don't mean to say anything about it? So much the better. Leave it all to me."

"If she calls me a thankless old woman," Mrs. Bread went on, "I shall have nothing to say. But it's better so," she added with supreme mildness. "She shall be my lady to the last. That will be more respectable."

"And then you'll come to me and I shall be your gentleman," said Newman. "That will be more respectable still!"

She rose with lowered eyes and stood a moment; then, looking up, she rested her gaze upon Newman's face. The disordered proprieties were somehow settling to rest. She looked at her friend so long and so fixedly, with such a dull intense devotedness, that he himself might have had a pretext for embarrassment. At last she said gently: "You 've not your natural appearance, sir."

"Why, Mrs. Bread," he answered, "I've not my natural balance. If you mean I don't look sunny I guess I look as I feel. To be very indifferent and very fierce, very dull and very violent, very sick and very fine, all at once — well, it rather mixes one up."

Mrs. Bread gave a noiseless sigh. "I can tell you something that will make you feel queerer still, if you want to feel all one way. About the poor Countess."

"What can you tell me?" Newman quickly asked. "Not that you've seen her?"

She shook her head. "No indeed, sir, nor ever shall. That's the dead weight of it. Nor my lady. Nor M. de Bellegarde."

"You mean she's kept so close?"

"The closest they keep any."

These words for an instant seemed to check the beating of his heart. Leaning back in his chair he felt sick. "They've tried to see her and she wouldn't — she couldn't?"

"She refused — for ever! I had it from my lady's own maid," said Mrs. Bread, "who had it from my lady. To speak of it to such a person my lady must have felt the shock. The Countess declines to receive them now, and now's her only chance. A short while hence she'll have no choice."

"You mean the other women — the mothers, the daughters, the sisters; what is it they call them? — won't let her?"

"It's what they call the rule of the house — or I believe of the order. There's no rule so strict as that of the Carmelites. The bad women in the reformatories are fine ladies to them. They wear old brown cloaks — so the *femme de chambre* told me — that you would n't use for a horse-blanket. And the poor Countess was so fond of soft-feeling dresses; she would never have anything stiff! They sleep on the ground," Mrs. Bread went on; "they're no better, no better" — and she hesitated for a comparison — "they're no better than tinkers' wives. They give up everything, down to the very name their poor old nurses called them by. They give up father and mother, brother and sister — to say nothing of other persons," Mrs. Bread delicately added. "They wear a shroud under their brown cloaks and a rope round their waists, and they get up on winter nights and go off into cold places to pray to the Virgin Mary. I hope it does *her* at least good!"

Newman's visitor, dwelling on these terrible facts, sat dry-eyed and pale, her hands convulsive but confined to her satin lap. He gave a melancholy groan and fell forward, burying his face and his pain. There was a long silence, broken only by the ticking of the great gilded clock on the chimney-piece. "Where is the accursed place—where is the convent ?" he asked at last, looking up.

"There are two houses," said Mrs. Bread. "I found out; I thought you'd like to know — though it's cold comfort, I think. One's in the Avenue de Messine; they've learned the Countess is there. The other's in the Rue d'Enfer. That's a terrible name; I suppose you know what it means."

He got up and walked away to the end of his long room. When he came back Mrs. Bread had risen and stood by the fire with folded hands. "Tell me this. Can I get near her — even if I don't see her? Can I look through a grating, or some such thing, at the place where she is?"

It is said that all women love a lover, and Mrs. Bread's sense of the pre-established harmony which kept servants in their "place," even as planets in their orbits (not that she had ever consciously likened herself to a planet), barely availed to temper the maternal melancholy with which she leaned her head on one side and gazed at her new employer. She probably felt for the moment as if, forty years before, she had held him also in her arms. "That would n't help you, sir. It would only make her seem further away."

"I want to go there, at all events," he returned. "The Avenue de Messine, you say? And what is it they call themselves?"

"Carmelites — whatever it means!" said Mrs. Bread.

"I shall remember that."

She hesitated a moment and then: "It's my duty to tell you this — that the convent has a chapel and that respectable persons are admitted on Sunday to the mass. You don't see the poor creatures in their prison or their tomb, but I'm told you can hear them sing. It's a wonder they have any heart for singing! Some Sunday I shall make bold to go. It seems to me I should know *her* voice in fifty."

Newman thanked her, while he held her hand, with a stare through which he, for a good reason, failed to see her. "If any one can get in I will." A moment later she proposed deferentially to retire, but he checked her, pressing on her grasp a lighted candle.

"There are half a dozen rooms there I don't use;" and he pointed through an open door. "Go and look at them and take your choice. You can live in the one you like best." From this bewildering privilege she at first recoiled; but finally, yielding to her friend's almost fraternal pat of reassurance, she wandered off into the dusk with her tremulous taper. She remained absent a quarter of an hour, during which Newman paced up and down, stopped occasionally to look out of the window at the lights on the boulevard, and then resumed his walk. Mrs. Bread's interest in her opportunity apparently deepened as she proceeded; but at last she reappeared and deposited her candlestick on the chimney-piece.

"Well, have you picked one out?"

"A room, sir? They're all too fine for a dingy old body like me. There is n't one that has n't a bit of gilding."

"It's only some shocking sham, Mrs. Bread," he answered. "If you stay there a while it will all peel off of itself." And he gave a dismal smile.

"Oh sir, there are things enough peeling off already!" she said with a responsible head-shake. "Since I was there I thought I'd look about me. I don't believe you know, sir. The corners are most dreadful. You do want a housekeeper, that you do; you want a tidy Englishwoman that is n't above taking hold of a broom."

Newman assured her that he suspected, if he had not measured, his domestic abuses, and that to reform them was a mission worthy of her powers. She held her candlestick aloft again and looked round the salon with compassionate glances; then she intimated that she accepted the mission and that its sacred character would sustain her in her rupture with her old dread mistress. On this she curtsied herself away.

She came back the next day with her worldly goods, and her friend, going into his drawing-room, found her on her aged knees before a divan, sewing up a piece of detached fringe. He questioned her as to her leave-taking with her late mistress, and she said it had proved easier than she feared. "I was perfectly civil, sir, but the Lord helped me to remember that a good woman has no call to tremble before a bad one."

"You must have been too lovely," Newman frankly observed. "But does she know you've come to *me?*"

"She asked me where I was going, and I mentioned your name," Mrs. Bread returned.

"What did she say to that?"

"She looked at me very hard, she turned very red. Then she bade me leave her. I was all ready to go, and I had got the coachman, who's an Englishman, thank goodness, to bring down my poor boxes and to fetch me a cab. But when I went down myself to those terrible great gates I found them closed. My lady had sent orders to the porter not to let me pass, and by the same orders the porter's wife, a dreadful sly old body, had gone out in a cab to fetch home M. de Bellegarde from his club."

Newman's face lighted almost with the candour of childhood. "She *is* scared! she *is* scared!"

"I was frightened too, sir," said Mrs. Bread, "but I thank the powers I felt my temper rise. I took it very high with the porter, and asked him by what right he used violence to an honourable Anglaise who had lived in the house for thirty years before he was heard of. Oh sir, I was very grand — I brought the man down. He drew his bolts and let me out, and I promised the cabman something handsome if he would drive fast. But he was terribly slow; it seemed as if we should never reach your blest door. I'm all of a tremble still; it took me five minutes, just now, to thread my needle."

Newman told her, in munificent mirth, that if she chose she might have a little maid on purpose to thread her needles; and he went away nursing this sketch of the scene in the Rue de l'Université and rejoicing in the belief that he had produced there what he might call the impression of his life.

He had not shown Mrs. Tristram the document he carried in his pocket-book, but since his return to Paris he had seen her several times, and she had not disguised from him that he struck her as in a strange way — an even stranger way than his sad situation made natural. Had his disappointment gone to his head? He looked like a man who was spoiling for some sickness, yet she had never seen him more restless and active. Some days he would hang his head and fold his brow and set his teeth, appear to wish to give out that he should never smile again; on others he would indulge in laughter that was almost rude and make jokes that were bad even for him. If he was trying to carry off his humiliation he went at such times really too far. She begged him of all things not to be "strange." Feeling in a measure answerable for the adventure that had turned out so ill for him, she could put up with anything but his strangeness. He might be tragic if he would, or he might be terribly touching and pierce her to the heart with silent sorrow; he might be violent and summon her to say why she had ever dared to meddle with his destiny: to this she would submit — for this she would make allowances. Only, if he loved her, let him not be incoherent. That would quite break down her nerves. It was like people talking in their sleep; they always awfully frightened her. And Mrs. Tristram intimated that, taking very high ground as regards the moral obligation which events had laid upon her, she proposed not to rest quiet till she should have confronted him with the least inadequate substitute for his loss that the two hemispheres contained.

"Ah," he replied to this, "I think we're square now and we had better not open a new account! You may bury me some day, but you shall of a certainty never marry me. It's too rough, you see — it's worse than a free fight in Arkansaw. I hope, at any rate," he added, "that there's nothing incoherent in this — that I want to go next Sunday to the Carmelite chapel in the Avenue de Messine. You know one of the Catholic clergymen — an abbé, is that it? — whom I've seen here with you, I think, on some errand for his poor; that motherly old gentleman with the big waistband. Please ask him if I need a special leave to go in, and if I do, beg him to obtain it for me."

Mrs. Tristram gave expression to the liveliest joy. "I'm so glad you've asked me to do something! You shall get into the chapel if the abbé is disfrocked for his share in it."

And two days afterwards she told him it was all arranged; the abbé was enchanted to serve him, and if he would present himself civilly at the convent gate there would be no obstacle.

XXIV

SUNDAY was as yet two days off; but meanwhile, to beguile his impatience, Newman took his way to the Avenue de Messine and got what comfort he could in staring at the blank outer wall of Madame de Cintré's present abode. The street in question, as some travellers will remember, adjoins the Parc Monceau, which is one of the finest quarters of reconstructed Paris. It has an air of modern opulence and convenience that sounds a false note for any temple of sacrifice, and the impression made on his gloomily-irritated gaze by the fresh-looking, windowless expanse behind which the woman he loved was perhaps even then pledging herself to pass the rest of her days was less exasperating than he had feared. The place suggested a convent with the modern improvements — an asylum in which privacy, though unbroken, might be not quite identical with privation, and meditation, though monotonous, might be sufficiently placid. And yet he knew the case was other; only at present it was not a reality to him. It was too strange and too mocking to be real; it was like a page torn out of some superannuated unreadable book, with no context in his own experience.

On Sunday morning, at the hour Mrs. Tristram had indicated, he rang at the gate in the blank wall. It instantly opened and admitted him into a clean, cold-looking court, beyond which a dull, plain edifice

met his view in the manner of some blank stiff party
to a formal introduction. A robust lay sister with
a cheerful complexion emerged from a porter's lodge
and, on his stating his errand, pointed to the open
door of the chapel, an edifice which occupied the
right side of the court and was preceded by a high
flight of steps. Newman ascended the steps and
immediately entered the open door. Service had not
yet begun; the interior was dimly lighted and it was
some moments before he could distinguish features
Then he saw the scene divided by a large close iron
screen into two unequal parts. The altar was on the
hither side of the screen, and between it and the
entrance were disposed several benches and chairs.
Three or four of these were occupied by vague,
motionless figures — figures he presently perceived to
be women deeply absorbed in their devotion. The
place seemed to Newman very cold; the smell of the
incense itself was cold. Mixed with this impression
was a twinkle of tapers and here and there a glow of
coloured glass. He seated himself; the praying
women kept still, kept their backs turned. He saw
they were visitors like himself, and he would have
liked to see their faces; for he believed that they were
the mourning mothers and sisters of other women
who had had the same pitiless courage as the person in
whom he was interested. But they were better off
than he, for they at least shared the faith to which
the others had sacrificed themselves. Three or four
persons came in, two of them gentlemen important
and mature. Every one was very quiet, with a perverse effect of studied submission. He fastened his

eyes on the screen behind the altar. That was the
convent, the real convent, the place where she was.
But he could see nothing; no light came through the
crevices. He got up and approached the partition
very gently, trying to look through. Behind it was
darkness, with no sign even of despair. He went
back to his place, and after that a priest and two
altar-boys came in and began to say mass.

Newman watched their genuflexions and gyrations
with a grim, still enmity; they seemed prompters and
abettors of the wrong he had suffered; they were
mouthing and droning out their triumph. The
priest's long, dismal intonings acted upon his nerves
and deepened his wrath; there was something defiant
in his unintelligible drawl — as if it had been meant
for his very own swindled self. Suddenly there arose
from the depths of the chapel, from behind the inex-
orable grating, a sound that drew his attention from
the altar — the sound of a strange, lugubrious chant
uttered by women's voices. It began softly, but it
presently grew louder, and as it increased it became
more of a wail and a dirge. It was the chant of the
Carmelite nuns, their only human utterance. It was
their dirge over their buried affections and over the
vanity of earthly desires. At first he was bewildered
almost stunned, by the monstrous manifestation,
then, as he comprehended its meaning, he listened
intently and his heart began to throb. He listened for
Madame de Cintré's voice, and in the very heart of
the tuneless harmony he imagined he made it out.
We are obliged to believe that he was wrong, since
she had obviously not yet had time to become a mem-

ber of the invisible sisterhood; the chant, at any rate,
kept on, mechanical and monotonous, with dismal
repetitions and despairing cadences. It was hideous,
it was horrible; as it continued he felt he needed all
his self-control. He was growing more agitated, the
tears were hot in his eyes. At last, as in its full force
the thought came over him that this confused, imper-
sonal wail was all that he or the world she had de-
serted were ever again to hear of the breath of those
lips of which his own held still the pressure, he knew
he could bear it no longer. He rose abruptly and
made his way out. On the threshold he paused, listened again to the dreary strain, and then hastily
descended into the court. As he did so he saw that
the good sister with the high-coloured cheeks and the
fan-like frill to her head-dress, who had admitted
him, was in conference at the gate with two persons
who had just come in. A second glance showed him
that these visitors were Madame de Bellegarde and
her son, and that they were about to avail themselves
of that method of approach to their lost victim which
he had found but a mockery of consolation. As he
crossed the court the Marquis recognised him; he
was on the way to the steps and was supporting his
mother. From Madame de Bellegarde he also received a look, and it resembled that of Urbain. Both
faces expressed a less guarded perturbation, something
more akin to immediate dismay, than Newman had
yet seen in them. Evidently he was disconcerting,
and neither mother nor son had quite due presence
of mind. Newman hurried past them, guided only
by the desire to get out of the convent walls and into

the street. The gate opened itself at his approach; he strode over the threshold and it closed behind him. A carriage which appeared to have been standing there was just turning away from the pavement. He looked at it for a moment blankly; then he became conscious, through the dusky mist that swam before his eyes, that a lady seated in it was bowing to him. The vehicle had got into motion before he recognised her; it was an ancient landau with one half the cover lowered. The lady's bow was very expressive and accompanied with a smile; a little girl was seated beside her. He raised his hat, and then the lady bade the coachman stop.

The carriage drew up again and she sat there and beckoned to Newman — beckoned with the demonstrative grace of the Marquise Urbain. Newman hesitated a moment before he obeyed her summons; during this moment he had time to curse his stupidity for letting the others escape him. He had been wondering how he could get at them; fool that he was for not stopping them then and there! What better place than beneath the very prison walls to which they had consigned the promise of his joy? He had been too bewildered publicly to fall on them, but now he felt ready to await them at the gate. Madame Urbain, with a certain attractive petulance, made a more emphatic sign, and this time he went over to the carriage. She leaned out and gave him her hand, looking at him kindly and smiling. "Ah, monsieur, you don't include me in your wrath? I had nothing to do with it."

"Oh, I don't suppose *you* could have prevented

it!" he answered in a tone which was not that of studied gallantry.

"What you say is too true for me to resent the small account it makes of my influence. I forgive you, at any rate, because you look as if you had seen a ghost."

"I *have* seen a ghost," Newman darkly returned.

"I'm glad then I did n't go in with my *belle-mère* and my husband. You must have seen them, eh? Was the meeting affectionate? Did you hear the chanting? They say it's like the lamentations of the damned. I would n't go in: one's certain to hear that soon enough. Poor Claire — in a white shroud and a big brown cloak! That's the full dress of the Carmelites, you know. Well, she was always fond of long, loose things. But I must n't speak of her to you; I must only say I'm very sorry for you, that if I could have helped you I would, and that I think every one has behaved infernally. I was afraid of it, you know; I felt it in the air for a fortnight before it came. When I saw you, at my mother-in-law's ball, take it all in such good faith I felt as if you were dancing on your grave. But what could I do? I wish you all the good I can think of. You'll say that is n't much! Yes; they've been abominable; I'm not a bit afraid to say it; I assure you every one thinks so. We're not all like that. I'm sorry I'm not going to see you again; you know I think you very good company. I'd prove it by asking you to get into the carriage and drive with me for the quarter of an hour that I shall wait for my mother-in-law. Only if we were seen — considering what has passed, and every one knows you've been *joué* — it might be thought I was going a little too far, even for me. But I shall see you sometimes — somewhere, eh? You know" —this was said in English—"we've a plan for a little amusement."

Newman stood there with his hand on the carriage door, listening to this consolatory murmur with an unlighted eye. He hardly knew what Madame Urbain was saying; he was only conscious she was chattering ineffectively. But suddenly it occurred to him that, with her pretty professions, there was a way of making her effective; she might help him to get at the old woman and the Marquis. "They're coming back soon — your companions? You're hanging about for them?"

"They'll hear the *office* out; there's nothing to keep them longer. Claire has refused to see them."

"I want to speak to them," Newman said; "and you can help me, you can do me a favour. Delay your return for five minutes and give me a chance at them. I'll wait for them here."

The young woman clasped her hands in sharp deprecation. "My poor friend, what do you want to do to them? To beg them to come back to you? It will be wasted words. They'll never come back!"

"I want to speak to them all the same. Pray do what I ask you. Stay away and leave them to me for five minutes. You need n't be afraid; I shall not be violent; I'm very quiet."

"Yes, you look very quiet! If they had *le cœur tendre* you'd move them. But don't count on them — you've had enough of that. However, I'll do

better for you than what you propose. The understanding is not that I shall come back for them. I'm
going into the Parc Monceau to give my little girl
a walk, and my mother-in-law, who comes so rarely
into this quarter, is to profit by the same opportunity
to take the air. We're to wait for her in the park,
where my husband is to join us with her. Follow me
now; just within the gates I shall get out of my carriage. Sit down on a chair in some quiet corner and
I'll bring them near you. There's devotion for you!
Le reste vous regarde."

This proposal Newman eagerly caught at; it
revived his drooping spirit and he reflected that
Madame Urbain was not quite the featherhead she
seemed. He promised immediately to overtake her,
and the carriage drove away.

The Parc Monceau is a very pretty piece of land-
scape-gardening, but Newman, passing into it, had
little care for its elegant vegetation, which was full of
the freshness of spring. He found the young Marquise promptly, seated in one of the quiet corners of
which she had spoken, while before her in the alley
her little girl, attended by the footman and the lap-
dog, walked up and down as if to take a lesson in
deportment. Newman seated himself by his friend,
who began to chatter afresh, apparently with the
design of convincing him that — if he would only see
it — poor dear Claire did n't belong to the most
pleasing type of woman. She was too long, too lean,
too flat, too stiff, too cold; her mouth was too wide
and her nose too narrow. She had n't such a thing
as a dimple, or even as a pretty curve — or call it

really an obtuse angle — anywhere. And then she was eccentric, eccentric in cold blood; she was a furious Anglaise after all. Newman was very impatient; he was counting the minutes until his victims should reappear. He sat silent, leaning upon his cane, looking absently and insensibly at Madame Urbain. At last she said she would walk toward the gate of the park and meet her companions; but before she went she dropped her eyes and, after playing a moment with the lace of her sleeve, looked up again at her visitor.

"Do you remember the promise you made me three weeks ago?" And then as Newman, vainly consulting his memory, was obliged to confess that this vow had escaped it, she mentioned that he had made her at the time a very queer answer — an answer at which, viewing it in the light of the sequel, she had fair ground for taking offence. "You promised to take me to Bullier's after your marriage. After your marriage — you made a great point of that. Three days after that your marriage was broken off. Do you know, when I heard the news, the first thing I said to myself? 'Ah, *par exemple*, now he won't go with me to Bullier's!' And I really began to wonder if you had n't been expecting the rupture."

"Oh, my dear lady — !" he merely murmured, while he looked down the path to see if the others were n't coming.

"I shall be good-natured," said his friend. "One must n't ask too much of a gentleman who's in love with a cloistered nun. Besides, I can't go to Bullier's while we're in mourning. But I have n't given it up for that. The *partie* is arranged; I have my cavalier — Lord Deepmere, if you please! He has gone back to his dear Dublin; but a few months hence I'm to name any evening, and he'll come over from Ireland on purpose. That's what I call really feeling for a woman."

Shortly after this Madame Urbain walked away with her little girl. Newman sat in his place; the time seemed terribly long. He felt how fiercely his quarter of an hour in the chapel had raked over the glowing coals of his resentment. His accessory kept him waiting, but she proved as good as her word. Finally she reappeared at the end of the path with her little girl and her footman; beside her slowly walked her husband with his mother on his arm. They were a long time advancing, during which Newman sat unmoved. Aching as he fairly did now with his passion — the passion of his wrath at the impudence, on the part of such a pair, of an objection to *him* in the name of clean hands — it was extremely characteristic of him that he was able to moderate his expression of it very much as he would have turned down a flaring gas-jet. His native shrewdness, coolness, clearness, his lifelong submission to the sense that words were acts and acts were steps in life, and that in this matter of taking steps curveting and prancing were exclusively reserved for quadrupeds and foreigners — all this admonished him that rightful wrath had no connexion with being a fool and indulging in spectacular violence. So as he rose, when the elder lady and her son were close to him, he only felt very tall and unencumbered and alert. He had been sitting beside some shrubbery in such a way as not to be noticeable at a distance; but the Marquis, at hand, had quickly enough perceived him. The couple were then for holding their course; at sight of which Newman stepped so straight in front of them that they were obliged to pause. He lifted his hat slightly and looked at them hard; they were pale with amazement and disgust.

"Pardon my stopping you," he dryly said; "but I must profit by the occasion. I've ten words to say to you. Will you listen to them?"

The Marquis blinked, then turned to his mother. "Can Mr. Newman possibly have anything to say that is worth our listening to?"

"I assure you I've something," Newman went on; "besides, it's my duty to say it. It concerns you ever so closely."

"Your duty?' said the Marquise, her small fine mouth contracting in its odd way as for a whistle. "That's your affair, not ours."

Madame Urbain meanwhile had seized her little girl by the hand, with a gesture of surprise and impatience which struck Newman, intent as he was on his own words, with its plausible extravagance. "If Mr. Newman's going to make a scene in public," she exclaimed, "I shall take my poor child out of the *mêlée*. She's too young to see such naughtiness!"—and she instantly resumed her walk.

"You had much better listen to me," he persisted with his difficult ease. "Whether you do or not your gain will be small; but at least perhaps you'll be prepared."

"If you mean prepared for your preposterous threats," the Marquis replied, "there's nothing grotesque from you, certainly, for which we're not prepared, and of the idea of which you don't perfectly know what we think."

"You think a great deal more than you yet admit. A moment," Newman added in reply to a sharp exclamation from Madame de Bellegarde. "I don't at all forget that we're in a public place, and you see I'm very quiet. I'm not going to tell your secret to the passers-by; I shall keep it, to begin with, for certain picked listeners. Any one who observes us will think we're having a friendly chat and that I'm complimenting you, madam, on your venerable virtues."

The Marquis gave a hiss that fairly evoked for our friend some vision of a hunched back, an erect tail and a pair of shining evil eyes. "I demand of you to step out of our path!"

Newman instantly complied and his interlocutors proceeded. But he was still beside them and was still distinct. "Half an hour hence Madame de Bellegarde will regret that she didn't learn exactly what I mean."

The Marquise had taken a few steps, but at these words she pulled up again, as if not to have the appearance of not facing even monstrous possibilities — as monstrous, that is, as a monster of rudeness might make them. "You're like a pedlar with something trumpery to sell," she said; and she accompanied it with a strange, small, cold laugh — a demonstration so inconsequent that it meant nothing, Newman quickly felt, if it did n't mean a "lovely" nervousness.

"Oh no, not to sell; I give it to you for nothing." And he had never in his life, no matter under what occasion for it, spoken so completely and so gratefully to the point as now. "You cruelly killed your helpless husband, you know; and I'm in possession of all the facts. That is you did your best, first, and failed; and then succeeded — by which I mean finished him — at a stroke and almost without trying."

The Marquise closed her eyes and gave a small dry cough which, as a piece of dissimulation and of self-possession, seemed to her adversary consummate.

"Dear mother," said Urbain as if she had been moved to hilarity, "does this stuff amuse you so much?"

"The rest is more amusing," Newman went on. "You had better not lose it."

The eyes she fixed on him might well have been, he recognised, those with which, according to Mrs. Bread, she had done her husband to death; and they had somehow no connexion with the stifled shrillness of her spoken retort. "Amusing? Have I killed some one else?"

"I don't count your daughter," said Newman, "though of course I might. Your husband knew what you were doing. I've a proof of it the existence of which you've never suspected." And he turned to the Marquis, whose face was beyond any he had ever seen discomposed, decomposed — what did they call it? "A paper written by the hand, and signed with the name of Henri-Urbain de Bellegarde. Written and dated after you, madam, had left him for dead, and while you, sir, had gone — not very fast — for the doctor."

The Marquis turned to his mother; she moved a little at random, averting herself and looking vaguely round her. But her answer to his appeal fell, after an instant, rather short. "I must sit down," she simply said, and went back to the bench on which Newman had been posted.

"Could n't you have spoken to me alone?" her companion then asked, all remarkably, of their pursuer, who wondered if it meant that there was suddenly, quite amazingly, a basis for discussion.

"Well, yes, if I could have been sure of speaking to your mother alone too," Newman answered. "But I've had to take you as I could get you, don't you see?"

Madame de Bellegarde, in a manner very eloquent of what he would have called her "grit," her steel-cold pluck and her instinctive appeal to her own personal resources, seated herself on the bench with her head erect and her hands folded in her lap. The expression of her face was such that he fancied her at first inconceivably smiling, but on his drawing nearer felt this display to be strange and convulsive. He saw, however, equally, that she was resisting her agitation with all the rigour of her inflexible will, and there was nothing like either fear or submission in the fine front she presented. She had been upset, but she could intensely think. He felt the pang of a conviction that she would get the better of him still, and

he would n't have been himself if he could wholly fail
to be touched by the sight of a woman (criminal or
other) in so tight a place. She gave a glance at her
son which seemed tantamount to an injunction to be
silent and leave her to her own devices. He stood
beside her with his hands behind him, quite making
up in attitude, as our observer noted, for what he
failed of in utterance. It was to remain really a
burden on Newman's mind to the end, this irritating, this perplexing illustration he afforded of the
positive virtue and the incalculable force, even in the
unholy, of attitude "as such." "What paper is this
you speak of?" the Marquise asked as if confessing
to an interest in any possible contribution to the
family archives.

"Exactly what I 've told you. A paper written by
your husband after you had left him that evening,
for dead — written during the couple of hours before
you returned. You see he had the time; you
should n't have stayed away so long. It declares in
the most convincing way his wife's murderous intent."

"I should like to see it," she observed as with the
most natural concern for a manifesto so compromising to the — already in his day, alas, so painfully
compromised — author of it.

"I thought you might," said Newman, "and I 've
taken a copy." He drew from his waistcoat pocket
a small folded sheet.

"Give it to my son," she returned with decision;
on which Newman handed it to the Marquis while
she simply added "Look at the thing." M. de Belle-

garde's eyes had a pale irrepressible eagerness; he took the paper in his light-gloved fingers and opened it. There was a silence during which he took it in. He had more than time to read it, but still he said nothing; he stood looking at it hard. "Where's the original?" his mother meantime asked in a voice of the most disinterested curiosity.

"In a very safe place. Of course I can't show you *that*," Newman went on — "a treasure the value of which makes it sacred to me. You might want to grab it," he added with conscious quaintness, "and I've too much other use for it. But this is a very correct copy — except of course the hand-writing: I'll get it properly certified for you if you wish. That ought to suit you — its being properly certified."

The Marquis at last raised a countenance deeply and undisguisedly flushed. "It will require," he nevertheless lightly remarked, "a vast deal of certi-fication!"

"Well," Newman returned, "we can always fall back on the original."

"I'm speaking," said the Marquis, "of the orig-inal."

"Ah, that, I think, will speak for itself. Still, we can easily get as many persons as possible — as many of those who knew the writer's hand — to speak for it. Think of the number it will interest — if I begin, myself, say, with the Duchess, that amiable, very stout lady whose name I forget, but who was pleasant to me at your party. She asked me to come to see her, and I've been thinking that in that case I should n't have much to say to her But such a matter as this gives me plenty!"

"You had better, at this rate, keep what you have there, my son," the old woman quavered with a strained irony.

"By all means," Newman said — "keep it and show it to your mother when you get home."

"And after enlisting the Duchess?" asked the Marquis, who folded the paper and put it away.

"Well, there are all the other people you had the cruelty to introduce me to in a character of which you were capable, at the next turn, of rudely divesting me. Many of them immediately afterwards left cards on me, so that I have their names correctly and shall know how to find them."

For a moment, on this, neither of Newman's friends spoke; the Marquise sat looking down very hard, while her son's blanched pupils were fixed on her face. "Is that all you have to say?" she finally asked.

"No, I want to say a few words more. I want to say that I hope you quite understand what I'm about. This is my vindication, you know, of my claim that I've been cruelly wronged. You've treated me before the world, convened for the express purpose, as if I were not good enough for you. I mean to show the world that, however bad I may be, you're not quite the people to say it."

Madame de Bellegarde was silent again, and then, with a return of her power to face him, she dealt with his point. Her coolness continued to affect him as consummate; he wondered of what alarms, what effronteries, what suspicions and what precautions she had not had, from far back, to make her life. "I need n't ask you who has been your accomplice in this clumsy fraud. Catherine Bread told me you had purchased her services."

"Don't accuse Mrs. Bread of venality," Newman returned. "She has kept your secret all these years. She has given you a long respite. It was beneath her eyes your husband wrote that paper; he put it into her hands with a solemn injunction that she was to make it public. You've had the benefit of her merciful delay."

The Marquise appeared for an instant to hesitate, and then, "My husband, for years, did what he — most remarkably! — liked with her," she declared dryly enough. "She was perhaps the meanest of his many mistresses." This was the only concession to self-defence that she condescended to make.

"I very much doubt that," said Newman. "I believe in her decency."

Madame de Bellegarde got up from her bench. "It was n't to your beliefs — however interesting in themselves — I undertook to listen; so that, if you've nothing left but *them* to tell me, this charming interview may terminate." And turning to the Marquis she took his arm again. "My son," she then oddly resumed, "say something!"

He looked down at her, passing his hand over his forehead to the positive displacement of his hat; with which, tenderly, caressingly, "What shall I say?" he too uncertainly enquired.

"There's only one thing to say — that it was really

not worth while, on such a showing, to have pulled us up in the street like a pair of pickpockets."

But the Marquis thought he could surpass this. "Your paper's of course the crudest of forgeries," he said to Newman.

Newman shook his head all amusedly. "M. de Bellegarde, your mother does better. She has done better all along, from the first of my knowing you. You're a mighty plucky woman, madam," he continued. "It's a great pity you've made me your enemy. I should have been one of your greatest admirers."

"*Mon pauvre ami*," she proceeded to her son, and as if she had not heard these words, "you must take me immediately to my carriage."

Newman stepped back and let them leave him; he watched them a moment and saw Madame Urbain, with her little girl, wander out of a by-path to meet them. The Marquise stooped and kissed her grandchild. "Damn it, she *is* plucky!" he sighed; and he walked home with a sense of having been almost worsted. She was so quite heroically impenetrable. But on reflexion he decided that what he had witnessed was no real sense of security, still less a real innocence. It was only a very superior style of brazen assurance, of what M. Nioche called *l'usage du monde* and Mrs. Tristram called the grand manner. "Wait till she has seen how he puts it!" he said to himself, and he concluded that he should hear from her soon.

He heard sooner than he expected. The next morning, before midday, when he was about to give orders for his breakfast to be served, M. de Bellegarde's card was brought him. "She *has* seen how he puts it and she has passed a bad night," he promptly inferred. He instantly admitted his visitor, who came in with the air of the ambassador of a great power meeting the delegate of a barbarous tribe whom an absurd accident had enabled for the moment to be abominably annoying. The ambassador, at any rate, had also passed a bad night, and his faultlessly careful array only threw into relief the sick rancour of his eyes and those mottled spots on his fine skin that resembled, to his host's imagination, the hard finger-prints of fear. He stood there a moment, breathing quickly and painfully and shaking his forefinger curtly as Newman pointed to a chair.

"What I've come to say is soon said and can only be said without ceremony."

"I'm good for as much or for as little as you desire."

The Marquis looked round the room and then: "On what terms will you. part with what you call your original?"

"Ah, on none!" And while, with his head on one side and his hands behind him, he sounded his visitor's depth of detestation, Newman added: "Certainly that's not worth sitting down about."

M. de Bellegarde went on, however, as without having heard him. "My mother and I, last evening, talked over your story. You'll be surprised to learn that we think your little document is — a " — and he held back his word a moment — "characteristic."

Newman laughed out as it came. "Of your mother and you, you mean?"

"Of my deplorable father.

"You forget that with you I'm used to surprises!" Newman gaily pursued.

"The very scantest consideration we owe his memory," the Marquis continued, "makes us desire he should n't be held up to the world as the author of an elaborately malignant attack on the reputation of a wife whose only fault was that she had been submissive to repeated outrage."

"Oh, I see! It's for your father's sake!" And Newman laughed the laugh in which he indulged when he was, if not most amused, at any rate most pleased — an intimate noiseless laugh with closed lips.

But M. de Bellegarde's gravity held good. "There are a few of his particular friends for whom the knowledge of so unfortunate an inspiration would be a real grief. Even say we firmly established by medical evidence the presumption of a mind disordered by fever, *il en resterait quelque chose.* At the best it would look ill in him. Very ill!"

"Don't try medical evidence," said Newman. "Don't touch the doctors and they won't touch you. I don't mind your knowing that I've not written to either of the gentlemen present at the event."

He flattered himself he saw signs in his visitor's discoloured mask that this information was extremely pertinent. The Marquis remained, however, irreducibly argumentative. "For instance Madame d'Outreville, of whom you spoke yesterday. I can imagine nothing that would shock her more."

"Oh, I'm quite prepared to shock Madame d'Outreville. That's just what's the matter with me. I regularly *want* to shock people."

M. de Bellegarde examined for a moment the fine white stitching on one of his black gloves. Then without looking up, "We don't offer you money," he said. "That we suppose to be useless."

Newman, turning away, took a few turns about the room and then came back. "What *do* you offer me? By what I can make out the generosity is all to be on my side."

The Marquis dropped his arms at his flanks and held his head a little higher. "What we offer you is a chance — a chance a gentleman should appreciate. A chance to abstain from inflicting a terrible blot upon the memory of a man who certainly had his faults, but who, personally, had done you no wrong."

"There are two things to say to that," Newman returned. "The first is, as regards appreciating your 'chance,' that you don't consider me a gentleman. That's your great point, you know. It's a poor rule that won't work both ways. The second is that — well, in a word, you're talking sad nonsense."

In the midst of his bitterness he had kept well before his eyes, as I have noted, a certain ideal of saying nothing rude, and he felt a quick scruple for the too easy impatience of these words. But the Marquis took them more quietly than might have been expected. Sublime ambassador that he was, he continued the policy of ignoring what was disagreeable in his adversary's replies. He gazed at the gilded arabesques on the opposite wall and then transferred his glance to his host as if he too had been

a large grotesque in a vulgar system of chamber-
decoration. "I suppose you know that, as regards
yourself, a course so confessedly vindictive — vindictive in respect to your discomfiture — won't do at all."

"How do you mean it won't do?"

"Why, of course you utterly damn yourself. But
I suppose that's in your programme. You propose
to throw at us this horrible *ordure* that you've raked
together, and you believe, you hope, that some of it
may stick. We know naturally it can't," explained
the Marquis in a tone of conscious lucidity; "but you
take the chance and are willing at any rate to show
that you yourself have dirty hands."

"That's a good comparison; at least half of it is,"
said Newman. "I take the chance of something
sticking. But as regards my hands, they're clean.
I've taken the awful thing up with my finger-tips."

M. de Bellegarde looked a moment into his hat.
"All our friends are quite with us. They would have
done exactly as we've done."

"I shall believe that when I hear them say it.
Meanwhile I shall think better of human nature."

The Marquis looked into his hat again. "My poor
perverse sister was extremely fond of her father. If
she knew of the existence of the few base words —
at once mad and base — of which you propose to
make this scandalous use, she would require of you,
proudly, for his sake, to give them up to her, and she
would destroy them on the spot."

"Very possibly," Newman rejoined. "But it's exactly what she won't know. I was in that hideous place
yesterday, and I know what *she's* doing. Lord of

mercy! You can guess whether it made me feel for-
giving!"

M. de Bellegarde appeared to have nothing more
to suggest; but he continued to stand there, rigid and
elegant, as a man who had believed his mere personal presence would have had an argumentative
value. Newman watched him and, without yielding
an inch on the main issue, felt an incongruously good-
natured impulse to help him to retreat in good order.
"Your idea, you see — though ingenious in its way
— does n't work. You offer too little."

"Propose something yourself," the Marquis at last
brought out.

"Give me back Madame de Cintré relieved of the
blight and free of the poison that are all of your
producing."

M. de Bellegarde threw up his head and his flush
darkly spread. "Never!"

"You can't!"

"We would n't if we could! In the sentiment
which led us to deprecate her marriage to you nothing
is changed."

"'Deprecate' is lovely!" cried Newman. "It was
hardly worth while to come here only to tell me that
you're not ashamed of yourselves. I should have come
to think of you perhaps as in your guilt-burdened
hearts almost pitifully miserable."

The Marquis slowly walked toward the door, and
Newman, following, opened it for him. "Your hawk-
ing that tatter about will be, on your part, the vulgar-
est proceeding conceivable, and, as having admitted
you to our *intimité*, we shall proportionately wince

for it. That we quite feel. But it won't otherwise incommode us."

"Well," said Newman after reflexion, "I don't know that I want to do anything worse than make you regret your connexion with me. Only don't be sure you know yet," he added, "how very much you *may* regret it."

M. de Bellegarde stood a moment looking on the ground, as if ransacking his brain to see what else he could do to save his father's reputation. Then, with a small cold sigh, he seemed to signify that he regretfully surrendered the late Marquis to the penalty of his turpitude. He gave a scant shrug, took his neat umbrella from the servant in the vestibule and, with his gentlemanly walk, passed out. Newman stood listening till he heard the door close; then for some minutes he moved to and fro with his hands in his pockets and a sound like the low hum of a jig proceeding from the back of his mouth.

XXV

He called on the immense, the comical Duchess and found her at home. An old gentleman with a high nose and a gold-headed cane was just taking leave; he made Newman a protracted obeisance as he retired, and our hero supposed him one of the high personages with whom he had shaken hands at Madame de Bellegarde's party. The Duchess, in her armchair, from which she did n't move, with a great flower-pot on one side of her, a pile of pink-covered novels on the other and a large piece of tapestry depending from her lap, presented an expansive and imposing front; but her aspect was in the highest degree gracious and there was nothing in her manner to check the effusion of his confidence. She talked to him of flowers and books, getting launched with marvellous promptitude; about the theatres, about the peculiar institutions of his native country, about the humidity of Paris, about the pretty complexions of the American ladies, about his impressions of France and his opinion of its female inhabitants. All this had a large free flow on the part of the Duchess, who, like many of her countrywomen, was a person of an affirmative rather than an interrogative cast, who uttered "good things" and put them herself into circulation, and who was apt to offer you a present of a convenient little opinion neatly enveloped in the gilt paper of a happy Gallicism. Newman had come to her with a grievance, but he found himself in an atmosphere in which apparently no cognisance was taken of such matters; an atmosphere into which the chill of discomfort had never penetrated and which seemed exclusively made up of mild, sweet, stale intellectual perfumes. The feeling with which he had watched Madame d'Outreville at the treacherous festival of the Bellegardes came back to him; she struck him as a wonderful old lady in some particularly "high" comedy, thoroughly well up in her part. He noticed before long that she asked him no question about their common friends; she made no allusion to the circumstances under which he had been presented to her. She neither feigned ignorance of a change in these circumstances nor pretended to condole with him upon it; but she smiled and discoursed and compared the tender-tinted wools of her tapestry as if the Bellegardes and their wickedness were not of this world. "She's fighting shy!" he said to himself; and, having drawn the inference, was curious to see, further, how, if this were a policy, she would carry it off. She did so in a masterly manner. There was not a gleam of disguised consciousness in the small, clear, demonstrative eyes which constituted her nearest claim to personal loveliness; there was not a symptom of apprehension he would trench on any ground she proposed to avoid. "Upon my word, she does it very well," he tacitly commented. "They all hold together bravely, and, whether any one else can trust them or not, they can certainly trust each other."

He fell at this juncture to admiring the Duchess for her fine manners. He felt, most accurately, that she was not a grain less urbane than she would have been if his marriage were still in prospect; but he was aware also that she led him on no single inch further. He had come, so reasoned this eminent lady — heaven knew why he had come after what had happened; and for the half-hour therefore she would be *charmante*. But she would never see him again. Finding no ready-made opportunity to tell his story, he pondered these things more dispassionately than might have been expected; he stretched his legs as usual and even chuckled a little quite appreciatively and noiselessly. And then as his hostess went on relating a *mot* with which her mother had, in extreme youth, snubbed the great Napoleon, it occurred to him that her evasion of a chapter of French history more interesting to himself might possibly be the result of an extreme consideration for his feelings. Perhaps it was delicacy rather than diplomacy. He was on the point of saying something himself, to make the chance he had determined to give her still better, when the servant announced another visitor. The Duchess on hearing the name — it was that of an Italian prince — gave a little imperceptible pout and said to him rapidly: "I beg you to remain; I desire this visit to be short." He wondered, at this, if they might n't then after all get round to the Bellegardes.

The Prince was a short stout man, with a head disproportionately large. He had a dusky complexion and bushy eyebrows, beneath which glowed a fixed and somewhat defiant stare; he seemed to be challenging you to hint that he might be hydrocephalic.

The Duchess, judging from her charge to our own friend, regarded him as a bore; but this was not apparent from the unchecked abundance of her speech. She caused it to frisk hither and yon as to some old rococo music and then pull up on a *mot* after the fashion in which a stage-dancer whirls, for breath and with arms arranged, into ecstatic equilibrium; she characterised with great felicity the Italian intellect and the taste of the figs at Sorrento, predicted the ultimate future of the Italian kingdom (disgust with the brutal Sardinian rule and complete reversion, throughout the peninsula, to the mild sway of the Holy Father) and, finally, took up the heart-history of their friend *cette pauvre Princesse*, a lady unknown to Newman, who had notoriously so much heart. This record exposed itself to a considerable control from the Prince, who was evidently not related to the heroine in question otherwise than by an intimate familiarity with her annals; and having satisfied himself that Newman was in no laughing mood, either with regard to the size of his head or the authenticity of his facts, he entered into the controversy with an animation for which the Duchess, when she set him down as a bore, could not have been prepared. The often so oddly-directed passions of their friend led Newman's companions to a discussion of the *côté passionel* of the Florentine nobility in general; the Duchess had lately spent several weeks in the very bosom of that body and gathered much information on the subject. This was merged, in turn, in an examination of the Italian heart *per se*. The Duchess, who had arrived at highly original conclusions, thought it the least susceptible organ of its kind that she had ever encountered, related examples of its Machiavellian power to calculate its perils and profits, and at last declared that for her the race were half arithmetic and half ice. The Prince became flame and rhetoric to refute her, and his visit really proved charming.

Newman was naturally out of the fray; he sat with his head a little on one side, watching the interlocutors. The Duchess, as she talked, frequently looked at him with a smile, as if to intimate, in the charming manner of her nation, that it lay only with him to say something very much to the point. But he said nothing at all, and at last his thoughts began to wander. A singular feeling came over him — a sudden sense of the folly of his errand. What under the sun had he after all to say to the Duchess ? Wherein would it profit him to denounce the Bellegardes to her for traitors and the Marquise into the bargain for a murderess ? He seemed morally to have turned a high somersault and to find things looking differently in consequence. He felt, as by the effect of some colder current of the air, his will stiffen in another direction and the mantle of his reserve draw closer. What in the world had he been thinking of when he fancied Madame d'Outreville could help him and that it would conduce to his comfort to make her think ill of the Bellegardes ? What did her opinion of the Bellegardes matter to him ? It was only a shade more important than the opinion the Bellegardes entertained of herself. The Duchess help him, that cold, stout, soft, artificial woman help him ? — she who in the last twenty minutes had built up between them a wall of polite conversation in which she evidently flattered herself he would never find a gate? Had it come to this — that he was asking favours of false gods and appealing for sympathy where he had no sympathy to give? He rested his arms on his knees and sat for some minutes staring into his hat. As he did so his ears tingled — was he to have brayed like that animal whose ears are longest? Whether or no the Duchess would hear his story he would n't tell it. Was he to sit there another half-hour for the sake of exposing the Bellegardes? The Bellegardes be deeply damned! He got up abruptly and advanced to shake hands with his hostess.

"You can't stay longer?" she graciously asked.

"If you'll pardon me, no."

She hesitated, and then, "I had an idea you had something particular to say to me," she returned.

Newman met her eyes; he felt a little dizzy; for the moment he was conscious of the high — or at least the higher — air in which he performed gymnastic revolutions. The little Italian prince came to his help. "Ah, madame, who has not that?" he richly sighed.

"Don't teach Mr. Newman to say *fadaises*," said the Duchess. "It's his merit that he does n't know how."

"Yes, I don't know how to say *fadaises*," Newman admitted, "and I don't want to say anything unpleasant."

"I'm sure you're very considerate," Madame d'Outreville smiled; and she gave him a little nod for all good-bye, with which he took his departure.

Once in the street he stood for some time on the pavement, wondering if after all he had not been most an ass not to offer to the great lady's inhalation his nosegay of strange flowers. And then he decided, he quite had the sense of discovering, that he should simply hate to talk of the Bellegardes with any one. The thing he most wanted to do, it suddenly appeared, was to banish them from his mind and never think of them again. Indecision had, however, not hitherto been one of his weaknesses, and in this case it was not of long duration. For three days he applied all his thought to not thinking — thinking, that is, of the Marquise and her son. He dined with Mrs. Tristram and, on her mentioning their name, requested her almost austerely to desist. This gave Tom Tristram a much-coveted opportunity to offer condolences.

He leaned forward, laying his hand on Newman's arm, compressing his lips and shaking his head. "The fact is, my dear fellow, you see you ought never to have gone into it. It was not your doing, I know -- it was all my wife. If you want to come down on her I'll stand off: I give you leave to hit her as hard as you like. You know she has never had a flick of the whip from me in her life, and I do think she wants to be a bit touched up. Why did n't you listen to *me*? You know I did n't believe in the thing. I thought it at the best a high jump in which you might bruise a shin. I don't profess to have been a tremendous *homme à femmes*, as they say here, but I've instincts about the sex that, hang it, I've honestly come by. I've never mistrusted a woman in my life that she has not turned out badly. I was not at all deceived in Lizzie for instance; I always had my doubts about her. Whatever you may think of my present situation I must at least admit that I got into it with my eyes open. Now suppose you had got into something like this box with your grand cold Countess. You may depend upon it she'd have turned out a stiff one. And upon my word I don't see where you could have found your comfort. Not from the Marquis, my dear Newman; he was n't a man you could go and talk things over with in an easy and natural way. Did he ever seem to want to have you on the premises? Did he ever try to see you alone? Did he ever ask you to come and smoke a cigar with him of an evening or step in, when you had been calling on the ladies, and take something? I don't think you'd have got much out of *him*. And as for that daughter of a hundred earls his mother, she struck one as an uncommonly strong dose. They have a great expression here, you know; they call any damned thing 'sympathetic' — that is when it is n't it ought to be. Now Madame de Bellegarde's about as sympathetic as that mustard-pot. They're a d—d stony-faced, cold-blooded lot anyway; I felt it awfully at that ball of theirs. I felt as if I were walking up and down the Armoury in the Tower of London — every one cased in ancestral steel, every one perched up in a panoply. My dear boy, don't think me a vulgar brute for hinting it, but, you may depend upon it, all they wanted was your money. I know something about that; I can tell when people want one's money. Why they stopped wanting yours I don't know; I suppose be-

cause they could get some one else's without working
so hard for it. It is n't worth finding out. It may be
it was not with your Countess, Lizzie's and yours,
that the idea of chucking you originated; very likely
the old woman put her up to it. I suspect she and
her mother are really as thick as thieves, eh? You're
well out of it, at any rate, old man; make up your
mind to that. If I express myself strongly it's all
because I love you so much; and from that point of
view I may say I should as soon have thought of making up to that piece of pale peculiarity as I should
have thought of wooing the Obelisk in the Place de
la Concorde."

Newman sat gazing at Tristram during this
harangue with a lack-lustre eye; never yet had he
seemed to himself to have outgrown so completely
the phase of equal comradeship with Tom Tristram.
Mrs. Tristram's glance at her husband had more of
a spark; she turned to Newman with a slightly lurid
smile. "You must at least do justice," she said, "to
the felicity with which he repairs the indiscretions of
a too zealous wife."

But even without the lash of his friend's loud
tongue Newman would have waked again into his
bitterest consciousness. He could keep it at bay only
when he could cease to miss what he had lost, and
each day, for the present, but added a ton of weight
to that quantity. In vain Mrs. Tristram begged him
to *se faire*, as she put it, *une raison;* she assured him
the sight of his countenance made her wretched.

"How can I help it?" he demanded with a trembling voice — "how can I help it when the sight of

everything makes *me* so? I feel exactly like a stunned widower — and a widower who has not even the consolation of going to stand beside the grave of his wife, one who has not the right to wear so much mourning as a weed on his hat. I feel," he added in a moment, "as if my wife had been murdered and her assassins were still at large."

Mrs. Tristram made no immediate rejoinder, but at last she said with a smile which, in so far as it was a forced one, was less successfully simulated than such smiles, on her lips, usually were: "Are you very sure that you'd have been happy?"

He stared, then shook his head. "That's weak; that won't do."

"Well," she persisted as with an idea, "I don't believe it would have really done."

He gave a sound of irritation. "Say then it would have damnably failed. Failure for failure I should have preferred that one to this."

She took it in her musing way. "I should have been curious to see; it would have been very strange."

"Was it from curiosity that you urged me to put myself forward?"

"A little," she still more boldly answered. Newman gave her the one angry look he had been destined ever to give her, turned away and took up his hat. She watched him a moment and then said: "That sounds very cruel, but it's less so than it sounds. Curiosity has a share in almost everything I do. I wanted very much to see, first, if such a union could actually come through; second, what would happen to it afterwards."

"So you had n't faith," he said resentfully.

"Yes, I had faith — faith that it would take place, and that you'd be happy. Otherwise I should have been, among my speculations, a very heartless creature. *But*," she continued, laying her hand on his arm and hazarding a grave smile, "it was the highest flight ever taken by a tolerably rich imagination!"

Shortly after this she recommended him to leave Paris and travel for three months. Change of scene would do him good and he would forget his misfortune sooner in absence from the objects that had witnessed it. "I really feel," he concurred, "as if to leave *you*, at least, would do me good — and cost me very little effort. You're growing cynical; you shock me and pain me."

"Very well," she said, good-naturedly or cynically, as may appear most credible. "I shall certainly see you again."

He was ready enough to get quite away; the brilliant streets he had walked through in his happier hours and which then seemed to wear a higher brilliancy in honour of his happiness, were now in the secret of his defeat and looked down on it in shining mockery. He would go somewhere, he cared little where; and he made his preparations. Then one morning at haphazard he drove to the train that would transport him to Calais and deposit him there for despatch to the shores of Britain. As he rolled along he asked himself what had become of his revenge, and he was able to think of it as provisionally pigeonholed in a very safe place. It would keep till called for.

THE AMERICAN

He arrived in London in the midst of what is called "the season," and it seemed to him at first that he might here put himself in the way of being diverted from his heavy-heartedness. He knew no one in all England, but the spectacle of the vaster and duskier Babylon roused him somewhat from his apathy. Anything that was enormous usually found favour with him, and the multitudinous English energies and industries stirred in his spirit a dull vivacity of contemplation. It is on record that the weather, at that moment, was of the finest insular quality; he took long walks and explored London in every direction; he sat by the hour in Kensington Gardens and beside the adjoining Drive, watching the people and the horses and the carriages; the rosy English beauties, the wonderful English dandies and the splendid flunkies. He went to the opera and found it better than in Paris; he went to the theatre and found a surprising charm in listening to dialogue the finest points of which came within the range of his comprehension. He made several excursions into the country, recommended by the waiter at his hotel, with whom, on this and similar points, he had established confidential relations. He watched the deer in Windsor Forest and admired the Thames from Richmond Hill; he ate whitebait and brown bread-and-butter at Greenwich; he strolled in the grassy shadow of the cathedral of Canterbury. He also visited the Tower of London and Madame Tussaud's exhibition. One day he thought he would go to Sheffield, and then, thinking again, gave it up. Why the devil should he go to Sheffield? He had a feeling that the link which bound him to a possible interest in the manufacture of cutlery was broken. He had no desire for an "inside view" of any successful enterprise whatever, and he would n't have given the smallest sum for the privilege of talking over the details of the most splendid business with the most original of managers.

One afternoon he had walked into the Park and was slowly threading his way through the human maze which fringes the Drive. This stream was no less dense, and Newman, as usual, marvelled at the strange dowdy figures he saw taking the air in some of the most shining conveyances. They reminded him of what he had read of Eastern and Southern counties, in which grotesque idols and fetiches were sometimes drawn out of their temples and carried abroad in golden chariots to be seen of the people. He noted a great many pretty cheeks beneath high-plumed hats as he squeezed his way through serried waves of crumpled muslin; and, sitting on little chairs at the base of the dull, massive English trees, he observed a number of quiet-eyed maidens who seemed only to remind him afresh that the magic of beauty had gone out of the world with the woman wrenched from him: to say nothing of other damsels whose eyes were not quiet and who struck him still more as a satire on possible consolation. He had been walking for some time when, directly in front of him, borne toward him by the summer breeze, he heard a few words uttered in the bright Parisian idiom his ears had begun to forget. The voice in which the words were spoken was a peculiar recall, and as he bent his

eyes it lent an identity to the commonplace elegance
of the back view of a young lady walking in the same
direction as himself. Mademoiselle Nioche, seeking
her fortune, had apparently thought she might find
it faster in London, and another glance led him to
wonder if she might now have lighted on it. A gentleman strolled beside her, lending an attentive ear to
her conversation and too beguiled to open his lips.
Newman caught no sound of him, but had the impression of English shoulders, an English "fit," an
English silence. Mademoiselle Nioche was attracting
attention: the ladies who passed her turned round as
with a sense of the Parisian finish. A great cataract
of flounces rolled down from the young lady's waist
to Newman's feet; he had to step aside to avoid
treading on them. He stepped aside indeed with a
decision of movement that the occasion scarcely
demanded; for even this imperfect glimpse of Miss
Noémie had sharpened again his constant soreness.
She seemed an odious blot on the face of nature; he
wanted to put her out of his sight. He thought of
Valentin de Bellegarde still green in the earth of his
burial, his young life giving way to this flourishing
impudence. The fragrance of the girl's bravery quite
sickened him; he turned his head and tried to keep
his distance; but the pressure of the crowd held him
near her a minute longer, so that he heard what she
was saying.

"Ah, I'm sure he'll miss me," she murmured. "It
was very cruel of me to leave him; I'm afraid you'll
think I've very little heart. He might perfectly have
remained with us. I don't think he's very well,"

she added; "it seemed to me to-day he was rather down."

Newman wondered whom she was talking about, but just then an opening among his neighbours enabled him to turn away, and he said to himself that she was probably paying a tribute to British propriety and feigning a tender solicitude about her parent. Was that miserable old man still treading the path of vice in her train? Was he still giving her the benefit of his experience of affairs, and had he crossed the sea to serve as her interpreter? Newman walked some distance further and then began to retrace his steps, taking care not to accompany again those of Mademoiselle Nioche. At last he looked for a chair under the trees, but he had some difficulty in finding an empty one. He was about to give up the search when he saw a gentleman rise from the seat he had been occupying, leaving our friend to take it without looking at his neighbours. Newman sat there for some time without heeding them; his attention was lost in the rage of his renewed vision of the little fatal *fact* of Noémie. But at the end of a quarter of an hour, dropping his eyes, he perceived a small pug-dog squatted on the path near his feet — a diminutive but very perfect specimen of its interesting species. The pug was sniffing at the fashionable world, as it passed him, with his little black muzzle, and was kept from extending his investigation by a large blue ribbon attached to his collar with an enormous rosette and held in the hand of a person seated next Newman. To this person our hero transferred his attention, and immediately found himself the object of all that of his neighbour, who was staring up at him from a pair of little fixed white eyes. These eyes he instantly recognised; he had been sitting for the last quarter of an hour beside M. Nioche. He had vaguely felt himself in range of some feeble fire. M. Nioche continued to stare; he appeared afraid to move even to the extent of saving by flight what might have been left of his honour.

"Good Lord!" said Newman; "are you here too?" And he looked at his neighbour's helplessness more grimly than he knew. M. Nioche had a new hat and a pair of kid gloves; his clothes too seemed to belong to an eld less hoary than of yore. Over his arm was suspended a lady's mantilla — a light and brilliant tissue, fringed with white lace — which had apparently been committed to his keeping; and the little dog's blue ribbon was wound tightly round his hand. There was no hint of recognition in his face — nor of anything save a feeble fascinated dread. Newman looked at the pug and the lace mantilla and then met the old man's eyes again. "You know me, I see," he pursued. "You might have spoken to me before." M. Nioche still said nothing, but it seemed to his ex-patron that his eyes began faintly to water. "I did n't expect," the latter went on, "to meet you so far from — from the Café de la Patrie." He remained silent, but decidedly Newman had touched the source of tears. His neighbour sat staring and he added: "What's the matter, M. Nioche? You used to talk, talk very — what did you call it? — very *gentiment*. Don't you remember you even gave lessons in conversation?"

At this M. Nioche decided to change his attitude. He stooped and picked up the pug, lifted it to his face and wiped his eyes on its little soft back. "I'm afraid to speak to you," he presently said, looking over the puppy's shoulder. "I hoped you would n't notice me. I should have moved away, but I was afraid that if I moved it would strike you. So I sat very still."

"I suspect you've a bad conscience, sir," Newman pronounced.

The old man put down the little dog and held it carefully in his lap. Then he shook his head, his eyes still watering and pleading. "No, Mr. Newman, I've a good conscience," he weakly wailed.

"Then why should you want to slink away from me?"

"Because — because you don't understand my position."

"Oh, I think you once explained it to me," said Newman. "But it seems improved."

"Improved!" his companion quavered. "Do you call this improvement?" And he ruefully embraced the treasures in his arms.

"Why, you're on your travels," Newman rejoined. "A visit to London in the Season is certainly a sign of prosperity."

M. Nioche, in answer to this superior dig, lifted the puppy up to his face again, peering at his critic from his small blank eye-holes. There was something inane in the movement, and Newman hardly knew if he were taking refuge in an affected failure of reason or whether he had in fact paid for his base accommodation by the loss of his wits. In the latter case, just now, he felt little more tenderly to the foolish old man than in the former. Responsible or not, he was equally an accomplice of his pestilent daughter. Newman was going to leave him abruptly when his face gave out a peculiar convulsion. "Are you going away?" he appealed.

"Do you want me to stay?"

"I should have left you—from consideration. But my dignity suffers at your leaving *me*—that way."

"Have you anything particular to say to me?"

M. Nioche looked round to see no one was listening, and then returned with mild portentousness: "*Je ne lui ai pas trouvé d'excuses.*"

Newman gave a short laugh, but the old man seemed for the moment not to heed; he was gazing away, absently, at some metaphysical image of his implacability. "It does n't much matter whether you have or not," said Newman. "There are other people who never will, I assure you."

"What has she done?" M. Nioche vaguely enquired, turning round again. "I don't know what she does, you know."

"She has done a devilish mischief; it does n't matter what. She's a public nuisance; she ought to be stopped."

M. Nioche stealthily put out his hand and laid it on Newman's arm. "Stopped, yes," he concurred. "That's it. Stopped short. She's running away—she must be stopped." Then he paused and again looked round him. "I mean to stop her," he went on. "I'm only waiting for my chance."

"I see," Newman dryly enough laughed. "She's running away and you're running after her. You've run a long distance."

But M. Nioche had a competent upward nod, "Oh, I know what to do!"

He had hardly spoken when the crowd in front of them separated as if by the impulse to make way for an important personage. Presently, through the opening, advanced Mademoiselle Nioche, attended by the gentleman Newman had lately observed. His face being now presented to our hero, the latter recognised the irregular features and the hardly more composed expression of Lord Deepmere. Noémie, on finding herself suddenly confronted with Newman, who, like M. Nioche, had risen from his seat, faltered for a barely perceptible instant. She gave him a little nod, as if she had seen him yesterday, and then, without agitation, "*Tiens,* how we keep meeting!" she sweetly shrilled. She looked consummately pretty and the front of her dress was a wonderful work of art. She went up to her father, stretching out her hands for the little dog, which he submissively placed in them, and she began to kiss it and murmur over it: "To think of leaving him all alone, *mon bichon* — what a horrid false friend he must believe me! He has been very unwell," she added, turning and affecting to explain to Newman, a spark of infernal impudence, fine as a needle-point, lighted in each charming eye. "I don't think the English climate does for him."

. "It seems to do wonderfully well for his mistress," Newman said.

"Do you mean me? I've never been better, thank you," Miss Noémie declared. "But with *milord*," and she gave a shining shot at her late companion, "how can one help being well?" She seated herself in the chair from which her father had risen and began to arrange the little dog's rosette.

Lord Deepmere carried off such embarrassment as might be incidental to this unexpected encounter with the inferior grace of a male and a Briton. He blushed a good deal and greeted his fellow-candidate in that recent remarkable competition by which each had so signally failed to profit with an awkward nod and a rapid ejaculation — an ejaculation to which Newman, who often found it hard to understand the speech of English people, was able to attach no meaning. Then he stood there with his hand on his hip and with a conscious grin, staring askance at the mistress of the invalid pug. Suddenly an idea seemed to strike him and he caught at the light. "Oh, you know her?"

"Yes," said Newman, "I know her. I don't believe you do."

"Oh dear, yes, I do!" — Lord Deepmere was sure of that. "I knew her in Paris — by my late cousin Bellegarde, you know. He knew her, poor fellow, did n't he? It was she, you know, who was at the bottom of his affair. Awfully sad, was n't it?" the young man continued, talking off his embarrassment as his simple nature permitted. "They got up some story of its being for the Pope; of the other fellow having said something against the Pope's morals. They always do that, you know. They put it on the

Pope because Bellegarde was once in the Zouaves.
But it was about *her* morals — *she* was the Pope!"
his lordship pursued, directing an eye illumined by
this pleasantry toward Mademoiselle Nioche, who,
bending gracefully over her lap-dog, was apparently
absorbed in conversation with it. "I dare say you
think it rather odd that I should — a — keep up the
acquaintance," he resumed; "but she could n't help
it, you know, and Bellegarde was only my twentieth
cousin. I dare say you think it rather cheeky my
showing with her in this place; but you see she is n't
known yet and she's so remarkably, thoroughly
nice — !" With which his attesting glance returned
to the young lady.

Newman turned away; he was having too much of
her niceness. M. Nioche had stepped aside on his
daughter's approach, and he stood there, within
a very small compass, looking down hard at the
ground. It had decidedly never yet, as between him
and his late protector, been so apposite to place on
record that, for his vindication, he was only waiting
to strike. As Newman turned off he felt himself held,
and, seeing the old man, who had drawn so near,
had something particular to say, bent his head an
instant.

"You'll see it some day *dans les feuilles.*"

Our hero broke away, for impatience of the whole
connexion, and to this day, though the newspapers
form his principal reading, his eyes have not been
arrested by any paragraph forming a sequel to this
announcement.

XXVI

IN that uninitiated observation of the great spectacle
of English life on which I have touched, it might be
supposed that he passed a great many dull days.
But the dulness was as grateful as a warm, fragrant bath, and his melancholy, which was settling to
a secondary stage, like a healing wound, had in it a
certain acrid, palatable sweetness. He had the company of his thoughts and for the present wanted none
other. He had no desire to make acquaintances and
left untouched a couple of notes of introduction sent
him by Tom Tristram. He mused a great deal on
Madame de Cintré — sometimes with a dull despair
that might have seemed a near neighbour to detachment. He lived over again the happiest hours he had
known — that silver chain of numbered days in
which his afternoon visits, strained so sensibly to the
ideal end, had come to figure for him a flight of firm
marble steps where the ascent from one to the other
was a momentous and distinct occasion, giving a
nearer view of the chamber of confidence at the top,
a white tower that flushed more and more as with a
light of dawn. He had yet held in his cheated arms,
he felt, the full experience, and when he closed them
together round the void that was all they now possessed, he might have been some solitary spare ath-
lete practising restlessly in the corridor of the circus.
He came back to reality indeed, after such reveries,

with a shock somewhat muffled; he had begun to know the need of accepting the absolute. At other times, however, the truth was again an infamy and the actual a lie, and he could only pace and rage and remember till he was weary. Passion, in him, by habit, nevertheless, burned clear rather than thick, and in the clearness he saw things, even things not gross and close — having never the excuse that anything could make him blind. Without quite knowing it at first, he began to read a moral into his strange adventure. He asked himself in his quieter hours whether he perhaps *had* been more commercial than was decent. We know that it was in reaction against questions of the cruder avidity that he had come out to pick up for a while an intellectual, or otherwise a critical, living in Europe; it may therefore be understood that he was able to conceive of a votary of the mere greasy market smelling too strong for true good company. He was willing to grant in a given case that unpleasant effect, but he could n't bring it home to himself that he had reeked. He believed there had been as few reflexions of his smugness caught during all those weeks in the high polish of surrounding surfaces as there were monuments of his meanness scattered about the world. No one had ever unprovokedly suffered by him — ah, provokedly was another matter: he liked to remember that, and to repeat it, and to defy himself to bring up a case.

If moreover there was any reason in the nature of things why his connexion with business should have cast a shadow on a connexion — even a connexion broken — with a woman justly proud, he was willing

to sponge it out of his life for ever. The thing seemed
a possibility; he could n't feel it doubtless as keenly
as some people, and it scarce struck him as worth
while to flap his wings very hard to rise to the idea;
but he could feel it enough to make any sacrifice that
still remained to be made. As to what such sacrifice
was now to be made to, here he stopped short before
a blank wall over which there sometimes played
strange shadows and confused signs. Was it a think-
able *plan*, that of carrying out his life as he would have
directed had Madame de Cintré been left to him ? —
that of making it a religion to do nothing she would
have disliked ? In this certainly was no sacrifice; but
there was a pale, oblique ray of inspiration. It would be
lonely entertainment — a good deal like a man's talking to himself in the mirror for want of better company. Yet the idea yielded him several half-hours'
dumb exaltation as he sat, his hands in his pockets and
his legs outstretched, over the relics of an expensively
bad dinner, in the undying English twilight. If,
however, his financial imagination was dead he felt
no contempt for the surviving actualities begotten
by it. He was glad he had been prosperous and had
been a great operator rather than a small; he was
extremely glad he was rich. He felt no impulse to
sell all he had and give to the poor, or to retire into
meditative economy and asceticism. He was glad he
was rich and tolerably young; if it was possible to
have inhaled too fondly the reek of the market, it
was yet a gain still to have time for experiments in
other air. Come then, what air should it now be ?
Ah, again and again, he could taste but one sweet-

ness; that came back to him and back; and as this happened, with a force which seemed physically to express itself in a sudden upward choking, he would lean forward, when the waiter had left the room, and, resting his arms on the table, bury his troubled face.

He remained in England till midsummer and spent a month in the country, wandering among cathedrals, hanging about castles and ruins. Several times, taking a walk from his inn across sweet field-paths and through ample parks, he stopped by a well-worn stile, looked across through the early evening at a grey church tower, with its dusky nimbus of thick-circling rooks, and remembered that such things might have been part of the intimacy of his honeymoon. He had never been so much alone nor indulged so little in chance talk. The period of recreation appointed by Mrs. Tristram had at last expired and he asked himself what he should next do. She had written to propose he should join her in the Pyrenees, but he was not in the humour to return to France. The simplest thing was to repair to Liverpool and embark on the first American steamer. He proceeded accordingly to that seaport and secured his berth; and the night before sailing he sat in his room at the hotel and stared down vacantly and wearily at an open portmanteau. A number of papers lay upon it, which he had been meaning to look over; some of them might conveniently be destroyed. But he at last shuffled them roughly together and pushed them into a corner of the bag; they were business papers and he was in no humour for sorting them. Then he drew forth his pocket-book and took out

a leaf of smaller size than those he haa dismissed.
He did n't unfold it; he simply sat looking at the back
of it. If he had momentarily entertained the idea of
destroying it this possibility at least quickly dropped.
What the thing suggested was the feeling that lay in
his innermost heart and that no reviving cheerfulness
could long quench — the feeling that, after all and
above all, he was a good fellow wronged. With it
came a hope, as intense as a pang, that the Bellegardes were enjoying their suspense as to what he
would do yet. The more it was prolonged the more
they would enjoy it. He had hung fire once, yes;
perhaps in his present queer state of mind he might
hang fire again. But he restored the safe scrap to his
pocket-book very tenderly and felt better for thinking
of the suspense of the Bellegardes. He felt better
every time he thought of it while he sailed the summer
seas. He landed in New York and journeyed across
the continent to San Francisco, and nothing he observed by the way contributed to mitigate his sense
of being a good fellow wronged.

He saw a great many other good fellows — his old
friends — but he told none of them of the trick that
had been played him. He said simply that the lady
he was to have married had changed her mind, and
when asked if he had changed his own inscrutably
answered, "Suppose we change the subject." He told
his friends he had brought home no "new ideas"
from Europe, and his conduct probably struck them
as an eloquent proof of failing invention. He took no
interest in discussing business and showed no desire
to go into anything whatever. He asked half a dozen

questions which, like those of an eminent physician enquiring for particular symptoms, proved he was master of his subject; but he made no comments and gave no directions. He not only puzzled all the prominent men, but was himself surprised at the extent of his indifference. As it seemed only to increase he made an effort to combat it; he tried to take hold and to recover, as they said, his spring. But the ground was inelastic and the issues dead; do what he would he somehow could n't believe in them. Sometimes he began to fear there was something the matter with him, that he had suffered, unwitting, some small horrid cerebral lesion or nervous accident, and that the end of his strong activities had come. This idea for a while hung about him and haunted him. A hopeless, helpless loafer, useful to no one and detestable to himself — this was what the treachery of the Bellegardes had made of him. In his anxious idleness he came back from San Francisco to New York, where he sat for three days in the lobby of his hotel and looked out through a huge wall of plate glass at the unceasing stream of pretty girls who wore their clothes as with the American accent and undulated past with little parcels nursed against their neat figures. At the end of three days he returned to San Francisco and, having arrived there, wished he had stayed away. He had nothing to do, his occupation had gone, had simply strayed and lost itself in the great desert of life. He had nothing to do *here*, he sometimes said to himself; but there was something beyond the ocean he was still to do; something he had left undone experimentally and speculatively, to see if it could content itself to remain undone. Well, clearly, it could n't content itself; it kept pulling at his heartstrings and thumping at his reason; it murmured in his ears and hovered perpetually before his eyes. It interposed between all new resolutions and their fulfilment; it was a stubborn ghost dumbly entreating to be laid. On the doing of that all other doing depended.

One day toward the end of the winter, after a long interval, he received a letter from Mrs. Tristram, who appeared to have been moved by a charitable desire to amuse and distract her correspondent. She gave him much Paris gossip, talked of General Packard and Miss Kitty Upjohn, enumerated the new plays at the theatres and enclosed a note from her husband, who had gone down to spend a month at Nice. Then came her signature and after this her postscript. The latter consisted of these few lines: "I heard three days since from my friend the Abbé Aubert that Claire de Cintré last week received the veil at the Carmelites. It was on her twenty-ninth birthday, and she took the name of her patroness, Saint Veronica. Sœur Véronique has a lifetime before her!"

This letter reached him in the morning; in the evening he started for Paris. His wound began to ache with its first fierceness, and during his long bleak journey he had no company but the thought of the new Sister's "lifetime" — every one's sister but his! — passed within walls on whose outer side only he might stand. Well, for that station *he* would live, if it was to be spoken of as life; he would fix himself in

Paris; he would wring a hard happiness from the knowledge that if she was not there at least the stony sepulchre that held her was. He descended, unannounced, on Mrs. Bread, whom he found keeping lonely watch in his great empty saloons on the Boulevard Haussmann. They were as neat as a Dutch village; Mrs. Bread's only occupation had been removing individual dust-particles. She made no complaint, however, of her solitude, for in her philosophy a servant was but a machine constructed for the benefit of some supreme patentee, and it would be as fantastic for a housekeeper to comment on a gentleman's absences as for a clock to remark on not being wound up. No particular clock, Mrs. Bread supposed, kept all the time, and no particular servant could enjoy all the sunshine diffused by the career of a universal master. She ventured nevertheless to express a modest hope that Newman meant to remain a while in Paris. He laid his hand on hers and shook it gently. "I mean to remain for ever."

He went after this to see Mrs. Tristram, to whom he had telegraphed and who expected him. She looked at him a moment and shook her head. "This won't do," she said; "you've come back too soon." He sat down and asked about her husband and her children, enquired even for news of Miss Dora Finch. In the midst of this, "Do you know where she is?" he abruptly demanded.

Mrs. Tristram hesitated; of course he couldn't mean Miss Dora Finch. Then she answered properly: "She has gone to the other house—in the Rue d'Enfer." But after he had gloomed a little longer she went on: "You're not so good a man as I thought. You're more — you're more —"

"More what?"

"More unreconciled."

"Good God!" he cried; "do you expect me to forgive?"

"No, not that. I've not forgiven, so of course you can't. But you might magnificently forget. You've a worse temper about it than I should have expected. You look wicked — you look dangerous."

"I may be dangerous," he said; "but I'm not wicked. No, I'm not wicked." And he got up to go. She asked him to come back to dinner, but he answered that he could n't face a convivial occasion, even as a solitary guest. Later in the evening, if he should be able, he would look in.

He walked away through the city, beside the Seine and over it, and took the direction of the Rue d'Enfer. The day had the softness of early spring, but the weather was grey and humid. He found himself in a part of Paris that he little knew — a region of convents and prisons, of streets bordered by long dead walls and traversed by few frequenters. At the intersection of two of these streets stood the house of the Carmelites — a dull, plain edifice with a blank, high-shouldered defence all round. From without he could see its upper windows, its steep roof and its chimneys. But these things revealed no symptoms of human life; the place looked dumb, deaf, inanimate. The pale, dead, discoloured wall stretched beneath it far down the empty side-street — a vista without a human figure. He stood there a long time; there were no

passers; he was free to gaze his fill. This seemed the
goal of his journey; it was all he had come for. It was
a strange satisfaction too, and yet it was a satisfaction; the barren stillness of the place represented
somehow his own release from ineffectual desire. It
told him the woman within was lost beyond recall,
and that the days and years of the future would pile
themselves above her like the huge immoveable slab
of a tomb. These days and years, on this spot,
would always be just so grey and silent. Suddenly
from the thought of their seeing him stand there again
the charm utterly departed. He would never stand
there again; it was a sacrifice as sterile as her own.
He turned away with a heavy heart, yet more dis-
burdened than he had come.

Everything was over and he too at last could rest.
He walked back through narrow, winding streets to
the edge of the Seine and there he saw, close above
him, high and mild and grey, the twin towers of
Notre Dame. He crossed one of the bridges and
paused in the voided space that makes the great
front clear; then he went in beneath the grossly-
imaged portals. He wandered some distance up the
nave and sat down in the splendid dimness. He sat
a long time; he heard far-away bells chiming off into
space, at long intervals, the big bronze syllables of
the Word. He was very tired, but such a place was
a kingdom of rest. He said no prayers; he had no
prayers to say He had nothing to be thankful for
and he had nothing to ask; nothing to ask because
now he must take care of himself. But a great church
offers a very various hospitality, and he kept his

place because while he was there he was out of the world. The most unpleasant thing that had ever happened to him had reached its formal conclusion; he had learnt his lesson — not indeed that he the least understood it — and could put away the book. He leaned his head for a long time on the chair in front of him; when he took it up he felt he was himself again. Somewhere in his soul a tight constriction had loosened. He thought of the Bellegardes; he had almost forgotten them. He remembered them as people he had meant to do something to. He gave a groan as he remembered what he had meant to do; he was annoyed, and yet partly incredulous, at his having meant to do it: the bottom suddenly had fallen out of his revenge. Whether it was Christian charity or mere human weakness of will — what it was, in the background of his spirit — I don't pretend to say; but Newman's last thought was that of course he would let the Bellegardes go. If he had spoken it aloud he would have said he did n't want to hurt them. He was ashamed of having wanted to hurt them. He quite failed, of a sudden, to recognise the fact of his having cultivated any such link with them. It was a link for themselves perhaps, their having so hurt *him,* but that side of it was now not his affair. At last he got up and came out of the darkening church; not with the elastic step of a man who has won a victory or taken a resolve — rather to the quiet measure of a discreet escape, of a retreat with appearances preserved.

Going home, he said to Mrs. Bread that he must trouble her to put back his things into the portmanteau she had unpacked the evening before. It was therefore as if she had looked at him on this, through bedimmed eyes, with the consciousness of a value, so far as she could see, quite extravagantly wasted. "Dear me, sir, I thought you said you were going to stay for ever."

"Well, I guess I omitted a word. I meant I'm going to stay *away* for ever," he was obliged a little awkwardly to explain. And since his departure from Paris on the following day he has certainly not returned. The gilded apartments I have so often spoken of stand ready to receive him, but they serve only as a spacious setting for Mrs. Bread's solitary straightness, which wanders eternally from room to room, adjusting the tassels of the curtains, and keeps its wages, which are regularly brought in by a banker's clerk, in a great pink Sèvres vase on the drawing-room mantel-shelf.

Late in the evening Newman went to Mrs. Tristram's and found the more jovial member of the pair by the domestic fireside. "I'm glad to see you back in Paris," this gentleman declared, "for, you know, it's really the only place for a white man to live." Mr. Tristram made his friend welcome according to his own rosy light, and repaired in five minutes, with a free tongue, the too visible and too innocent deficiencies in Newman's acquaintance with current history. Then, having caused him to gape with strange information — all as to what had been going on in "*notre monde à nous*, you know" — Tristram got up to go and renew his budget at the club.

To this Newman replied that Mrs. Tristram was

his club and that he had never wanted a better: a statement he felt the truth of when he was presently alone with her and even — or perhaps all the more — when she asked him what he had done on leaving her in the afternoon. "Well," he then replied, "I worked it off."

"Worked off the afternoon?"

"Yes, and a lot of other troublesome stuff."

"You struck me," she confessed, "as a man filled with some rather uncanny idea. I wondered if I were right to leave you so the prey of it, and whether I ought n't to have had you followed and watched."

This appeared to strike him with surprise. "Surely I did n't look as if I wanted to take life."

"I might have feared, if I had let myself go a little, that you were thinking of taking your own."

He breathed a long sigh of such apparent indifference to his own as would have ruled that out. "Well," he none the less after a moment went on, "I *have* got rid of about nine tenths of something that had become the biggest part of me. But I did that only by walking over to the Rue d'Enfer."

"You've been then," she stared, "at the Carmelites?" And as he only met her eyes: "Trying to scale the wall?"

"Well, I thought of that — I measured the wall. I looked at it a long time. But it's too high — it's beyond me."

"That's right," she said. "Give it up."

"I *have* given it up. But on the spot there I took it all in."

She rested now her kindest eyes on him. "On the

spot then you did n't happen to meet M. de Bellegarde — also taking it all in? I'm told his sister's
course does n't suit him the least little bit."

Newman had a moment's gravity of silence. "No,
luckily — I did n't meet either of *them*. In that case
I *might* have fired."

"Ah, it is n't that they've not been keeping quiet,"
she said; "I mean in the country, at — what's the
name of the place? — Fleurières. They returned
there at the time you left Paris, and have been spending the year far from human eye. The little Marquise
must enjoy it; I expect to hear she has eloped with her
daughter's music-master!"

Newman had gazed at the light wood-fire, and he
listened to this with an apparent admission of its
relevance; but he spoke in another sense. "I mean
never to mention the name of those people again and
I don't want to hear anything more about them."
Then he took out his pocket-book and drew forth
a scrap of paper. He looked at it an instant, after
which he got up and stood by the fire. "I'm going
to burn them up. I'm glad to have you as a witness.
There they go!" And he tossed the paper into the
flame.

Mrs. Tristram sat with her embroidery-needle suspended. "What in the world is that?"

Leaning against the chimney-piece he seemed to
grasp its ledge with force and to draw his breath
a while in pain. But presently he said: "I can tell
you now. It was a proof of a great infamy on the part
of the Bellegardes — something that would damn
them if ever known."

She dropped her work with a reproachful moan. "Ah, why did n't you show it to me?"

"I thought of showing it to you — I thought of showing it to every one. I thought of paying my debt to them that way. So I told them, and I guess I made them squirm. If they 've been lying low it 's because they have n't known what may happen. But, as I say, I 've given up my idea."

Mrs. Tristram began to take slow stitches again. "Wholly renounced it?"

"Wholly renounced it."

"But your 'proof,'" she went on after a moment, "what was it a proof of?"

"Oh, of an abomination not otherwise known."

"An abomination?"

"An abomination."

She hesitated but briefly. "Something too bad to tell me?"

He considered. "Yes, not good enough now."

"Well," she said, "I 'm sorry to have lost it. Your document," she smiled, "did n't look like much, but I should have liked immensely to see it. They 've wronged me too, you know, as your sponsor and guarantee, and it would have served my revenge as well! How did you come," she then asked, "into possession of your knowledge?"

"It 's a long story. But honestly at any rate."

"And they knew you were master of it?"

"Oh, but rather!"

"Dear me, how interesting!" cried Mrs. Tristram. "And you humbled them at your feet?"

Newman was silent a little. "No, not at all. They

pretended not to care — not to be afraid. But I know they did care — they *were* afraid."

"Are you very sure?"

He looked at her hard. "Why, they fairly turned blue."

She resumed her slow stitches. "They defied you, eh?"

"They took the only tone they could. But I did n't think they took it very well."

"You tried by the threat of exposure to make them come round?" Mrs. Tristram pursued.

"Yes, but they would n't. I gave them their choice, and they chose to take their chance of bluffing off the charge and convicting me of fraud, that is of having procured and paid for a forgery. Forgery was of course their easy word — but words did n't, and don't, matter. They're as sick as a pair of poisoned cats — and I don't want any more 'revenge.'"

"It's most provoking," she returned, "to hear you talk of the 'charge' when the charge is burned up. Is it quite consumed?" she asked, glancing at the fire. He assured her there was nothing left of it, and at this, dropping her embroidery, she got up and came near him. "I need n't tell you at this hour how I've felt for you. But I like you as you are," she said.

"As I am — ?"

"As you are." She stood before him and put out her hand as for his own, which he a little blankly let her take. "Just exactly as you are," she repeated. With which, bending her head, she raised his hand and very tenderly and beautifully kissed it. Then.

"Ah, poor Claire!" she sighed as she went back to her place. It drew from him, while his flushed face followed her, a strange inarticulate sound, and this made her but say again: "Yes, a thousand times — poor, poor Claire!"

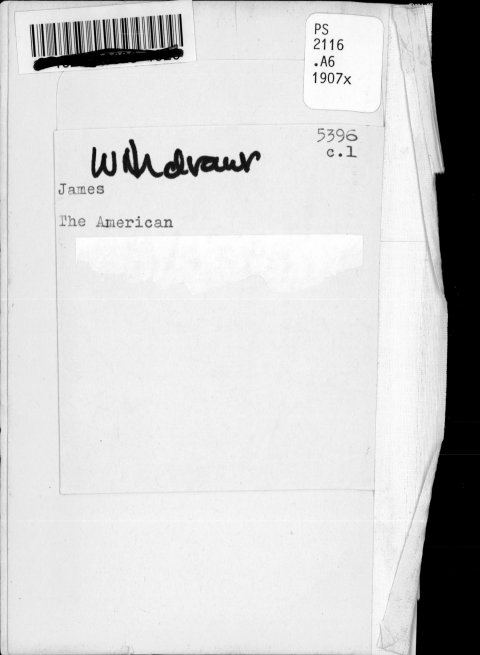